PRAISE FOR EDWARD CHRISTOPHER WILLIAMS'S

When Washingt[illegible] W[illegible] In Vogue

"*When Washington Was in Vogu*[illegible]
to life. . . . *A Great Gatsby* with [illegible]

[illegible]l

"*When Washington Was in Vogue* brims with life."

—*Boston Globe*

"An engaging, eminently readable work, and Williams is no less elegant a storyteller for having been forgotten. The book's rediscovery, too, is inspiring; one can only hope for further belated additions to the rich literature of the Harlem Renaissance."

—*San Francisco Chronicle*

"As delightful as it is significant." —*Essence*

"Richly rewarding." —*Honey*

"Deep in detail, an invaluable addition to period scholarship. . . . McKible's discovery is sure to provoke scholarship and discussion, and attract well-deserved attention." —*Publishers Weekly*

"*When Washington Was in Vogue* offers a welcome and consistently entertaining glimpse of a pivotal era in our recent past."

—*The Crisis*

"A love story with the sensibilities of an all-black-cast *Vanity Fair*, rendered with the keen eye of a sociologist." —*Booklist*

"A realistic portrayal of the black middle class in 1920s Washington, D.C. . . . Charming and conventional protagonist Davy Carr . . . often speaks of the pleasures of sitting before a crackling fire in the hearth, and that would be a good place to enjoy this sincerely delightful book." —*Library Journal*

"Dramatic frisson for historians and black studies scholars."

—*Kirkus Reviews*

"A pictorial of very colorful and impressive characters. . . . Entertaining. . . . Alluring, refreshing, and humorous."

—*Atlanta Daily World*

"Not everything found is a discovery, but *When Washington Was in Vogue* is just that. With language that beckons to be read aloud, Edward Christopher Williams captured an era of love, life, and the complexities of both, in an engaging and vibrant peek into a world known to exist yet rarely presented with such vivid and unapologetic detail."

—Brian Keith Jackson, author of *The Queen of Harlem*

"Adam McKible's recovery of this fascinating and complex narrative does a great service to all of us who value the African American literary tradition. Our classrooms, libraries, book clubs, and scholarly debates will surely benefit from this text's availability. Edward Christopher Williams's lively and insightful account of Davy Carr enhances the African American canon—not only in its innovative interpolation of the epistolary with the novel of manners but also in its demonstration of the nuances, challenges, and joys that have always characterized the New Negro Renaissance."

—Kathleen Pfeiffer, Associate Professor of English, Oakland University

"An absolutely fascinating novel. A rare window to the world of upper-middle-class African Americans in the 1920s. It reads like an Edith Wharton novel for its attention to the details of the social life of Americans emerging from the grip of Victorian morals and manners into the modern age. Williams's characters, though, must make their way through the labyrinths of racism. A page-turner, witty and charming."

—Elizabeth Nunez, author of *Bruised Hibiscus* and *Discretion*

EDWARD CHRISTOPHER WILLIAMS was born in Cleveland, Ohio, in 1871. He was schooled at Western Reserve University, in Ohio, where he was Phi Beta Kappa and valedictorian, and at the New York State Library School. Williams is documented as the first Black American to graduate from a library school. He was a notable scholar, a brilliant teacher, and a pivotal developer of education for librarians at Case Western and Howard Universities. He was also an active member of the American Library Association and founding member of the Ohio Library Association. Williams was married to Ethel Chestnutt Williams, the daughter of Charles W. Chestnutt, author of the seminal novel *The House Behind the Cedars.* In 1929 Williams died of a sudden illness in Washington, D.C., at the age of forty-eight.

ADAM MCKIBLE received his B.A. and his M.A. in English from SUNY–Binghamton and his Ph.D. in English from the University of North Carolina at Chapel Hill. He is assistant professor of English at John Jay College of Criminal Justice, where he teaches courses on African American, American, classic, and immigration literature. McKible uncovered *When Washington Was in Vogue* in 1998 while researching his dissertation. He is the author of *The Space and Place of Modernism: The Russian Revolution, Little Magazines, and New York*, and lives in Brooklyn, New York, with his wife.

EMILY BERNARD was born in Nashville, Tennessee. She has a B.A. and a Ph.D. in American Studies from Yale University. She has received fellowships from the Ford Foundation, the National Endowment for the Humanities, and the W. E. B. Du Bois Institute for African and African-American Research at Harvard University. Bernard teaches in the English Department and in the ALANA U.S. Ethnic Studies Program at the University of Vermont. She is the editor of *Remember Me to Harlem: The Letters of Langston Hughes and Carl Van Vechten, 1925–1964* and *Some of My Best Friends: Writings on Interracial Friendships.*

Edward Christopher Williams

WITH COMMENTARIES BY

ADAM McKIBLE AND

EMILY BERNARD

AMISTAD
An Imprint of HarperCollins*Publishers*

When Washington Was In Vogue

A Lost Novel of the Harlem Renaissance

A hardcover edition of this book was published in 2004 by Amistad, an imprint of HarperCollins Publishers.

WHEN WASHINGTON WAS IN VOGUE. Written by Edward Christopher Williams; previously published anonymously as *The Letters of Davy Carr* in *The Messenger*, January 1925–June 1926. For information, address HarperCollins Publishers, 195 Broadway, New York, NY 10007.

HarperCollins books may be purchased for educational, business, or sales promotional use. For information, please e-mail the Special Markets Department at SPsales@harpercollins.com.

FIRST AMISTAD PAPERBACK EDITION 2005

Designed by Jennifer Ann Daddio

Printed on acid-free paper

Library of Congress Cataloging-in-Publication Data is available upon request.

ISBN 0-06-055546-7 (pbk.)

HB 07.24.2020

You sang far better than you knew.

—JAMES WELDON JOHNSON,

"O BLACK AND UNKNOWN BARDS"

ACKNOWLEDGMENTS

Literature is a profoundly collective endeavor. I am grateful to the following people and institutions for their help in making the republication of this novel possible. For their initial interest while I was in graduate school, thanks go to James Thompson, William L. Andrews, J. Lee Greene, and Robert Scholes. At John Jay College, I have been encouraged by all of my colleagues, especially Jon-Christian Suggs, Tim Stevens, Robert Crozier, John Matteson, Cristine Varholy, Erica Class, and Jacob Marini. I am also grateful to my union, the Professional Staff Congress; my project was funded (in part) by a grant from the PSC-CUNY Research Foundation. I could not have found a home for E. C. Williams's novel without the help of Regina Bernard, to whom I am eternally grateful. Thanks to another former student, Tedrina Da Costa, with whom I spent an enjoyable semester analyzing the novel from myriad angles. My thanks to all of the librarians who helped keep Williams's memory alive; I am particularly grateful to Teddy Abebe at Howard University and E. L. Josey, who carried Williams's torch for many a year. I am fortunate to know Sian Hunter, Paul Harrington, and Kathleen Pfeiffer; their encouragement and advice helped me to keep the faith. Thanks to Barbara Foley for sharing information about the Williams-Toomer connection, and to Ganda Suthivarakom for her invaluable, last-minute help.

I owe my dear friend Richard Simon a debt of gratitude, because, without him, I would not have met Tanya McKinnon, dispenser of wisdom and agent extraordinaire.

Thanks to Kelli Martin at HarperCollins, who has understood from the outset the importance of this book.

My family has been with me every step of the way, and I am forever grateful to them.

Thanks, finally, to Julie, my life's song and the love without whom I cannot live.

—Adam McKible

CONTENTS

INTRODUCTION

by Adam McKible

When *Washington Was in Vogue* is an extraordinary book of firsts. It was originally published anonymously under the title *The Letters of Davy Carr: A True Story of Colored Vanity Fair* in serial form in the African-American little magazine *The Messenger,* from January 1925 through June 1926. Written as a series of letters, it is most likely the first epistolary novel in the African-American literary tradition. It is also one of the first novels to offer an extensive and realistic portrayal of the black middle class in Washington, D.C., during the 1920s. And its author, Edward Christopher Williams, was the first professionally trained black librarian in America. Perhaps most extraordinary of all, however, is that *When Washington Was in Vogue* has lain dormant and unrecognized for almost eighty years.

I was in graduate school at the University of North Carolina when I originally came across *When Washington Was in Vogue*, and from its opening pages I realized that I had discovered an important but lost voice of the Harlem Renaissance. Here was a story of African Americans in Washington, D.C., the likes of which I had never seen before. I was not, however, thrilled by my discovery. At the time—about 1994 or 1995—I was as resistant to diving into *When Washington Was in Vogue* as Walker Percy was many years before when John Kennedy Toole's mother coerced him into reading the barely legible draft of *A Confederacy of Dunces*. Acquiescing to Toole's persistent mother, Percy agreed to read the manuscript, all the while hoping that he would be able to dismiss it as the amateur scribbling of a talentless hopeful:

> *There was no getting out of it; only one hope remained—that I could read a few pages and that they would be bad enough for me, in good conscience, to read no further. Usually I can do just that. Indeed the first paragraph often suffices. My only fear was that this one might not be bad enough, or might be just good enough, so that I would have to keep reading.*
>
> *In this case I read on. And on. First with the sinking feeling that it was not bad enough to quit, then with a prickle of interest, then a growing excitement, and finally an incredulity: surely it was not possible that it was so good.*

I, too, was ambivalent and a bit bewildered by the treasure I had just unearthed. When I first found *When Washington Was in Vogue*, I was a harried graduate student with very little time and even less money. My greatest desire was to finish my dissertation—already far too many years in the making—and then throw my hat into the crowded and dismal academic job market. I simply didn't have the time or resources to devote myself to undiscovered Harlem Renaissance novels, no matter how good they might be.

But *When Washington Was in Vogue* was so very good, and it was good from the first paragraph. I was immediately drawn in and compelled to read it from beginning to end, and I was richly rewarded, because *When Washington Was in Vogue* boasted a new narrative voice, a new kind of story, and a setting that had not been seen before in American literature. I had no choice but to adopt *When Washington Was in Vogue* as a personal cause, and decades after it was first published, to help it find its way toward a new readership. This is the first time it has been published in book form.

When I found *When Washington Was in Vogue*, I was researching what would become my first book, *The Space and Place of Modernism: The Russian Revolution, Little Magazines, and New York*, a scholarly analysis of how small-circulation magazines of the 1910s and 1920s responded to the Russian Revolution. At the time, I was working on a chapter on *The Messenger*, one of the most important little magazines of the Harlem Renaissance, and my focus was on a series of articles about black life in America entitled "These 'Colored' United States." Because I wanted my research to be thorough, I decided to read all of the other serialized pieces in the magazine's eleven-year run. Like Walker Percy, I was not really hoping to find anything that I could or would need to use; I figured I had done enough research and that I was ready to write the chapter, move on to the next one, and then get my much overdue Ph.D. Hunkering down to my work, I read through George Schuyler's long running "Hobohemia," Floyd J. Calvin's "Eight Weeks in Dixie" and "The Mirrors of Harlem," and Zora Neale Hurston's "Eatonville Anthology." While some of these series were certainly wonderful to read, they were also unnecessary for my work, and I could happily set them aside and write my chapter.

But then along came *When Washington Was in Vogue*. While first reading *The Messenger* on microfilm, I had printed out copies of each installment of what I thought was another series of articles, just in case they might prove useful or necessary to my chapter. I felt it was my obligation to give *When Washington Was in Vogue* at least a quick scan before setting it aside for good and for ever. So, one afternoon, I settled down with fifty-five barely legible photocopied pages of what I was hoping would be a quick and dismissible read. Before very long, however, I was drawn into the vibrant social world of African-American Washington, D.C., in the 1920s, and I found myself in equal parts charmed with and amused by the keen insights and emotional obtuseness of Captain Davy Carr, the narrator and protagonist of what was not—as *The Messenger*'s publishers promised—a mere series of letters written by an anonymous observer. Instead, as I soon discovered, I was reading a finely crafted novel that demanded my attention. Despite the illegibility of those photocopied pages, I could not put them down.

Set in the fall and winter of 1922–1923, *When Washington Was in Vogue* tells the story of Davy Carr's experiences in the lively black community of the nation's capital. Davy, who served as a commissioned officer in the United States Army in France, has come to Washington in order to research his book on the African slave trade. In his letters to Bob Fletcher, a former comrade-in-arms, Davy relates his encounters with and observations about the people he meets. As the story unfolds, he also falls in love with his landlady's daughter, Caroline Rhodes, a development that is apparent to everyone but Davy. Much of the book's pleasure derives from Davy's ability to write about his milieu so perceptively while also being unable to see the love blossoming right under his own nose.

As I read *When Washington Was in Vogue*, I realized that I had never heard about a book like this before. Here was an epistolary romance novel set in Washington, D.C., during the era commonly referred to as the "Harlem Renaissance." Had anyone written about this book before? The novel was published anonymously—had anyone ever located its author? I scoured the shelves of my university library. I consulted with experts of African-American literature. I came away empty-handed. Nonetheless, I knew this was a novel that should be published, and I thought someone might be interested in reissuing it. I made a few tentative approaches to publishers, but without the author's name, no one was interested. Turning my attention to the more pressing business of my dissertation, I set *When Washington Was in Vogue* aside, hoping to return to it before too long.

A few years passed, I received my degree, and then I moved to New York to teach at John Jay College of Criminal Justice. My photocopies of *When Washington Was in Vogue* languished while I attended to all the problems and challenges a new professor must inevitably face. I worked on other projects, all the while hoping to come back to my anonymous, undiscovered gem. Then, one day, a former student paid me a call. Regina Bernard had taken a number of classes with me at John Jay, and after graduation she went to Columbia University where she would become one of the first students to earn a master's degree from that institution's newly founded African-American Studies program. Because of our shared interest in African-American literature, Regina asked me if there were any projects she could help me with, and that's when I told her about the anonymously published novel I had discovered a few years back. She quickly volunteered to help me search for its mysterious author.

Owing to my previous experience researching *When Washington Was in Vogue*, I imagined that Regina would encounter the same dead ends, and I did not expect to hear back from her any time soon. Much to my surprise, however, she contacted me within forty-eight hours with the name of the author: Edward

Christopher Williams. Between my initial discovery of *When Washington Was in Vogue* and my conversation with Regina, the Internet had blossomed, and Google was on its way to becoming a household name. Regina did what now seems so sensible: She logged on to Google, typed in "Davy Carr," and found a number of Web pages devoted to Edward Christopher Williams who, it turns out, was the first professionally trained black librarian in America. This was in the summer of 2001.

E. C. Williams was born to a mixed-race couple on February 11, 1871, in Cleveland, Ohio.* His father, Daniel P. Williams, was from a well-established black family in Cleveland, and his mother, Mary Kilkary, was born in Tipperary, Ireland. Williams graduated with honors from public schools in Cleveland and went on to Western Reserve University (now Case Western Reserve University), where he made a name for himself as both a student and a varsity baseball player. In 1892, Williams graduated Phi Beta Kappa and valedictorian, and shortly thereafter he secured a position as assistant librarian at Western Reserve's Hatch Library.

Within two years, Williams became head librarian, a post he held until 1909. During those years, Williams earned a reputation as an outstanding librarian dedicated to enlarging that institution's holdings and improving its physical condition. Originally self-taught as a librarian, Williams left Cleveland temporarily in 1899–1900 in order to study at the New York State Library

* There are a number of bio-bibliographic sources on Williams. My sketch draws from "Some Schoolmen," July 1915, *Crisis* 10, 118–120; Porter, Dorothy B., 1947, "Phylon Profile, XIV: Edward Christopher Williams," *Phylon* Vol. 7 (4), 315–321; Russell H. Davis, 1969, *Memorable Negroes in Cleveland's Past*, Cleveland, Ohio: The Western Reserve Historical Society; and E. J. Josey, March 1970, "Edward Christopher Williams: Librarian's Librarian," *Negro History Bulletin* 33, 70–77.

School in Albany, where he completed the two-year course in a little over a year. He also taught courses in librarianship during his time at Western Reserve.

In 1902, Williams married Ethel Chesnutt, the daughter of author Charles W. Chesnutt, who wrote many short stories and such novels as *The House Behind the Cedars.* In 1909, Williams resigned his position as librarian and became principal of the M Street School (now the Paul Lawrence Dunbar High School) in Washington, D.C. One of Williams's best biographers, E. L. Josey, wonders what prompted this move, and he considers it "one of the ultimate questions of [Williams's] life which remains unanswered." When Josey visited Washington in 1967, he spoke with a number of Williams's former colleagues, but "no one seemed to know or would run the hazard of a guess" about why Williams changed jobs (Josey, 73). There are hints, however, that racism played a role in Williams's resignation from Hatch Library, and at least one source claims that he was "forced from his position" (Davis, 40). Unfortunately, this would not have been a surprising development in Jim Crow America, when so many African Americans were legally and culturally denied many rights and opportunities.

Williams served as principal until 1916, when he was lured away from M Street by Howard University, where he eventually fulfilled many roles. In addition to being head librarian, Williams taught numerous classes in library science and foreign languages. He remained at Howard until 1929. Although his biographers—particularly fellow librarians—point to Williams's time at Western Reserve as the days of his greatest achievement because of his work at Hatch Library, he appears to have hit his real stride as a creative writer once he moved to Washington. During these years, he saw three of his plays performed: *The Chasm, The Exile* (a drama about Renaissance Italy), and *The Sheriff's Children*, an adaptation of Chesnutt's short story of the same name. In addition, Williams contributed a number of anonymous pieces to magazines such as *The Messenger*, the most important being *When Washington Was in Vogue*. He may have also published under the pseudonym "Bertuccio Dantino."

In 1929, Williams left the District in order to pursue a Ph.D. in library science at Columbia University. While in New York, he succumbed to an illness and returned to Washington, where he died on December 24, 1929, at the age of fifty-eight. Williams was survived by his wife; their son, Charles; and a granddaughter, Patricia Ann Williams.

Williams's biographers routinely speak of him in superlatives, and he was undoubtedly a brilliant and accomplished man who received steady and unconditional praise for his work as a student, athlete, librarian, scholar, teacher, translator, and writer. For all of his achievements, though, Williams seems to have been quite modest. In a 1931 eulogy for Williams, C. C. Williamson, Director of Libraries and the School of Library Service at Columbia University, quotes a former classmate of Williams's, whose sketch represents a typical assessment of Williams's character:

> *He was an outstanding member of my class on account of his achievements in scholarship and on the athletic field. . . . He bore his honors in a very modest and unassuming manner and was well liked by all members of the student body. . . . He had a very friendly nature, perhaps a little retiring, but a nice sense of humor and gentle manners.*

The picture of Williams that arises out of his various biographies is of a dynamic but gentle, perhaps even genteel, man who gained people's attention without seeming to demand or need it. He also appears to have been quite proud of his racial inheritance, because although he was fair enough to pass for white, he did not hide his background from anyone, despite the consequences. Judging from his literary output, I am tempted to suggest that he had become even more proud about being black after coming to Washington, but this is another aspect of Williams's life that will have to be decided by future biographers.

There is one more facet of Williams's character to consider, and it comes from probably his most famous literary acquaintance, Zora Neale Hurston. While she attended Howard University in the early 1920s, Hurston became familiar with Williams, and in her autobiographical *Dust Tracks on a Road*, she paints a picture of him as something other than modest and genteel. In her recollection, Williams seemed magisterial to the undergraduate Hurston, but he was also witty, flirty, and playful:

> *The man who seems to me to be the most overpowering was E. C. Williams, Librarian and head of the Romance Language department. He was cosmopolitan and world-traveled. His wit was instant and subtle. He was so inaccessible in a way, too. He told me once that a flirtation with a co-ed was to him like playing with a teething-ring. He liked smart, sophisticated women. He used to lunch every day with E. D. Davis, head of the Greek and German department. Davis was just the antithesis of Williams, so shy, in the Charles S. Johnson manner, in spite of his erudition. They would invite me to come along and would pay for my milk and pie. Williams did most of the talking. I put in something now and then. Davis sat and smiled. Professor Williams egged me on to kiss him. He said that Davis would throw a fit, and he wanted*

to be present to see it. He whispered that Davis liked to have me around, but from what he ever said, I couldn't notice. When I was sick, Professor Davis came to see me and brought me an armload of roses, but he sat there half an hour and scarcely said a word. He just sat there and smiled now and then.

One day a pretty Washington girl visited me on campus and joined us at lunch. She laid down a heavy barrage around E. C. Williams. He leaned back in his chair in the midst of her too-obvious play and said suddenly, "Girlie, you would flirt with the Pope."

Williams was in his late forties or early fifties when Hurston met him, and her picture of him gives us a fuller sense of Williams as something more than just the sum of his many accomplishments and talents. Williams was also clearly a man who was sometimes fascinated and often amused by young, modern women, and this particular interest extends across his life and fiction. In two of his unpublished short stories, "The Colonel" and "The Incomparable Dolly,"* Williams's protagonists are older, slightly stuffy men who fall in love with younger, fashionable women. This dynamic is also at play in the relationship between Davy and Caroline in *When Washington Was in Vogue*. Although it is always perilous to equate an author with his characters, I cannot help but wonder if Williams's characters act out the desires of their creator—a fifty-year-old librarian surrounded by undergraduates—to participate in the social experimentation of the Jazz Age rather than merely observe it from a safe distance.

I do not mean to suggest, however, that Williams might have felt as though time was passing him by. Born just eight

* These stories can be found in manuscript in Howard University's Founders Library.

years after Abraham Lincoln signed the Emancipation Proclamation, Williams became the first professionally trained African-American librarian in America, and he must have understood that he was a living example of the historical development of black life in America. Indeed, it would have been impossible for Williams not to feel like an active participant in the course of history. Two phenomena in particular should be considered in conjunction with *When Washington Was in Vogue*: African-American military service during World War I, and the Great Migration of African Americans from the South to the North. Williams's protagonist is a product of both of these developments. Captain Davy Carr was one of the two hundred thousand African Americans who served in Europe during the war, and he and Bob Fletcher may have been among the first black officers to be trained by the United States Army. As many scholars have noted, black service in World War I provided an enormous psychological boost to African Americans, and this military service has been named as an important contributing factor toward the rise of the "New Negro" movement of the 1920s.*

Davy Carr is also a part of the Great Migration of 1915–1930, a mass movement of African Americans from the mostly rural South to the urban centers of the North and West. A number of factors produced this migration: economic and ecological disasters were ravaging the farming economy of the South; anti-immigration laws were closing off U.S. borders to foreign workers; and World War I was draining northern factories of their labor pool. Most important of all, Jim Crow conditions of

* For an excellent discussion of World War I and its relationship to the Harlem Renaissance, see David Levering Lewis, 1989, *When Harlem Was in Vogue*, New York and Oxford: Oxford University Press. I am also grateful to Tedrina DaCosta for her research on this subject.

peonage, segregation, violence, and rabid discrimination made life unbearable for African Americans in the South. Although the North and West were certainly not free of such problems, they did offer living conditions that were infinitely more desirable than did the states of the former Confederacy. According to Alain Locke, whose anthology, *The New Negro,* signaled the arrival of a "New Negro Renaissance," the Great Migration was "a mass movement toward the larger and the more democratic chance—in the Negro's case a deliberate flight not only from countryside to city, but from medieval America to modern."* Like hundreds of thousands of African Americans, Davy Carr makes his way north in order to pursue a life of his own choosing.

Davy's story, however, is not set in the North, but in Washington, D.C., a place that bore many of the South's more despicable aspects of racial intolerance in the 1920s. A useful portrait of Washington during this period can be found in *The Messenger,* the same magazine that originally serialized *When Washington Was in Vogue* under the title *The Letters of Davy Carr.* From 1923 through 1926, *The Messenger* ran a series of articles, "These 'Colored' United States," that provides a panoramic, state-by-state analysis of black life in America; in October, 1923, it published Neval H. Thomas's "The District of Columbia—a Paradise of Paradoxes." As it happens, Thomas's biography bears an uncanny resemblance to Williams's, and so his depiction of Washington is particularly worth noting. Thomas, who would eventually rise to prominence in the NAACP, was born in Ohio in 1874, just three years after Williams was born in the same state. Both men eventually made their way to Washington, where

*Alain Locke, 1992, *The New Negro.* Intro. Arnold Rampersand. New York: Atheneum, 6.

Thomas pursued his education while working at the Library of Congress. Also like Williams, Thomas died a relatively young man in 1930; he was fifty-six.*

Neval Thomas's depiction of Washington, D.C., in the 1920s highlights the many social ills that prey at the margins of the vibrant social world portrayed in *When Washington Was in Vogue*. Thomas describes the nation's capital as a city marred by violent racism and legally enforced segregation, warped by lack of opportunity in education and the workplace, and pervaded by a mean-spiritedness that informs both its history and its contemporary daily life. He notes with bitterness that the slave trade flourished in the capital for many years, and that auction blocks could be found throughout the city. "Save a few years of Reconstruction," Thomas writes, "the national capital has been to the Negro a scene of sorrow" (79). But Thomas also argues that African Americans managed to flourish in Washington, and in doing so, he describes a thriving, if also necessarily self-contained, world very much like the one found in *When Washington Was in Vogue*:

> *Our people are grouped in numbers of organizations and clubs, some for social service, others for self-improvement, like book lovers' clubs; and in beneficial societies. We have many forward-looking men and women who study the world movements from such able and progressive magazines as* The Messenger, The Nation, The New Republic, *and* The Liberator, *and at the Bethel Literary Society we hear messages from every thinking group in the world. Washington's social life*

* See Tom Lutz and Susanna Ashton, eds., 1996, *These "Colored" United States; African American Essays from the 1920s*, New Brunswick, New Jersey: Rutgers University Press, 76-80.

is the most cultured in the country. To attend any social function is to see a marvel in self-culture, for we see women of various colors, without social contact outside the race, the equal in physical beauty, refinement of conduct, grace in manner and dress, and exquisite social charm of the highest bred Anglo-Saxon woman anywhere in the world. The white man keeps the full weight of his superior numbers, oppressive spirit, and unjust monopoly of political power, hard pressed against this suffering, yet beautiful little world of striving, but we grow to fuller stature in spite of it all. Though he closes such splendid educational agencies as the opera, and such refining experiences as the exercise of civil privileges, to this struggling people, we acquire culture, not through *segregation and oppression, but* in spite *of them.*

In *When Washington Was in Vogue*, E. C. Williams gives us our first extensive view of the "fictional beautiful little world of striving" described by Neval Thomas. Davy Carr comes from the South during the Great Migration, faces combat during World War I, and then arrives in a center of African-American culture that rivaled the renaissance in Harlem. In fact, *When Washington Was in Vogue* might just help dispel the notion that the New Negro Renaissance was ever really as localized as the term "Harlem Renaissance" implies, because the novel and Williams's own life demonstrate just how culturally vibrant the District of Columbia was in the teens and twenties.

Thomas's essay on Washington, D.C., also highlights two of the most important themes in *When Washington Was in Vogue*: the intra-racial politics of skin tone and the experience of modern love in an African-American community. I want to suggest that the novel can be read as having two parts devoted to these themes. In the beginning chapters of the novel, Davy makes frequent observations about variations in skin color, and, considering himself something of an amateur sociologist, he notes the ways in which the politics and mores of color manifest themselves among his friends and acquaintances. In one of his letters to Bob Fletcher, Davy describes Caroline, her sister, Genevieve, and Thomasine Dawson, three of his closest female friends in Washington, by noting their differing shades. Davy then moves on to an analysis of color that consumed many black authors of the period:

> *There was Genevieve, who, barring a little tropical warmth in the lines of her mouth, would pass for a descendant of English or American stock; Caroline, whose vivid coloring, dark skin, and flashing eyes would suggest Spain, or Sicily; and Thomasine Dawson, who might have graced the throne of one of the ancient rulers of the Nile! . . . Why, why, why, with such a variety of beauty of every type under the blue canopy, must we discard as worthless all but one, and that the one in which we can hope least of all to compete with the other race groups environing us? I do not believe, and never have believed, that women of their own choice make of themselves neither fish, flesh, nor good red herring, but they do so through a sort of moral and social compulsion, because so many colored men of the more prosperous class seem to be attracted only by fair women approximating the white type.*

Davy's observations about the intra-racial preference for fair-skinned mates echo a concern that pervaded the era. For even though there was, as Langston Hughes suggested, a Negro "vogue" in the 1920s, opportunities were more likely to elude those African Americans with darker complexions. Indeed, many of the political and cultural luminaries of the so-called "Talented Tenth" (W. E. B. Du Bois's term for the emerging black vanguard in the first decades of the twentieth century) were fair; Williams himself was fair enough to pass for white, which is also true for his protagonist, Davy. Claude McKay, the most important sonneteer of the Renaissance, makes a similar observation in his review of Noble Sissle and Eubie Blake's all-black Broadway hit, *Shuffle Along*. Praising the musical on a number of levels, McKay nonetheless takes the production to task for its "disappointing" casting: "Instead of making up to achieve a uniform near-white complexion the chorus might have made up to accentuate the diversity of shades among 'Afro-Americans' and let white audiences in on the secret of the color nomenclature of the Negro world."*

As both Williams and McKay indicate, black women in particular were victims to the preference for lighter skin. The most well-known fictionalized treatment of this subject is Wallace Thurman's 1929 novel, *The Blacker the Berry,* which begins with Emma Lou Morgan's acute awareness of the drawbacks presented by her "luscious black complexion." Her painful self-consciousness owes directly to her family's sense of shame and inferiority at having such a dark daughter:

> *She wasn't the only person who regretted her darkness either. It was an acquired family characteristic, this moaning and grieving over the color of her skin. Everything possible had been done to alleviate the unhappy condition, every suggested agent had been employed, but her skin, despite bleachings,*

* Claude McKay, 1921, "A Negro Extravaganza," *The Liberator,* Vol. 4 (12): 24–26.

> *scourgings, and powderings, had remained black—fast black—as nature planned and effected.*
>
> *She should have been a boy, then color of skin wouldn't have mattered so much, for wasn't her mother always saying that a black boy could get along, but that a black girl would never know anything but sorrow and disappointment? But she wasn't a boy; she was a girl, and color did matter. . . .**

Although Caroline Rhodes is not as dark as Thurman's main character, she is noticeably darker than Davy, her unwitting suitor, who describes her as having a Mediterranean complexion. Davy is, however, admirably indifferent to the putative values assigned to Caroline's skin tone, and thus Williams's novel can be read as a celebration of "the secret nomenclature of the colored world."

But if Davy is personally unconcerned about Caroline's coloring, he is almost painfully aware of her modern temperament and behavior. Describing himself as an "older person" with "mid-Victorian notions," Davy tells Bob that Caroline has "all the best and the worst points of the modern flapper." Such points are on display from the outset. During Davy's first private meeting with Caroline, when she invites herself into his room, Caroline smokes in front of him while deriding her mother and sister for being too old-fashioned. Davy finds all of this charming, but he also suspects that Caroline's progressive thinking might be merely the last vestiges of her adolescence rather than a clearly articulated challenge to convention: "[S]he sat, swinging her silk-clad legs with the abandon of a small boy, and regaled me in terms pi-

* Wallace Thurman, 1996, *The Blacker the Berry*, New York: Scribner Paperback Fiction, 21–22.

quant and interesting, if a trifle startling at times, with her very modern views of the woman question, fellows, and marriage. Viewed from some standpoints, it was decidedly refreshing, but I am not sure that it was not more shocking than anything else."

For Davy, Caroline embodies the questions he asks her in the early chapters of the book: "Is the love of an up-to-date, modern girl worth having? Or, if worth having, is there any way in which to be sure of it?" Davy's answers come in the second half of the book, when he has been in Washington long enough to feel more like an accepted insider than like a sociological observer of an alien culture. As his involvement with Caroline becomes deeper and ever more complicated, Davy loses his interest in reporting on the black community of D.C. to Bob, and his letters become instead the transcripts of a man who does not realize he is in love.

Davy's inability to recognize his own feelings has everything to do with the historical differences between Caroline and him. Even though he is a participant in two of twentieth century America's most important modern developments, the Great Migration and black service in the war, Davy happily thinks of himself as out of step with many recent developments of modern behavior, which he considers too uncouth for polite society—a social construct he heartily endorses. He is gentlemanly to a fault, dislikes cabarets and most contemporary music, and blushes at the smallest social improprieties. Whatever his actual age, Davy considers himself much older and rather old-fashioned in comparison with Caroline, who bobs her hair, wears abbreviated clothing, drinks bootleg liquor, and smokes cigarettes whenever her mother isn't looking. Williams's novel appears to share the anti-modernism of its protagonist, because as the novel progresses, Caroline alters her behavior to suit Davy's tastes and win his affection. Modern flappers may fascinate Davy Carr, but at the end of the day, he is far more comfortable in the company of women who behave according to traditional expectations. Although it is a delightful novel, *When Washington Was in Vogue* is not a particularly feminist novel.*

But *When Washington Was in Vogue*, if not entirely forward thinking in terms of gender, is also more than just a good read. It is, in fact, an extraordinary novel. Published almost sixty years before Alice Walker's *The Color Purple* (1982), *When Washington Was in Vogue* is quite probably the first example of an epistolary novel in African-American literary history. Writing a novel composed almost entirely of letters (the last pages of the book are a diary entry), Williams mastered a form that has its origins in the eighteenth century but had largely fallen into disuse by the twentieth. Although this literary strategy may not seem as innovative as the modernist experimentation found in such contemporary works as Jean Toomer's *Cane* and Langston Hughes's blues poetry, the epistolary form perfectly suits the subject matter of *When Washington Was in Vogue*. Davy is, after all, an old-fashioned man reacting to the modern world; his formal letters to Bob reflect the state of his psyche, give a good indication of his physical bearing, and demonstrate Davy's self-presentation with immediacy and verisimilitude. Davy's letters to Bob are an excellent measure of both his strength of character and his weakness of emotional insight. *When Washington Was in Vogue* is indeed an important addition to the twinned canons of American and African-American literature.

When Washington Was in Vogue is also a welcome addition

* For an excellent discussion of gender and politics in Williams's novel, see Christina Simmons, "Modern Marriage for African Americans, 1920–1940," *Canadian Review of American Studies* 30:3 (2000). My thanks to A. Crew, whose crazedloveblog pointed me toward Professor Simmons's essay.

more specifically to the literature of the Harlem Renaissance; in fact, as I hinted earlier in this introduction, Williams's novel offers a definitive challenge to the idea that the explosion of African-American creativity in the first decades of the twentieth century can accurately be called the "Harlem" Renaissance at all. When Williams was writing, terms such as "Negro Renaissance," "New Negro Renaissance," and "New Negro Movement" were used to describe the cultural phenomenon that was, perhaps, centered in Harlem but had pockets of black creative and intellectual activity throughout the African Diaspora. The literary ferment in Washington, D.C., that encouraged Williams to write plays and fiction had important links to the Negritude movement of the Francophone world, to developments in Pan-Africanism, as well as to the vibrant culture of Harlem.

The connection between Williams's book and other African-American novels of the period are myriad. Like the middle section of Toomer's *Cane* (1923), *When Washington Was in Vogue* is set in Washington, D.C. According to an unpublished letter written by Toomer* in 1921, he met with a small group of intellectuals, including Williams, to discuss the status of people with "mixed-blood," which is a central concern of Williams's book. Until now, Toomer's experimental novel, which largely condemns the bourgeois stuffiness of Washington's black community, was our only extensive fictional view into that place and time. With *When Washington Was in Vogue*, we acquire an entirely different perspective from Toomer's, because the world Toomer paints in *Cane* as insular and narrow-minded is portrayed by Williams as one marked by accomplishment, creativity, and aspiration. Williams, however, is no Babbittesque booster of

* My thanks to Barbara Foley for sharing this letter with me.

the District. He sees its flaws and writes about them, but the community's foibles are set in a wider and more generous perspective than Toomer's. In this sense, *When Washington Was in Vogue* more closely resembles Nella Larsen's 1929 novel *Passing,* which offers both praise and blame for the black bourgeoisie in New York and Chicago.

When Washington Was in Vogue and Larsen's novel also share a relationship as examples of the "passing" narrative, a common genre in African-American literature, particularly during the early twentieth century. Like Clare Kendry and Irene Redfield in *Passing,* many of Williams's characters—most notably Davy—can, and sometimes do, pass for white. In this way, *When Washington Was in Vogue* also bears a resemblance to James Weldon Johnson's *The Autobiography of an Ex–Colored Man* (1912). Johnson and Williams's novels were both originally published anonymously and were presented as nonfiction, and in each, the narrator/protagonist looks white. However, Johnson's Ex–Colored Man eventually decides to pass permanently as white; in *When Washington Was in Vogue*, Davy, who does not condemn this behavior in others, is firmly set against choosing this path for himself.

While connections can be made between Williams's text and many of the black novels of the era, there is one way in which it is sui generis. Unlike every other novel written by an African American during this period, there is not a single white character in *When Washington Was in Vogue*. There are, certainly, characters that look white, but none identify themselves as such. White characters are common in the novels of the Harlem Renaissance, and, from the sympathetic Stephen Jorgenson in Wallace Thurman's *Infants of the Spring* (1932) to the violently racist John Bellew in *Passing,* they demonstrate a wide range of traits and dispositions. Even Claude McKay's *Home to Harlem* (1928), which focuses almost exclusively on the black demi-monde, has at least one white minor character. *When Washington Was in Vogue* stands alone as a Harlem Renaissance novel comprised entirely of African-American characters. Perhaps the only surprise is that during an age of entrenched Jim Crow legislation, violent racism, and profound discrimination, more African-American novelists did not take a similar tack.

Despite this seeming racial insularity, *When Washington Was in Vogue* is nonetheless a quintessential American novel that reflects its time and place with great insight and a deft style. Narrated by a World War I veteran who feels like an outsider among the beautiful and talented in an unfamiliar urban setting, *When Washington Was in Vogue* shares more than a little with another novel published the same year: F. Scott Fitzgerald's *The Great Gatsby* (1925). Although they resolve quite differently, both novels tell stories of social glitter and emotional blindness, and for all of its mid-Victorian trappings, Williams's novel is a tale of the Jazz Age. Or, perhaps—considering Davy's feelings about jazz—Williams's text is better understood as an anti–Jazz Age novel. *When Washington Was in Vogue* is also a tale of the Harlem Renaissance, but it may well be the book that contributes to the future disuse of that particular term. But these are issues that readers will decide for themselves. One thing is certain: Edward Christopher Williams has captured a time, a place, and a psyche previously undocumented by authors of his era, and he has preserved for us a part of our shared history. *When Washington Was in Vogue* is indeed an American novel of the first order.

COMMENTARY

by Emily Bernard

W*hen Washington Was in Vogue* is a novel. Disregard the original title, *The Letters of Davy Carr: A True Story of Colored Vanity Fair*. Ignore the teasing of "The Publishers" about the "pains" taken to conceal the identities of protagonist Davy Carr's friends. Resist the letters themselves as they silently exhort you to enjoy them as authentic correspondence. This is not as easy as it sounds. The world that Edward Christopher Williams has created in these pages is vivid and exhilarating, and the characters that populate this world are sometimes outrageous, sometimes compassionate, and always wonderfully and poignantly human. It requires real effort to remember that *When Washington Was in Vogue* is only a story, albeit a most remarkable one.

One of the most remarkable features of *When Washington Was in Vogue* is its geographical setting. It has become almost obligatory in the world of Harlem Renaissance scholarship to argue that the term "Harlem Renaissance" is something of a misnomer; that as much of the period's cultural achievements took place outside of the borders of New York City as within them. *When Washington Was in Vogue* is the first piece of fiction to put flesh on this thesis, and present a portrait of black life and culture that is as thrilling as anything Harlem could have conceived. If anything, the intensified insularity of black Washington society serves as an even more fertile ground for intrigue, African-American style. As Adam McKible points out in his introduction, "Unlike every other novel written by an African American during this period, there is not a single white character in *When Washington Was in Vogue.*" In Harlem Renaissance novels, white characters are often present to underscore the disadvantages and hypocrisies of segregation that are at the heart of their tragic plotlines. White racism is only a backdrop in Davy Carr's world, and plays, at the most, only an implicit role in the drama of daily life for privileged black Washingtonians.

The absence of white antagonists in *When Washington Was in Vogue* does not mean that the story is bereft of villains. Colored society in Washington, seemingly, does not need white racism to supply *all* of its venom. Here, Langston Hughes describes black Washington as he experienced it when he lived there in the mid-1920s:

> *. . . the "better class" of Washington colored people, as they called themselves, drew rigid class and color lines within the race against Negroes who worked with their hands, or who were dark in complexion and had no degrees from colleges. These upper-class colored people consisted largely of government workers, professors and teachers, doctors, lawyers, and resident politicians. They were on the whole as unbearable and snobbish a group of people as I have ever come in contact with anywhere. They lived in comfortable homes, had fine cars, played bridge, drank Scotch, gave exclusive "formal" parties, and dressed well, but seemed to me altogether lacking in real culture, kindness, or good common sense."*[*]

[*] Langston Hughes, *The Big Sea* (New York: Knopf, 1940), 207.

The dramas of this heartless group make up the world of *When Washington Was in Vogue*. Just as Langston Hughes suggests, its members can be quite dreadful. But Hughes's description above leaves out a few things, namely the style, wit, and charm that characterize this group as much as its bad behavior. The devils described above are anything but dull. Betrayals are carried out with colorful language and in fetching evening wear. As Hughes himself admitted in a scathing 1927 indictment of the same crowd, "Our Wonderful Society: Washington," published in the August 1927 issue of *Opportunity*, he found himself "awed" by these self-described "best people." Even in their ugliness the "better class" of black Washingtonians captivate. Shallow creatures they may be, but what they represent is hardly frivolous. The contradictions they embody—a simultaneous dedication to race unity and rigid intraracial hierarchies—have always been, and may always be, fundamental aspects of black society. *When Washington Was in Vogue* pulls back the curtain and unapologetically reveals the timelessly unattractive underside of black elitism and the poignant contradictions that are an inherent feature of the project of "race uplift."

Captain Davy Carr enters this world largely unprepared for the social complexities he is about to encounter. He is fresh from a stint as an officer in World War I, but he has neither the weapons nor the battle plans he needs to navigate the gender and class wars that are Washington's black subculture. For a Harlem Renaissance novel, *When Washington Was in Vogue* has a most unusual protagonist. Davy Carr is, first of all, older than the young men and women with whom most Harlem Renaissance fiction is preoccupied. He bears no resemblance to the hedonistic, dissipated, cynical young men and women that play both major and minor roles in other Harlem Renaissance novels, like

The Blacker the Berry; Infants of the Spring; Home to Harlem; Quicksand; and *Nigger Heaven.* Davy Carr is a model of focus, sobriety, and industry: having served in World War I, he is in Washington to research a book on the African slave trade. The bawdy pursuits that characterize the Jazz Age, activities that readers turn to these books to experience vicariously, hold no interest for the captain. Here Davy Carr describes his reactions to an evening spent at a cabaret:

> *The songs were of a type whose cheapness, vulgarity, banality, and utter lack of wit, humor, harmony, or distinction of any kind, simply defy description. . . . The themes were hackneyed beyond the power of my poor pen to depict, and how any human being with a spark of intelligence—I don't say decency—could sit and listen to them, except under actual compulsion, is more than I can fathom.*

In his utter conservatism, Davy Carr is actually an intriguing addition to the panorama of memorable characters in Harlem Renaissance fiction. Davy's priggishness is somehow refreshing and even daring when juxtaposed with the reverential manner in which cabaret scenes are often experienced and narrated in novels from this period. But most importantly, the voluptuous language Davy uses to describe his distaste for the scene hints to his true ambivalent feelings about such scenes, and the changing social world they represent.

The object of Carr's passionate prose is Bob Fletcher, Davy's former comrade-in-arms and present correspondent. The relationship between Davy and Bob recalls the dynamic between Jake and Ray in Claude McKay's *Home to Harlem,* similarly suggesting, at times, a homoeroticism that lies beneath the surface of both novels' ostensible plots. *When Washington Was in Vogue* resembles *Home to Harlem* by Claude McKay in its preoccupation with the smorgasbord of women its male protagonist encounters. E. C. Williams's sirens are not the dizzying "chocolate browns" that Jake beholds but rather a set of chic, urbane women whose reserved, subtle ways are no less enticing and bewildering than the more explicit come-hithering that Jake navigates in *Home to Harlem*. Davy Carr may lack Jake's smoothness and confidence, but he is, privately, an eroticist, much like his counterpart in *Home to Harlem*. Here, Davy writes to Bob about one memorable evening:

> *I had the exquisite pleasure of being fed from time to time by the loveliest hands in the world—on both sides of me—and if in the process of taking marshmallows from the fingertips of Beauty, I now and then missed the marshmallows and got more than my share of the fingertips, who can blame me?*

However attenuated, Davy Carr's sensuality is clear in his language, and it is also evidenced by the care with which he reproduces this moment for his friend. He recounts his life to Bob Fletcher with the kind of doting tenderness and exacting detail that suggests more than a casual bond—it signifies an intimate connection. The epistolary form this novel takes contributes to the sense of intimacy between the two men, and enables readers to appreciate this story on a more subtle level than a conventional novel. *When Washington Was in Vogue* reminds us of the important role correspondence has always played in our deep, human need to testify to our experience, and to assign order and meaning to the things that happen to us. In this book, letters are not only records of love and desire, but expressions of it, as well.

When Washington Was in Vogue is singularly preoccupied with the doings of one Caroline Rhodes, even though she is not the possessor of either set of fingertips that found their way into Davy Carr's mouth during the evening Davy remembers above. Even though, as Adam McKible asserts in his introduction, *When Washington Was in Vogue* is not a feminist novel, there are fascinating women everywhere in this book, frankly sensuous, free-thinking, plain-speaking women. But none of these women has as much to offer readers as does Caroline Rhodes: "the prettiest, trimmest, shapeliest little brown girl you ever saw, with the boldest black eyes I ever looked into," Davy Carr gushes to Bob Fletcher shortly after his first encounter with Caroline. All of the women in the Rhodes family are exceptional but Caroline is the "flower of the flock." Indeed, Caroline Rhodes may be among the most memorable characters in Harlem Renaissance fiction. Like Clare Kendry in *Passing*, she is a young woman who fails to heed conventional attitudes about decorum and female behavior. She smokes, makes off-color jokes, and glories in a variety of male company. When she is with Davy, she lodges sarcastic barbs, teases him into doing her schoolwork, and steals his cigarette holder. Davy's hesitant sensuality is outdistanced by Caroline's no-holds-barred approach to racy banter. Early in the novel, when Davy suggests the he might give her a spanking if she were his daughter, Caroline keeps the joke alive, inflecting Davy's "innocent" comment with raunchy sexual innuendo. To put it simply, Caroline Rhodes is a delight.

Importantly, Caroline is also brown-skinned, unapologetically so. She is not "tragically colored," to use the phrase coined by Zora Neale Hurston in her essay, "How It Feels to Be Colored Me." Caroline Rhodes is a refreshing, ribald antidote to the panorama of black women in Harlem Renaissance fiction who lament blackness, their own or others'. She is no Emma Lou Morgan who, in *The Blacker the Berry,* swallows arsenic wafers to lighten her complexion. She would only pity Olivia Blanchard Cary, who in Jessie Fauset's *Comedy: American Style* drives her own son to suicide, so disgusted is she by his brown skin. Caroline Rhodes wears her blackness beautifully. When she comes across the color prejudice of other women, she understands it as the manifestation of their helpless jealousy over her beauty and popularity, and walks away, untraumatized. If novels like *The Blacker the Berry* and *Comedy: American Style* wring their hands over the color question, then *When Washington Was in Vogue* turns on its heel and leaves the question for others to fret over, and makes its way to the next party, the next gripping romance, the next "toothsome repast."

For much of the novel, Caroline's primary pursuit is pleasure. She may be a hedonist, but *When Washington Was in Vogue* refuses to allow you to take her for a mindless little flapper. She carefully fashions the persona that she parades in front of Davy, the object of her desire, and she delights in the confusion it causes him. As a seductress, Caroline Rhodes is a diligent student of the lusty tradition; early in the novel, we find her in her parlor reading *Madame Bovary.* Caroline may actually have some tips for the romantic heroines she studies. As Davy swoons in a letter to Bob, "Indeed, she is a type of whom Jane Austen never dreamed, for all her dainty feminine beauty."

The union of Caroline Rhodes and Davy Carr is a case of opposites attracting, but it is also a uniting of generations and ideological trajectories in African-American culture. Will they or won't they? The novel turns on this question, which finally concerns not only the possibility of the romantic coupling of Caroline and Davy, but also the generations they stand for, and ideological preoccupations these generations represent. Will the collective dreams of the race be realized? Will true racial unity be achieved? *When Washington Was in Vogue* imagines, through the characters of Caroline and Davy, that the conflict between the younger and older generations is not so much a rift, but a frustration of mutual curiosity, and that within this frustration itself lies the possibility for its solution.

In its romantic significance alone, the "Will they or won't they?" question is gripping. As a novel about romance, in all of its exquisite pain and pleasure, *When Washington Was in Vogue* is hypnotic. The reader *is* Bob Fletcher, receiving Davy's panting, love-filled missives, rooting for him, anticipating his liberation from the blindness inspired both by his romantic thickness as well as by his generational anxieties about the dramatic cultural revolution African-American society seemed to be undergoing during the Jazz Age. "Yours, in deep trouble, Davy" is how Carr signs one of his letters to Bob. Trouble beckons Davy throughout these pages, trouble in the form of his own desire, as well as his conflict over the changing times and his role within them. Trouble calls Davy, and he answers willingly. As readers, we find ourselves urging Davy along into more and more dangerous, thrilling, unknown territory. Eagerly, we follow.

When Washington Was In Vogue

A Lost Novel of the Harlem Renaissance

The following prefatory note was written by the editors of *The Messenger,* the Harlem Renaissance journal that published this novel anonymously as serial excerpts in 1925 and 1926.

THE LETTERS OF DAVY CARR

Prefatory Note

It has long been asserted that in the city of Washington, Colored American Society has reached the point of greatest complexity, if not the highest development. The reasons for this are not far to seek, for the population of the national capital is a conglomerate of elements from every state in the Union. This explains, at least in part, the interest manifested in this favored group by society everywhere. In these days of ease and fatness, following an era of small things, we sometimes have asked ourselves if the race which survived centuries of slavery and adversity might not succumb under the degenerative influences of freedom and prosperity. It is a source of great pleasure, then, to be able to offer our readers a real judgment in the case, for the "Letters of Davy Carr" present a rather brilliant cross section of Washington's Vanity Fair. Since the publishers of contemporaneous personal letters oft-times suffer under the imputation of indelicacy, it was with some hesitation that we ventured even to consider the present undertaking. After due reflection, however, we are convinced that, through the exercises of competent and discriminating editorial censorship, the principal objections to publication could be removed.

In this connection we were fortunate in securing for this difficult and delicate task of editing a person intimately acquainted with the social life of the capital city. After making a careful study of the letters, he decided that certain alterations were imperative. First, all the names must be changed, of persons, clubs, cities, and even streets, except in the few cases in which the real name could work no harm. Next, he must distort and dislocate, so to speak, such descriptions as might make too obvious the identity of certain characters. Finally, he excised entirely a few passages which seemed too revelatory. While doing this he has striven to preserve unspoiled the flavor of the letters, by retaining the carelessness, the colloquialism, and the unstudied art of the originals, even at the cost of an occasional split infinitive, or other bugbear of the teacher of syntax and composition. What the resulting document loses in polish, and in finish of diction, it should more than gain in naturalness.

We realize that whatever pains we may take to conceal the identity of Davy Carr's friends, there are those of our readers who will insist that they see resemblances even where none exist. This, of course, we cannot help. All we can do is to wish them joy in their difficult if fascinating task. To forestall possible questions from the over-curious, perhaps we might say now that the publishers and the editor are under pledge not to reveal the identity of anyone mentioned in this unique correspondence.

In conclusion, we feel that we are presenting to our readers something absolutely new in the field of writing as it relates to our race group. But let the letters speak for themselves. They are before you!

The Publishers

N.B. The headings are furnished by the editor.

ONE

In which Davy, having arrived in Vanity Fair,
looks for lodgings and finds a home.

Washington, D.C., Monday, October 2, 1922

Dear Bob:

You certainly were right when you advised me to wait until I found just what I wanted. I was getting impatient and I should have taken the place on T Street, if it had not been for your letter. So I decided to hold out a few days longer, and my waiting has been rewarded, for I have found the best place imaginable. This self-congratulation may seem a little premature, but somehow I do not think it is. My good luck came from an unexpected source, too.

I called on the Wallaces the other night, and in the midst of a very interesting conversation Mrs. Wallace happened to ask me if I were located satisfactorily. I told her my troubles, and gave her an idea as to what I wanted. She reflected a minute, and then said she thought she could help me out. So she excused herself and, while Wallace and I talked and smoked, I could hear her in the next room telephoning. After a while she returned and handed me a note. I glanced at the envelope and noted that it was inscribed to a Mrs. Margaret Rhodes, at an address just around the corner from the T Street house I was considering. So I went there the next afternoon at about five. I was met at the door by a handsome, rather stately young woman with a very dignified manner, who ushered me into the back parlor, where I was asked to have a seat. She left me for a moment, but reappeared almost immediately to say that her mother would see me in a few minutes. She then returned to the parlor, where she was entertaining a lady caller.

Thus left to my own devices, I took the opportunity to look about me, and to say that I was delighted with what I saw expresses it mildly. Rarely have I seen a room—it was evidently a library-living room—that I have liked better. Solid, substantial furniture, walls lined with bookcases filled with good books, and more good pictures and art objects, well selected and in the best of taste, than I have seen in an ordinary home for a long time. Nothing seemed new, but, on the contrary, everything showed signs of use, and looked as if it were an integral part of the room. An open fireplace, in which a fire was laid ready for lighting, gave the final touch of coziness. To say I was charmed is putting it mildly. Mrs. Rhodes, when she entered, seemed quite in place in the picture. She is an attractive, motherly person of quiet manners and refined speech. My mind was made up the moment I saw her and I was afraid only that she might refuse me. In fear and trembling, so to speak, I gave her Mrs. Wallace's note. She read the note attentively, and then arose and offered me her hand.

"I am pleased to meet any friend of the Wallaces, Mr. Carr. I was not planning to take anyone else," she continued. "We have one lodger, and we have just begun to get used to him. You see, we never had anyone in the house except our own family while Mr. Rhodes was alive, and it is hard to break old habits. What Mrs. Wallace says puts a different face on it, of course. Mr. Rhodes knew your people well, I believe. I have heard him speak often of your father." She hesitated, and looked at me again smilingly. "We have only one room available, and I don't like to think of renting it. It was Mr. Rhodes's private den." Again she hesitated, and again she looked at me. "Well, let's look at it, anyway, since you are here."

She arose, and I followed her—two flights of stairs to the third-floor back. The room itself finished me, and I decided then and there that I must have it. It was appointed to suit me exactly—wallcases, couch, table, revolving bookcase and all.

"This is just what I want," I said. "If only you will let me have it, I promise you I shan't give you a bit of trouble. I am a quiet person, and you won't know I am here."

To make a long story short, the good lady agreed to take me in, and I hastened to clinch the bargain by paying my first month's rental, which was most reasonable, and making immediate arrangements for the moving in of my traps.

As we reached the lower hall, the young woman who had let me in was just taking leave of her visitor. As she turned from the door, Mrs. Rhodes called her.

"Genevieve, let me present Mr. Carr. Mr. Carr, this is my daughter, Miss Rhodes."

That dignified young person received the introduction with a cool graciousness which was a curious mixture of perfect courtesy and impersonal indifference.

Then Mrs. Rhodes explained my errand, told who I was, and otherwise oriented me for the benefit of the handsome young woman with the coldly gracious manner, who withdrew as soon as she could do so without too much abruptness.

So two days later I moved in, and had a rather enjoyable time unpacking my books, and bestowing my belongings properly. All is now in order, and I hope sincerely that I am settled for the winter. Somehow I feel that I am going to like this place. The house is certainly homelike and attractive, and the Rhodes family are surely "easy on the eyes," for they have as high an average of good looks as any household I have seen in many a day. Mrs. Rhodes must have been a belle in her youth, and she is still good looking, with the dearest, most motherly manner in the world; Genevieve, as I have said, is very handsome, stately, fair, with fine chestnut hair and dark eyes; but the flower of the flock is Caroline, the younger daughter, who is a real beauty, much darker than her sister, more petite, and livelier. She has, apparently, all the best and the worst points of the modern flapper.

I saw her first the day I moved in. I was unpacking and arranging my books when Mrs. Rhodes came in to see how I was getting on. She was followed closely by the prettiest, trimmest, shapeliest little brown girl you ever saw, with the boldest black eyes I ever looked into. She received her mother's introduction with the savoir faire of a duchess, and took me in with her appraising eyes in such wise that I was almost embarrassed, though, as you know, I have not a reputation for lack of poise.

There is a boy, too, it seems. He is twenty, so his mother says, and he has just matriculated in the medical school. Since he spends most of his time at the chapter house of his fraternity, I have not seen him yet. As the youngest member of the household, and a boy in a trio of doting women, I have no doubt that he has been indulged to a degree, and is consequently a spoiled darling. I am glad, then, that he spends little time at home.

There is another lodger here. He has the third-floor front, and seems quite luxuriously housed. He is surely a swell dresser, and must be popular to judge from the mail and messages he gets. Maybe you know him. I have passed him twice in the hall in the last two or three days, and I know only his name, which is Morris H. Jeffreys. I have noted through his open door two Atlanta pennants adorning his walls. Since you know almost everyone from that neck of the woods, maybe you have come across this M. H. Jeffreys. He is a tall, well-built, brownskin chap with a quick step, and a rather assured manner. His voice is very musical and soft—almost too soft, somehow. At any rate, that's the way it strikes me. Though maybe that is just the little human touch of envy that would pick a flaw in a chap who is handsome, well dressed and unusually prosperous looking.

Of course I know the danger of judging young chaps—Jeffreys looks under twenty-five—by their outward appearance. You and I know the wonderful front that was put up by some of those impecunious, scheming, grafting birds with whom we consorted in the good old days in the Sunny South. And I guess the North is not so different. Human nature is about the same everywhere, and I have never heard that state boundaries make any difference in that particular. At any rate, "yours truly" has learned to shy at a suave, soft-spoken boy who is *too* well dressed. Do you remember Milton Upshaw and the vanished semester fees money to which we bade such a fond farewell? Every time I think of Milt I smell hair burning, and it isn't a nice odor, is it, Bob? So, while I realize that it is not fair to him, maybe, I cannot help saying that every time I have seen this Jeffreys I have thought of Milt Upshaw and our vanished coin. If Jeffreys could only see my thoughts he certainly would have good grounds for a suit for slander. But enough of him!

I have heard it said many times that Washington has more pretty women than any city in the country, and I am beginning to think it is true. I had another illustration of it last night. The Wallaces, who have been very kind, invited me to supper, and there I met Dr. and Mrs. Morrow, the Hales, Miss Lillian Barton, and Mr.

Morton Reese, an eligible bachelor. It was an unusually interesting group, I assure you, and such as one would not be likely to meet around one table in many cities with which I am acquainted. For example, the conversation happening to turn to France and the war, it transpired that, of the nine people present, including myself, at least six have been to Europe—I am not sure as to the other three—and one or two of them more than once. They are all highly cultivated people.

The Wallaces you know already, having met them in Boston last summer. Dr. Morrow is a very distinguished-looking dark man, tall and graceful, with the manner of an aristocrat, and Morton Reese you know by reputation. The ladies, except Mrs. Wallace, are all very fair, and would not be likely to be taken for colored, and in manner and dress they all of them showed real class. I am not sure that Miss Barton is not, taking her in all, the most brilliant woman I have ever met in colored society, but I speak, remember, after only one meeting. She is not only clever and witty, with a real sparkle about her, but she is undeniably handsome. In fact, I am not sure that one might not call her beautiful. Mrs. Hale is a rather stately beauty, with a fine color and a pair of interesting gray eyes. We took a liking to each other on sight apparently. At any rate, I am sure that I took a liking to her, and I *think* she did to me, but I don't wish to appear conceited.

This much I know, that I had a ripping good time, and a very nice supper—creamed oysters, and wonderful cocoa, and other good things—and last, but by no means least, plenty of the most stimulating conversation. Wallace himself is a man who does not deal in gossip or small talk, but is a well-read chap with real brains and genuine intellectual interests, and he rather set the pace. I must confess that most of those present were quite able to hold their own.

Taking it all in all, I was quite elated over my evening. The company was certainly a choice one, and I was accepted without question as "belonging." The Morrows took all the guests home in their car, and as they left me at my door, they gave me a very cordial invitation to call, which I shall certainly not let go by default.

This letter was interrupted by a voice at my door, and the entrance of Miss Caroline Rhodes, my landlady's younger daughter. She came to bring me your telegram. She delayed her going by some errand or other in the big storeroom opening off the hall just outside my door long enough to pop her head in again, and say that she hoped it was not bad news. It is a curious thing about telegrams and long-distance telephone messages. So many people seem to have a horror of them, as expedients resorted to only in matters of life and death. In this, as in other things, we are progressing. I know that I did not get over my provincial feeling of excitement over a telegram until I had sent and received some scores of them in that very exciting winter of 1917–1918.

At any rate, Miss Caroline asked me if the news was bad, and, the ice thus broken, sat down on a corner of my couch and chatted a few moments. She is really quite a striking little beauty, with the most flashing black eyes you ever saw, and the prettiest feet and ankles imaginable. Extremes surely meet in that last sentence, don't they?

As an older person I took the liberty of asking questions, all of which she answered very frankly, and at the same time quite as frankly took in everything in my room. She teaches in a graded school, so she says, and her sister teaches in the high school. She, Caroline, is planning through evening work at the University to get her college degree, so that she may take the high school examinations, and thus put herself in line for the better salaries the secondary school positions pay.

"Genevieve gets $2,740 a year," she said in her sprightly manner, "and she does not need it half as much as I do. It takes money to keep up in this town!" Verily, I believe it does, to judge from what I have seen thus far! "And you have not a ghost of a show to get married nowadays if you can't cash a nice fat paycheck once a month," she added, laughing.

"Has it come to that?" I queried.

"It has, indeed," she answered. "Mother raves over what she calls 'such a state of things.' But I tell her that the Middle Ages are over—this is 1922. *She* used to go buggy riding with her best fellow when she was coming up, but that does not prove that there's anything wrong with a 1923 Packard, does it?"

Of course, you know my flair for what you call "things social and sociological." So I commenced to question her in real earnest, trying to get her point of view, if, indeed, these flappers have any such thing. While talking, I asked her permission to light a cigarette.

"Surely," she laughed, "if you will give me one. I love Melachrinos." She had recognized the box across the room.

Then she noticed my cigarette holder, the one that pretty French girl at Granges gave me. She sized it up with a discerning eye, noticed my monogram engraved on it, and I had to tell her all about it.

"By the way," she said, "Mother and Genevieve fuss a lot about my smoking, so please keep mum. Genevieve thinks I am headed straight to perdition, and says so, while Mother thinks so, I am afraid, without saying so. It's a chore getting along with two Victorian females in one house. One's a great plenty, I'll say!"

And so she sat, swinging her silk-clad legs with the abandon of a small boy, and regaled me in terms piquant and interesting, if a trifle startling at times, with her very modern views of the woman question, fellows, and marriage. Viewed from some standpoints, it was decidedly refreshing, but I am not sure that it was not more shocking than anything else. Hearing a step on the stairs, she hastily put her half-smoked cigarette back among the books on the shelf behind her. At the moment, Jeffreys appeared at the head of the stairs. She greeted him cordially and most informally, and he returned the greeting with that flashing smile of his, and stopped in the doorway for a few seconds. After introducing us to each other, Caroline resumed her cigarette.

"He surely is a good-looking fellow," I thought, as I took in his lithe gracefulness as he leaned carelessly against the door frame, and his manners and "manner" are perfection. And yet, somehow, I don't like him.

"Jealous," you will say.

"Of what?" say I.

This is a shockingly long letter, and I know you are overcome by this time, so I shall close. Be good, old fellow, even if you are a bit lonesome at times. A word to the wise—the Brown Boulevard is almost as alluring and quite as dangerous as the gay White Way! Keep that thought in your mind. Remember the words of that catchy song some of the boys used to sing:

If you haven't been vamped by a brownskin,
You haven't been vamped at all!

There is not a great deal of poetry in that song, Buddie, but there's a whole lot of truth. So keep your lamps working, and watch your step! If that Harlem life gets you, you won't amount to a tinker's damn—excuse my perfect Old English!—but if you can weather that particular trouble, there's no telling what you may not do. But I have said it all before, you know it, and I know it—so why repeat it, you may say. True, but I am older than you are, and I have seen many a good fellow break his neck over that same old log.

Write soon, and tell me what you are doing.

With all good wishes,

Davy

TWO

A day out-of-doors, with music by moonlight and two fair faces. Sunday supper seasoned with gossip.

Washington, D.C., October 9, 1922

Dear Bob:

I am glad you found my last letter entertaining. It surely was long, and I feared it might be tedious. Life has many charms hereabouts, socially speaking. I miss the theater, of course, and envy you your opportunities on the little old island of Manhattan. When I look over the Sunday edition of the *New York Times*, and note the theatrical page, I could weep. The downtown theaters here segregate colored people, and some of them will not sell them seats anywhere but in the gallery. Naturally, that lets me out. You will say, of course, that since I can "get by," such a rule should not bother me. But for some reason difficult to explain, it does. Needless to relate, scores of folks here go to the theater whenever they want to, and sit where they please, and no one notices them. Who, indeed, can blame them?

And that brings me to a question which has interested me very much, the existence of color lines within the color line. It is a very fascinating subject, and one on which I am going to write someday, for nothing that I have seen in print thus far seems to do the theme anything like justice. Then, too, the whole face of the matter is undergoing ceaseless transformations, as might be expected. The complexity of our social life is amazing. It makes one think of the kaleidoscopes we used to have when I was a very small boy. As you looked through them, the colors and forms changed moment by moment. To my mind, and I speak, as you well know, from a varied experience, this town presents a better opportunity for the study of this question of color lines within the race group than any city in America, so I am keeping eyes and ears open.

I have had a very fine outing since my last. This bachelor man of whom I wrote, Morton Reese, has a bungalow south of the city in a suburb called Anacostia. You may recall the name as being associated with that of Frederick Douglass, for his old mansion is situated there. Well, Reese has a fashion of inviting his friends to motor out now and then for week-ends. Last week the Morrows, the Wallaces, the Hales, and Miss Barton, all of whom you will remember were at the supper party I described in my last, were invited, and I was fortunate enough to be included. Naturally, as a stranger in a strange land, I should like to know who are my friends, and so I should give a good deal to know to whose interest I owe my invitation. Reese himself phoned me Friday night, but somehow I do not believe the initiative came from him. At any rate, not to burden you with too much detail, which may not interest you, I cannot imagine who suggested me as a member of the party, and I would give something handsome to find out.

But to return to the party itself. The Wallaces, so Reese said, would come for me shortly after three Saturday. So about three-thirty they arrived, bringing with them the Hales. The ride out was delightful in the bracing October chill, and our party was a merry one. Mrs. Hale was strikingly handsome, with her rosy cheeks and dark hair, Mrs. Wallace was as jolly as could be, and Wallace is always the best of company. Hale himself was lively enough for that matter, but his face was flushed, as if he had been drinking, and I noticed that Mrs. H. looked furtively at him from time to time. But the ride was exhilarating, and for my part too soon over.

The bungalow, as they called it, was after all not a bungalow at all, for it was a tiny two-story affair, with a wide veranda covering the front on both floors. Downstairs there was a tiny kitchen and a pantry, and a small front room with an open grate; and upstairs one bedroom and a big sleeping porch. We sat on the lower porch and waited a few minutes for our host, who brought Miss Barton with him in his very trim roadster, and he was followed immediately by the Morrows, who brought with them someone of whom we have heard more than once from Marcia. I refer to her friend Donald Verney. He is an interesting-looking fellow, surely. He may be a trifle older than Wallace, but he has such a youthful manner that it is hard to guess his age. He is a little above the medium height, fair, yet with a kind of ruddy brownness, good features, and keen eyes. He seems to be a general favorite, is a lively talker when the mood takes him, and a very good storyteller. Altogether, it was about as lively a crowd of reasonably mature people as I have ever seen.

The Morrows, Wallaces, and Hales, being householders, had brought generous hampers of provisions. Following Reese's suggestion I had brought some nuts and candy, and each of the others had a contribution. There was enough and to spare. While the women folks opened up the house, and dusted and swept a bit, the men chopped wood, shook out the beds, hung out the bedding to air, made fires in the kitchen range and in the parlor grate, and swept off the porches. It was great fun. The three married ladies are all accomplished housekeepers, and before long we sat down—on boxes and rickety chairs, to be sure—to as toothsome a repast as I have ever eaten in my life.

The dinner disposed of, in the midst of a running fire of banter, we men were told to wash the dishes, for which service a large tin of water had been set to boil on the range. As we were all in sweaters, we needed to make no special preparations for work, but set to with a will. While we did the dishes in a clumsy, man-fashion, the ladies arranged the sleeping quarters for the night, and dressed for the evening.

Soon they were down again, attractive in sweaters, tam-o'-shanters, and leggings. The dishes were soon put up, and Reese and the men who had been at the bungalow before scurried about getting together the paraphernalia for the evening. I was soon staggering under a load consisting of a lot of firewood and a pile of heavy blankets and steamer rugs, and under the leadership of Wallace, Dr. Morrow, Hale, Verney, and I started on ahead, leaving Reese to lock up the house and escort the ladies. We crossed the road and walked down a path through a little clump of woods until we came to a clearing on the brow of a hill, which gave a fine view of all the country around. It was now growing dark, and the edge of the moon could be seen just peeping over the horizon. On the brow of the hill there was a small square enclosed by a low parapet of brick and stone, and close to the trunk of a fallen tree. Here we piled newspapers and a large amount of small wood, and when this had begun to blaze, we put on two or three of the logs we had brought. In a few minutes we had a bonfire of no mean proportions. Then we pulled the fallen tree trunk into a better position, arranged the rugs and blankets, lighted our pipes and cigarettes, and stretching ourselves out luxuriously in the comforting heat and the cheerful light happily awaited the coming of the ladies.

We had not long to wait, and soon we were all leaning against the fallen trunk, enjoying the fire and the beautiful night. I sat between Miss Barton and Mrs. Hale, and for once in my life I realized to the full the meaning of the old saying: "Oh, I could be happy with either, were t'other dear charmer away." Surely never in my mundane existence have I had the honor of being the thrice fortunate thorn between two such roses—real American beauties! The looking was deadly to the right or to the left. And such a good time we had! Repartee—and not the cornfield or levee variety, either, my boy—kept one's wits going constantly. Miss Barton sang—a rich mezzo-soprano, well trained. Verney told stories, and then I had the temerity to sing. I really made a hit with "Duna" and one or two of Tosti's old ones. I don't believe I quite appreciated my voice before. But I suppose a gorgeous moon and a bonfire will make pretty rotten music sound like the heavenly choir.

Reese sat on the other side of Miss Barton, but I was conscious that I was getting more than my full share of her company. However, don't think, please, that I take too much to myself, for I realize, of course, that as a stranger I might get more attention than home folks. Then we toasted marshmallows and roasted peanuts, and I had the exquisite pleasure of being fed from time to time by the loveliest hands in the world—on both sides of me—and if in the process of taking marshmallows from the fingertips of Beauty, I now and then missed the marshmallows and got more than my share of the fingertips, who can blame me? Certainly not you, Old Pal!

If Miss Barton were not engaged to Reese, I fear that I should make a fool of myself over her, for she is a real fascinator. And then when I look at Mary Hale, I get another dizzy spell, but she is still safer, being married. By the way, I noted a bit of byplay which interested me. It may have meant much or nothing—probably nothing. You have sometimes said that I have a gift for seeing things overlooked by most people. Perhaps I have. At any rate, I have always been more interested in *people* than in anything else in this world, and I guess that I watch them more than do my fellow mortals, even when, as individuals, they are utterly unknown to me. But to return to the little byplay. I noticed that Mrs. Hale frequently fed marshmallows and peanuts to Verney, and once or twice she even bit them in half and gave him one part, usually, in fact, put it to his lips with her fingers, and neither she, nor he, seemed to hurry the process much. Seated as we were in a row, such a thing might easily escape notice. By pure accident I saw it once, and then I watched for it. Then I noticed that she always appealed to him with questions, that when he talked she listened to no one else, and when a good story or joke was told, her eyes sought his when the laugh went around. Perhaps I overstate *her* side of it, for he certainly did his part, but he seems to have a shy streak, and is usually very quiet when not actively drawn into the conversation.

But, alas, even the most delightful of evenings must have an end and thus it was with this most delectable one. So, we scattered the glowing embers, picked up our wraps and belongings, and "with reluctant steps and slow" wended our way back through the woods in the light of the now-risen moon, which shone resplendent over the valley. Reese and I escorted Miss Barton, and I, in my role of investigator, noted that Mrs. Hale leaned heavily on Verney's arm, and he, though laden down with rugs and blankets, seemed in nowise incommoded thereby.

Since we men were to sleep on the porch, and therefore would have to pass through the one inside sleeping room, we went up first and turned in early. I lay awake longer than usual, thinking very pleasant thoughts, in which Lillian Barton and Mary Hale were agreeably commingled, and with the strains of Tosti's "I Dream of the Day I Met You" running melodiously through it all. Then I fell asleep, the fathoms-deep slumber of the health-giving out-of-doors.

I shall not burden you with a further relation of the events of Sunday, a gorgeous October day, and the tramps in the woods, and the long walk up the country road with Lillian Barton to get milk, and the long talk with Lillian Barton sitting on the brow of the hill. Old Pal, she's a wonder! I have never met anyone just like her. I have tried to think up a word or two by means of which to give you an idea of her personality, and I can think only of scintillating, sparkling. You will laugh, I know, but you should see her. When you do, I predict your immediate and complete subjugation.

It was with regret, accompanied by a feeling of keen satisfaction, that I alighted from Wallace's car Sunday night at eight. Our house was brightly lighted and I knew the girls had visitors. I dodged through the hall quickly, for I felt somewhat bedraggled, and not dressed for company. As I did not feel sleepy, I washed up, changed my clothes, and had started a letter to you when Caroline appeared in the doorway with an invitation to Sunday supper.

"Nothing special," she said, "but we need another man."

And while she talked, she coolly robbed my cigarette case, and smiled at me coquettishly the while. As she stood in the doorway waiting for me to give a final "lick" to my hair and to adjust my tie, I noted that she was attired in the extreme modern mode — a waist with no top and no back, a skirt extremely abbreviated, the sheerest of fine silk stockings, and the thinnest of French pumps. The amount of bare flesh was amazing and yet this is cold-weather attire in Washington, my boy! However, I suppose we have nothing on Harlem when it comes to displaying our natural advantages, eh? If you were not in New York, I might surprise you, but I realize that a few days in the subway trains leave one without further capacity for shock.

I went downstairs with Caroline, and was ushered into the very attractive dining room. As in certain Washington houses, it is in the basement, and this was the first time I had seen it. It is done in café au lait, and is, I think, quite satisfying to the eye. There were some strange faces around the table, and I was glad that I had fixed up a bit. Besides Mrs. Rhodes and her two daughters, there was my fellow lodger, Jeffreys, a chap named Johns, and two younger women, Misses Clay and Young. The latter was rather frumpy, but Miss Clay was quite as stylish as Caroline. She would be a pretty brown girl if she would stop trying to be white. I noted her critically, having in mind my proposed study of the color line within the race. She was bleached several shades lighter as far as her face was concerned, for, happening later in the evening to stand directly behind her, I noticed that her neck was a very dark brown. She was dressed to the minute, and carelessly thrown over the back of her chair and half dragging on the floor was a Hudson seal coat, which must have knocked the spots out of five hundred dollars. Her dress, stockings, slippers, hat, and jewelry were all the most expensive type, if I am any judge. You will ask with me, "How do they do it?" It is a question one asks here a dozen times a day, and only echo answers.

"Did you have a good time?" asked Genevieve, with her quiet, courteous manner, after I had been presented and had taken my seat.

"The time of my young life!" I responded with enthusiasm.

"Mr. Carr has been spending his weekend among the 'dicties,'" piped up Caroline in explanation. Everybody laughed, and Miss Clay asked who was meant. So Caroline, who had gotten her information from the Lord knows where, proceeded to give an accurate account of our party. Then, with what seemed to me execrable taste, under all the circumstances, Miss Clay proceeded to tear my friends, figuratively speaking, limb from limb. I do not believe that I was ever so scandalized in my life. Here were these people whom I knew only as kind and pleasing hosts to a newcomer, and I had to sit, a guest at a strange table, and listen while still a stranger woman dissected them to the very nerves and arteries. For a few moments I was completely nonplussed, and busily attacked the supper, trying to ignore the monologue, which was plainly intended for me. Mrs. Rhodes and Genevieve intervened as best they could, and finally did succeed in blanketing the loquacious Miss Clay. I have heard more than once, as have you, of the class feeling in Washington, and this was my first contact with it.

The rest of the evening was pleasant enough. I was especially taken with Genevieve Rhodes, who has a lovely manner when once awakened. But there is something almost sullen in her usual bearing. She is usually not friendly in any way, and makes no advances whatever. On this occasion she seemed to drop the cloak of indifference she appears, for some purpose of her own, to have assumed.

When the visitors had departed, and Caroline and Jeffreys were up in the parlor at the piano, Mrs. Rhodes, Genevieve, and I lingered at the table, eating nuts and raisins, and indulging in small talk. When I finally rose to go, Genevieve held out her hand and said:

"I am so glad you did not rise to Helen Clay's gossip. Nobody pays any attention to what she says, and when she starts, it is a case of 'the least said the soonest mended.' But I am very sorry it happened at our table."

I slept like a top that night, and felt much invigorated by my little outing. But this is an unconscionably long letter and an imposition on any human creature, even if he does happen to be one's best friend. So I guess I might better cut off here, and save the rest for next time.

Give my regards to Broadway—and Lenox Avenue! If you see Marcia, tell her I mentioned her in my letter, and that she owes me a long one.

With best wishes, Buddie, I am,

Davy

Washington, D.C., October 15, 1922

Dear Bob:

I see that I shall have to condense my information, for I realize that in my last letter I was really diffuse. Is not that the word? If only I had power comparable to my facility, I might be somebody before I die. But, as they say, one can't have everything. In the ardor of writing, the thoughts outrun my pen, and there is so much that I feel would interest you that I do not seem able to select. I am afraid that my letters are a hodgepodge in which the best and most important things are not properly stressed. However, it's a comfort to think that if you are bored, you can stop reading at any point, for I put the personal things at the beginning and the end, so that you can skip the middle without missing anything vital.

I went to my first dance the other night—mostly college fellows and flappers. Some of the latter, if the clock had been turned back ten years, would have been arrested on two counts—appearing in public without sufficient clothing, and indecent dancing. However, as Caroline says, this is 1922, and the Middle Ages are over. We have left their old-fashioned ideas behind. Sometimes I feel that I am too old for these new things. That is due, no doubt, to my provincial upbringing. It is all a puzzle to me. I can see some good in many of the innovations of the past five years, and it is no doubt true that every generation suffers from accretions of conventionalisms which must be removed at regular intervals, like the barnacles from the hull of a ship. But I must confess that a few of the new ideas and tendencies leave me gasping in a maze of wonder as to how the whole thing will end. After watching one young girl whose dancing was especially atrocious, I asked one of the older men present, "How do they get away with it?" He laughed.

"They don't," he said, "but then," he added, "they don't want to."

With this cryptic remark he left me. I am still thinking it over.

Caroline and Jeffreys were present, and danced often together. Her dancing was a trifle too modern to suit my medieval views, but I can say this much at least for her, that she was not the worst. As none of my friends of the weekend party was present, I had to be presented to many strangers, and I had several dances with pretty girls. The woods around here are full of them, Old Man! You ought to come down and look us over—indeed, you should!

Jeffreys presented me to a certain Miss Riddick, whom he and Caroline called Billie. She was a pretty girl, I must admit, but not my style. I suppose you will say that that is a very vague description. Well, I can't tell you much about her complexion, for she was a strictly modern up-to-date product of the beauty culturist's art, but she had a pretty figure, and furnished the usual guarantees, for her waist was lacking in the proper places. However, there was something hard and sophisticated in her level glance, which struck a wrong note with me. You are always rigging me for being what you call sentimental, and I guess you are right about that. Call it sentiment, or what you will, but I have always liked women who are better than I am. So when a woman, pretty or not, looks at me with a bold glance which says: "I know all you know, and I defy you to shock me," then I am through. I yawn politely, and look around for something better.

But I don't presume to dictate to anyone else what he shall do, as you well know. "There should be no disputing concerning tastes," said the old medieval monks. In good American: "Choose your own poison," or "Go to hell your own way."

However, as Jeffreys and Caroline made rather a point of this introduction to Miss Riddick, politeness seemed to demand that I pay some little attention to the lady. She is a good dancer, and she is not stupid, for she has a ready wit and a caustic tongue. Yet when Caroline and Jeffreys came up at the close of the dance and proposed that we four go somewhere to eat, I was not so pleased, for I should have preferred to choose my own company. But there was nothing to do but acquiesce.

Jeffreys called a taxi and we all hopped in. As I was a stranger, I merely followed the leader. We were only a few moments reaching our destination, which I found to my mild dismay was a cabaret. I can hear you laugh now. Of all places in the world—a cheap cabaret! I have often marveled why decent people go to them. This one was typical of the breed. A lot of fresh boys and flashy girls composed most of the patronage, with a few people of more class thrown in. The singers were the usual kind, with hard, unintelligent over-made-up faces, raucous voices, and coarse, ungraceful, suggestive gestures. The songs were of a type whose cheapness, vulgarity, banality, and utter lack of wit, humor, harmony, or distinction of any kind simply defy description. A high-class bagnio would not have tolerated them for a minute. The themes were hackneyed beyond the power of my poor pen to depict, and how any human being with a spark of intelligence—I don't say decency—could sit and listen to them, except under actual compulsion, is more than I can fathom. But as I was under a kind of social compulsion, I tried to forget them, and so I paid more attention to Miss Riddick than I might otherwise have done.

The waiter came to take our orders. We all ordered something to eat, and then Jeffreys said a few words in a low tone to the waiter, who looked at me questioningly. Jeffreys laughed.

"That's all right," he said. "He is a friend of mine."

Then he asked me if I would not like something "red" to drink. Thinking of the girls, and reflecting on the possible deadliness of bootleg liquor, I declined politely, whereat he shrugged his shoulders, and said laconically to the waiter, "Bring three!"

But I shall not burden you with a prolonged account of this painful experience, nor do I want you to misunderstand me. I have not the least doubt that in another mood I might have found the evening moderately entertaining. But, possibly because of my aversion to Jeffreys, I just could not get myself in the humor for it. The singers became more distasteful as the time went on, their voices seemed to grow rougher and harsher with every moment, and their gestures and attitudes coarser and more objectionably suggestive, and, finally, when one of them planted herself right beside our table, I could endure it no longer. So I made some conventional excuse about it being very late and about an early morning appointment. By this time the "red" liquor had had its effect on at least one member of our party, for Caroline had become quite noisy. It is queer how little alcohol is needed to muddle the brains of some folks, and yet these same individuals have not the good sense to let it alone. Women with Caroline's responsibility ought to shut themselves up alone in their rooms, with doors double-locked, before they take a drink, for if they are in company, they surely make a holy show of themselves.

Jeffreys readily acceded to my suggestion that we start for home. On the way Caroline rested her head quite boldly on his shoulder, and I, for one, was very glad when the taxi dropped us at our door. I hurried up to my room and hastily retired, rather disgusted with all the world, and particularly with myself. Somehow I felt that either I should have refused to go with them, or, having gone, I should have been a good sport, and have fallen in with their program. I had done neither, but I had been simply a "spoil sport," an unenviable role, indeed!

Next morning I heard Genevieve telephoning Caroline's principal that she would not be at school that day. Oh, the morning after the night before! I dressed more quickly than usual, and hurried out to breakfast, managing to elude both Genevieve and Mrs. Rhodes, for I had an uneasy feeling that I did not want to see them. That afternoon, coming home somewhat earlier than usual, I found Caroline, attired in a most attractive negligee, curled up on my couch reading Flaubert's *Madame Bovary*, which she had picked out of the bookcase. Though she was evidently surprised to see me thus early, she greeted me with careless geniality, asked if she would be in the way, and, receiving a negative answer, said with the utmost sangfroid:

"Then please smoke up, for I am dying for a cigarette. It isn't much fun smoking out of the window, and I was afraid Mamma might come up. If she comes now, I have an alibi."

I opened my cigarette case and held it out to her, and she rested her pretty dark curls against my arm while, with great deliberation, she took a light from the match I held for her. Then she stretched out luxuriously on the couch, and heaved a sigh of profound content.

"This is the life, eh?" Then she added mischievously, looking up at me from under her long lashes, "How is the old grouchy bear today? Still growling?"

"I never growl," said I decidedly, calmly lighting a cigarette for myself, and stretching out in my armchair.

"Well, if you don't actually growl, you go through all the motions. I love a grouch less than I do Monday morning in school, and I hate wet blankets worse than I do grouches."

"It's nice to get one's exact place," said I, coolly, and then I added, "but before you go too far on the wrong track, let me make certain things plain. I don't care two whoops what anybody in this world does, and I shall never interfere with any fellow mortal going to perdition by his own chosen route, but I do object sometimes to accompanying him. You are expecting me to 'jump' you about last night, but I am going to do nothing of the kind. You can frequent any kind of cheap joint that suits your taste. You can drink all the bootleg liquor you want, and be as maudlin as you please. I shall probably think you're a damned little fool who ought to know better, but I shall not interfere with you at all, for it's really none of my business. If you were my daughter or sister, I should probably give you a good spanking, make you put on more clothes, and stop dancing like a—but I can't think of a nice word to express the kind of woman some of you girls dance like. But you are not my daughter or my sister, and it is, therefore, none of my affair, as I said before. So you have my permission to go to the demnition bow-wows in your own sweet way, unhampered by any mid-Victorian notions of mine. I shall, however, be interested in watching the procession, I assure you. My grouch last night was due to the fact that I was an unwilling participant. Do you get me?"

Caroline did not move for a moment. I watched her out of the corner of my eye. She lay reflectively blowing smoke rings toward the ceiling. Then she spoke without turning her head.

"You don't believe in—ah—circumlocutions, do you? What are you up to? Trying to convert me?"

"No indeed, my dear. When I try my hand at that sort of thing, I shall practice on something easy."

"Then you positively refuse to try to reform me?"

"I do, most decidedly. It would be a hard job, certainly; a thankless job, in addition; and after all, the game might not be worth the candle."

"I thank you. You are very plain."

"Don't mention it. They say that a burnt child dreads the fire, and this child was certainly burnt. I tried once in my callower youth to reform a girl. I have but one consoling thought connected with that most painful episode. I was not sent to jail. So I said, 'Never again for me!' Thus far I have kept my word, and Heaven helping me, I intend to keep on keeping it!"

"Old Bear, you're just the man I've been looking for. Everybody in this house has either tried to reform me—witness Mother and Genevieve—or help me faster down the primrose path. But like dear old Bert Williams, you declare yourself neutral. You for me, and me for you! I thought I'd never live to see you, though I have often dreamed of finding you, and even—in my poor, unregenerate way—*prayed* for you!"

There are difficulties, as you will have observed, my friend, in talking seriously to Caroline. While she makes not the slightest outward show of culture in her ordinary social relations, she has a quick and ready wit, and a perfectly uncanny fluency of speech, as I have found out to my discomfiture on more than one occasion. But in this case the worst was yet to come. Our conversation continued, more or less in the same vein, with good-natured satire on my side and an absolutely poised and cynical sarcasm on hers, when her mother called her from somewhere below stairs. She cried an answer, jumped up from the couch, walked over to the table and threw her half-smoked cigarette into the ashtray, and stood looking down at me with laughing, mischievous eyes.

"For such a prosy, dull, conservative old dear, you look very young—and do you know, if you would only awaken from your long sleep, one could like you a whole lot."

And without warning, quicker than my slow-following thought, she stooped, put both arms around my neck, making me curiously conscious of a mingled odor of cigarette smoke and perfume, and kissed me squarely on the mouth. In another second she had disappeared down the stairs, laughing gleefully!

Now what, in the name of all the great and little gods, is a poor fellow to do with a girl like that? I ask you! What indeed?

At about seven that evening, I was called to the telephone, and had the pleasure of listening to Lillian Barton's well-modulated voice, inviting me to come over Sunday evening at five. "Just a little tea," she said. We had a few minutes' chat before hanging up. I have been promising myself for several days to call on her, but for one reason or another have been prevented from carrying out my intention. This invitation makes it nicer and easier.

Genevieve met me in the hall as I was turning away from the telephone and spoke, so it seemed to me, rather coolly. I wonder if she blames me for last night's performance. Since she and Caroline have the same room, she could hardly help noticing that young lady's condition, unless, indeed she were sound asleep. The thought that she may believe that I had any willing part in it makes me most uncomfortable, but I suppose there is nothing to do but grin and bear it.

Revolving these thoughts in my mind, I went up to my room with the idea of spending the evening reading and writing. Then I changed my mind, dressed hurriedly, and paid a call on Don Verney, of whom you will recall my speaking in connection with the weekend party. Verney is most comfortably—indeed most luxuriously—located. Imagine an oblong room, with low bookcases on three sides, a bed couch at one end, a handsome library table with a fine light, a few unusually beautiful pictures, and very comfortable chairs. I, of course, was most interested in the books, for Verney has the best personally selected library of its size I have ever seen. It is not composed of odds and ends of rubbish handed down from the previous generations, but of some hundreds of live books and the best and most modern reference books. On the table I noted recent numbers of *The Nation, The Dial, The New Republic, The Atlantic,* and several other periodicals of the highest type.

"How did you achieve it?" I asked, after I had taken a quick glance at his shelves.

"What do you mean—exactly?" he asked

"Why, the wheat without any chaff," I answered.

"Well, for one thing, I never buy any trash, and if trashy books do drift in, I either give them away, or throw them in the wastebasket. It takes resolution at first, but one soon gets used to it."

A hobby in common is the very best basis, I imagine, for starting a friendship, and soon we were deep in a conversation which

I, at least, found most stimulating. I have heard Verney's friends talk a great deal about him, and he certainly "makes good." He has a wonderfully well-stocked mind, the gift of keen observation, and an unusual facility in expression. I enjoyed my hour with him hugely, and left with one or two leads for future reading, and a most cordial invitation to call again.

Then I took a walk up You Street while finishing my cigar, and watched the crowds coming out of the three movie theaters and at the entrances of the two or three well-known dance halls. As I look on our folks in these days of prosperity, it is borne in upon me that we are indeed a pleasure-loving people, that we love display for its own sake, and fine clothes and the gauds of life even more than our friends the Jews, and they, alas, can better afford all these things than we can. Of course, I believe in pleasure as a natural and proper element in a well-ordered and normal life, but I fear, somehow, that we have the proportions wrong. Maybe not—I should be glad to know that I had overstated the case against us. Does it not look, though, as if we have mistaken the shows for the substance?

In imagination I can hear you say, "The old preacher is at it again!"

Well, so long, and be good to yourself.

Davy

THREE

Pervasive Caroline. A fair lady's parlor. Enter a fascinating brown girl.

Washington, D.C., October 23, 1922

Dear Bob:

Caroline is the most pervasive personality I have run across lately. She has the faculty of being underfoot at the most inopportune times, and yet, what is one to do? She has quite taken possession of my quarters. I don't recall if I mentioned it before, but she uses some special kind of perfume, and whenever I come into my room, I can tell if she has been there recently. There is something strangely alluring in this kind of intimate contact with a pretty woman, and yet, somehow, I resent it as an invasion of my privacy. If she were ugly and unattractive, I suppose I should close my door and thus shut her out, and of course if her mother knew how much time she spends here, she would soon put a stop to the practice, or try to. Most of the time, naturally, I am out of the house, and as Caroline knows my hours pretty well by now, she times herself accordingly. Today's experience, for instance, was typical.

I came in about five and found my French dictionary open on the table, the inkwell open, a penholder, blotter, and several sheets of monogrammed paper scattered about, in the midst one of Caroline's dainty little handkerchiefs, and pervading the whole room the very faintest trace of that wonderful perfume which I am beginning, by some occult psychological process, to associate with her personality. I had a moment of irritation, for you know how I like to have my personal things for myself, and you recall how often the folks at college used to say that I was not a bit Southern in some of my ways. My irritation increased considerably when I saw that my pet copy of Amiel's *Journal*, the one I bought in that queer little shop in Geneva in the spring of 1919, was lying facedown on the rug beside the couch. I swore softly, stooped to pick it up, and then suddenly changed my mind. So I left everything just as I found it, and went out to dinner. I met Reese, who now and then eats where I do, and after our meal was over, we walked around the block while he finished his cigar. When I reached home it was about seven.

My room was straight, the table in perfect order, and the two books back in their respective places. Resting against the base of my lamp I found this note:

Dear Old Bear:

I really did not mean to be careless, but the phone rang for me, and then Mamma sent me out on an errand, and I forgot to come back and straighten up. But I am usually very careful, indeed I am. Your Amiel must have slipped from the couch, for I certainly did not throw it on the floor. But it was mean in you to leave it there—as a reproach! You owe me an apology.

Caroline.

The note made me laugh, of course, it was so characteristic, and I settled down to a cigarette and an hour's reading in my very comfortable chair. A few minutes before eight in breezed

Caroline. She had on something extra fetching, which I should set forth in words if I could, but I am aware that the angels weep when I try to describe a lady's gown, so I shall refrain, much as I am tempted.

"Going to the show at the Howard tonight," she said laconically, as she sat on the corner of my couch and reached for my cigarette case. "Let me take a dozen puffs while I am waiting for the others. They won't be here until after eight. Well, why don't you tell me I'm 'the class'? Where were you brought up, anyway?"

I laughed. I guess I had been *looking* my approval, for she was smiling contentedly. Then I said:

"Well, you are 'the class'—whatever that means. That's an awfully pretty rig, and not badly placed, either."

"You don't use a trowel, do you? But thanks anyway, even for small favors. But look me over, Old Bear, for I am so afraid you might someday be really displeased, and actually give me that—ah—chastisement you spoke of the other day."

"You are all right, little girl. I have no criticisms to offer. If I had a sister, and she looked half as well as you do, I should be proud to acknowledge the relationship."

"Be careful there, or you will compliment me before you know it."

Then she stood up to go, and I arose from my chair. She came over close to me, and looked up in that superlatively devilish way she has.

"See, Old Grouchy, there's not a tiny bit of rouge."

And she took my hands, and rubbed my fingertips over her velvety cheek. It was true, as she said, that she was not rouged, and Heaven knows she did not need it.

"Why don't you?" I asked, hardly knowing why.

"Why don't you wear spats?" she asked, with seeming irrelevance.

I laughed.

"Because I can't endure them," I answered.

"Well, I don't rouge for the same reason. Maybe someday necessity may overrule choice, but for the present, Old Grouchy, you can kiss me without the least risk of being poisoned."

Then with mischievous determination in her eyes she took a step toward me, and said, "I have half a mind . . ."

Involuntarily I stepped back, startled, and she gave me a merry laugh and ran down the stairs. Why I am unable to stand my ground against her, I cannot for the life of me determine, but she always manages to startle me, to "get my goat," as she would put it. I swore softly over my lack of poise, and sat down to write to you.

But the real purpose of this letter was to tell you about my Sunday-evening tea at Barton's. I wish I might show you Lillian Barton's parlor, for I am sure I cannot describe it adequately. I am like the actor who made you laugh so hard that last wild night on Broadway, and who sang—don't you remember it?—a silly song with the refrain:

I cannot sing the old songs,
For I do not know the words!

That is just my trouble. I don't know the words. Now if I had Leroy's command of the King's English and his vocabulary of modern art terms, I could make sure you see a perfect picture.

In a few undistinguished words, it's an old house, a rich man's house, made over, and redecorated on modern lines—some ultra-modern, I should say. Dark walls, with a few good paintings;

heavy furniture in keeping with the size of the room; a wonderful rug; and a big fireplace with a real fire. Altogether it is the most attractive room I have been in—as a guest—and you know I have seen most of our handsome houses between New Orleans and Boston, and as far west as Chicago. Most of our pretentious residences are too ornate, or too luxurious, and the element of conspicuous expenditure is somewhat too pronounced. But here there were evidences of intelligent planning coupled with a cultivated individual taste. It was pleasing to the eye, and would have rejoiced your heart, I know. Somehow—and I suppose you would have said that this was the final test of the room—it seemed a perfect setting for Miss Barton.

There were, including our hostess, just six of us, the others being the Hales, Reese, of course, and Verney. We had a most delightful tea served in a sort of library-dining room, which was quite as attractive in its way as the parlor, but we spent most of the evening seated in a semicircle around the most hospitable hearth, in the glow and warmth of a fine wood fire. It was perfect!

We told stories, sang songs, and discussed everything in this mundane sphere, ending of course, where we always do, with the race question. Verney made one or two statements which stimulated debate. He contended that this generation is not going forward, except in the conspicuous, showy ways; that our progress is more apparent than real, except in the matter, perhaps, of mere intellectual training; and that even there we are vastly outpointed by the Jews and the Japanese. He holds that we read only those things which concern us *directly*, and that we have no interest in the story of the past politics of Europe and Asia; while, on the other hand, the Jews and the Japanese seem to feel the absolute necessity for understanding completely the civilization of the Western European races which now dominate the world.

He said, further, that our most prosperous class takes little real interest even in the race question, but that many of the women think only of "getting by" the color line by painting their faces, while the men, for the most part, studiously avoid it, and live strictly within their own self-sufficient circle; that better incomes are making us more cowardly, rather than more bold, for we can now procure in our own circle the satisfactions we once could get only outside, and so we shut our eyes to what we do not wish to see, and then assert that it does not exist; that we love pleasure too much, and that we will spend more both of time and money in following it than any other struggling race in the world.

But I shall not unduly burden this letter with the details of his contention. Of course, there are rather obvious answers to most of the assertions advanced by Verney, but for every answer made he had a telling rejoinder. Someday I am going to draw him out again, for I am interested to know what is the basis of his claims.

But let me get back to our Sunday-evening tea. Reese, whom I noted especially on this occasion, seemed to assume a distinctly proprietary manner, and certainly would give a stranger to think that the story of his engagement to Miss Barton is no mere canard. He is a cool, rather unimaginative chap, and I can quite believe what they say of him, that he is a fine man of business, who has already accumulated a snug fortune. He is a pretty good imitation of a Yankee money getter, and from all I can hear, he is regarded as a man of the highest integrity, whose word is as good as his bond.

He does not act as if he had much sentiment, though maybe his own special virtues are more dependable. Somehow I foresee that, while Miss Barton is rather inclined to act the grand lady with everyone, if she ever assumes the matrimonial harness, it will be the old story of Greek meeting Greek. Men of Reese's type have rather a fashion of letting a woman deceive herself all she pleases regarding their eagerness to meet her every wish, but after the ceremony they quite frequently uncover a very complete assortment of wishes of their own. Reese is probably unimaginative, as I said before, and not overshrewd or overobserving, maybe, in social matters in which he is not deeply interested, but, if I am any judge, he is nobody's fool, and he is going to be nobody's slave.

I have seen nothing to indicate any effusive affection on either side. That "catty" little Miss Clay, whom I mentioned in a previous letter, said that Miss Barton was interested only in Reese's prospects, and that he would see it if he were not stone blind. I am wondering if this is true. Of course, you are wanting to know how she treated *me*. Well, I'll tell you. I have indicated that she is unusually interesting, which means, in other words, that she says and does interesting things. Every time I have talked with her she has said something to whip up my interest.

When we were all standing up to take our leave, for one moment it happened that I remained alone in front of the fire, while the others were in the next room putting on their wraps, Reese helping Hale on with his coat and Verney assisting Mrs. Hale. Miss Barton left them quickly, and came over to me and held out her hand. As I took it she said:

"Do you know what I have been thinking as we looked into the fire tonight? I have been thinking that we two could have some wonderfully interesting times together. What do *you* think, my friend? It has been so nice to know you."

Then without another word, she turned to greet her guests coming from the other room. I am afraid that I stood openmouthed, an attitude in which few men are conscious of looking their best. Now, Old Fellow, I ask you—what do you think of that?

As we left rather early, Reese remained behind and we four—

the Hales, Verney, and I—walked home together. They invited us to come in, but we declined with thanks, and went on to his quarters, where we smoked and talked for a while. I had an impulse to draw him out about Miss Barton and Reese, but thought better of it, and decided to watch for another opportunity.

When I reached home the house was full of company, as it usually is on Sunday evening. I slipped upstairs, hoping to find time for a little reading or writing before I retired. I had just settled down to work when I heard my name called from below, and, on answering, was invited by Mrs. Rhodes to come down to supper. Don't you wish you had a landlady like mine? I went to the head of the stairs, and thanked her as nicely as I could, giving as an excuse for declining that I had been out to tea. She said something about my being welcome anyway, if I wished to come down. I thanked her again in a noncommittal fashion and went back to my work.

In a few minutes I had become so absorbed in what I was doing that I was startled by a voice close to my ear, and here was my friend Caroline with a small tray of two dishes of unusually fine homemade ice cream flanked by two huge pieces of real cake. Who—being human—could refuse? So while I attacked one dish, she seated herself calmly on the arm of my big chair, and regaled herself from the other, talking and laughing incessantly about everything and nothing. Then she insisted on dragging me downstairs to meet a particular friend of hers. I at first essayed a mild refusal.

"Now if I were a real 'cat,' like Helen Clay, I should say that you are so taken up with your 'dicty' friends that you don't want to meet anyone else. But then I am not a real 'cat.' But, come on, Old Grouchy, or I shall be compelled to resort to extreme measures."

Such is my helplessness in the hands of this young minx, that, when she takes this tone, there seems to be nothing to do but yield. So I arose with a cheerful grin, and prepared to follow her.

"I don't in the least care what you think about other folks," she went on, "but *this* girl is my very dearest friend, and if you don't like her I shall feel very badly." And then, in a peculiar tone, which puzzled me somewhat at the time, she added impressively, "She is not very good looking, you know, and I shall be heartbroken if you treat her indifferently on account of it. When you realize the beauty of her character, you will agree with me that she is the sweetest girl in town."

This showed the flighty, careless, irresponsible Caroline in a new light, indeed, and I was somewhat touched by her solicitude. I hastened to assure her that I was the last person in the world to be unduly influenced by mere outward beauty, or the lack of it. But I could not help wondering what special type of physical deformity would make her feel such a warning necessary, and I prepared myself accordingly. Then I was ushered into the dining room, and found quite a company gathered about the table. A trifle self-conscious, I was led to the head of the table, where sat the loveliest brown girl it has ever been my privilege to meet. Shut your eyes for a moment to the ugliness of the everyday world about you and construct in your mind's eye a girl of medium height, with a figure which would make the *Venus de Milo* hunt a new corsetier, the most wonderful rosy velvety-brown complexion, and a pair of flashing black eyes. Use your imagination a moment longer, and picture her attired in a costume which is the last word in simple good taste and elegance. I am aware that this paragraph might be blue penciled for excessive use of superlatives, but I refuse to remove a single one!

You can, of course, imagine my slight confusion when Caroline put her arm around the girl's neck and said in a voice in which she could not quite control the note of mischief triumphant:

"Tommie, let me present Mr. Carr. Mr. Carr, this is my dearest friend, Miss Dawson."

Then the saucy baggage looked straight into my face and exploded in a perfect gale of laughter, somewhat to the mystification of everyone present, including Miss Dawson, who blushed a deep red and offered me her hand. Mrs. Rhodes, poor woman, who is being scandalized continually by Caroline, looked from one to the other of us with a sort of helpless bewilderment, but Genevieve, who always has the right word ready, said very sweetly:

"We should all enjoy a good laugh, Carrie. Don't be selfish."

But Caroline only laughed the more, and finally had a mild fit of hysterics, and had to be slapped on the back and given cold water. After a few lively minutes, order was restored, and then Genevieve returned to her request, this time pointing it my way.

"Please, Mr. Carr, we are dying of curiosity. Won't you tell us the joke?" I looked at Caroline, and she laughingly nodded acquiescence. I turned to Miss Dawson and bowed slightly, and then I answered Genevieve.

"Caroline," said I, "made me promise very solemnly that I should be nice to Miss Dawson, even if she was very homely."

The spontaneous and hearty laugh which followed was a perfect tribute to the lady's beauty. The rest of the evening was pleasant enough, I must say. Carolyn made me sit next to Miss Dawson, and the ice being so completely broken by the former's prank, we were soon fast friends. Another item or two, Old Pal —she has a nice voice, a well-furnished mind, and, judging from her countenance, she has character. A paragon, you will exclaim. I am not quite sure as yet, but thus far I have been able to check every requirement. Caroline and I took her home, and we had a lively time. Miss Dawson is quieter than Caroline, and seems to have more control over that rather willful young person than does anyone else. I turned in when I got back, and slept the sleep of good digestion and a clean conscience.

I had just finished writing the above lines when the folks came in from the theater, and it was not long before I heard Caroline's little slippers tripping up the stairs. This time she had a handful of macaroons, which she was munching with every sign of enjoyment. She sat calmly on the arm of my chair and fed me macaroons in the most nonchalant way in the world. It is a fact that her "pervasiveness" ofttimes irritates me, and she frequently interrupts me when it is disagreeable to be interrupted. Then, too, I somewhat resent her perfectly assured manner, as of one who either has no doubt of her welcome, or is quite indifferent to what I may think or feel. And yet, I guess I should not be absolutely ingenuous if I tried to make you believe that her presence is always unpleasant or tiresome.

"I saw Tommie tonight," she said, among other things. "She likes you, but I warned her against you. In spite of that she sent you her love. I told her that I should not deliver it, but as you see, I have. Take it for what it is worth."

"I feel honored to be in Miss Dawson's thoughts at all," I said, "but tell me, is the love of an up-to-date, modern girl worth having? Or, if worth having, is there any way in which to be sure of it?"

"Now you're too deep for me, Old Grouchy."

And with this answer Caroline bade me good night, and ran down to her own room, whence I could hear Genevieve's voice raised in tones of expostulation and reproof.

I have not seen Jeffreys for several days, in fact, but once since the night of the dance. From something Mrs. Rhodes said, I think he is in Baltimore. Personally, I should like it better if he were not in this house. But, after all, I suspect that is a selfish desire. Though I express it, I am duly ashamed of it.

This is a dreadfully long letter, and, as I look it over, seems rather full of Caroline, perhaps too much so to be interesting to you. If you knew the young lady herself, you would realize how hard it is to control her in letters or anywhere else. I am going to a rather nice dance this week Friday. The Merry Coterie is giving a "dove" party, but inviting the menfolks to come late to dance and eat. It sounds promising, for it's a lively bunch, and I expect to meet a good many people I have been wanting to know.

Be good to yourself. I am glad the people up that way are beginning to appreciate you. It's a true saying, Buddie, that "you can't keep a good man down"! So long until next time!

Davy

Sunday, A.M., October 29, 1922

Dear Bob:

I am happy to note that you survived my last letter. You must be a glutton for punishment to come back for more. While I am not sure I agree with your "diagnosis" concerning my friends, and especially your estimate of Miss Barton, still I am glad that I have succeeded in making you see them somewhat vividly, even if a trifle out of focus. I don't remember all that I wrote about Miss Barton, and, though I admit that one or two of my experiences with her might suggest the flirt, you would have to *see* her for yourself to get a *total* effect which would be reasonably just.

So you like Caroline best? I guess that's because I have written more about her, and I have written more because she is always around, and because she has a rather aggressive—I was about to say "obtrusive"—personality. But, my dearest friend, if you should at any one time see Caroline, and Lillian Barton, and Mary Hale, and Tommie Dawson—not to mention Genevieve and a half dozen others I have met—I'll wager you would have a brainstorm such as you have never experienced. I should give quite a tidy sum to see you in such a pickle.

Last Tuesday I spent the early part of the evening with Don Verney and I tried to get his ideas regarding the present phase of our social life in cities like Washington and New York. His views are certainly interesting, though I am not quite prepared to say that I agree with him completely.

According to Don, we are suffering—and especially those of us who call ourselves the "best people"—with a dreadful "inferiority complex," to use the phrase of the celebrated Dr. Freud. We imitate the white American in everything, except the few points in which he really excels. Indeed, we have a gift for picking the wrong things to imitate. For example, we (our so-called "best people," I mean) have run wild on lavish spending and frivolous pleasures, in the modern American fashion, but we have not learned the art of hard work which underlies these things in the typically American life. Socially we are beginning to imitate the rather "sporty" classes of Americans, such as infest the ordinary summer resorts and are obtrusively present in all places of public entertainment, under the erroneous impression that these people are typical Americans, whereas in fact they are only the parasites who live on the great body of the American social organism. They spend from their superfluity, which has been piled up often through the efforts of generations of toilers, of which this present generation is but the last bitter dregs. Our women spend as much for a gown as a white woman with many times as great resources, and the wives of men with limited salaries feel constrained to make the conspicuous display which in the case of white Americans would be made only by the very rich or by irresponsible women of the underworld, who live but for the hour. Pretty dresses are all very well, and most of us realize their aesthetic and social value, but no middle-class group seems to be justified in any great amount of *display for its own sake,* and quite apart from real needs. For example, during the festivities attendant upon the last inauguration, when there were many elaborate functions given within the space of a few days, one local lady wore five *different* costumes, each one expensive, to five successive dress affairs, and yet her husband is a man living on a salary which, to a white American of the business world, would be moderate indeed. We have the lavishness of Jews, without their acquisitive ability, and the love of pleasure of the tropical races, while trying to compete with the hardest-headed and most energetic people in the world, the Yankee Anglo-Saxon. Since the law does not permit Sunday dances, one hall on You Street advertises dances to begin at midnight Sunday, and last until dawn on Monday, as if an eighteen-hour day is not long enough to satisfy our lust for pleasure. In no *similar* middle-class community among any other race in the world could such performances be made to pay, but the midnight show is a regular institution in colored Washington and New York.

As we talked, I noted Shands's *White and Black* lying on the table. I opened it at the passage in which the author makes one of his characters, an educated colored preacher, rebuke his brethren for wanting to be white, and for wanting only the fairest mulatto or quadroon women for wives.

"What do you think of that statement?" I asked, handing him the open book.

"I guess it's true of too many men in Washington as well as in Texas. There are circles here in which one rarely sees a woman of brown complexion, and the men choose the women, you know. Of course, the reasons and motives back of such a selection are complex. It isn't mere color prejudice in probably most of the cases, though it is in some, no doubt. In a country with such a hellish system of discrimination, not only in social life, but in employment, in places of public entertainment and service, on railways, ships, in schools, in stores, in courts of law, in the army and navy—in every possible relation of life, in fact—the possibility of approximation to the white type becomes a very practical ideal. Who can blame a man if he wants his children to be as nearly white in appearance as possible, or, at any rate, perhaps more nearly white than he is himself?"

"From a practical viewpoint, certainly no one!" I said. "But what of those who, while living *socially* as colored people, in their desire to be treated as white in public places 'cut' their too palpably colored friends? Do you uphold them?"

"No, I don't!" he answered. "But if I don't uphold them, and if I could not find it in my heart to imitate them, I at least understand. Some of these people are holding government jobs which they would lose if they were known to be colored, so they have to protect themselves. They are, therefore, white downtown and colored uptown, which is a most regrettable situation, whatever the extenuating circumstances. But it is not only those who are dependent on their apparent whiteness for their chance to make a living who do this sort of dodging. There are those who do it merely because they want to be able to pass as white in restaurants, theaters, and stores. Their reason is not quite so good, but after all, they would say, and with some justice, that *it is a reason.* There is no doubt that, especially in the upper strata of society, and particularly among the women, a very fair skin is regarded as a distinct and indisputable evidence of superiority. Just as the Germans tried—and almost succeeded—in making the French believe that they were a degenerate people, so has white America for the moment succeeded in making some of us feel our inferiority, even though we refuse to admit it. Yes, we have—many of us—a distinct inferiority complex!"

"What would you say should be the attitude of those fair enough to 'pass'? Should they never go anywhere where their whiteness will procure them better treatment than would be accorded them if they were known to be colored?"

"No, I should not take such an extreme position. If that were the case, there would be very few places left for us in Washington. My rule is not so far to seek, after all. I go where I please, when the notion strikes me, and in all places where one must pay for what one gets, I accept gladly the best treatment my appearance procures for me. But if by chance any friend or acquaintance comes in whose color clearly indicates his race connection, I make it a point to treat him just as cordially as our previous intimacy would warrant."

When you think it over, that's a pretty good rule. Many more things Don said and many were the illustrations he gave, but I shall not overload this one letter with them. Too much solid food in one meal is a bad thing.

I believe I said in my last that I had not seen Jeffreys for several days. Well, he turned up the other evening a trifle haggard, perhaps, but more dapper and prosperous looking than ever. As Caroline would say, if it's a question of mere clothes, he surely is "the class"! I was in the lower hall talking to Mrs. Rhodes and Caroline when he dropped out of a taxi in front of the door. To the questions as to where he had been, he gave serene and untroubled responses.

"To tell the exact truth," he said, with his widest smile, "I have been to my tailor in Philadelphia. I was getting positively shabby, you know."

If that were the case, he surely brought home clothes enough. He had on a new fur-lined overcoat whose cost would dress an ordinary young fellow for a whole year, and then some, and a diamond ring such as only a champion pugilist or a circus owner might wear. It was easily worth the price of an ordinary automobile. I have noticed before that Jeffreys is very much given to wearing expensive jewelry, especially rings, of which he seems to have a great variety.

Well, he laughed and joked for a few minutes, fished from his bag a five-pound box of Huyler's most expensive candy for Caroline, and ran upstairs where he spent the time before dinner getting straight. I happened to be looking at Caroline as she followed him with her eyes—a steady, half-puzzled, reflective look. She caught me watching her, and blushed, I thought, just a trifle.

Caroline, as I said, is taking evening work at the University in order to make up some needed credits on her college record. She goes to classes every evening but Saturday, all of which does not prevent her from having company after eight-thirty or nine o'clock several nights a week. Very often she comes in with some young chap who has brought her home in his car. She is indeed a popular young lady. But I should hate to have a sister of mine pawed over as she is by these modern youngsters. I heard one of the older men refer to them as cubs, and it's a good name, when one sees them maul the girls around. The whole arrangement between girls and fellows seems to have changed since I came up in a little provincial Southern city. The girls do all the leading, a good deal of the inviting, and more than their share of the wooing, and the boys seem to expect it. When you speak to them, they laugh and say, "Oh, well, this is 1922!" That answer seems to fit almost any situation. While Caroline seems rather independent in most ways, she does let the fellows maul her about too much. I never like to see it. I am not used to it. In my early days a fellow who tried it would get called down pretty fast and pretty hard.

Caroline is taking French and history in her classes, and she often asks my help on some point or other. In fact, she has the habit of coming up to my room to study or write when I am out in the evening, for if she is in her room on the floor below, she is more likely to be disturbed. On the night of Jeffreys's arrival, she came up about nine o'clock, having sent away her escort as soon as she reached home.

"I didn't know you were in," she said. "Would I bother you if I curled up here to study? Genevieve has two or three teacher friends downstairs, and if I am in sight, I can have no peace."

I was busy writing, but I assured her that she was welcome. Before settling herself down, she looked inquiringly at Jeffreys's door.

"Did he look as if he were going out for the evening?" she asked.

When I assured her he did, she stretched out with her book under the wall electric as if relieved, and said no more for some time. After a long while she came over and sat on the arm of my chair, which seems to be her favorite post, and asked me to translate a troublesome passage from her French text. While we looked on the book together, she leaned against me, and put her right arm over my shoulder. It was very sweet and very intimate, but I could give Saint Anthony a few pointers about temptations. When the difficulties had been satisfactorily smoothed out, and she had gone back to her place on the couch, I said, in a teasing mood, "Don't you ever read and study in Mr. Jeffreys's room?"

"No," she answered quickly, looking up at me.

"Why not?" I persisted.

"Because he would not understand."

"Understand what?"

"Well, because he might *misunderstand*."

"And you think *I won't*?" I continued, taking a sort of malicious satisfaction in cornering her—or rather, trying to corner her.

"No, I *know* you won't."

"But—*why*?"

She smiled at me serenely, and was it indulgently?

"Because Old Grouchy, *you* are *you*."

I was checked for a moment. Then I returned to the attack.

"You have only known me a few days, let us say, and yet do you assume that you know me so precisely? Am I so transparent, so shallow as all that? May I not be, for example, a monument of deceit and duplicity? How do you know I am not? I am afraid your conclusions are not entirely flattering to me."

She laughed a merry little laugh, and turned on her elbow to look at me.

"Old Grouchy, I thought you were old and wise. Or are you just trying to draw me out? Well, I have seen transparent water that was not shallow as far as that goes, so your analogy does not hold exactly. More than that, I am by way of being complimentary, but you, like most weak mortals, would rather be thought inscrutably wicked than naively good. And yet you have the nerve to preach to *me*!"

"You're wrong there, little lady. I never *preach* to you!"

"You may call it by another name, but I choose to call it preaching! Of course it is not always expressed orally. You have very eloquent eyes, Old Grouchy, did anyone ever tell you that? You surely can *look* disapproval!"

She laughed, and I laughed, and I dropped the subject as being too personal.

Everyone here is talking about the Thanksgiving Day game between Howard and Lincoln. I suppose you recall how our New York friends tried to persuade us to go to Philadelphia last year. Well, this year's game will be in Washington, and the University folks and the society folks are getting ready for "big doings." The Rhodeses expect a house full of company to judge from the talk downstairs. Caroline is having new dresses made, and I have recently heard her complaining that her fur coat is not "fit to wear to a dogfight," to quote her exact words. If Genevieve is making any preparations, she makes no outward display, but "little sister" is not so reticent. Mrs. Rhodes, usually so cheerful, was complaining today of the high cost of living, which in this particular case means the high cost of clothing. It seems the boy, who, as you may remember is a medical student, must have a new outfit, for his "frat" is turning on some great stunts during the Thanksgiving recess. I sympathized with her as one who knew what trouble and expense it is to bring up a boy. Well, have you not given me lots of trouble, old fellow, not to say expense? So using you as my particular burden, I listened to the good lady with the most sympathetic consideration, and thus, I hope, advanced myself several grades in her good graces. And we both know, don't we, Buddie, that it pays—yea, even a thousandfold—to try to please one's landlady!

Just to prove how very right I am in this last assertion, as the upshot of our conversation, I was invited to partake of some very special extra fritters, with "gobs" of butter and some heavenly syrup. Let me tell you, my friend, the Rhodes house is completely appointed for living, from the outermost part of the kitchen porch to the attic door. (As I have never been in the attic, I can't say as to that.) Don't you envy me from the very bottom of your soul? You know you do! I know that third-floor front in Harlem which you inhabit—one could hardly say you *live* there!

But before I forget it—can't you come down to the game? I know I ought not tempt you from the hard path of virtue and devotion to learning which you are now following, but this once won't hurt. We had about decided, had we not, that you were to come Christmas anyway, but I am wondering if you might not enjoy the Thanksgiving festivities more. From what I hear, there will be college folks from everywhere and we are sure to meet many old friends. Think it over, and write me in your next, so that I can have time to make plans.

Monday, October 30, 1922

As I write these lines, it is nearly twelve o'clock, and the whole house, except Jeffreys, whom I hear whistling softly in his room, is asleep. Before me lies a note written in a pretty but not too legible hand. "Dear Old Grouchy (it says): If you don't write me a very brief essay in your best Baton Rouge French, on

'Rousseau and the Romantic Movement,' I shall surely get an F, and then, of course, I shall die of mortification. Certainly you will not wish to have my untimely demise on your conscience. In serene confidence, I await your decision. Your devoted pupil, C." *Pupil*—indeed. Now what—I ask for the one-hundredth time—is a poor man to do?

So I close this long, and, I fear, rather prosy, letter in order that I may write, in my *"best Baton Rouge French,"* an essay on "Rousseau and the Romantic Movement" for a lazy girl who is getting her beauty sleep in order that she may ensnare some other unsuspecting man tomorrow.

Don't forget to tell me your decision about the football game. By the way, Caroline says she brought Tommie Dawson into my room yesterday when I was out—oh this plague of women!—and the handsome Miss Tommie admired your picture very much. But I have not told how my room is arranged, have I? Well, I'll save that for next time. Do you remember that lovely brown beauty in Savannah you were so crazy about in the hectic fall of 1917? Well, Tommie Dawson has her backed off the boards! Enough said! Good night, my friend!

Davy

FOUR

Davy's third-floor back. The subjection of women. A social philosopher. Some more jazz. A modern Saint Anthony.

Monday, November 6, 1922

Dear Bob:

I promised to tell you about my room, and this is just the night to do it, for it seems infinitely cozy and desirable, with the cold rain driving against my windows and the wind rattling the sash. It is indeed a night to stay indoors and read or write. Imagine me in smoking jacket and slippers, with a package of Pall Malls within easy reach, and my trusty fountain pen in hand! Here goes!

My apartment is a reasonably good-sized square room with a long and most comfortable bed couch along one wall. The couch is quite luxuriously furnished with pillows of all kinds—for Harvard, Fisk, Shaw, Tuskegee, Wellesley, and the U. of P. are all present. The last two were contributed by Caroline, who says that since she uses my room so much, she feels she ought to donate something to its furnishings. Genevieve is a Wellesley graduate, and the U. of P. pillow is all that is left of a former attachment of Caroline's. The result of this conglomeration is a perfect riot of color, and suggests thoughts of a conference of the League of Nations. Over the couch, and well placed for reading, are two very satisfactory electric lights with rather attractive shades.

Between the corner of the foot of the couch and the back windows is a wall bookcase, which holds over three hundred volumes. A revolving case nearby holds my dictionaries, atlas, and similar much-used books in addition to a tobacco jar, and such conveniences. Then there is a small, but quite serviceable, library table with one long drawer, and two smaller drawers very cleverly contrived at one end. Two small stout chairs, my beloved armchair, and my trunk, with a heavy linen cover, complete the visible furniture equipment. Behind a screen, in a sort of recess between my clothes closet and the closet of the room adjoining, is my dresser. In the clothes closet, which is equipped so as to get the limit of capacity, I keep another chair, in the very unusual event of a multitude of callers. There is a mantel on one side of the room on which are kept books of the moment, library books and the like, and these I maintain in neat array by means of two Florentine bookends. There are only three pictures—the *Salome* you used to like so much, my mother's picture, and a photograph of you, which usually adorns one end of the mantel. You should feel honored, Old Pal! Your picture is one you had taken that wonderful day in April 1918, at Dijon! Will you ever forget it? You always did look like "somebody" in your regimentals—as all the French lassies seemed willing to testify—and it was this portrait which took Tommie Dawson's eye.

That reminds me that I saw that same lady this very day. When I came in from dinner, she and Caroline were in the parlor, and as I stopped at the hall table to get my letter they hailed me. I don't wonder they run together. They are both good looking, but such entirely different types that each sets the other off by contrast. There is a curiously vital something about a handsome brown woman which seems not to be possessed in the same degree by her fairer sister. What is it? Is it the greater physical vigor of the darker race which shows through?

We say—we men of the so-called better class—that there are more beauties among the fair women of our group, but are we good judges? Are we not so prejudiced against *mere color* that we cannot really judge fairly in such cases, thus, on the one hand, exhibiting our slavish adherence to the ideals set up by the Western European, and, on the other hand, through our enforced segregation within our own group, lacking the perspective which enables even some white men to see the beauty in our diverse and to him exotic types. I cannot forget one or two passages in *Batouala,* that unlovely thing, which show the reaction of the unspoiled native African toward the physical appearance of the white man. I suppose it would be pretty difficult for us to realize how far we have imbibed the white man's ideals through education and environment, and I should certainly be willing to admit without argument that this was perfectly right and proper, and as it should be, if it were not for the fact that it is just our *darker brothers* who seem to lack utterly the capacity to appreciate the beauty of the darker types of women.

I heard someone say the other day that even the darker women themselves acknowledge the inferiority of their type by trying so hard to approximate the other. That is hardly a fair rejoinder, I think. Women the world over, and since the world began, have been slaves to the conventions of their own milieu, and to achieve social success (which means still, in most cases, to get husbands) they must conform. If that means slitting their cheeks, wearing rings in their noses, binding their feet until they become miniature monstrosities, twisting their internal organs all out of shape by confining their bodies in a steel-and-canvas cuirass called a corset, they will do these things, any one of them or all of them, not only uncomplainingly, but eagerly. All civilized and cultivated races ridicule such practices, and very rightly, indeed, but—mark you, my friend!—each group ridicules the conventions of the other groups and *not its own.*

We read about the hideous foot-binding process of the aristocratic Chinese and shudder, but how many women of your acquaintance have the feet with which they were born? If Dame Nature had intended women to walk with their heels elevated two inches above the ball of the foot, don't you imagine the old lady would have made the proper adjustments herself? Don't misunderstand me! Heaven knows the result, as seen by the masculine eye, is all that one could wish, and personally I have no objection. But for that matter, neither have I any active objection to a man slaving in the mines of West Virginia to furnish the coal to keep me warm! If the result pleases me, why worry about the process?

But to return to my muttons! All this tirade apropos of Miss Thomasine Dawson! Caroline gave me an opening by referring to Miss Dawson's comments on your picture, and I said I hoped you might be here for the game on Thanksgiving. Then I asked the ladies' permission to read your letter, which I had just taken off the hall table.

When I opened it, such exclamations there were at the number of closely written pages.

"What, in Heaven's name, do you men find to say to each other?" Caroline cried. "It is useless for me to pretend I never noticed them—such fat letters they are. And of course, I thought they were from your best girl."

Then she laughed, and Miss Dawson laughed, quite boisterously. There was evidently some joke between them which they did not see fit to explain to me. When, after glancing hastily over the letter, I told them you had decided not to come for the game, they were voluble with regrets. I need not say that I, myself, was very much disappointed. However, let us hope that Christmas will bring a different story.

Have I ever written about Verney's diary—I suppose that's what you might call it. He says it is a sort of spiritual and intellectual diary, and that he keeps another and separate record of his social life. This intellectual diary is an unsystematic record of the books he reads with the thoughts suggested by them. As I looked it over, it reminded me of the big book kept by the Philosopher in the movie of *Blood and Sand*. Do you recall it? There are some interesting things in it. I wonder what has given Verney his point of view. He's a curious mixture of idealism and cynicism. Here are a few extracts, which I copied the other day, with his permission:

During the heyday of the Victorian era we were afraid to call a spade a spade. Somewhat later on we commenced to poke fun at all verbal prudery which was too pronounced, and began to insist upon calling a spade a spade, whenever it was absolutely necessary to mention it at all. Some twenty years ago we seemed to discover that young folks were getting worse in some respects, and it was generally agreed that our reticences were at the bottom of all their shortcomings. So we began giving them the plain truth as to the physiological and biological facts of life. Today we discuss, openly and publicly and before any type of audience, subjects which, a generation ago, would have been out of place before any but a most carefully selected group. The "flappers" of this age seem to know far more than their mothers do, and they read books which their grandmothers would have burned, and go to plays which—thirty years ago—would have been debarred from any stage. But in this case, if the truth has made them free, it has not made them clean. There is only this difference noticeable to me—they are far coarser than the generations which have gone before. Personally, I cannot see that this is a gain. Is it a gain for purity to get used to filth?

Whenever I read after Dr. Freud, or his follower Dr. Jung, I hold my head and ponder: "Am I crazy, or is he crazy? We cannot, both of us, be sane."

Race hatred in this town is worse than in mid-Georgia. Down there a white man can kill a colored man for any cause or no cause, and with absolute impunity, and he can with the same impunity abuse, beat, cheat, humiliate, and degrade him at will. Knowing this, he does not hate him, unless the colored man shows too great skill or resolution in thwarting his white neighbor in carrying out his most amiable intentions. Up here no white man will try to beat or abuse a colored man unless the odds on his side (the white man's) are at least five or ten to one. If they are less than five to one, the scion of the superior race is liable to get the most of it. Being thus thwarted in his God-given right to beat, cheat, abuse, mutilate, or kill his inferior, his hatred, lacking a vent, eats in. This was the reason why the riots of 1919 were so popular, until the colored people awoke.

These are just a few bits chosen at random from hundreds of closely written pages.

"With so many ideas," said I to Don, "you ought to write for publication."

He smiled indulgently and shook his head.

"I am afraid I have no great desire to do creative work," said he. "If I have any 'itch for writing,' as Horace so aptly calls it, I seem to get rid of it in this harmless fashion."

As for me, I only wish I had one half of Don's wealth of ideas. After noting his equipment and his diffidence, it makes any ambitious literary plans seem rather presumptuous.

The other evening while I was very busy composing the first draft of an important letter, Caroline came in, looking a little bored or tired, or something of the kind, and taking my French dictionary from the revolving bookcase, disposed herself comfortably on the couch, and began picking out the stories in Maupassant's *La Maison Tellier.* This has been her favorite amusement during the past two or three days. What it will be next, Heaven only knows!

"Are you cutting classes tonight?" I stopped long enough to ask.

"Partly. One of my teachers is ill, and I am not prepared anyway, so I am going to cut the other class. I feel dopey. I'll have to cut out these midweek frolics, or I'll be old before my time. I ought to sleep, but I prefer to read and give you the pleasure of my presence, Old Grouchy."

I grunted, as is befitting an "old grouchy."

"Oh, you're very welcome," said Caroline sweetly, with her head buried in her book. I looked around, started to speak, then thought better of it, and went on writing. I finished my letter, and began to read in the first volume of that frivolous work by Westermarck entitled *The Origin and Development of the Moral Ideas.*

By and by, Caroline yawned portentously, stretched herself luxuriously, and came over and consulted the big dictionary, at the same time scribbling some words on a bit of paper. Then she resumed her comfortable place on the couch.

"Old Grouchy, I have finally found a name for you," she said, after a few moments.

"Yes?"

"Yes—it's been troubling me for some time. You see, the name Old Grouchy, though in this case accurately expressive, as a name should be, is inelegant, exceedingly unaesthetic, in fact. Then, too, it is not comprehensive enough, it does not include all the factors. Now 'godfather' seems to be the word I want. The dictionary says"—here she consulted the bit of paper—"'godfather, a man who becomes a sponsor for a child at baptism, and makes himself a surety for its Christian training.' Omitting the trivial matter of presence at baptism, the rest is all right. So please consider yourself, from now on, my official godfather."

"I agree, at any rate, that it is better than Old Grouchy."

"I hope you will not fail to perform seriously the duties imposed by your new office."

"You have not given me an easy job."

"No. Godfather, dear, there is all the more reward for *difficult* duties well done."

"No doubt there should be, in all fairness."

And thus did "Old Grouchy" pass away and "Godfather" take the place thus vacated. The minx introduced me last evening to the famous Dr. Weld, her pastor, as "my godfather, Mr. Carr." The reverend gentleman stared at us both in apparent perplexity, but Caroline never once blinked. So he received the introduction without more ado. I saw Mrs. Rhodes, who was present, open her mouth as if to speak, but she evidently thought better of it. Everyone who lives in this house has discovered that the easiest way is the best where Caroline's pranks are concerned.

I have been to three dances within the past two weeks, two of them small, private affairs, and the other semipublic, given for the benefit of the NAACP. Perhaps one comment which might interest you is the rather general observation that there are a great many good-looking people in this town, and that your folks, Old Fellow, have emerged from the barrel. One other thing might interest you. I danced at two of these affairs with Thomasine Dawson, and, for all the same lady is no abnormally ethereal creature to look at, she is veritable thistledown on a dancing floor. We two seem to be on perfectly easy terms, somehow, and we are becoming great pals. Caroline really seems pleased that I have taken such a liking to her friend, though, if such be virtue, me for the straight and narrow henceforth and forever more!

Jeffreys, who has been rather scarce about the house lately, which fact accounts for my not saying much about him in recent letters, was at the two private dances, and to use Tommie Dawson's phrase, "He's a regular jazz hound!" To give him credit, he is an unusual dancer, and, if his dancing is now and then objectionable, he gets away with it, and it does not seem to lessen his popularity. At one of these dances, he was rather busy with some strange people, of somewhat unprepossessing appearance, who, in my humble opinion, seemed a trifle out of place. He must have thought so, too, for, at any rate, I did not see him present them to either Caroline, or Tommie, and I know he did not introduce them to me. On that occasion he and Caroline had a tiff. I am not sure what it was about. She did not offer to tell me, and of course I did not ask. What I noticed was that right in the middle of a one-step they stopped, and she went over to one corner and sat down, while he trailed after her, as if reluctantly. As I passed them, dancing with Miss Dawson, Caroline's face was flushed, and Jeffreys was smiling rather sarcastically, it seemed, and he looked both flustered and angry. When the music stopped, Miss Dawson excused herself, and she and Caroline went into the dressing room together. Jeffreys seemed a bit sulky for the rest of the evening, but Caroline was soon showing her usual high spirits. I noticed also that she and Jeffreys did not dance together again until after supper was served.

Tommie and I ate supper together, and we were separated from Caroline and Jeffreys by the width of the room. I noted Tommie eyeing them speculatively, and I caught her eye and then I, too, looked at them and back again at her inquiringly. She understood my unspoken question at once, but did not respond to it. Naturally, I did not repeat it in words. By one of those sudden feminine twists, which often, to us unseeing men, are unintelligible, but which in women are the result of a perfectly logical, though silent and therefore invisible, process of reasoning, she was especially cordial in her manner, and I was quite charmed by it. When we arose at the sound of the orchestra's opening bars, she squeezed my arm and whispered, "Godfather, you are a dear, and no mistake!"

To which I replied, without hesitation, "Virtue, my dear child, is indeed sometimes its own reward!"

We both laughed, and were whirled away on the magic wings of a waltz. To you, poor mortal, who have never had that divine experience—a waltz with Tommie Dawson—these words mean little. Someday my friend, you may know. When the music stopped again, I held her hand for a moment and looked into those wonderful black eyes, with the tiny flashing diamond point of light deep down in the heart of each one. Then I said:

"Tommie, dear, I am just beginning to understand about Heaven!"

"That is no proper speech for a godfather, Mr. Sir!" But she squeezed my arm again, and turned, laughing, to greet her next partner.

Late that night when I came in, Jeffreys and Caroline were standing inside the parlor, which was dark, though there was a light in the hall. Though I hastened upstairs, I could hear that they were indulging in mutual recriminations, for both were speaking in low, but rather tense, tones.

I often read very late, especially after a dance, for I am rarely sleepy then. So on this occasion, I turned on my light, and tackled Westermarck—a good nightcap, I assure you. It was not long before I heard the front door slam. This surprised me, for I was wondering who was going out so late. Then I heard Caroline's step, and rather dragging it sounded. Then my name was called softly, and I went to the door. Caroline was standing near the foot of the last flight, hesitating as to whether she might come up. When she saw me she continued her ascent. Considering the lateness of the hour, this seemed to me an indiscretion, and I was not a little annoyed by it, knowing that neither Mrs. Rhodes nor Genevieve would approve. My welcome, therefore, was a trifle cool, and I remained standing, hoping that thus I might abbreviate the interview.

But I seemed destined to have my trouble for my pains. Caroline came up to me and putting her arms about me snuggled her head close against my shoulder. She had been crying, it was plain. Her face was flushed, but, in the midst of my annoyance and discomfort, I recall noticing how unusually pretty she was.

"Grouchy, dear, am I so very bad? Tell me, honestly."

Why this girl takes me for a sort of wooden Saint Nitouche the Lord only knows!

"Yes," I replied irritably. "You are very bad! You have no business to come up here at this hour of the night. Suppose Jeffreys"—for I confess I was thinking very hard of him—"suppose Jeffreys should come up, what would he think?"

"*I* don't care *what* he thinks about *anything*. I hate him! But you needn't *worry*. He's gone to that nasty cabaret with his flashy friends from Baltimore. He wanted me to go. I told him I had to draw the line somewhere. Then he got angry, and—I never thought—"

Here Caroline, after twisting her face into the most dreadful contortions, commenced to cry, and real tears dropped steadily down my immaculate shirtfront, and glistened on the satin facing of my dinner jacket. I was decidedly more annoyed than moved, and, as this cloudburst showed no immediate signs of abating, apprehension got the upper hand of annoyance. Suppose Genevieve should hear? I thought of her coolness after the night of the cabaret experience, and I confess that I felt wretchedly uncomfortable. The little clock on my table showed a quarter of two! Shades of my puritanical Presbyterian grandfather! I said some more or less meaningless things meant to be comforting, and tried at the same time to disengage myself from the confining arms, but she only held me tighter, shifting her grasp from my shoulders to my neck, and buried her face against my shirt bosom, and sobbed unconstrainedly. I assure you that under the existing circumstances, I did not enjoy it a bit. But I patted her on the back, and wiped her eyes with my handkerchief.

Finally, she calmed down and smiled rather wanly at me.

"Go to bed, Caroline, you're all tired out!" I said in the most fatherly tone I could assume.

"All right, Old Grouchy." Then she looked ruefully at the "havoc that was my shirtfront," and tried most ineffectually to rub the stains of combined powder and tears from my coat.

"Poor fellow," she murmured, "it's a terrible thing to be a godfather, is it not? Good night, I feel better, thank you." So I led her to the door, and with one last paternal pat on the shoulder, bade her good night.

In my brief but checkered career, and in an experience extending from the levees of the Mississippi to the rice swamps of South Carolina, and from Jacksonville in Florida to Idlewild in the heart of Michigan, not to mention New York, Philadelphia, Boston, Paris, Metz, Nice, and way stations too numerous to mention, I have had occasion a thousand times to ask this question: Why does a woman like nothing better than to see how far a supposedly decent, gentlemanly fellow will let her go? I have observed it in women of every class and of many races. A certain type of woman just cannot help tempting a man who is supposed to be on his good behavior.

I suppose the lure is, on the one side, somewhat like that which entices one to the very outermost edge of the deepest abysses, and is related on another side to that fascination which draws us irresistibly to touch any painted surface marked "wet." If a man is labeled "safe," such women must find out just *how* safe he is, and they will take any risks to do it. And I am talking now about reasonably nice women and not the other kind. Caroline is an organized bundle of fascination, and having studied me and made a careful estimate of my safeness, she thinks it her duty to test that safeness to the very breaking point. Sometimes I think she realizes how she teases me, and then again I think the opposite, for she has a rare assortment of inconsistencies and contradictions in her makeup.

I have just been looking up Saint Anthony, the famous hermit of the Theban desert. As a fellow sufferer, and one with a record, I thought I might well get a few pointers from the career of this august personage. I note in my encyclopedia that he lived and died in the odor of unusual sanctity at the advanced age of nearly one hundred years. Buddie, I don't know much of his temptations, but I venture the assertion that if he had had wished on him the job of being the godfather to Caroline

Rhodes, he would have never been heard of outside of the bush leagues.

But, enough of my troubles! Tell me more of what you are doing. I had a long letter from Marcia today. She says she had a bat with you the other evening. I envy you, my boy. She's a smart child, and no mistake, and it is no pain to look at her, and those elegant little frocks! Give her my best, tell her I am working hard and living like a monk, but that I shall leave my cloister long enough to answer her very welcome epistle. Be good to yourself!

Davy

The game's the thing! More kisses. Three fair ladies vis-à-vis. On the trail of the villain.

Sunday, November 12, 1922

Dear Bob:

Everyone is talking about the game. There are parties coming from Chicago, Pittsburgh, New York, Philadelphia, Baltimore, and all intervening points, so it seems. The Rhodeses are going to have their full share of company, surely. Tommie Dawson is to be Caroline's houseguest over the holiday, Wednesday to Sunday, and there are three girls, friends of Genevieve, coming from New York, and Mrs. Rhodes's brother and his wife from Brooklyn. Jeffreys has asked permission to have a friend over Thursday and Friday, and Mrs. Rhodes, who wants to make everyone happy, has consented. Everybody who is to be in the house will dine here Thanksgiving Day, except myself, the Hales having invited me to dinner that day. I was glad to have an invitation out, for, though I feel it would be an imposition on Mrs. Rhodes's good nature to accept her bid, still she would probably be offended should I do otherwise. When I told them I was invited out, they all expressed regret, and I really believe they are sincere. But I think it is better all around that I do not have to be an added burden. It makes me feel a bit more independent, at any rate. After they had been discussing these things in a sort of family council in the parlor, at which I was present, I went up to my room to read awhile, and shortly thereafter, hearing Caroline whistling in her room—a regular practice of hers—I called her. In a few minutes she came in, attired in a very stunning walking suit and the chicest little bonnet you ever saw stuck over one ear. (There looks to be something wrong with that word "chicest," but if c-h-i-c spells "chic," you must surely add "est" for the superlative. I note that old man Webster says nothing about it, but we'll let it go at that. It's not the first word I've coined or you either.)

But to return to Caroline.

"What do you want, Old Bear?" was her characteristic greeting. "I feel so excited at being sent for—summoned, as it were, to the venerable presence of my august godfather. I hope it's not anything in the nature of that—ah—chastisement you once mentioned."

She threw the two books she was carrying on the couch, and sat down, wonderful to relate, in a straight chair. Even a hoyden will think of her clothes now and then.

"I have been thinking over what you are planning for Thanksgiving," I said. "Where are you going to put all these people? Your mother will have to work her head off managing the house, and attending to the meals for so many, and she, certainly, ought not to have to give up her room, for she will be played out at night, or I am much mistaken. Now I suppose if I offered to give up my room, and go elsewhere, you would not want to let me—eh?"

"No, indeed," said Caroline. "Mamma would not hear of it, I know. Besides, where could you go? Everyone will be overrun with visitors."

"Well, I have just been thinking that if you and Thomasine Dawson would condescend to use this room, I could bunk in that little storeroom off the hall. It's a perfectly good room, with enough light, and it's well enough ventilated for this season of the year. In an hour I could fit it up so that it would be quite habitable. But—though I don't like to offer anything with a string to it—I should rather hate to give up my room to strangers. My godchildren (I was including you in that plural, old fellow) say I am rather fussy, and maybe I am, but you, or Tommie, or your mother, or Genevieve, would honor me by accepting this, my humble abode." I made a mock bow, and ended with a flourish of my right arm, in regular elocutionist style.

If I judge from its reception, my speech was a perfect artistic success. Caroline left her sedate pose on the straight-backed chair, and quicker than you could think it, much less write it, she was on my lap with both arms around my neck.

"You dear old darling, you."

And she kissed me twice on the mouth!

Then, before I could formulate a thought, she was back in her chair again, looking at me with a quizzical expression which defies description and which has eluded thus far my best efforts at a satisfactory interpretation.

"I have been twice paid," I said, bowing, and regretted the remark on the instant, for I think it is best to ignore these emotional outbursts as the most effective way to limit them.

"We were rather put to it, for we must give Uncle and his wife a nice room, and then Genevieve's friends must have reasonably comfortable quarters. Mother was going to ask Jeff (that is Caroline's regular name for my fellow lodger) if he could not help us out, but before she got a chance, he asked *her* if he might not put his friend up. Tommie did not want to come, but I told her that there would be a room for one more anywhere, and she would just have to come. But this will fix it all right. Genevieve and three girls can use the two beds in our room, and Uncle and Aunt can have the middle room, for Brother is going to spend the whole holiday at the 'frat' house. And that will leave Mother her own room, which she will surely need, as you say. Tomorrow we'll put our heads together, and fix up that little room. I wouldn't mind taking it myself, but it would hardly do for Tommie, would it?"

So we settled the matter, and—I am thankful to say—without further osculatory pyrotechnics, and Caroline went off to her classes whistling merrily.

I have been puzzled as to just what to do about the game. Of course I have seen these things often enough to know that men are very desirable as escorts. Jeffreys and his friend will probably take Caroline and Tommie, though I have not heard that definitely stated. However, it is safe to assume it. I have not the least idea who the New York girls are, and until I do, I don't like to commit myself. I should be glad to take Genevieve, of course, but until I know more about the visitors, I guess I won't get myself tied up. I'll find out from Caroline who the New Yorkers may be, and if they are unknown to me, you can look them up at your end.

Some wit, long since dead, had a bright thought which has been hauled down from generation to generation in this town, and quoted to each newcomer in turn. Though a bit hackneyed by now, of course, it was clever in its day, and is still perfectly descriptive. It is this: The District of Columbia has no climate, but only *weather*. Now, when you have lived here awhile, you realize that the ancient wit who said that was positively inspired. Caroline had not been gone fifteen minutes when what had promised to be a perfect fall evening turned out badly, and it came on to rain in torrents. I had planned to take a walk, and perhaps call on some of my friends, but this did not look promising for anything like a stroll for pleasure. Then I thought of Caroline and the nobly new hat, the trim little suit, and those dainty little French pumps. Really, Old Friend, that is where Caroline shines. You have seen nothing "classy" until you have seen her feet. But that is an irrelevant aside! Of course some admirer might bring her down in a car, but admirers, or at any rate desirable admirers, are not always present when needed. I read awhile longer, and then went down to the 'phone. I called the University, and asked if I could speak to Miss Rhodes. In a few moments I heard her clear, almost boyish, treble. She was surprised when she knew who it was, then quickly asked if her mother was ill. I reassured her, and asked her if she had anyone to bring her home.

"No," she answered. "I was just wondering what I should do."

"It would be a crime to spoil that pretty rig of yours. What can I bring you?"

"Oh, I wouldn't think of having you come out in such a storm."

"Nonsense. I was coming out anyway. I need the exercise."

So after a few more perfunctory objections, she told me what to bring, and told me at what time she would be free. I hunted up Mrs. Rhodes, and she got the rain attire together, a pretty mackintosh and a pair of the most ridiculously little overshoes you ever saw—I could put one of them in my vest pocket. I donned my old army storm coat—what memories it conjures up!—and sallied forth into the gale, enjoying the high wind and the pelting rain. When I got to Florida Avenue and Seventh Street it had not slacked a bit, so I went around to the T Street corner, where the waiting taxis stand. In that respect it reminds one of Lenox and 135th in New York. My watch showed 8:25, and Caroline had said she would be ready at half past. I hunted up a chap whom I have employed once or twice since I have been here, and in two minutes we were up the long hill and on the University grounds. Caroline was in the vestibule waiting for me, and in a moment, having been duly invested with overshoes and mackintosh, and protected as to the cute little hat by my perfectly good umbrella, she was comfortably seated in the taxi, and we were on our way home.

"I knew what I was doing when I picked *my* godfather," she said, laughing. "But it's really awfully nice of you." And she snuggled up close to me, and slipped her hand through my arm. She reminded me of a nice, purry kitten when she is in a good humor.

"It's such a wild night," said I. "How would you like to get Tommie, and some eats, and go home and have a spread?"

"Oh, that would be jolly," she said, and clapped her hands. So we took in Tommie's house on our way, and, to save taxi hire, I took the girls home first and then had the man drive me back to a delicatessen store, where I paid him off, and sent him on his way.

In a few minutes I was back home again, laden down with good things. What a time we had preparing that stuff and setting the table. When everything was ready, we called Genevieve—

Mrs. Rhodes had retired and begged to be excused. That was really a delightful evening. Just as a woman likes nothing better in this wide world than to be the center of attraction for a group of men, so I suppose we men like now and then to have the undivided attention of two or three attractive women. I admit I enjoyed the situation to the full.

We enjoyed the collation in the cozy dining room, with the rain dashing against the windows and the wind rattling the frames. They were interesting faces which looked at me from the three sides of the table, and nowhere else in the wide world but in colored America would you be likely to see such contrasting types in one room. There was Genevieve, who, barring a little tropical warmth in the lines of her mouth, would pass for a descendant of English or American stock; Caroline, whose vivid coloring, dark skin, and flashing eyes would suggest Spain, or Sicily; and Thomasine Dawson, who might have graced the throne of one of the ancient rulers of the Nile!

And as I looked at them I began to wonder at what has been to me one of the insoluble mysteries in the attitude of our race group. Why, why, why, with such a variety of beauty of every type under the blue canopy, must we discard as worthless all but one, and that the one in which we can hope least of all to compete with the other race groups environing us? I do not believe, and never have believed, that women of their own choice make of themselves neither fish, flesh, nor good red herring, but they do so through a sort of moral and social compulsion, because so many colored men of the more prosperous class seem to be attracted only by fair women approximating the white type.

Does it not strike one as a dreadful confession of admitted inferiority? For the life of me I cannot see how else to regard it. Maybe it is more true here than elsewhere. In fact, I feel reasonably sure that it is, local society being somewhat more sophisticated. But again I recur to my thesis, that I feel that the men have imposed this monstrous thing on their women.

When I reflect on this, I can forgive Caroline a lot of her foibles, as, with the usual aids, she could surpass most of the devotees of the Great God Enamel, for she has the features, and a shape and poise of the head hard to surpass. The fact that she is vastly prettier in her exotic way than she would be if whitened to the dull American level would, of course, make no difference with most of them, and I imagine they actually disapprove of her for not making the change. As for Tommie, she is perfect as she is. Her skin is like brown satin, only there never was satin half so fine, and it would be ridiculous, if it were not a thing to weep over, to reflect that the Anglo-Saxon civilization of America has made such beauty a badge of inferiority, and has made us regard any lying imitation of the white man's type, however spurious to the most casual glance it may be, as a real achievement. But pardon this aside!

In the midst of our conversation, Tommie started as if she suddenly had recalled something, got her handbag from the side table where she had thrown it on coming in, and produced therefrom a letter, which she tossed across the table to me.

"I thought our sociologist might be interested in it," she said, laughing.

I opened and read. As I have not the letter by me, I can only reproduce the gist of it, which was somewhat as follows: The undersigned (writing from an address in New York, not two blocks from you, old fellow) announces that he is going to be in Washington on the Tuesday before the game, and will have on hand a remarkably fine assortment of high-grade fur coats, evening gowns, silk lingerie, stockings, and the like at unusually low prices. If responsible persons, having in mind definite wants, will communicate with him, he will try to meet their individual needs. Terms, of course, in consideration of the really nominal prices asked, must be cash down. When I had finished reading, I looked inquiringly at Tommie.

"Those same chaps operated in Philadelphia last year. I saw some of the things they sold," she said.

"What is the idea?" I asked, just to see what she would say, for I recalled what some of our New York friends told us the past summer.

"What idea would you get if a man had a $500 fur coat for sale for anything above $75 each? And $50 gowns for $10 cash? And $4 silk stockings for 75 cents a pair? And everything new and absolutely up-to-date?"

"I should say it looked rather bad for somebody."

"I can make it more pointed than that," said Tommie. "In Philadelphia I saw one of those coats sold to a well-known New York woman for a mere song. Later on in the winter, she was accosted by detectives in a theater on Seventh Avenue, and the coat identified and taken from her on the spot."

"Yes, I recall hearing about it from New York friends. The interesting, though somewhat disheartening, fact is that their only reaction was that the poor woman had rotten luck," I said.

"Any number of people got these letters. The broadcast sending of them seems to suggest a feeling of security on the part of the seller."

"How much of this sort of thing is done?" I asked.

"I have no idea," said Tommie. "But too much, I fear, for our self-respect. You have seen one, at least, of these fur coats, yourself—oh, I shan't say whose it is!"

"Well, I suppose when folks must keep up with the Joneses,

or die, the method or process is of comparatively little importance. It's only another instance of the demoralizing influence of our anomalous position in American life. Truly, in many ways we are Ishmaelites, with every man's hand against us, and our hands against every man, so that even our own crooks feel safe in the shadow of this situation, confident that if we will have no share in the spoils of their crimes, we will not, at any rate, betray them!"

"Did it ever strike you," interjected Genevieve, "that when a people really religious, both by temperament and training, come into close and forced contact with a soulless civilization like that of the Anglo-Saxon, that they are in very grave danger? They are likely to lose their own warm spiritual feeling completely, while, on the other hand, they do not gain, as an offset, the colder ethical standards of the other race. It's the old case of swapping horses while crossing a stream."

"Your explanation certainly fits many of the points in the case," said I. "Well, it is an unpleasant subject. It's dreadful to have to wonder where some of your good friends get their pretty clothes."

Then we went up into the parlor, and turned on the Victrola and—oh fortunate mortal—I danced with Caroline and Thomasine and Genevieve in turn. Genevieve is a fine dancer, though she is so very quiet one would never suspect it, but Tommie, as I have already said, is a nine days' wonder. She's a ball of thistledown animated by the combined spirits of Grace and Rhythm. I could dance with her forever, and never tire!

I have been studying my fellow lodger, and, without having the most definite material premises for my conclusions, I feel sure that there is something wrong with him. If he were not living here, or were not so very attentive, even though somewhat intermittently so, to Caroline, I should not bother my head about him. Even as it is, with the painful memory of one unhappy experience of a similar kind, in connection with which I registered a solemn vow that I should never, Heaven helping me, interfere in any way in another person's concerns, it is a question of whether I ought to bother about him or not. But ordinary human curiosity is sometimes hard to overcome, and when you add to it a touch of the temperaments of Sherlock Holmes, Monsieur Lecoq, and the immortal Dupin, what are you to expect? I did not at all like the gentleman's deportment on the night of the quarrel of which I have already told you. He has been, for some reason of his own, unusually attentive to Caroline recently. I suppose that might be explained by the very simple reason that he is fond of her, in love with her, or whatever you would call it. She does not lack attractions, as you may have gathered from what I have said about her, and certainly, even without being acquainted with her at all, one might infer the fact of her attractiveness from the large numbers of young men who dance attendance upon her.

To make a long story short, I saw Jeffreys yesterday with the flashy friends of whom Caroline was complaining the other night. They were eating dinner in a restaurant where I sometimes dine. Jeffreys had his back to the door, and consequently to me, as I went in. I took a seat so that I might see them fairly well without being conspicuous myself, allowing a hat tree to intervene somewhat between us. Then I ordered my dinner, and observed the party at my leisure, spreading out my newspaper before me the better to mask my intentions, and hoping that someone might come in who could tell me who the strangers were. I had just about come to the conclusion, from sight and hearing, that Mr. J.'s friends were decidedly off-color, when in walked Reese, and when he saw me he took a seat at my table.

I asked him if he knew any of the strangers.

"The big man," he said, "is a sport, which means that he makes his living by gambling on the races, and in other similar ways. The woman is nobody in particular, I think, just a kind of cheap adventuress, and the other man I don't know. The first two are from Baltimore. I am surprised that young Jeffreys would be seen with them in a place like this."

I have been recasting what the folks at the house have told me about Jeffreys. He has a very unimportant government clerkship from what I hear, certainly not one to furnish him with such an elaborate wardrobe, and the money for his almost weekly trips. I have noted that his articles of jewelry, of which he seems inordinately fond, are unusual in number and variety, and many of them, while not in the best of taste, are evidently quite costly. On two or three occasions, I have seen him display a roll of bills amounting into the hundreds. For example, the night we were in that ill-omened cabaret, he slipped the twenty-dollar bill which he handed the waiter from a thick roll in which I plainly saw two or three century notes. So you can see why he may be an interesting problem. I have figured out to my own satisfaction that his trips to Baltimore are "business" trips. Without connecting J.'s name in any way with the matter, I brought up the general question à propos of the party at his table, and Reese said that several well-known men of sporting propensities make these regular trips to Baltimore, and that at least one local character was completely ruined in business by being fleeced by the sharpers of that hustling city. But that sort of thing is an old story—and ever new. The real gambling mania seems about as hard to overcome as the "dope" habit. I hope J. is not an adventurer of this type, for I should hate to think of a man like that imposing upon a household like the Rhodeses'.

How goes the world with you, Buddie? Life is very interesting hereabouts, what with absorbing work, and the possibility of meeting new people every day. I have not been able to tell you about everything and everybody, naturally, but someday when you come this way, I will show you my diary, which is a condensed record of the most important things.

Speaking of diaries, I have often planned to keep a "*journal intime*," as our French friends call it. Of course it is more than a notion, for one has always to take into account the chance of it falling by accident into alien or unfriendly hands. However, as an experiment, I have begun one on a very small scale, and someday, perhaps, I shall try it out on you.

I see my friends the Wallaces, Hales, and Morrows every few days somewhere. Lillian Barton has been out of town for over a week, but I am hoping to see her Saturday or Sunday. Verney and I have struck up a very nice friendship, and I am finding it both enjoyable and profitable, I assure you. He has lived just enough longer than I to make his philosophy, gathered by the way, both enlightening and stimulating to me.

I almost forgot one important thing. Tommie Dawson said that when next I write I should say "Hello" for her to that good-looking soldier boy. I hope you appreciate your good fortune, my friend, but to measure it adequately you will have to see Tommie.

My literary work is going swimmingly, especially the research side. The Americana collection in the Library of Congress is unusually rich, and, while the local history sections in which I am particularly interested occasionally fall short of my desires, I find quite enough to keep me busy. The slave-trade material is fascinating, and I have located one or two rich "finds" in the special collection at Howard. I am enclosing a list of books which I wish you would try to locate in the New York libraries—between the University and the Public Library you ought to be able to find one or two, at least. What you don't succeed in locating I am going to try to borrow from Harvard. It looks as if, to put the finishing touches on the local color, I may have to go to Charleston and Columbia. But there is still much I can do here, and I can decide about the rest later on.

I am sending you herewith parts of two sample chapters. Tell me frankly what you think of them, both as to matter and manner. Don't try to spare my feelings, but if you think it necessary, "Lay on, Macduff!" I await your criticism with interest.

Davy

FIVE

Love and life. Bob and Davy "over there."
Memorabilia. The prettiest woman in town.

Sunday, November 19

Dear Bob:

Love, Buddie, is the mainspring of most human action that is not selfish and that is really worthwhile. Don't get excited! I am not raving. This is merely a quotation from the wisdom of my friend Verney.

We were all at Lillian Barton's last Sunday evening, and the talk turned on great men, and the springs and motives of action. Dr. Morrow, who is a worshiper of Napoleon, spoke interestingly upon his career, and then Lincoln, and George Washington, and Cromwell were discussed. Wallace developed some clever points about the great Corsican, but my friend Don came back to Napoleon with the assertion that he had done nothing but impoverish a whole continent, and develop the spirit of nationalism throughout Europe, and that this, in its turn, has been the cause of the most bloody, destructive, cruel, savage, inhuman wars the world has ever seen, and that this same nationalism is probably destined to be, before it disappears from the world forever, the father and mother of still more inhuman deviltries. Then he propounded the assertion which begins this letter.

Somebody cited the lives of Christ and Buddha, but Verney contended that in their case it was love of the people, love of humankind, as contrasted with the love of the individual. That Lincoln, in his latter days, might reasonably be put in a similar category. He says that, as far as he has observed and read, no man does the very highest type of work of which he is capable until he is in some way touched by love. That without the element of love, human ambitions are utterly selfish, and, as such, dangerous to all who come in contact with them. That, though we all of us now and then see the effect of love upon individuals, there are many more affected by it whom, in the nature of things, we are unable to see. Just as the most advanced students now agree that the secretions from the reproductive glands in some mysterious way vitalize and energize the whole physical mechanism of life, just so does the emotion of love vitalize and energize life itself. Life without love is conceivable, but it is life senescent.

Then Don took out his notebook, and read us a quotation from Jung, which he characterized as a "rare bit in five hundred pages of rot!" Here it is:

> *It is the incapacity to love which robs mankind of its possibilities. This world is empty to him alone who does not understand how to direct his desire towards objects and to render them alive and beautiful for himself, for Beauty does not tend to lie in things, but in the feeling that we give to them.*

By some accident my eye fell upon Lillian Barton, and she, curiously enough, with her own eyes half hidden behind her hand—we were all seated in front of the big grate—was watching Mary Hale, who in her turn was staring with unwinking eyes into the fire. What did she see there? I wonder. I, too, have watched her many times, not from mere impertinent or idle curiosity, but because I like her and I like Verney very much, and because I see in them, or at any rate, I *think* I see, an unselfish love manifesting itself across insurmountable barriers. Her voice when she speaks to him contains a note of such unspeakable sweetness that his name is a caress, and his eyes, to anyone not entirely blind, are a trumpeting declaration of love! It is really one of the prettiest things I have ever witnessed.

I suppose that if they two could express their feelings in the more obvious and ordinary ways, one might not observe this tense emotion compacted into the commonplace exchanges of social intercourse. At any rate, it is tremendously interesting to me, and I am very sorry for them both, somehow.

On this same evening we had tea in the library-dining room at Barton's, and during the stirring about after tea was over, Mary Hale and I happened to be seated side by side in front of the fire while the rest were still in the other room.

"Don has been telling me how much he has enjoyed knowing you," she said, looking at me with the utmost friendliness.

"I appreciate the compliment," I said with a modest bow. "I think I am very lucky to know him, and to find him so kind. After all, it is only *people* who are worthwhile—I mean, real people."

"I think you are both very lucky," she said, again with that friendly look.

As I am really very much pleased with Don, I launched out into a little eulogy of him, and I assure you I had a most sympathetic listener. Not only did she listen, but she asked a word or two in the right places. Then she asked me how I liked the Rhodeses, and I was properly enthusiastic. Altogether we had a nice time, and I was sorry when the coming in of the others interrupted our tête-à-tête.

Before we left Miss Barton's, Reese took me aside, and told me some interesting news. He has found out, through inquiries downtown, that my friend Jeffreys does function very largely not only in a so-called "private" gambling hell in Baltimore, but sometimes also in one of the well-known places connected with a big resort in the business section of that city. Reese's informant says that Jeffreys is used often as a decoy to rope in a certain class of victims. This information puts me in an unenviable position. If I make use of it in the way that I should, if I were a son in the house, instead of a mere lodger, it might not be received in the spirit in which I should offer it; on the other hand, if I do *not* use it, and any unpleasant scandal should develop, all the Rhodeses would blame me, probably, for withholding it from them. And yet, when I simmer it all down, what I call "information" is, for the present at least, mere hearsay. If I actually knew these things at firsthand, I might feel constrained to act, however unpleasant the consequences might be.

When I arrived home from Barton's, it was early, and the usual Sunday crowd was present, as I noted through the windows of the basement dining room. I slipped upstairs quietly, thinking I might write one or two brief notes before turning in. Do you recall Scott Green, whom you knew as Lieutenant Green? He was on duty at St. Nazaire when we came through, and I procured us baths, and eats, and good beds on that most wretched night in the snow and mud. I know you'll remember the bath, Buddie, if you don't remember anything else! Well, this same chap is in Baltimore, and I met him here at a football game "on the hill"—that's Washingtonese for "on the University campus." He has been trying ever since to get me to come to Baltimore, and the other day I received an invitation in his name to a big dance in that burg on next Friday night. I thought it would be pleasant to go, but I should have to go alone, and probably come back by trolley the same night. So I decided to decline Green's bid and I sat down and wrote him as nice a letter as I could, showing him "wherein and whereas." I had just sealed the letter, addressed and stamped it, and laid it aside for mailing when here comes Caroline—her regular Sunday-evening stunt—but this time closely followed by Thomasine Dawson. I jumped up to receive them.

"We didn't know you were here. You must have sneaked upstairs in your stocking feet. You always feel so exclusive Sunday evenings that you don't want to associate with the plain people. We should never have known you were in the house if Tommie had not insisted on coming up to my room to rouge her lips."

This was the basest of slanders, but it is Caroline's little way with her friends, so Tommie smiled cheerfully, and I hastened to do the honors, as it was Miss Dawson's first visit. Since the girls were both there, I brought up the matter of Thanksgiving arrangements, and we examined the little skylight room opening off the hall, and planned what we should do with it, Tommie agreeing to come over next Wednesday and help. Not that we needed her help, but is a really beautiful woman ever in the way?

Then Caroline brought up a subject they had apparently been discussing below stairs. Said Caroline:

"Godfather dear, don't you think they ought to let me go to the dance Friday night in Baltimore?"

"What dance?" I asked, pricking up my ears.

She told me, and it was the same one the invitation to which I had just declined. My eyes involuntarily sought the letter lying on the table, but something told me to say nothing about it.

"Who wants to take you?" I asked.

"Jeff."

"What's the objection?"

"I can't just make out. Mother does not want me to go on general principles, Genevieve says I don't know who is going to be there, and Tommie does not approve of my company, though she won't say so in so many words."

Tommie looked at me as if to read my thoughts, but I was quite noncommittal, for I realized I was on dangerous ground. Then she said, addressing her remarks to Caroline:

"You know even you did not like his Baltimore friends the other night, and I certainly did not. How do you know that they, too, will not be at this party? Would you like to be forced to associate with them all evening?"

Caroline looked stubborn. Finally, she said:

"Well, I'll give Jeff a chance to say about that first. But I am going, for I think all your reasons are silly."

And by the tone of the boyish voice, and the set of the very defiant little chin, I felt that she meant it.

Realizing, as an old campaigner, that much may happen in five days, I did not unmask my batteries, but let the girls talk it out between them. Suddenly, I noticed my letter to Scott Green lying on the table. I picked it up and sat for a few moments looking at it reflectively. Then I tore it into little bits, while Caroline and Tommie looked at me in some perplexity.

"What's the matter?" said Tommie. "That looked like a perfectly good letter."

"Oh, I just changed my mind, that's all," I said.

"I am glad you are not a correspondent of mine," said Caroline. "You are the most abrupt person. Do you get that way very often?"

"Quite often," I said, smiling. "Besides, I finished writing that letter just before you came in. Many things have happened since then."

The girls looked puzzled and amused, and then laughed. Then Caroline said:

"By the way, Old Grouchy, Tommie is crazy about your soldier-boy friend. Show us that great big book you've got full of pictures. It was on your table the first day you came. I was dying to look at it then, but I didn't like to ask. You looked so dignified—and—venerable, I was afraid. I love scrapbooks!"

Caroline thoroughly understands the ultimate psychological bases of human conduct. Her manner of request suggests not even the shadow of the possibility of a refusal. You know I never was crazy about showing my keepsakes to the multitudes, but Caroline is such a coaxing little kitten, and Tommie—well, you have not seen her yet, so you can't understand. To make a long story short, I fished out the big brown book, Caroline switched on the electrics over the couch, and I sat down between them, and took up the epic of the great war as it crossed the life currents of Bob Fletcher and Davy Carr. It is a mighty interesting book, if I do say it myself, who shouldn't. I'll bet you can guess the pictures they stopped longest over. Well, I'll let you get through your blushes quickly by admitting that several were yours, of course. They asked one million questions about you, which I answered as truthfully as considerations of loyalty and friendship would permit. The other pictures were those of your friend Claire and of Mademoiselle Hortense de Figuieres. I didn't realize how many pictures of Hortense I had, nor did I ever before see so many of the things those two girls read into the pictures.

"She was looking at someone when that picture was snapped," said Caroline of one of the photos taken that glorious Sunday after the armistice was signed. "Was it you?" And she persisted until I had to answer. So I lied, and said she was looking at *you.* Since you are not here, the lie will cause you no embarrassment.

"There's a whole lot in that expression," she said, very judicially, as she examined it intently. "Godfather, in spite of your disclaimer, I fear you have been a sad flirt!"

One does need perspective to see things in their true proportions—is it not a fact? For the first time I really understood how much I saw of Hortense, what good pals we were, and what wonderfully expressive eyes she has. And the worst of it is that in some of these Kodak pictures it is apparent even to a dull person that these friendly looks are meant for the holder of the camera. Trust Caroline and Tommie not to miss a little thing like that. After looking silently and without comment—they had commented volubly on most of the other pictures—at Hortense in Captain Carr's overseas cap and Sam Brown belt, and Hortense pinning a spring flower on Captain Carr's manly bosom, and Hortense in that wonderful evening gown with the inscription, *"À Davy, m'ami, de son Hortense,"* Tommie gave a curious kind of throaty sound impossible to reproduce phonetically, and Caroline said, in her blandest manner:

"Teacher, what does *'son'* mean in French?"

"Hers or its," I answered, very glibly, and cursed the effusiveness of the Gallic temperament.

"From *his* Hortense," murmured Caroline to herself, as if in deep reflection. "Oh, you soldier boys, making the world safe for democracy!" Then she said quickly, "I suppose she's the one who writes you those fat letters with the French stamps?"

I evaded somewhat.

"She writes now and then," said I, "but I have several correspondents in France."

"And this," said Caroline with much seriousness, looking

across me at Tommie, "is the man who has been trying to preach moral lessons to me."

Of course it was a nice bit for them and they made the most of it, and I was glad enough when somebody called them and they had to go downstairs. But since that time Caroline calls me nothing but Lothario, or Don Juan. I am not so sure about the desirability of keeping a memorabilia book, and as for a private, intimate diary, I'd like to see any system which would keep Caroline Rhodes from getting underneath its inmost secrets with those gimlet eyes and boring wits of hers. She's a saucy minx, and that's a fact!

On Tuesday night I was invited to go late to a meeting of one of the numerous social clubs, composed largely of young married women. These ladies usually invite their menfolks to come about ten-thirty, and they have refreshments and dance. By chance I found that Verney was going, so we went together. On the way he said, "You will probably see tonight, if you have not already met her, the woman many folks consider the best-looking in Washington."

"That is interesting, indeed," I said. "What do you think of her? Do you think the popular judgment is good?"

"She is undeniably good looking," he said, but without committing himself. "But I should like to know what you think of her."

When we reached our destination, the house of one of the very socially minded younger set, and when I say that I mean that the host and hostess average around thirty-five, and they have recently "arrived," we were ushered into a bright parlor, full of very noisy people. The house was done in white, and the lights, while beautiful, were perhaps too numerous and too brilliant, if one should venture a criticism. I have been in three or four of these houses now, and, while they are all in the latest mode and are quite luxurious, they are more or less of a pattern, and do not evince a great deal of individual taste. This particular group—the women, I mean—seem to strive to make themselves noticed through sheer noise, and they lacked the social restraint visible in other circles I have had the pleasure of knowing. The note of gaiety seemed rather feverish, and with some of them, even forced. One woman, whom I have seen in gatherings of both kinds, has evidently decided that being in Rome, one must copy the Romans, and she was shouting and "carrying on" like the rest, though in other surroundings she exhibits the most perfect poise.

I was introduced to a few new people, and finally, under Verney's guidance, was brought face-to-face with one of the prettiest women I have seen in a long while. She was laughing and talking at such a rate that it was a moment before Verney could get her attention, but when he finally succeeded, he said:

"Mrs. Burt, may I present my friend, Mr. Carr? I have been telling him about you, and I told him he could not possibly afford to leave the 'zoo' without seeing the 'elephant.'"

"You've not lost your nerve, Don Verney," she said with a laugh. "Are you referring to my size, sir?" Then she turned to me, and held out her hand. "Pleased to meet you, Mr. Carr. I hope you like the elephant."

"The 'elephant,' dear lady, is all that it is advertised to be," said I, with my best bow.

Now you will want to know about the belle of this particular set. Well, she is a "peach," and no doubt. She has a handsome face, a fine color, pretty hair, a striking figure, a trifle voluptuous, let us say, and vivacity plus. I watched her off and on for quite a while. I stood in the same circle and talked with her, and I danced with her. But, somehow, I did not get a thrill. For sheer physical beauty, Tommie Dawson is quite her match, though you could not get many people in that crowd to admit it, for Tommie's undisguised brownness would disqualify her at once. Later on in the evening I noticed her standing by Caroline, and, to my mind, Caroline outshone her, and two or three older women in the room seemed, taking them all in all, more attractive. Why? It is hard to tell.

What is beauty, and wherein does it reside? That is a hard question to answer, when we think that the mere shadow of a line makes a difference between beauty and the lack of it. But that greater question: What is personality? How many good men have addled their brains puzzling over it! I looked at Sophie Burt and Caroline Rhodes, and the other attractive women in the room, and as I ate my salad, I wondered. While I thus ate, and between the volleys of small talk, pondered, Don Verney came up, and managed to find a seat beside me.

"What are you thinking about, young man?" he said cordially. "You looked puzzled."

"I have been wondering," I said, "why your belle, with all her undoubted beauty, leaves me quite cold."

"I was awaiting your judgment, but I did not want to prejudice it by the expression of any views of mine. But since you have expressed yourself so plainly, I'll tell you. The reason is simple. She has the soul of a hummingbird, if, indeed, she has any soul at all! When she's forty-five, she will be ugly, and when she's a bit older, she will be a catty, sharp-tongued, grasping, selfish old woman. If I were an artist, I could sit here now, looking at her, and draw her picture fifteen years hence, and it would not be a pretty one. There is only one thing which might, perhaps, save her from her otherwise inescapable fate."

"And that is?" I interjected, when he hesitated.

"An absorbing, honest-to-goodness love for a man of real worth. You see she has one chance in a million."

I looked about me, and, spying Caroline seated not far away in a bevy of flappers, I said, "Now there's Caroline Rhodes opposite us, do you regard her as beautiful?"

"Caroline—yes, you might say that without stretching the truth too far. She's undoubtedly very pretty, at any rate, and she has a kind of charm which is felt, if it is difficult to analyze."

"Has she a soul?"

"A flapper a soul! Well, the matter's still a moot question. The authorities disagree. But this particular flapper has brains and personality and the rudiments of a character. Someday I think she may develop even a soul."

We both laughed aloud, and looked at Caroline, who observed us, and called over:

"Are you two wise owls making fun of me?"

We laughed still louder, and she left her place and came over to where we were seated. We squeezed out a place for her to sit down.

"Mr. Verney was just debating the point as to whether you possess a soul or not. We had not settled the question—quite—when you interrupted. Won't you help us out?" I asked.

Caroline laughed easily.

"We modern women," she said, "never display our souls except to those equipped to see them. Now are you answered? Does one, for example, need a soul for this?" she swept her hand in a semicircle, and looked about her.

"Out of the mouths of babes—" began Verney.

Then Caroline, with that caressing intonation which would make a slave of old Bluebeard himself, said, looking at my companion with her sloe-black eyes:

"Now if only Don Verney would deign to take an interest in me, I might develop a great many attributes until now hidden from a waiting world."

Verney bowed.

"I am too old a bird, little lady, to be caught with chaff."

"I have never heard that mere age conferred immunity from folly. Doesn't the sight rather lose its keenness with the advance of years? My dear Don, the older they are the harder they fall."

This time the laugh was on Don, and we all joined in it heartily.

I had noticed while we were talking that the Hales had come into the next room. It was not long before Verney had excused himself gracefully, and a few minutes later I saw him seated by Mary Hale, looking quite as if he had been there all evening. Caroline caught my roving glance, and looked at me meaningfully. Then she spoke with more feeling than one might expect from a flyaway like her.

"They were made for each other. It's a mortal shame there must be barriers between them. Fate plays us curious tricks, eh? The disadvantage of civilization is that he can't carry her off, as he would have done long ago if we had been living in the Stone Age."

"Do you believe in Stone Age methods?"

"Well—there are advantages and disadvantages in all situations. Unfortunately, we can't adopt the system suited to each need as it occurs." She laughed.

"To change the subject slightly," I interjected, "I did not know you knew Verney so well."

"Oh, Old Don!" said Caroline with an affectionate intonation. "Everybody knows him, and I suspect many of us would meet him more than halfway if he made the least sign that he cared. He is kind and encouraging and tones you up when you are feeling blue. He was the first real grown man to ask me for a dance, and he paid me the first real compliment I can recall. His compliments have point and individuality, so that you believe he's sincere, and of course you remember them."

"What did he say to you that you remember so well?"

"Can one in cold blood repeat a compliment to one's self? It sounds silly and vain, and just as if one believed every word of it. But the best part of nice compliments is that you *wish* they might be deserved, and maybe you try a bit to make them so."

"That is true, though I had never thought of it. But what did he say? I shan't think it silly or vain. I'm just interested."

"I believe you," she said simply. "He said just these very words as we finished dancing, and he seemed awfully big and important, and I was just a high school girl: " 'Caroline, you're a beautiful dancer, and a lovely girl, and if you don't let the young fellows turn your head by telling you so, you will someday meet a sure enough man who will appreciate you. But don't choose your life partner to the sound of a jazz orchestra. Don't forget that!' "

"It was a very nice compliment," said I, "and capital advice."

"Yes, so much better than telling a girl that she has pretty hands, or pretty eyes!"

"But if she has," said I, laughing, and looked directly at her, "do you object to simple statements of mere obvious fact?"

"I declare," said the incorrigible, "if Old Grouchy isn't paying me another compliment!"

"What are you two having such a good time over?" said a sweet, laughing voice. We glanced up to see Mary Hale looking down at us, smiling, with Don Verney close behind her. As I jumped up to give Mrs. Hale a seat, Caroline answered without hesitation, but with a hint of mischief in her tone:

"We were talking about you two—you looked so cozy over

there in the corner. What is that English tag—'We two, and the world well lost!' We said some other things, but it would be indiscreet to repeat them. And my godfather is very particular that I should be discreet."

"Your godfather, you saucy little minx," said Mary Hale, with flushed cheeks, but plainly not offended by the friendly badinage. "Who is your godfather, the luckless mortal!"

"Mr. Carr is my godfather," said she demurely, looking at me.

Well, it was altogether a ripping evening, with pleasant memories and no regrets, but I don't know why I should inflict it in such minute detail on you. As I look over what I have written, I think I might have spared you a good deal of it, but it was enjoyable in the living, and though I am afraid I have been unable to set it forth adequately on paper, I have found the attempt pleasant.

Won't you tell me more about your new friend in Richmond Hill—or should one say *on* Richmond Hill? I don't know much about Long Island. Evidently she has made a hit with you. As Thanksgiving approaches I regret more and more that you're not coming. The only thing that consoles me is the thought that Christmas is only a short time off, and then I'll surely see you.

Write soon, and don't forget to tell me more about your new acquaintance.

Davy

A damsel in danger, with a true knight to the rescue. The passing of Jeffreys.

Sunday, November 2

Dear Bob:

You surely recall, in your wide reading, how many celebrated men have been prouder of their achievements in some side issue of life than they have of the activities which have brought them fame. As, for example, Richelieu, the great statesman, was inordinately proud of his dramas, which the world deemed quite mediocre; Nero was vain of his supposed poetic gift; Goethe of his writings on scientific subjects; and so one might go on indefinitely. It is a foible characteristic of the human animal.

Thus it seems to be with your humble servant and he can only plead in extenuation the example of the world's great men. I wonder if you recall the achievement of which I have always been most vain, perhaps because it is one of which few people would suspect me to be a master—I mean my prowess as a boxer? It is a curious fact that proficiency in this art seems to be second nature with me, and I cannot recall the day when I was not so adept at it as quite to outclass all my playmates. As I was not oversized as a boy, it has saved me many a licking, I am sure. Although by nature peace loving, and quieter in my tastes than most of my companions, I have never faced a man on equal terms, both of us unarmed, and felt afraid.

But I know your ears are itching to know what in the world this preamble means. Well, I shan't commit the fault in dramatic technique of telling you at this point, so you will have to wait.

Everything in its own time. Let this suffice—that uncanny ability in *"l'art de boxe"* saved me maybe a term in jail or the hospital, or perhaps even the jail by way of the hospital. But let us take things in order.

You will recall that in my last letter there was a question of an invitation to a dance in Baltimore, and that I had discovered that Caroline was planning to go to the same dance with Jeffreys, to whom I have taken a violent dislike. I felt so sure that Jeffreys meant Caroline no good that I wrote Scott Green that I hoped to be able to accept his invitation, and should probably bring a lady. Then I called on Tommie Dawson, and told her what was in my mind. As Tommie can be trusted—at least I am willing to risk my judgment on that assertion—I told her everything I knew. She, without even so much definite knowledge as I had, had already come to somewhat the same conclusion, for it seems that Jeffreys has tried repeatedly to get Caroline to go to some function or other in Baltimore, but up to now either her mother, or Genevieve, or Tommie had succeeded in "blocking" these plans. Not to go into much detail, Tommie accepted my invitation to go to the dance, and we agreed on a line of action. We were both to be very friendly with Jeffreys, and see if he would meet us halfway, or whether he would not—as we thought likely—try to shy off from us, and inveigle Caroline into closer intimacy with his Baltimore friends. Of course we were to tell no one anything about our trip.

Meanwhile Caroline was making preparations to go, having thrown down the gauntlet of defiance to the whole household, and, when she wants to be stubborn, I assure you that she can be one of the worst hardheads in the world. Tommie smoothed down Genevieve, and got her to reduce her objections to a mere silent attitude of disapproval. Mrs. Rhodes insisted that the two young folks promise to leave Baltimore not later than one o'clock, which Jeffreys quite volubly agreed to do.

On Friday evening I dressed immediately after dinner, called for Tommie, and we took an early train from 11th Street, in order to avoid the possibility of meeting Caroline and Jeffreys. We thought it best to surprise them. The ride over, usually so tiresome, was very delightful to me, for Tommie is exceptionally good company, and as sensible a girl as one could find in a day's journey. The man who gets her for a wife will be lucky, indeed!

We had no trouble finding the hall, for Tommie knows Baltimore very well—which I do not. After Washington, with its wide, asphalted, clean-swept streets, Baltimore makes a very bad impression by contrast, though it is a bigger and busier city in many respects. But I shan't take time to dilate on that topic now. The hall was beautiful, the crowd very attractive. My friend Scott Green was most kind, introduced us to everybody, and seemed to get a terrible crush on Tommie. We were quite in the middle of things, and enjoying a most "scrumptious" time, when Caroline and Jeffreys arrived. Of all the surprised people you ever saw, they were the worst. Caroline was plainly pleased, especially to see Tommie, but somehow Jeffreys' cordiality did not ring quite true to me, even after I had made generous allowance for my prejudice against him. Fortunately, I had just engaged a dance with Tommie, so we were able to compare notes without exciting Jeffreys's suspicions. We both agreed that Caroline, whom her worst enemy could not call deceitful, was really *glad* we had come, and we agreed just as completely that Jeffreys was annoyed, and that he could be annoyed only because our presence might interfere with private arrangements of his own. So we planned to keep them both, and especially Jeffreys, in sight, and if Tommie noted them leaving she was to stop dancing to let me know.

I observed that Jeffreys was terribly busy talking during the intermission between dances with the flashy man and woman I had seen in the restaurant in Washington. He had presented Caroline to these people and to one or two others who were, to me, no more prepossessing. To tell the truth, I wondered how they had gotten into an affair of this kind. I noted that he did not present these friends to either Tommie or me, though he did introduce two other friends, a young chap named Lacy and a Miss Hunt, a smart-looking person with a rather taking manner. Just before the intermission for refreshments, Lacy brought Miss Hunt up to where Tommie and I were standing, and as I had not yet asked the lady for a dance, I did so, and was told I could have the second dance after the intermission. At the same time Lacy asked Miss Dawson if he could not have that dance with her.

I noted at the close of the intermission that Jeffreys had been drinking, and Caroline gave every sign of overstimulation. She is a regular little hoyden when she wants to be, but in a large gathering such as this she has the manners one would expect from a girl brought up in a cultivated home. So when she commenced to laugh rather noisily, I looked at Tommie and Tommie's glance confirmed me in my suspicion. I don't think I was ever in my life more angry over anything which was not directly a personal concern of mine. Why do men of a certain type take peculiar delight in spoiling girls whose worst fault is really a foolish giddiness? But, as I judge the thing by the event, I suppose I cannot in all truth ascribe this to mere moral vandalism on Jeffreys' part, for rather it must be regarded as just one step in a carefully matured plan.

To omit nothing in the way of a precaution, I sought out my

friend Scott Green, and asked him what was the cabaret resort usually visited by parties composed of people like Jeffreys' Baltimore friends. He thought a place called Martin's would be the most likely place, and he gave me the exact address. Then I went to the coatroom and got my wraps, and gave them to the doorman, together with a half dollar. "I may have to make time," I said to that worthy, "and I want these where I can grab them in passing." I told Tommie that if Jeffreys was planning anything crooked, he would have to spring it sometime before the close of the dance, so one of us ought to be near the exit. Unfortunately, we both had the second dance after the intermission engaged, but I promised Tommie that I should not dance again after that. As it turned out, however, I did not have to keep my promise, for just in the middle of that particular dance, I heard my name called, and here was Tommie, followed by the reluctant Lacy, "blocking traffic" in a fashion no doubt extremely irritating to the other dancers.

"They've gone!" she said simply.

In a flash I swung the startled Miss Hunt into the arms of the surprised Mr. Lacy, and with the sketchiest kind of "Pardon me," I was on my way to the door, with more disturbance of traffic en route. I snatched up my coat and hat, and took the stairs two and, I imagine, even three at a time. When I emerged into the street, I saw an automobile moving off from the curb. As luck would have it, there were several taxis standing near. I made a flying jump into the first one, and ordered the man to follow the moving car. It was evident that Jeffreys did not know he was being followed, for his car was going at an ordinary pace, and it was easy to keep in sight. Soon it stopped before a brightly lighted place which looked like a restaurant. My driver told me it was Martin's. I thrust a bill into his hand, and told him to wait for me. Then I got out in the shadow of the car, and watched the party of six, in which I plainly recognized Caroline and Jeffreys, alight. I followed them as closely as I dared.

To my chagrin, the third man in the party, who was unknown to me, stopped in the entrance walk with someone coming out, and the rest went on. Fearing he might know who I was, even though I did not know him, I waited in an agony of impatience. Finally, he, too, disappeared inside. Then I went back to my waiting car, and asked the driver if he knew how the land lay in Martin's. He did—and he told me the best way to proceed. I went in the same entrance in which Jeffreys's party had disappeared, and, turning to the left, as I had been directed, opened a small door and saw a sleepy man standing there at the foot of a stairway. I said to him, "I'm with Mr. Jeffreys's party," and, without hesitating, went boldly up. For some reason he did not stop me, but at the top of the stairs I had a different experience. The guardian of the upper landing was the real Cerberus, and he stood resolutely on the top step, effectually blocking the road.

"I belong with Mr. Jeffreys' party," I said, smiling genially.

"I don't know Mr. Jeffreys," he said, with a sort of unflickering wooden stare.

I described Mr. Jeffreys and I described the party.

"Nobody in any such party said they were expecting anyone," he said, calmly.

I fingered two bills—one a two, the other a five. I handed him the two. "Go to Mr. Jeffreys' room, and ask him if he is not expecting Mr. Lacy, and if he says, 'No,' I'll give you the fiver." He hesitated, fingered the bill a moment, looked at the fiver in my hand, looked me up and down, and, I suppose, noted that I was in evening dress, as were the members of the party I was seeking. I think this last detail probably decided him.

"What name did you say?"

"Lacy," said I. "Mr. Lacy."

He turned on his heel, and walked quickly down the heavily carpeted hall, and I followed him as noiselessly as I could, and not too closely. Just before we reached the door of the last room on the right, I heard a voice which made every nerve in my body jump! It was Caroline's voice and the tone was half anger, half fear. It was hard to control my impulse to rush forward, but somehow I managed it. The guardian of the landing paused at this very door, and knocked. After a moment's delay the door was opened less than halfway, and there was a distinct sound of a struggle, smothered exclamations, and finally a half-articulate cry—this time of real fear. This was too much for me, and with one motion I had thrown myself past the attendant, and into the doorway. One more swing of my shoulder and I was in the room. I shall not do violence to my own feelings, much less yours, by describing in detail what I saw. Everyone started back when they saw me, of course, but I had eyes only for Caroline—and Jeffreys. In the twinkling of an eye, he released her, and she fell, half fainting, to the floor. Jeffreys had plainly been drinking heavily, for I had never before seen him so lose his unshakable poise. His expression was not pretty to see. I was shocked beyond words, and then, when I saw Caroline lying helpless on the floor, all the devil that is in me—and I guess we all have aplenty lurking somewhere about us—came to the surface in one burst of blind, yet calculating, rage. And here comes the one dizzy, inspired moment for which my preamble was written so many pages back! I took Jeffreys' powerful figure, his face, almost bestially ferocious in its expression of balked desire, and I picked out the spot where I knew I was going to hit him—an inch to the right, just under his chin. I made a lightning feint with my left hand, which brought both his hands up, and then, with every minutest ounce of weight and muscle and will, I drove my right fist on the very dot I had chosen. It was the hardest, cleanest blow I have ever struck. Jeffreys seemed to rise from the floor and then crumpled up in a limp heap, without sound or motion. I never looked at him again, for I knew by the "*feel*" that he wouldn't trouble anybody again that night. His two male companions started forward, and then stopped dead in their tracks, and stood looking down at him as if awestruck. The two women cowered together in one corner, whimpering. I took Caroline's wrap from the floor beside her, rolled her up in it—her waist had been torn practically off in the struggle with Jeffreys—picked her up tenderly in my arms, and without a word or a look went out of the door, while Jeffreys' four friends stood, looking stupidly with open mouths.

When I got out into the hall, here was Cerberus again and for a second I anticipated trouble. But I might have spared myself even this very momentary apprehension. He was standing staring at me with eyes wide open. Then he spoke.

"Foh Gawd, Mistuh, you swings a nasty right. Wid dese eyes I seen Bob Fitzsimmons break de flo wid Jim Hall's haid down in Noo Yawlins, an' way back dere in '97, I seen him paralyze Jim Corbett wid dat turribul solah plexus blow, but in all my bawn days I nebber seed no such cut down as dat. Who is you, Mistuh?" And he followed me respectfully to the stairs.

I suppose I shall regret that my concern for Caroline, and my anxiety to avoid any public scandal, prevented me from enjoying this moment of real, unalloyed triumph, and this perfect, wholly unsought tribute. But, to tell the truth, it was only later that the scene and the quaint words of the attendant came back to me.

I ran down the stairs, and, in my excitement, though Caroline is no featherweight, she impeded me no more than would a small doll baby. I asked the doorman to get my car as quietly as possible, showing him a dollar bill. In a moment, and with absolutely no publicity, I had Caroline in the car. Then I asked the chauffeur to get me a glass of cold water from the restaurant. In a few minutes the young lady was thoroughly conscious, but a little dazed, and it was pitiful the way she clung to me. I have never in my life struck a man when he was down, but I really believe that if I had had Jeffreys right there in front of me, even helpless as he was, I should have struck him again and again.

We drove back to the hall, and I started to alight to get Scott Green and Tommie, but Caroline seemed so averse to my leaving her that I sent the chauffeur. It was not many seconds before both of them came flying out, and in a moment Tommie had Caroline in her arms. Green and I conferred. I did not want to take Caroline on the train, and yet I did not want to pay taxi hire to a Baltimore car for a trip to Washington. Green said he could fix that, for he knew two or three Washington cars which were always waiting about, looking for chance passengers for the home trip. Soon he was back with a man he could recommend, and had brought extra robes for the trip—I must really do something nice for Green, for he certainly acted like an officer and a gentleman! Well, I paid off my Baltimore chauffeur, and we started for home, with Tommie and Caroline snugly wrapped up, and Caroline between the two of us. At a big restaurant we stopped, and sent the chauffeur in for some steaming cups of hot coffee, which did us all good, even Caroline.

I had told Tommie about the condition of Caroline's waist, and we both thought it was best not to take the time to fix it in Baltimore, but Tommie said she would take Caroline to her house for the night, and everything could be all fixed up by morning, when I could bring over one of her school suits, and the necessary changes. I need not say that I breathed prayers of thanksgiving all the way over at the manner in which everything had turned out. Such a nasty mess as it might have been, had the cat just once jumped the wrong way!

At first Caroline was so silent I began to get nervous, but just before we got to the District line, she commenced to cry, not hysterically, but softly, and she snuggled down close against me. So I put my arm around her, and let her cry to her heart's content, while Tommie looked over at me and smiled approval. Before we got to Tommie's we were all talking and laughing, more or less as usual, but none of us referred to Jeffreys nor his friends nor the nasty incident of the evening.

Then my hand commenced to pain me, or rather, I suppose, I just became aware of it, and, inadvertently, I spoke of it, a fact I instantly regretted, for nobody present knew of the "haymaker" that had put Jeff out of the picture.

"Your hand?" said Tommie, unsuspectingly. "Have you hurt it, and how?"

"I was just trying to think," I lied glibly.

Soon we arrived at Tommie's and we all went in. Tommie made a light in the hall, and I told the taximan to wait for me for a moment or two, for I wanted to be sure everything was all right.

Tommie left us to light up her room.

Caroline came over to where I was standing, and, putting up her hands, pulled my face down.

"Old Grouchy," she said, "I have been a bad girl, and I've been punished, so don't scold me! I did not know when I adopted you as my godfather that I was adopting an angel—a real guardian angel—in disguise. How did I ever do without you so long! Someday I'll thank you, but I shan't try it now."

I had an insane impulse to kiss her, she did look so like a forlorn little girl, but thanks to my own guardian angel, I resisted. These cute little girls are always playing the devil with a man's good sense.

So I bade her good night, and went out to the waiting car. When I got home I knocked on Mrs. Rhodes's door and told her that Caroline was back in town and at Tommie Dawson's house.

"Where is Mr. Jeffreys?" she asked.

"For some reason, he did not come back tonight. We left him in Baltimore."

"But did *you* go? I did not know you and Tommie were to be there, or I should not have made such a fuss about Caroline's going."

"Well, we did not know it until the last minute."

So I bade her good night—repeated the same message to Genevieve, who had heard me talking, and who spoke to me through her closed door—and I went up to my room.

When I had turned on the light, I examined my hand and wrist, which were throbbing away at a great rate. My knuckles were badly skinned, and smarted considerably. It looked as if I had sprained my hand. Well, it was a good cause, and I could only wonder how Jeff's jaw felt. Plenty of witch hazel and a firm bandage made me feel better, and I went to bed, "dog tired," and slept like a log.

Next morning the wrist was much better, and I rubbed it down hard with a healing balm, put on a simpler bandage, and took good care to put on my glove so that Mrs. Rhodes would ask no questions. In spite of her perfunctory protest against what she called my "spoiling that bad girl," I took a small handbag of clothes to Tommie's for Caroline. The girls were not up when I left it at the door.

This letter was written Saturday and Sunday morning. I have

not seen the girls since I left them at Tommie's. My wrist is better, so much better that writing causes me little trouble. I am going to Lillian Barton's at about five today, and I shall mail this as I go out. Jeffreys has, of course, not appeared, but, fortunately, his habits are so regularly irregular (to use a paradoxical expression) that his absence will cause no special comment. I am curious to know what he will do.

This is a long letter, but I have lived so quietly now for these two or three years that even a near adventure is quite exciting. I like what you say about the Richmond Hill girl. I should like, indeed, to see her. But first come down here, and let me show you a thing or two. Till next time, Bob, I am, etc.

Davy

SIX

Virtue is its own reward. Thanksgiving. The big game.
On with the dance. A doctor with heart trouble—
a bad case. Fiddling while Rome burns.

Sunday morning, December 3, 1922

Dear Bob:

Well, Buddie, Thanksgiving has come and gone since last I wrote to you, and we certainly did have a "whale" of a time! I wish you might have been here. However, there is one consoling thought, that if you had been here then, you would not be coming for Christmas, and do you realize that Christmas is just three weeks off?

I hardly know where to begin, there is so much to tell, and I guess the best I can do, in any event, is to give you a mere synopsis, for the four days from Wednesday to Saturday, inclusive, were a whirling panorama of functions of every kind.

Of course I had been wondering what Jeffreys would do, especially as he had already invited his friend to spend the weekend with him. I had no idea that Caroline would say anything to her mother about the Baltimore affair, but, as I have since discovered, that young lady's reactions cannot be forecasted as accurately as one might imagine. Naturally, I did not think that even Jeffreys would have the nerve to expect to remain here as a lodger, though I did feel that he might have nerve enough to stay the month out, since there were only three or four days left, and since he had invited his friend for the weekend. If he should do this, it would of course be awkward for Caroline, Thomasine, and me, for we knew so much about him, while Mrs. Rhodes and Genevieve did not. So all day Sunday I was in a mild state of wonder over the matter.

But two things happened to make further wonder unnecessary. In my letter mailed last Sunday, I told you I had not seen the girls since Friday night. Well, on Sunday afternoon I went to Lillian Barton's, as has been my custom for several weeks now. The usual crowd was present and we had a very nice time, I assure you. I got home about ten, and saw the dining room lighted up. I let myself in quietly, and went up to my room to write a letter home. I had been busy for some time when a voice spoke to me from the doorway, and I turned and saw Tommie smiling at me. I know even Saint Peter is going to be glad to see Tommie. I jumped up and greeted her very warmly.

"Thank you very kindly for your cordial welcome," she said, "but I cannot stay. Genevieve wants you to come down. She has prepared the supper tonight, and wants you to sample it."

"I am afraid I won't be able to do justice to a supper," said I, "but I shall be happy to go down, if only for the honor of having such a charming escort."

"Now you are stepping out of your role, Godfather," said Tommie as I followed her down the stairs.

But if only I had suspected what I was letting myself in for, I should not have followed so willingly. I expected, of course, the usual Sunday evening crowd, and was naturally surprised to see only Mrs. Rhodes, Genevieve, and Caroline at the table. Caroline's face was flushed and she looked, for her, strangely embarrassed. It was evident that Mrs. Rhodes had been crying, and

Genevieve was even more serious than usual. I looked from one to the other, and felt ill at ease. But the suspense was not of long duration, for Genevieve spoke up very quickly, in that precise, matter-of-fact way she has.

"We have just learned from Caroline the whole story of the affair in Baltimore Friday night. I need not say that we were shocked beyond words, nor shall I try now to express our gratitude to you, Mr. Carr. Tommie has made us understand very clearly what a service you have rendered us all, and to what pains you have gone on Caroline's account. If we do not say much, you must not think us unthankful."

I was embarrassed, naturally, and stammered something about it being a privilege to have been of the slightest service, and that I was sorry that Caroline had told them, and thus had given them pain which they might have been spared.

"I think she did perfectly right to tell us," said Genevieve in her gentle, but prim voice.

Caroline is surely a bundle of inconsistencies, but among her many and diverse qualities, she seems not to number deceitfulness. She looked at me, blushing vividly, and without a trace of that bold manner she usually assumes toward me.

"I didn't know quite how to show you that I was grateful, except to make a clean breast of it. I asked Tommie, and she said it was the right thing to do. So I did it, Old Grouchy. I know a dozen girls who would give a small fortune to be able to blush as you do. Will you look at him, folks?"

There was a general laugh, which broke the tension, and I think we all felt better for it, for Caroline seems so much more natural when she is bantering with someone.

It is nice to be a hero, even in a small way and in a tiny domestic circle, and I should not be truthful were I to deny that these moments were very sweet. Caroline had me sit by her mother, who, though a woman of few words, made her appreciation felt none the less. Genevieve presided over the meal. Caroline insisted on waiting on me herself, and it was not long before the atmosphere had lost its tension completely and we were laughing and talking quite normally.

Caroline's confession, then, removed the necessity for any further secrecy, and when on Monday night a friend of Jeffreys came to say that the latter was remaining in Baltimore for several days, and had commissioned him to pack up his belongings, the last troublesome question was settled. My plan to give up my room was reconsidered, and Caroline and Tommie decided to take the room vacated by Jeffreys, for it was assumed that of course his friend, who was expected for Thursday and Friday, would not come.

Tuesday, Mrs. Rhodes had the third-floor front thoroughly cleaned, and in the evening we all pitched in and arranged it for the use of the two girls. At Caroline's solicitation, I even loaned them two pictures of you. I found that, while Jeffreys and his friend were to take Caroline and Tommie to the game, the gap left by their defection was quickly filled by other eager aspirants, so my invitation was too late. We had a jolly lark fixing up the room, and then I phoned the delicatessen not far away, and had some things brought in by a small boy, and I showed them how an old campaigner can fix up a light collation. Since Sunday last Mrs. Rhodes has been treating me more like a son than a mere lodger, and while it is nice in a way, it is a trifle embarrassing, for it makes me feel as if I am being overpaid for the service I have been able to render. Even Genevieve treats me with distinguished consideration. Caroline and Tommie must certainly have laid it on! Trust them to see that a friend got all that was due him!

On Wednesday afternoon the three New York girls arrived, and late Wednesday night, Mr. and Mrs. Thomas Downs, from Brooklyn. I wonder if you know the New York girls—two of the three are sisters, Sallie and Antoinette Cole, and Jessie Chester. The Cole girls are not half bad, and Miss Chester is a typical Manhattan girl as to clothes and general style. There has been a perfect cloudburst of young men hereabouts since early Wednesday evening. Genevieve, who is a quiet but very effective person, has evidently been doing some planning, for the whole crowd went to the Benedicts' dance on Wednesday night under the escortage of personable young gentlemen. Tommie, having been invited by someone whom she did not deem desirable company, declined to go. As Verney had gotten me a bid, and as I had no company, I tried to get Tommie to go with me. Caroline, who had been depressed because Tommie was not going, helped me to persuade her, though I realize now that it was not the proper thing to do. Tommie has a very fine sense of what is right, and only the combined efforts of all of us succeeded in breaking down her resolution.

We had a wonderful time. In addition to the ladies of our own party, who in themselves would have been sufficient to ensure my having a delightful evening, I danced with Mary Hale *three times,* Lillian Barton *twice,* Mrs. Burt, the belle mentioned in a previous letter, and two or three others whose names are unknown to you. Under ordinary circumstances it was a time long to be remembered, but so much has happened in the few days that have elapsed since Wednesday that it has become a rather shadowy memory.

Thursday morning everybody went to the game, and it would take a letter in itself to tell you all the interesting things, but I can do no more than give you the sketchiest idea of it. The scene was the American League Ball Park on Georgia Avenue, situated a short block from the center of colored Washington, on the edge of its best residential district, and on the road from that district to the University. The park seats, I am told, twenty-two thousand people. While I lay no claim to proficiency in estimating crowds, I should say there were about twelve thousand people present. However, it was not the size, but the average quality of the crowd which was interesting and significant. Almost everyone was well dressed, large numbers were richly dressed, and too many were overdressed. All the great centers of colored population were represented, from Atlanta to Boston, and from Chicago to Atlantic City. Most of the women came to show their clothes, and, with the exception of the students, and those who had bets on the game, the major part of the crowd paid little attention to the contest itself, for the people and not the game were the real center of interest for most of them. From the viewpoint of the majority of the spectators, it was a social function, and not an athletic contest.

Hundreds of women, young women and mature women, were made up as if for a full-dress ball, and somehow "makeup" does not look well at ten o'clock in the morning on a sunny day. Clarice and Aloysius McGinnis were there, I assure you, and Clarice was too busy watching "the Joneses" to pay any attention to such an unimportant thing as a college football game. The tickets to the game ran from two dollars to one dollar and I judge that most of the people paid about a dollar and a half. I think the only mistake the management made was in not asking five dollars for the best seats, for, if I have sensed correctly the psychological reaction of that crowd, most of those in the two-dollar seats would rather have paid five dollars, just to show the world how little it would mean to them.

Being a free lance, without attachments, I spent most of the time in the reserved box section and saw there practically all of my friends. Then during the intermission, I wandered about a bit, and looked them over. I saw signs of prosperity on every hand. Outside on Georgia Avenue and the streets adjoining there were hundreds of automobiles parked. Altogether the affair had its impressive features.

From the game I went home to freshen up a bit for a three o'clock dinner at the Hales'. Our house was a busy place, for there were to be twelve people at the table. While her mother, Genevieve, and Tommie helped with preparations for dinner, Caroline did the honors in the parlor. I managed to get her aside for a minute, and inquire about plans for the evening, and asked if I could be of service as an escort for any of them. She thanked me, and said she was sure I could. So I agreed to be ready by nine o'clock to go to the Coliseum, where the official university dance was to take place.

The dinner at the Hales' was most enjoyable. They have a thoroughly attractive home, not so extravagantly furnished as some I have seen, but in very excellent taste. There were four other guests, all from out of town, and people I am sure you never heard of, so I shan't waste any time over them. The dinner was fine, and beautifully served, and the good cheer was abundant. Mrs. Hale gave me the place at her right hand, and of course, I liked that. After dinner we had some music, two of the ladies sang, Hale played, and I sang. I left at about seven, with the promise that I should see them all again at the Coliseum, where everyone was going, it seemed.

When I arrived at the Rhodeses', the house was full, what with the six guests and all the young fellows who had dropped in. In the group were chaps from New York, Baltimore, and Pittsburgh, besides the local contingent. All the outsiders had come down especially for the game, and several were planning to stay over Saturday. They surely had all the outward signs of prosperity. Most of them were in evening dress, for they planned to take in the various dances, and I found out that there were to be three big ones, at the Coliseum, Convention Hall, and the Lincoln Colonnade respectively. The first was under the official auspices of the University, the second was a public dance, and the last given by the university alumni association. Several of the young folks present were planning to go to all three.

A little after nine we all set out for the Coliseum, a very large hall in the downtown district. It was full when we arrived and the folks kept coming. Before we left it was estimated by someone that there were more than a thousand people present. It was practically impossible to dance, except in a most circumscribed area, and if you once lost your friends, you were likely not to find them again. I saw numbers of people I knew—just a flash, and then they had disappeared again. I had one dance with Mrs. Hale and I tried to find Miss Barton, but finally gave it up. I danced with our New York visitors, Genevieve, and Tommie. Caroline was not in sight most of the evening, being kept busy by both old and new admirers. Among her hangers-on were two very ardent wooers, both physicians, one a young fellow from New York, and the other a solid-looking middle-aged man from one of the North Carolina cities, Raleigh or Wilmington—I don't know just which. The latter was at the Benedicts' dance on Wednesday night and seemed quite bowled over by the little lady's beauty. He came to the house Thursday right after dinner, Tommie tells me, and he just camped there until time for the dance, when he took most of the party in his Packard, a gorgeous car which must have cost at least four or five thousand dollars. Like many mature men, he seems to know what he wants when he sees it, and he is rather direct in his methods. He has eyes for nobody but Caroline, and she is enjoying the fun immensely. He said on Wednesday, I recall, that he was on his way to New York, and had just stopped over for the game, but Thursday night he said he thought he would see the festivities out. When he said that, I looked hard at Caroline, and she returned my look with an expression of the blankest and most demure innocence you ever saw.

From the Coliseum, which by eleven o'clock was so crowded as to be uncomfortable, most of us went to the Colonnade, where there was another crowd, and we finished the evening there, and went home thoroughly tired. I, for one, had a perfectly satisfactory day. As the pleasantest "nightcap" possible, I had a hearty good night handshake from Tommie, and a pat on the arm from Caroline, as they left me at my door to go to their temporary quarters in Jeffreys' old room.

"You have been very kind, Mr. Carr," said Tommie. "Thank you." And she gave me her hand.

"Nice old Godfather," chimed in Caroline, patting me on the sleeve.

I said the things obviously demanded by the occasion, and bade them good night. They had reached their door when I called them again.

"By the way, Caroline," I said, "there is one problem in mathematics you won't find in the school arithmetic."

"What is that? What do you mean?" she asked unsuspectingly.

"It is this: Does a young fellow plus a Mitchell touring car equal an old fellow plus a Packard limousine?"

Tommie shouted with laughter, and Caroline blushed, and then made a face at me!

Next morning the girls went to a so-called breakfast dance at the Casino, given by a crowd of college fellows, under the auspices of one of the college fraternities. To judge from all accounts, they had a lively time at this affair. Personally, I decided that four evenings straight were enough punishment for me, without going to daylight dances also, but it seems that I am a "piker." As far as I can learn, there were plenty of folks who have attended everything given thus far, and a lot of them are old enough to know better! Well, "There's no accounting for tastes," as the old woman said when she kissed the cow!

By the way, to change the subject a bit, I was at the Capitol Friday, watching the progress of the Dyer Bill. I say "progress," but, Bob, those scheming birds in Congress are planning in cold blood to do it up. I have been following it pretty steadily now for some days, and there is really no hope, as I see it. I firmly believe the word was passed around some time ago, that the Republicans were to let the Democrats do it to death, while some of the former went through the motions of mourning. I met James Weldon Johnson as I left the Capitol, and he looked pale and worn, completely done up, in fact. He agrees that the bill is done for.

Genevieve and Caroline had planned a house dance for Friday night, so when I got home the place was quite transformed. The furniture had been shifted about, some of it moved out, the rugs taken up, and the floors polished. I never before realized how big the house was. As there was to be another big "frat" dance Friday night, Genevieve asked her guest to come early so that those who had to go to the "frat" affair could take in both. The biggest crowd was about nine-thirty, but by ten-thirty a large part of the college crowd had gone, and we had a very good time, indeed. Some of the girls were a little listless, having been dancing pretty steadily since Wednesday, but Caroline is a living wonder. Where she gets her vitality from I don't know, but she is a regular fountain of energy.

The two rival physicians were present, and they came early and remained late, as if each was trying to outstay the other. It was like a play to watch them, and Tommie and I had a good time observing the fun. I have bet Tommie a five-pound box of Brownley's best against two neckties that the old fellow wins. You should see him! He knows what he wants, and he is a fighter, a ruthless two-fisted fighter, and though the youngster is good looking and attractive, he is going to lose out, for he will get discouraged first. I can see already that he is losing his nerve. The old chap evidently has an important engagement in New York, for they phoned him over long distance twice on Friday night while he was at the house, but he is staying over until Sunday morning, I heard him say.

I never saw a man worship a girl more with his eyes than he does Caroline. It is amazing to see the grip she has gotten on him in these few hours. And she knows it, too, the minx! To my mind, she looks too young and dainty and sweet for a grizzled chap like Dr. Corey, but, as I judge him from these few hours of observation, he is a rather high-minded man of real character. He is a widower, I hear, and has two grown children. For some unexplained reason, he seems to have taken a fancy to me, and to have the very mistaken notion that I have influence at court. At any rate, he has been cultivating me steadily, and when he's not dancing attendance on Caroline, he hunts me up and talks about her. It's very funny! Tommie has caught on to the situation, and has had a great deal of fun out of it.

After the dance was over Friday night—and we had a hard time getting rid of the doctor men—the family party, and I was honored by being included in it, assembled in the dining room, where

Tommie and Caroline served us some very refreshing cocoa, and those who wanted it had more salad, ice cream, and cake.

"What is the program for tomorrow?" asked Antoinette Cole, looking at Caroline.

"A breakfast at ten tomorrow at the Whitelaw, as the guests of Dr. Corey, the Wellmans' dance at three, and the fancy-dress party at night. If you are bored in the meantime, I am sure the doctor will take you sightseeing in his car."

"Bored!" said Sallie Cole. "If ever I get a chance to sit down again, I know my poor feet will appreciate it. I just know I have danced at least halfway around the globe since Wednesday evening. If Mr. Carr will regulate his blushes, I'll tell you something. I have had my slippers off ever since we've been sitting here."

So they all turned in to try to get some much-needed sleep, for the next day bade fair to be the biggest day of all.

I went to my room, and got ready to turn in. After I snapped out the light, I went to the window, threw up the shade, and stood looking out over the city. Very, very faintly there came to my ear the sounds of dance music from some belated function. Then the loud guffaw of someone in the street broke the stillness, followed by the shriller laughter of a girl. By some curious shift, my mind went back to Johnson's haggard face, and the Dyer Anti-Lynching Bill, being slowly strangled to death, strangled to death to the sound of jazz music played by a dozen orchestras, while hundreds and hundreds of educated, refined, prosperous colored people danced themselves haggard and lame between Wednesday night and Sunday morning! I felt a curious sense of dissatisfaction with myself and mine, a feeling as of impending misfortune. I went to bed, to sleep restlessly and to awake unrefreshed.

As I write these words, Caroline is singing love songs and accompanying herself on the piano, to the infinite delight and unrest of Dr. Corey, who has been here since twelve o'clock. It is now two, and I have been writing since early morning. I guess I might better stop here, and mail this today, hoping to be able to finish my recital tomorrow. If I add any more to this episode I won't have an envelope big enough to hold it.

While I was writing the above lines, Thomasine passed my door, and stopped long enough to say that Dr. Corey is going to stay over until tomorrow. Caroline is going to have him in for supper tonight, and wants me to be sure and come in early, as they are going to sit down about nine. So I have promised to be here.

I hope you do not feel as dissipated as I do. Tell me more about your new friend. I like her immensely. By the way, look up Antoinette and Sallie Cole. You will find them very nice girls. I told them about you, and they promise you a warm welcome. Until next time, Bob, I am, etc.

Davy

More Thanksgiving. Dr. Corey again. Davy warns the boys. An old-fashioned proper lover. Conversational spending.

Monday, December 4, 1922

Dear Bob:

I have had an early dinner, and shall devote the rest of the evening to finishing up the narrative of the Thanksgiving festivities. I believe I left off with a description of Friday evening's party.

Caroline had told me that Dr. Corey wanted me to come to the breakfast at the Whitelaw Saturday morning, but I begged off. I promised to do some lobbying at the Capitol, and as I said before, I felt that I did not care to compete with the college boys and the flappers in my devotion to the Goddess of Pleasure. Four riotous evenings and one whole day in one short week seemed quite enough. After all, every element of human life has its value, and the whole trouble comes in connection with the proportions of each. That's quoted from Don Verney. If you will think it over carefully, you will agree that it is hard to dispute successfully.

So I left the household to its unbroken round of gaiety, to follow the harder path of virtue, and I saw none of the family again until six, when I stopped in at the Wellmans' dancing party, which was given at one of the local balls. It was a very pretty party, and I saw most of my friends there. Some of them were a bit groggy by this time, and showed it, but they were determined to do or die. In the social game one must never show the white feather, and these folks surely play the game to the limit.

Dr. Corey's big car was the first thing I saw as I approached the theater which shelters the Colonnade, and within the hall the doctor was certainly showing the proper zeal. He danced every dance, and spent every possible minute with Caroline. However, he had a hard time, for she was surrounded by the young fellows practically all the time she was not dancing. In the short while I was there, she seemed, to judge from the attentions she got, easily the most popular person present. If she had planned to show her older suitor how high a valuation is set on her by her own crowd, she could not have staged the exhibition better. Corey is quite evidently a person who thrives on discouragements. A man of his type rarely fails to get what he wants, and he has made up his mind that this world without Caroline Rhodes is a very empty place indeed!

I took the crowd to dinner at the Whitelaw. I had arranged for special service, and it was very nice. Dr. Corey was included, and he took us all in his car. We did not dally too long at the table, for the ladies wanted a few minutes to relax and rest before the evening function.

The final affair of the week was a fancy-dress party at the Casino. As I had heard that most of the men would go in evening dress, and leave the fancy-costume dressing to the ladies, I decided to follow the crowd, and, as it turned out, I was glad I did so. However, I have noticed that a fancy-dress party loses somewhat in effectiveness when any large proportion of the guests are in ordinary conventional dress. Thus it was at this one, though many of the fancy costumes were very pretty.

Many of the guests, in spite of their makeup, and the fancy-dress feature gave them unusual opportunities for that, looked jaded and haggard, and it was plain that some were just going through the motions of enjoyment. But exhausted or not, they were game to the end. Dr. Corey had evidently inveigled Caroline into promising him several dances in advance, for she danced with him oftener than with anyone else, and she was surrounded, as usual, between dances. The young doctor from New York, I almost forgot to tell you, gave up in discouragement, and went home Saturday morning. Youth—which has so much more of time—is so much more impatient than maturity. Queer, is it not?

I had a very delightful evening, personally. I danced three times with Lillian Barton, and since Miss Chester, who was my special company for the evening, was very busy flirting with some chap from Philadelphia, and since Reese was so busy dancing attendance on his numerous out-of-town friends, I was able to have one or two little tête-à-têtes with that same lady.

By the way, Scott Green was present, and so was the chap Lacy, whom I mentioned in connection with the Baltimore adventure. I had not seen Lacy since the exciting moment when I actually threw Miss Hunt into his surprised arms. Under ordinary circumstances I suppose I should have gone back to the hall that night to apologize to Miss Hunt, or, at any rate, have sent her an explanation through Scott Green, but to tell the truth, I felt then, and still feel, that she and Lacy were helping out Jeffreys.

I discovered that Lacy was present in this wise. I saw a crowd of the men, among whom I recognized Verney, Reese, and two or three other friends. They were listening with evident interest to a story told by a man in the center of the group, whose face was hidden from me. This is about what I heard as I came within earshot:

"This old chap used to follow pugilism, and had been in his day at times sparring partner, trainer, or rubber in the camps of some of the biggest fighters years ago. Bob Fitzsimmons, especially, is his particular hero. When I got there, they had sent for the boss to look Jeff over. To tell the truth, we all thought he was dead. I never saw any man with life in him look quite as dead as he looked. The boss was frightened, for he did not want any police scandal, so he sent for a crooked doctor whose office is a few doors away, and who could be counted on to help him hush up the matter. While we were waiting for the doctor, this old geezer was telling us all about it. 'Wish day might strike me daid, ef I evah saw a man hit so quick and so ha'd. Ef he wuz a black man, I'd say it mus be dis here French nigger Seekee dey's all talking about.' Well, the doctor came, and he revived Jeff, but he was the sickest man you ever saw. I don't believe he knows yet just what happened."

You can imagine how I felt to have Lacy retailing the story to that crowd. Not that I am trying to work any false modesty on you, Bob, but I had hoped to have Caroline and her family spared this unnecessary publicity. I learned since that Lacy was considerate enough to withhold her name, but, from what I know of the folks in this burg, once they have gotten hold of one end of the string they won't rest until they find the other.

While Lacy was talking, I turned and slipped away, but of course, it was not many minutes before all the men, and some of the women, too, were joking me about the matter. Tommie got wind of it, and talked to Lacy, and then I saw them both talking to Caroline. I could only imagine what they were talking about from the way Caroline looked at me the next time we passed each other dancing. One of her characteristics has some very good points in its favor. I refer to her directness. "The soonest said, the soonest mended," is her motto. The silences of repression are the most uncomfortable things in the world. I think we would all of us admit that. Well, Caroline never suffers in that way, nor permits anyone else to suffer so. The next time we met face-to-face, she said:

"Godfather, if you'll promise never to chastise me, I'll promise to be very good. They tell me you are a very rough old dear." And she smiled her most winning smile, as did all the other ladies whom I knew. And this is the tribute of the gentler sex to a brutal manifestation of mere animal strength!

I feel sorry for Dr. Corey. He is completely subjugated. He worships Caroline. It is touching to note how he follows her with his eyes. I firmly believe there is nothing in the world he would not do to please her. I have a new opinion of her from watching her since this new adorer appeared on the horizon. She does not tease him, nor make a show of him, nor try to make him ridiculous in any way. Indeed, it seems rather as if she realized how likely the discrepancy in their ages is to lay him open to ridicule and laughing comment, and she tries very hard to forestall the possibility of such a thing. Either she is really touched by his admiration, or she respects him very much. As I have watched her, I have wondered how many young girls would give up the opportunity of making such a spectacular sacrifice to their own vanity.

While I was writing to you Sunday morning, Corey took them all sightseeing and they got back at noon, and then the others considerately gave him the field. When I left the house at three he had just gone, with the expectation of returning in the evening for supper. The girls' room is full of evidences of his admiration, for he has sent flowers every day, and candy galore. It's a very bad case indeed!

I had invited Scott Green to remain overnight with me Saturday, so, while I was writing to you Sunday, he accompanied the folks on the sightseeing tour as the special company of Thomasine Dawson, with whom he is very much smitten. I asked Miss Barton if I might bring him to tea in the evening, and she said she would be delighted to have him. We spent a very pleasant evening, and Green, like everyone else, was charmed with Miss Barton and pleased with my other friends. It was with regret that we left early, to keep our promise to be in time for supper at the Rhodeses'. As the New York and Brooklyn folks were going on the midnight train, the house was full of callers, and the supper, in consequence, was a kind of informal stand-up, catch-as-catch-can affair, but we had a very jolly evening for all that.

At eleven-thirty the visitors, including my friend Green, took their leave, and were taken to the station by the very useful Dr. Corey. His car holds seven very well, but he assured us that eight would be comfortable. Genevieve was, of course, thinking of going, but the good doctor looked so heartbroken at the thought of leaving Caroline behind that Genevieve said she would let Caroline represent the family. Green very properly insisted on taking a cab, but the rest would not hear of that, so they crowded in, and were whirled away, leaving Mrs. Rhodes, Genevieve, Tommie, and me to close up the house, which seemed so quiet and empty after the lively scenes of the past two days.

I went up to my room to smoke a quiet pipe before turning in, and, when Tommie came up to go to her room, I invited her in. So she sat down to wait for Caroline. Naturally, the talk turned on that young lady and her ardent new flame.

"What do you think of it?" said I.

"I hardly know," said Tommie, "but she will have to face the question seriously, for he is crazy about her, and wants to marry her. He says he knew it five minutes after he laid eyes on her. You ought to hear him rave about her."

"Oh, I have," I said, and we both laughed.

Then I queried, "Has he asked Caroline yet?"

"I don't believe he has," said Tommie, "but he quite probably will tonight. He is going tomorrow noon, I believe."

Tommie thinks he is not only a real man, but also a gentleman, and I agree. He leaves one in little doubt as to his character. There is a very attractive directness about him—I liked him my-self very much, and when Tommie said she liked him, that settled it. We both agreed, however, that he seemed too old for Caroline and that was our one objection. To my mind Caroline is such a rare embodiment of the very spirit of youth that such a match seems really incongruous.

We were still discussing the subject when Caroline came in. I looked at the clock. They had not taken many minutes from the station and the doctor did not linger at the door. These thoughts flashed through my mind when I heard her coming up the stairs: "Either he is a very *proper* lover, or he has asked and been rejected." When Caroline came in, she threw herself on the couch and heaved a deep sigh of relief.

"My, but won't it be nice to stretch out tonight!" she said.

Tommie, usually so calm and patient, could hold in no longer. "Well," she asked, "did he pop the question?"

Caroline laughed, looked at me, blushed, then laughed again. For some occult reason, I felt embarrassed, and under the battery of the two pairs of black eyes, I could feel myself growing red. Tommie looked from one to the other of us, and then said:

"What are you two people trying to do? Run a race? Which one is the redder I can't, for the life of me, tell!"

Then we all three laughed and Tommie returned to her original question.

"No," said Caroline, looking mischievous this time, "he didn't, but he says he is coming tomorrow morning to talk to Mamma—whatever that means."

So the ardent doctor turned out to an old-fashioned *proper* lover.

It was really nice to get back to the grooves of regular normal life once more, after the strain of the past few days. I should not care to try to keep up such a pace indefinitely. After a really profitable day, I knocked out about four o'clock and went home. Mrs. Rhodes was on my floor straightening up the front room when I came in. On her way downstairs, she stopped at my door for a few moments. She says she is going to keep the front room for her son, whenever he is home. He spends most of his time at the chapter house of his fraternity, where he has quarters, but now and then he spends a night at home. He has been using a second-floor room up to this time.

Of course, I was interested in Dr. Corey's wooing, and I was hoping she would say something about it, though naturally I did not like to ask questions. Sure enough, she did bring up the subject herself, and asked me what I thought of it. Dr. Corey, in good old-fashioned style, made his declaration to the mother. It sounds curiously formal in these days, does it not, when most girls get married first and announce it afterward even to their own parents? The doctor is a straightforward chap, it seems. He gave her a brief account of himself, his age, the facts about his family and his fortune. His two children are of age, and if he should marry again, he has planned to deed a share of his property to each of them at once, and a similar share to the new wife. He made the most explicit statements as to his resources, which are reasonably large, and he gave references to two or three of the largest banks and business houses in North Carolina. He is considerably over fifty, it seems. She asked me what I thought of it all. I told her that of course it was not for me to have an opinion, that I had been most favorably impressed by the doctor himself, that of course the discrepancy in age seemed very great, in spite of the vigor and apparently fine health of the suitor, but after all, the one person to be pleased seemed to me to be Caroline. Further than this I would not go.

It is a fact that I think most mothers do not object to their daughters marrying men much older, and that I think this is especially true of the mothers of girls who are very willful or unusually lively. I suppose to the mother, the older suitor does not look so old, after all, as he would to a younger person. If it were Genevieve, now, I should say, with her overserious, mature nature, that it would not be such a bad match. To say more—the good doctor might go further and fare worse! Before she left, Mrs. Rhodes said that Corey was coming back this way before the end of the week. About five o'clock an enormous box arrived from one of the big florist stores downtown—the doctor's parting gift—one dozen American beauties!

Tuesday, A.M.

I was feeling "dopey" last night, so I stopped writing about eight o'clock. The house was so quiet by contrast. I suppose that I got lonesome, so I thought I should take a walk. I went around to Verney's, and found him in. We talked awhile, and then we thought we might run over to You Street and take in a movie. We cut through Twelfth Street and went into the Lincoln Theater. This is one of the best houses in the city. Washington has two movie houses, the Lincoln and the Republic, which surpass any of those in Harlem for beauty and the quiet elegance of their appointments. They were built by white firms on the lines of the best downtown theaters of modern construction. Each is about as large as the Renaissance in New York, but far more perfectly appointed and more tastefully decorated.

As the house seemed to be crowded, we took box seats, and found ourselves seated just behind a very gay crowd of young women, two or three of whom I recognized as members of one of the clubs whose affairs I have attended. They were very well dressed, and very lively. This is a sample of the conversation we overheard during a lull in the music.

"Yes, I was terribly disappointed. You know I have been looking for a nice piece to go in that old corner in the library, and I just found it—the most wonderful bargain you ever saw. It was originally priced at $1,275, and marked down to only $800—a *ridiculously* low figure. But what do you think! When I went back to get it, it was gone! I almost cried."

"You don't say so—that *was* aggravating. But I had the identical experience last Tuesday. You know I've been crazy for a four-poster, but I have never seen one which suited me, and last week at Henderson's I ran across a perfect dream. It could not have pleased me better if it had been made to order for me. Henderson's are selling out, you know, and it was marked down to $1,230. Why I did not take it on the spot, I cannot for the life of me determine, but you know how one dallies sometimes. Next day I hurried down to get it, and as soon as the man saw me he said, 'Oh, Mrs. Manley, I am so sorry, but your bed is gone!'"

Then there was a chorus of sympathetic exclamations from the listeners, one of whom proceeded, when she could be heard, to tell how her husband had a perfectly wonderful chance to buy a certain house on Sixteenth Street for only $24,000 cash. Whether he had bought the house, or not, I could not hear, for the orchestra started up a jazz piece, and drowned out the conversation.

I need not say I was impressed—very much impressed. I had recognized none of these ladies as being anybody in particular, but the careless way in which they disposed of these trivial sums of money convinced me that prosperity in Washington was more general and widespread than I had thought. So I looked at Verney, and he met my eye with a smile.

"Did you catch that?" he asked.

"Yes, indeed," I said. "Are we in a nest of bootleggers?" I asked laughingly.

"No," he said, leaning over to me, and speaking in a low tone so as not to be overheard. "The first speaker is the wife of a schoolteacher, the second is a schoolteacher herself, and the last is a schoolteacher and the wife of a government clerk."

I looked my astonishment.

"That, my dear Carr, is what I call conversational spending. These women can keep that up all night and never turn a hair. You will notice, however, that their experiences did not cost them a single dime between them. It's the cheapest form of amusement I know. All it requires is nerve and a little practice. The first time you essayed it you would feel self-conscious, but after a few minutes' effort you would find yourself enjoying it. Someday, when you are particularly 'broke,' try it!" He laughed heartily, and I pondered over the artificiality of some phases of our modern life.

We enjoyed the show, and I enjoyed Verney's company, and when the lights went up for a moment we spied Dr. and Mrs. Morrow and Miss Barton in a box ahead of us. After a bit, two seats in the same box were vacated, and we went forward and took them. I talked to Miss Barton, and Verney to the Morrows, who invited us all to go home with them, which we did. Mrs. Morrow is a wonderful housekeeper, and she fixed us up one of the finest suppers I ever ate, and this, seasoned with such good company, made a perfect evening. I don't recall whether I have ever told you about the Morrows' house. It is very handsome, beautifully furnished on the older lines, and has every modern convenience. It is very satisfying indeed. Someday I hope I may be able to show it to you.

I took Lillian Barton home, and though it was very late, she insisted on my coming in, so I sat for a while in front of the grate, and had a delightful chat. It was a most unholy hour when I left, but I did not mind having lost one or two hours of sleep, for the dopey feeling was all gone. When I crept upstairs the house was still as a tomb. I turned in quickly, and slept the sleep of the just.

I shall try to get a picture of Tommie. I know whose line will help me. Three weeks from yesterday is Christmas, Bob, and I am certainly looking forward to seeing you then. If you should run into Dr. Corey up there, treat him nicely, won't you? And don't forget the Cole girls and Miss Chester. I must stop, so that I can mail this on my way out.

Sincerely, etc.

Davy

SEVEN

The color line in Afro-America. Crossing the line again.
The claws of a lovely woman. Before the grate.
A tropical beauty.

Sunday, December 10

It is a great pleasure indeed to know that you are getting on so well. You are one of those fortunate mortals who have all the gifts of the gods, and need only to put them to proper use to ensure yourself success in whatever you undertake. I see you, in my mind's eye, making a deprecatory gesture, but what I have just said is nevertheless true. You have a sound body, a strong mind, and a nicely balanced temperament. These should be quite enough, goodness knows, but old Dame Nature in an overgenerous mood decided to add a pleasing exterior. That was the crowning touch. When she allotted you that dimple and that smile, she was giving you an unfair advantage over the rest of us.

A boyish touch around chin and mouth and eyes is a thing few mortal women can withstand—witness the fascination of Rudolph Valentino! And sometimes I think even men are swayed by it. I often laugh to myself when I think of some of our war experiences. How the women, the old crones as well as the young lassies, used to fight for the privilege of waiting on you! It was nothing but that ineradicable boyishness in you, which will most likely accompany you to your grave. It's a mercy you have a strong will with it all, otherwise you would have gone to the dogs long ago, I suspect.

Apropos of one of my favorite subjects, the question of the existence of color lines within the race, I forgot to mention in my last letter a conversation I had with Tommie Dawson some days ago. As you may have gathered from remarks of mine, Tommie is as sweet a girl as I know, and I have never known one who seemed more sensible. She has no queer caprices and quirks in her disposition, and does not bawl one out for some little thing just because she happens to be in a bad humor. In other words, she is normal and natural, and you can count on her. I have heard it said so often, in New York and other places, that colored society here itself draws color lines—I mean among the women. I have studied the situation, without asking questions, but each time just when I thought I had hit upon something definite, some inconsistency or discrepancy would render the evidence useless. So one evening, being alone for a while with Tommie, I made so bold as to ask her.

If there ever was a person who could test such a rule, or custom, it would be Tommie herself. She has health, beauty, brains, character, a fine disposition, and is pleasing in dress and deportment. Last of all, she comes of nice people, who have more than one generation of good breeding and well-ordered social and family life behind them. The only possible objection to her could be her color, and, while it would seem an utter absurdity to find such an objection among colored people, still, from things I have noted, no absurdity is too impossible to pass current somewhere or other.

"Miss Dawson," I asked, "is it a fact that certain groups of people here draw the color line? People away from here say so."

"Well, that's a difficult question to answer, Mr. Carr."

"Difficult—why?"

"The point is this: They do and they don't. It would not be fair to give either a categorical yes or no as an answer to your question. But I shall be glad someday to point out some things which make outsiders think and say what they do. What happens here often gives an *effect* which is immediately referred back to a certain cause. I think people too often jump at conclusions, and unjustly attribute motives which frequently do not enter into the question at all."

I was about to ask her to elucidate the subject further when someone interrupted us, and we never got back to it. On Tuesday, however, Caroline entertained one of her card clubs, and some of the husbands of the members called for them after the games were over. It happened that two of the men are very good friends of Caroline, and she insisted on their coming out into the dining room and having refreshments. So they, their wives, and several other young women were collected around the table, talking and laughing while the men ate. I had been working in my room all evening, and Caroline called me down to have a bite after most of the company had gone. I recalled afterward what I had not noted at the moment, that every woman in the room happened to be distinctly fair, by which I mean white or nearly white, except Tommie Dawson, who is distinctly brown, and Caroline, who is somewhat less so. Someone started the ball rolling—I don't recall just how—and one of the very fair women commenced telling about the shows at Poli's Theater (one of the well-known legitimate theaters downtown). This was the cue for what followed.

Every woman around the table—I know, for I checked them off on my fingers after they had gone—told experiences involving the large theaters downtown, the best restaurants, or one of the hotel grill rooms. They discussed the relative merits of the different places, and at least three turned to Caroline and Tommie, and asked them if they had ever been to so-and-so's, though all of them knew that neither Tommie nor Caroline would be allowed, on account of their color, to enter any of these places. They even went so far as to use such phrases as "Oh, you really should go," knowing all the time that it would be utterly impossible for them to go.

It took me a few minutes to realize that, while perhaps the conversation was *started* without the slightest malicious intent, it was kept up to permit each one of the fair ones present to show how *she* could do these forbidden things, and to make the others feel that they were out of it. It is a form of boasting too often indulged in by fair-colored women, so I have since been told by others, and, as there are usually some persons present who could not indulge in such practices, the protraction of such a conversation must certainly be characterized as in execrably poor taste, to use no harsher word. In the particular case in point, both the husbands present were dark men. I somehow feel that in their place I should have resented the indelicacy of the ladies, but they did not seem to be the least troubled by it, as well as I could judge.

When the company had gone, and only Genevieve, Caroline, and Tommie were left in the room, Tommie turned to me and said:

"What you have just heard is a sample of the thing we were talking about the other day. You can hear such talk in more than one parlor in Washington. All it needs is for one woman to start it. No one of the others will let herself be outdone, so each must have her turn. Of course it's a form of boasting, and as such might be deemed too trivial to notice. But, did you ever reflect that it's just that sort of boasting that produces most of the feeling in cities like this between people of different colors? Take a girl like Helen Clay, who was compelled to listen to what we have just heard. You could not blame her for being a bit sore—indeed, the other women would be unhappy if they thought she did *not* feel sore—and she would give vent to her ill-feelings by saying nasty things about them and insinuating what she did not say. When a colored woman, or a group of colored women, are always boasting about going places where colored people are not allowed, places where their husbands or brothers cannot go, places where practically none of their friends can go, is it not quite in the natural order of things that evil-minded persons are going to suggest the possibility of their going to places they don't talk about, and doing things they don't tell about? I can think of two or three definite individuals who achieved scandalous reputations in this town because they spent all their spare time in white amusement resorts and white grill rooms where they would not, in the nature of things, expect to meet any of their friends. Personally, I do not believe the things that were insinuated about those women, because I know them, and yet I do not believe that even they can complain very justly about the slanderous things that were said, for they surely laid themselves open to such talk in a very special way. But I recur to my original statement, that not a little of the really vicious malignancy noticeable in the attacks on fair-colored women is attributable to such manifestations as you witnessed tonight."

That was the longest speech I ever heard Tommie make, and I shall leave it to you to say whether it was a good one or not. Personally, I should not have taken so much stock in her contention if I had not just had under my own eyes a striking example of the phenomenon she was citing, and had I not been myself so acutely aware of the irritation it caused. It is a valuable sidelight on a subject which interests me very much.

Before Caroline's ardent wooer, Dr. Corey, had been gone thirty-six hours, he had already managed to send her two reminders of his existence. The man is surely demented. But then, you know, these old fellows are hit hard when they are hit at all! After the company had gone, we tried to tease Caroline about him, but she is a cool one, and there is not much satisfaction in such a game. She did act a little puzzled though, as if the gentleman's persistence had impressed her, and she did not quite know how to convince him that his suit was hopeless. When Genevieve had gone upstairs, and there was no one but the three of us in the dining room, she confessed her misgivings, and ended with these words, "I guess the only way to settle him will be to tell him I am in love with someone else."

Things do not happen singly in this world. No sooner are you made aware of something for the first time than all nature seems to be conspiring to make you repeat your experience several times within a short space. The incident I have just related concerning colored women crossing the line happened on Tuesday, and on the next evening, Wednesday, something else happened to deepen the impression already made upon my mind. One of the numerous women's clubs had a regular meeting at Mary Hale's on that night, and I had been asked to come at ten-thirty, as they were going to dance for an hour or so. As Verney was going, too, I called on him, and we spent an hour in his room before stepping over to Mrs. Hale's.

As I have been around quite a bit by now, I know most of the people at these smaller affairs. Caroline is a member of this particular club, and there were a number of invited guests, among whom were Lillian Barton and Mrs. Morrow. They were just getting ready to dance when Verney and I arrived, though several of the men had not yet put in an appearance. To give more space it was proposed to move the piano into the hallway. Three or four of us essayed this job and it was hot work, so we were invited by the hostess to repair to a little washroom off the hall to remove the marks of our labors. When I came out of this room, and was giving a touch to my tie, to be sure it had not gotten awry, Lillian Barton came up to me, and, with a laugh, stopped me and adjusted the tie herself, giving it a little pat in conclusion. To quote a certain famous line of Edgar Allan Poe, "Only this and nothing more!"

Human society is a curious thing. There are few things in social life which have an absolute value, apart from their connections or associations, indeed, values seem to be assessed almost entirely because of these same relationships. Then, too, a thing has significance in one, or both, of two ways—as a *fact,* and as a *sign.* As a fact it may be of trifling importance, apparently, yet be tremendous as a sign. For example, an eye trouble, in itself slight, may point to a serious affection of the kidneys; the passing dizziness, which is not sufficient to check even momentarily the man of business in his rush for wealth, may suggest the high blood pressure which soon will incapacitate him completely. And so we might go on indefinitely. The thing which as a fact of this present hour is of the least importance may be an indicium of the supremest moment.

In certain phases of life it is not the act, but the motive behind it which determines whether or not it is worthy of notice. The mere fact that her lover fails to pick up her glove may be of minimum importance to a young woman, for, after all, the omission is negligible, but if, for example, she realizes suddenly that this failure on his part is due to his growing lack of interest in her, and the consequent flagging of his hitherto eager attention to her minutest concerns, then this defection, apparently trifling, assumes a significance impossible to exaggerate.

Now for a lady to stop for one second and, in friendly fashion, straighten a gentleman's tie, seems to be a matter of the most trifling concern, but, as a matter of fact, the social significance of such an act may be tremendous. Who the lady is, and who the gentleman, makes a vast difference, it seems. At any rate, in this particular case I was made to realize that ladies who straighten gentlemen's ties do so at their own peril. I caught several significant glances directed my way. One or two were expressive merely of amusement delicately tinged with malice, but two were distinctly disapproving, and I wonder if you can guess whence those two came. Well, one was from Mary Hale, and the other from Caroline Rhodes. Caroline's face flushed visibly, and I was made acutely conscious of the merest shadow of a sneer trembling about the base of her very aristocratic little nose. A sneer is one method of expressing emotion which is never attractive, even in the prettiest woman. Did you ever think of that? Since I was not the offending party, but only the innocent "victim," as I suppose the others would call it, I went on my way serenely. But Caroline was saucy all evening, and expended a good deal of sarcasm on me whenever we were near enough to exchange remarks. All of which I took with my usual good nature.

But when the refreshments were served, another turn was given to the matter. We were pretty well bunched together in one corner, Don Verney, Caroline, Lillian Barton, Mrs. Morrow, and two or three others, and the talk was rather lively. After a few minutes it was apparent—and I have noticed similar phenomena more than once even in the case of the best-bred women—that Lillian Barton seemed to be monopolizing the spotlight, so to speak. She did not give anyone else a chance, and she overrode any venturesome person who tried to say anything. Did you ever see a good-looking woman do that?

Well, it did not bother me a great deal, for I was busy eating, anyway, and most men don't find it very hard at such times to let someone else do the talking. Mrs. Morrow tried to express herself about something, but Miss Barton eliminated her, and then Verney put in a word, but was quickly blanketed. Even uninterested as I was at the moment, I soon seemed to become aware that the lady had taken on that sort of bullying manner which society women know so well how to assume on occasion. I stole a furtive look at the others, wondering if it affected them as it did me. Mrs. Morrow looked irritated, Verney had that inscrutable smile he sometimes wears, though he was to all outward appearances interested only in the very satisfying things on his plate, but Caroline's cheeks were flushed, and the defiant set of her mouth was easily to be noted. After a bit she took advantage of a very momentary break in the other lady's remarks to disagree with something she said. The subject of the conversation I have forgotten. It does not matter, anyway. Miss Barton tried to smother Caroline as she had done the others, but it would not work, that little lady's incisive voice would be heard, and, for all she seems the very embodiment of flighty frivolity, she has a good brain, knows how to use it, and knows how to express herself. All the members of the Rhodes family talk very well, and show the unmistakable marks of association with their cultivated father. This time my friend Miss Barton had caught a Tartar. She could not down Caroline, for Caroline refused to be downed. Then she tried a trick which shows how ruthless women—even nice women—can be under certain conditions.

She commenced to talk about the play at the Shubert-Belasco theater, and drawing Mrs. Morrow into the conversation, discussed the desirability of getting up a theater party for the following week. Of course that left Caroline with nothing to say, for in the nature of things, she could not be of that party. To a mere man the whole thing was an exhibition of cruelty—and shall I say cowardice—but how many nice women I have seen do things like that.

Of course I was not going to leave any friend in such a defenseless position, so, apparently without observing what the others were talking about, I drew Caroline into a private conversation about Dr. Corey, and we left the rest to their own devices. But Miss Barton, once started, was not so easily stopped. She actually interrupted our conversation long enough to ask Caroline if she would not be one of their party at the Belasco the following week. I braced myself for the shock of the answer, but I need not have had any apprehension, for Caroline said, in the most nonchalant manner in the world, and without turning a hair, "No, thank you! I have two dances and a card party for next week, and five nights at school. That's quite all I can manage, I guess. But there goes the music. Godfather, dear, let's make the most of it!" And in another moment we were whirling away to the strains of "Three o'Clock in the Morning."

The rest of the evening was uneventful. I had a nice time. Everyone was very gracious to me, and particularly my good friends. When we had our wraps on in the lower hallway, waiting to take our leave, I asked Caroline if I might see her home. She thanked me very prettily, but said she had company.

"However," she added, "I shall ask Will King if he will mind your coming with us, for I think you need someone to look after you, Godfather!"

And she looked at me as saucily as the proverbial jaybird.

So I walked home by myself, and mused more or less idly

on the eccentricities of women. As Caroline's friend Dr. King has a car, they beat me by a few minutes, and he was just driving off as I reached the house. I found Caroline warming herself—the night was quite bleak—before the remains of a grate fire in the back parlor. She removed her coat from the place beside her and made room for me. I thanked her, but declined the proffered seat, on the grounds that it was late, and I had better turn in.

"You know you don't go to sleep after a dance, and you know you are going to read some of your old books. You are not a good liar, Godfather!" She motioned me again to the seat beside her and I capitulated, after handing her, at her request, the last big box of bonbons recovered from Dr. Corey.

It was two o'clock and the house was strangely still. Caroline held out the open box to me, and, after I had taken a piece, she selected one and commenced to nibble at it daintily. I sat back in the extreme corner of the davenport, and half-turned so that I could look at her. I don't believe I ever realized what a beautiful girl she is. It's queer how things strike one sometimes all in a heap, and produce a sensation which must be akin to that of a blind man suddenly endowed with sight. From the top of her shapely little head to the soles of her incomparably pretty feet, she had all the unmistakable bodily marks of aristocracy. Of course, we know that the best, as well as the worst, blood of the South, from the Lees, Washingtons, Pages, and Randolphs of Virginia, to the Simon Legrees of the Red River cotton country, flows in our veins. Surely no one who has noted carefully the types of manly and womanly beauty in our race group can doubt it for a moment. Nor were all the slaves brought from that terrible West Coast hewers of wood and drawers of water, but there were captive kings and chiefs and great warriors as well. As I watched the play of the firelight on the lovely girl at the other end of the big davenport, I could not help realizing that here was no descendant of a peasant people. Anyone with half an eye could discern *race* in every line of her face and figure. That clean-cut profile, with the masterful curve of that firm little chin, surely came from forebears out of a ruling class. Those slim but shapely fingers, and those dainty, high-arched feet, were not a heritage from ancestors who worked with their hands or walked barefoot over ploughed fields. In the yellow light of the fire, she might well be the proud lady of the "big house." Only the dusky velvet of her skin and the warm richness of her pomegranate mouth, which to a discerning eye was the final and crowning touch of beauty, betrayed the presence of the more ardent blood of the tropics.

Suddenly, she looked up, and caught me fairly in the very act of regarding her dreamily. Did she blush, or was it only the warm firelight playing over her cheek?

"Whatever are you staring at, Godfather? Is there anything wrong with me?"

"Not one blessed thing, dear lady," I said. "I was just noting how many and how great are your physical perfections."

"Mercy on us, will you listen to the man rave! What was it, think you, the salad? Or was there too big a stick in the punch? Or could it be the candy? Have another piece!"

And she held it so that I should either have to stretch the length of the davenport to reach it, or move nearer. I half arose from my place, reached over for the box, and resumed my former seat. When I had selected what I wanted, I placed the box midway between us. She looked at me quickly and gave a queer little laugh. Then I asked her when Dr. Corey was coming back, and she said either Thursday or Friday.

"Are you going to accept him?" I asked.

"What do you think I ought to do?" she queried, looking at me again rather intently.

"I don't believe a third person can answer a question like that," I countered cautiously.

"Do you think he is too old for me?"

"Of course I do. But if you love him better than anyone else in the world, other considerations might not matter. In fact, in my humble opinion, your feeling toward him is about the only thing that does matter."

She was silent for a moment, and then heaved a deep sigh.

"Nobody wants to be just friends—except you, Godfather—and it's a dreadful nuisance!"

Then she arose slowly, smothering a yawn with her hand.

"It's fearfully late, and I have to teach tomorrow. I'll be a wrinkled old woman before I am thirty if I keep this up."

She picked up her coat and the box of candy, and came over close to me, enveloping me in the delicate aura of that exquisite perfume which seems to be part and parcel of her.

"What is that wonderful sachet of yours called?" I asked, for the want of anything better to say.

"Fleurs d'Amour," she answered, looking at me with a bewitching smile.

"Fleurs d'Amour!" I repeated the words after her, and to avoid looking at her, looked into the fire. She stood a moment, gazing down at me, and then turned with a low, "Good night, Godfather!" and went up to her room.

I sat for a long time staring into the fire, and I must have fallen asleep, for the embers in the hearth were dying fast when I realized where I was again.

Fleurs d'Amour—what a name, what an inspired name!

I hope no one in the house knows at what an unholy hour I turned in.

Dr. Corey came back Friday, and I gather that he must have received his dismissal. Happily, I did not see him while he was here. I was glad of that, for it would have pained me to see him suffer. But it seems in Caroline's "*affaires du coeur,*" it is merely a case of "*Le roi est mort, vive le roi!*" She has been escorted somewhere practically every night for a week by this good-looking Dr. King, who, according to Tommie, is a former favorite of hers, in her high school days. His father is a very prominent man down home, and the son, who has recently graduated in medicine, has just opened up his office here, after a few months looking over the ground in other places. It's a nice thing to have a wealthy father! The boy has a perfectly appointed office, they say, and a beautiful new car, a Cole Eight. If he does not succeed, it won't be the fault of the old man. But they say the youngster is smart as fresh paint. He certainly looks it. He is a tall, well-built chap, with a ruddy brown complexion, a good face, and most engaging manners. Like numerous other folks in this town, he is "dippy" about Caroline.

They talk hereabouts of the paucity of men, and the methods to which the girls have to resort to keep a "steady," but these observations do not, it seems, apply to Caroline Rhodes. I heard one of the young women commenting on her the other night. "Just to think," she exclaimed, "of a girl having three doctors as suitors at one and the same time! It's outrageous! There should be a law against it!"

But I must close this long letter. It is nice to think that it won't be long before I see you, Bob. Tell Marcia I am sorry she does not like this town enough to drop in now and then. I am so glad you like the Cole girls. I thought you would. Let me know as soon as possible just when you will come.

The sample chapter and your observations thereon reached me yesterday, and you may be sure I have read very carefully all you say, and, indeed, more than once. On the purely literary side, I have always rated your taste above mine, so I am pleased accordingly that you are reasonably well satisfied with what I have done. If it really commends itself to you, I shall have no need to offer apologies for it. As concerns the general plan, I am not sure that I agree with your views as to the proper points to stress. I think that my original idea is best—to feature the Middle Passage and the slave station of Da Souza at Whydah. However, as I work up the material, I can tell more precisely just what points will lend themselves best to elaboration. In such matters I suppose the feeling of the writer must have some weight, for he is more than likely to do best what he best enjoys doing. That seems reasonable, don't you think so?

Davy

EIGHT

La donna è mobile! *As others see us.*
Fair Lillian and the clever Caroline. Americans all—one hundred percent.

Sunday, December 17

Dear Bob:

It is a cheering thought to know that within a week you will be here. While it looks now as if I shall not carry out my original plans exactly as I had hoped, still I am sure I shall be able to show you a good time. Once more it is borne in upon me that woman is an uncertain creature. And is it a compliment to man, noble man, to have to add that that is probably the secret of the fascination which she exerts over us? We had a lively discussion one evening last week as to the relative uncertainty of the two sexes, young Dr. King and I proposing the thesis that women are inordinately changeable and inconsistent, while Thomasine and Caroline stoutly defended their sex.

The handsome doctor is here now practically every evening after his office hours, and his big car stands so often and so long in front of our house that Helen Clay pretended to believe that he had an office here. He is about as pertinacious a wooer as Dr. Corey, and he has, apparently, no handicaps to overcome, as had that hard-hit gentleman. Tommie says King fell in love with Caroline the first time he saw her some six or seven years ago, when he first came to Washington to enter school, and that he has been faithful ever since. It is difficult to say exactly how Caroline regards him, though she is evidently fond of him. He is a real gentleman, and one could hardly help liking him.

On the particular evening in question, we four had a lively time. For some reason the whim seized the doctor to sing. He has a light tenor voice, not unpleasing, and he sang several recent hits fairly well, with Caroline accompanying him on the piano. While I have sung two or three times at the Bartons', Hales', and Wallaces', I have never had occasion to do so elsewhere, and so neither Caroline nor Tommie knew that I made any pretensions in a musical way. King seemed to be holding the center of the stage so completely that I got impatient after a bit, and in a momentary lull in the concert I seated myself at the piano and began on my repertory. It did not take me many minutes to put the genial doctor out of the running completely. But I must admit that he is a real sport, a thoroughbred and "dead game." If he felt a bit sore at me for taking the spotlight from him, he did not show it, for he was quite generous and apparently as sincere in his applause as were the others. Tommie and Caroline were very much surprised.

"To think, Mr. Carr, that you have never let us know until now that you had such a voice. Is it selfishness, excessive modesty, or just natural secretiveness?" asked Tommie.

"Tommie, dear, what have I always told you about Godfather? He is, as I verily believe, a perfect monument of duplicity," was Caroline's rejoinder.

As I look back over what I have written, I note that I started this letter with the observation that it looked as if I might not be able to carry out my holiday plans as originally conceived and that *la donna è mobile!* This latter reflection is apropos of the very erratic conduct of Caroline Rhodes. What has gotten into her lately, I cannot for the life of me determine. The word "erratic" as used in this paragraph is absolutely in place—absolutely. You crave details, I suppose. They are easy to supply, so I append a few.

First of all, Caroline has stopped smoking, *mirabile dictu!* I discovered this first in this wise. There was a committee meeting of some woman's organization or other at Lillian Barton's the other night, and Don Verney and I, intent upon paying a call, happened in on the fag end of it about eight-thirty. As we went in, two or three of the ladies were standing in the hallway exchanging a few parting words with Miss Barton. When we entered the parlor, there sat Caroline and Sophie Burt, almost the two sauciest women in the District of Columbia, so we had a lively few minutes until Lillian came in after having taken leave of the others. She passed around the cigarettes, and you can imagine the shock when Caroline was the only one who reneged. I have a notion that my surprise was evident, for it seemed to me that for all she is so rosy under her dusky skin, her color heightened visibly when her eye caught mine.

"I'm off smoking," she said simply.

"What ails you, Caroline? Has your doctor given you orders?" asked Sophie Burt, a trifle maliciously, knowing full well that the double meaning of the word "doctor" would not be lost on a single person present.

"No," answered Caroline coolly. "I'm just off, that's all. I never cared much for it anyway, you know."

The subject was dropped, ostensibly, but I can answer for myself that I, at least, pondered over it for quite a few minutes.

Secondly, Caroline no longer believes in young ladies indulging in alcoholic beverages. It was by pure accident that I discovered this. We were at one of the club dances at Sophie Burt's, and Will Burt had concocted a punch which had a kick like an old Springfield rifle. Several of the men, of course, sampled it freely, and while many of the ladies were wary, knowing Burt's proneness to make the "stick" very large, a few of them seemed to find the punch bowl rather alluring. Two of the very young girls present were offered glasses by their escorts. Caroline was standing near, and protested.

"Put that glass down, Madeleine!" she said to the youngest Clements girl, a cute little bob-haired flyaway who is just beginning to go to grown-up-parties. "You're silly enough now, Heaven knows! Bobby, what do you mean by giving her that stuff? You ought to know better!"

While Bobby laughed and emptied the glass himself, Miss Rhodes proceeded to give the two "debs" a lecture which would have done credit to Genevieve. I could only look on with amazement.

Last of all, Caroline has developed a temper. The temper itself, to be sure, is nothing new, but it is the constant showing of it to me that strikes me as queer. The little lady has suddenly become very sensitive, and seems to take special delight in using me as the shock absorber, or whatever else one might like to call it.

So I say again, women are most uncertain creatures. It is impossible to place them with any certainty. What this capriciousness and inconsistency mean, in Caroline's case, I have no very definite notion. Is she trying to impress young Dr. King? I wonder. At any rate, it is a fact that he is the only new personality which has come into her circle within the past month. It is certainly a case of *post hoc*. Is it a case of *propter hoc* as well? When you come this way, you can judge for yourself.

For two or three of the holiday parties, I have been lucky enough to secure as our company Thomasine Dawson and Lillian Barton. In the case of the former, I forestalled my friend Scott Green, who has the disadvantage of living in Baltimore. In the case of the latter, also luck was with us, for Reese is going to be away on business in the far South during practically the whole of Christmas week. Mary Hale told me that two weeks ago. It is through her kindness, too, that I got an invitation for you for the Benedicts' ball, so you must be nice to her. I imagine, somehow, that you won't find that duty a very irksome one. Caroline and Tommie, too, have done their share in helping me get our social calendar filled up properly. I am sorry I could not get Caroline's company for at least one of the parties, but Dr. King is the most forehanded man I know. He takes nothing for granted, and he is the real early bird. However, I am sure you will find opportunities enough to see Miss Rhodes, or any other of my friends, for they will be, all of them, at the same affairs. So that leaves it up to you, young man, to get busy. But I warn you beforehand that you will have to move fast, and keep moving if you want to avoid being snowed under in this burg. This is just a word to the wise, as Mary Hale said to me when she told me about Reese's trip South.

One characteristic of this town is a sort of social ruthlessness. The girls here do not give visiting girls any edge on them, and the men—well, it's every man for himself, with a vengeance. If you comment on this seemingly inhospitable attitude, the local people only laugh. Their excuse is that everyone visits Washington sooner or later, and if "home folks" made way for visitors, they would never be able to do anything else. However, I am not worrying *about you*, Bob, for I know from long experience that you can take care of yourself. At least one "somebody" in Washington is going to lose his girl during this Christmas season. I am wondering idly who that person is to be. Personally, I am glad that I have no girl to lose.

I almost forgot to tell you that I had a delightful walk last Sunday with Lillian Barton. When I went out to mail my letter to you I called her up to ask some question or other, and we had a nice little chat over the telephone. Incidentally, I mentioned the fact that it was such a bracing day that I thought I should take a walk up Sixteenth Street to Rock Creek Park.

"It sounds rather nice," she said. "It surely will be nice, if you have good company."

"Unfortunately," I rejoined, "I have only the very poorest of company—myself. I was just wishing I might persuade some kind young person to go with me."

"I am sure you could if you tried," she said. "You have two or three charming young persons not so very far from you."

"They are busy, it seems, with one thing or another. One of them, for example, is motoring with her best fellow."

Well, the upshot of it was that Miss Barton said she would be delighted to go with me if I could find no other company. It was a very satisfying afternoon. Sixteenth Street hill is very attractive, with its magnificent residences, the palaces of the foreign embassies, and the endless stream of automobiles. From the park entrance it is a long walk to the buildings which house the "zoo," and there we sat on a bench on the brow of a long grass-covered hill, and watched the Sunday crowd. Miss Barton was very handsome in a "spiffy" outing costume of gray, with a gray hat faced with deep red. But, great as is her physical beauty, her chief charm, in my opinion, resides in her conversation, which is stimulating in the highest degree. I realize that it is futile to attempt to convey by the written word even an approximately adequate impression of such an afternoon as I spent, for even could I recall and record word by word the dialogue, it would lack the seasoning of Lillian Barton's vivid personality. So you will have to take my word for it that I had a wonderful time.

After we had rested for a while on the bench, we strolled over toward the hillside where the bears have their dens. On our way we stopped at the refreshment booth, and bought peanuts and popcorn, with which I stuffed my pockets. We had just tarried for a moment before the first of the long line of cages, and Miss Barton was throwing peanuts to a rather mournful-looking bear, when I heard my name called. On looking around, whom should I see but Caroline Rhodes and Dr. King.

"What are you two doing here?" asked Miss Barton, after greetings were exchanged.

"I have been trying to cure the doctor of his nervousness," said Caroline, "and so I insisted that he come over here to see himself as others see him. Come with me, and let me demonstrate how he acts."

We all laughed of course, and trailed after her to the railing behind which the great white bears were walking up and down, up and down, ceaselessly on either side of the pool which occupied the center of their enclosure.

"There," said Caroline, pointing, "that is just the way you act when you are waiting for anyone. Don't you agree that it is a senseless waste of energy?"

Dr. King grinned with sheepish good nature.

"Well, I'll admit, at any rate, that it is not pretty," he said. "Do you mean to say that I look like that?"

"Exactly," answered Caroline. "You know," she continued,

"when I was a high school girl, Genevieve used to bring Tommie and Brother and me out here Sunday afternoons, and Tommie and I discovered that the different animals reminded us of many of our friends. So we spent hours making comparisons. It was very interesting. You can't imagine, until you have tried it, what fun it is to bring people out here and introduce them to themselves. As a cheap and satisfying outdoor sport, I recommend it to you."

And as Caroline talked, she looked from one to the other of us quite as if she might be making mental comparisons. Miss Barton seemed to me to fidget uncomfortably.

"Of what do I remind you?" I queried.

The little lady's black eyes snapped mischievously. She giggled in a disconcerting fashion.

"I know, but I shan't tell," she said.

"Why?" I insisted.

"Why? Because it's too good to tell—yet." And she giggled again.

I waited for Miss Barton to ask, in her turn, what might be her animal double, but I waited in vain. For all Lillian's wit and poise, even she hesitates to measure herself against the clever Caroline when the latter is in one of her irrepressibly mischievous moods. As we fell into step with each other in front of the cages, the two ladies paired off together, and Dr. King and I walked behind them. From time to time, as we stopped for a few moments to feed the bears, I noted Miss Barton's unusual silence, and caught her looking earnestly at Caroline, who, utterly unconscious of that scrutiny, was busy tossing peanuts between the bars of the cages. Many times during the past week have I recalled that look in Lillian's eyes, and I have tried hard to analyze it, with this result: I think that

I saw in it perplexity and disapproval, mingled with a reluctant admiration.

When we had finished our round of the cages, and had ascended to the drive where the doctor's car was parked, the latter gave us a most cordial invitation to drive with them, and Caroline heartily seconded it. As she spoke, she stood on the step of the car, and had it been someone like Helen Clay, for example, and not Caroline Rhodes, I should have wagered that her pose was not entirely an unconscious one, for, from the feather on her velvet tam, canted rakishly over one ear, to the tips of her dainty beaded kid slippers, her costume was perfect to the minutest detail, and set off in a specially becoming fashion that slim graceful figure, vibrant with life.

As it was not my place either to accept or decline Dr. King's offer, I stood quietly and watched the ladies. Somehow I sensed the pressure of a feeling of antagonism whenever these two are together, and yet, except in the most general social sense, they are not rivals. Somehow, too, in these almost unseen silent contests, there is a serene confidence in the attitude of the saucy Caroline, and it is Lillian Barton, the cool, witty, perfectly poised Lillian, who shows signs of—what shall I say—diffidence? Why should she be diffident, or about what, the Lord only knows, but my feeling is a very definite one, and is exactly as I have herein before stated.

So, as you may have guessed already, the fair Lillian declined the apparently cordial invitation with suitable and gracious words of thanks. Just as the car started, Caroline turned, and with the unspeakably impish smile which precedes or accompanies any especially impudent sally of hers, called back to Miss Barton:

"Oh, Lillian, be sure and take Mr. Carr to see the owls!"

The car was, of course, out of reach of our voices before we could answer, if indeed, either of us had an answer ready. Strange to relate, Miss Barton seemed more sensitive than I to the implications of Caroline's parting words. Whether because she felt that perhaps she was somehow included in my owlishness, it is impossible to say. I laughed heartily, but my fair companion's merriment did not ring true, somehow, and she flushed perceptibly. I was for going straightaway to see the owls, but it is almost needless, I know, for me to tell you that we did not go. Is there any system of logic by which one may explain women? It surely is a liberal education of one's powers of observation and deduction to be thrown in with a group of highly developed females of the species, as I can testify.

As we walked home, the conversation was rather one-sided, for I did most of the talking, and Miss Barton's responses were laconic to a degree—in fact, almost monosyllabic—and she acted like one whose voice and thoughts were not working together. However, when we reached her house, her mood seemed to have passed. She served me tea in front of the big fireplace, and we had a very jolly hour together before the regular Sunday evening crowd arrived. Then I had a delightful tête-à-tête with Mary Hale, who was looking unusually handsome. We talked sotto voce, mostly about our friend Don, a subject on which I invariably find the lady most eloquent. As I looked, now and then, into her eyes, I could understand how Verney is so fond of her. Altogether it was a most interesting and eventful day, and, as such, has been recorded at some length in my diary.

The book is coming on famously, but the study of the slave trade is so fascinating and so infinite in extent that if I am not careful, I shall be in danger of being diverted from my original theme. I have quite enough material now to serve my purpose, but the subject seems to carry me away. In my researches in this field, I have come across much of curious interest that is no longer familiarly known—if, indeed, it ever was! How quickly man forgets his devilries! I heard Dr. Du Bois say once that Western European exploitation—slaves and ivory and red rubber—has cost Africa at least one hundred million souls, in about four hundred years, not to mention the complete destruction of whole civilizations quite equal to most of the European civilizations of the fifteenth century.

For the past few days I have been reading the life of Captain Canot, as edited from his journals and conversations by Brantz Mayer, and first published in the early fifties. The editor says in his dedicatory preface that *"setting aside his career as a slaver,"* he was convinced that Canot was a man of unquestionable integrity. There is a delicious irony in those words in quotation marks, for there was no crime in the calendar which a slave trader did not commit against the helpless blacks. And yet some of the very cruelest of them were psalm-singing deacons in their New England homes.

I guess an all-wise Providence knew what he was doing when he evolved the Nordic type, with its watertight, noncommunicating compartments in morals and religion, but to me it still remains the greatest of all the riddles of humanity. Accustomed as one is to the presence of inconsistencies in one's self and one's friends, one is continually amazed at the appalling and monstrous inconsistencies in human conduct as evidenced in the history of the slave traffic, and of the white man's exploitation of the hapless African. One could not believe that such things could be, did one not know of them from the testimony of the white man himself. But I did not intend to inflict so much of this on you, who know quite as much about it as I do.

A bit of human nature which has not such tragic elements came to my notice last Sunday at Barton's. I shan't give names, except to say that the usual crowd was present. You must deduce what you please from that. Apropos of something or other, the question of ages came up, and there were the usual jokes passed, of course. One of the ladies seemed a trifle piqued at the implication that she would not dare tell her real age, and in spite of any disclaimers the gentlemen might make that they were not at all interested in that subject, she insisted on telling and actually *did tell it*. Naturally, everyone smiled, and Don laughed that funny little laugh of his—which must be heard to be appreciated. I think the lady in question noticed the laugh, and as she and Don are very good friends, she looked at him rather sharply. He immediately grew grave, and very coolly introduced another topic.

During supper I noted him scribbling something on the back of an old envelope, looking pleasantly reflective all the while. As I appeared curious, he handed me the paper, with the caution to read and return it immediately. This was what I read:

> *When an ordinary* truthful *woman insists on telling you her age, add at least two years to the figure she gives you. If she is ordinarily* untruthful, *the Seven Wise Men of Greece cannot tell you what to add.*

We looked at each other and exploded into laughter, and I handed the paper back to him.

"What are you two discussing that is so funny?" asked our hostess.

"Suffragette arithmetic," I answered, whereat Don laughed again.

I intended to finish this yesterday, but a number of things intervened to prevent it. Caroline's brother, Philip, who, as I think I have told you already, is a medical student, made the house one of his rare visits Saturday and invited me to give a little Sunday morning talk at his fraternity house. As I like him very much, I allowed myself to be persuaded, though perhaps a curiosity to see the local college boys in their natural "habitat" had something to do with my acceptance. So I spent an hour or two very pleasantly with a group of rather wholesome chaps. If I judge them aright, they have a thoroughly twentieth-century American view of life, and such as one might expect to find in a typical group of Amherst, or Dartmouth, or Ohio State students. In other words, "none genuine without our trademark," which is, as you well know, *the dollar sign.* As I listened to one or two of the leaders talk, I murmured to myself, "One hundred percent American!"

In my little talk I tried to suggest other visions of life and other incentives for work besides the usual financial one, but I was conscious that it was time wasted. What are the feeble words of one man against the steady roar of the waves of a *civilization*? Of all the useless things I have done in my life, I feel that talk I gave the boys was the most futile. But I enjoyed them, and their "joie de vivre," and their eagerness to get out into the world and subdue it—immensely.

I sat in Lillian Barton's parlor last night, and enjoyed the open fire and one or two of Don's good stories. It was pleasant to reflect that you have a special invitation to be present *next* Sunday. The fair Lillian gave it to me for you as I was leaving. Tell Marcia that I wish she might come this way during the holiday season, but I suppose that there is little chance of that. Since this will in all likelihood be my last letter until I see you, I may quite properly say—au revoir.

Davy

P. S. Write me or wire me your train.

NINE

Blood will tell. Is it love, or what? Enter the girl with the green-gray eyes.

January 4, 1923

Dear Bob:

The old room seems very empty without you, and in spite of several engagements which are on my calendar for this week, things seem quite quiet after the wild rush of the past ten days. Everyone enjoyed having you, and a dozen people at least have told me to be sure to send regards when next I should write. Among the latter I might mention Thomasine, Caroline, Mary Hale, Lillian Barton, Don Verney, Mrs. Morrow, Helen Clay, and—you would never guess this one—Genevieve! As I predicted, you made your customary impression, and, if I mistake not, this time you got a pretty hard jolt in exchange.

Serves you right! When I asked Tommie yesterday evening if she had heard from you, she laughed and blushed. When I offered to bet her a box of candy against a German paper mark, and decide the bet on her word, that you had written every day, she only laughed again. As Tommie either can't or won't lie, I knew I had made a good guess and a safe bet.

I walked home with her two nights after you had left, and the exclusive topic of conversations was—you! I spent a very pleasant hour in that very charming old-fashioned parlor. While Tommie was in the kitchen fixing up what proved to be a most appetizing collation, I strolled into the library, turned on the Victrola, and while listening to "O Sole Mio," as sung by the one and only Caruso, I looked at the family portraits. There were, as you may remember, Tommie's grandfather, who received a Congressional Medal of Honor for distinguished service in the Civil War; her great uncle, who was a member of Congress in the exciting days of Reconstruction; and an uncle who was the first man of color to receive a diplomatic appointment from the United States government. As I looked at the portraits, and the books, and the various memorials of two generations past, I could easily understand why the beautiful brown girl gives one such a well-defined impression of "class."

I don't want to make you envious, Bob, but I had one of the nicest evenings in all my Washington sojourn. We talked, and we listened to the Victrola, and we had one of the loveliest waltzes in my experience, and we sang to her piano accompaniment. As a last touch, I told her to imagine that I was Bob Fletcher, and I sang my whole repertory of Italian love songs, ending with "O Sole Mio." Since I know you will want to ask questions, I shall forestall them by saying that when I told her to imagine that I was you, she laughed and said, "Don't be silly, Davy!" But she sat down in the big chair by the piano, closed her eyes, and did not move for whole long minutes, and she made me sing "O Sole Mio" three times! This much I will say, that if this one time in your checkered career of amourettes you should find that you have fallen a victim to a real, honest-to-goodness love, I should compliment you on your taste, and, as your closest friend, be more than delighted. I say this because I really believe that you have been very hard hit. Come on, confess!

Sunday morning

In spite of the suffragettes, and the whole great world movement aiming to show the absolute equality of men and women, I, for one, am not convinced. Lillian Barton would say that the great differences we seem to note are due to the influence of past ages upon the two sexes, and not to inherent qualities. Perhaps she is right, but for all practical purposes the results are the same. The reactions of woman to ordinary stimuli seem to be different from those of the average man. Man, so I think, reacts largely to the act, while woman reacts to the motives she sees, or thinks she sees, behind the action. Most men are not audacious enough to feel that they can evaluate motives, but women are not so faint-hearted. So it happens that often the reaction of one is exactly the opposite of the reaction of the other. Further, women are less consistent than men, and it is futile to judge from today's attitude what tomorrow's may be. The movie writer speaks of a process in the construction of a picture play which they call "putting in the punch." The plot in general may be all right, and the best dramatic sequence thought out, but still that little ingredient is lacking which so grips the waiting audience—and that is the "punch." Well, so I suppose it was with the creating of the world. First land and water, then the animate creation, fauna and flora, then *man*. So far, so good, but still something is lacking, and the world's a well-ordered but dull place. Then comes the crowning inspiration—woman, lovely woman! And, as we all well know, and some of us to our sorrow, the big world play has not lacked punch since that moment.

All this, you will ask, is a preamble to what? *"Quien sabe?"* as the vaqueros used to say down on the Texas border, and with such an expressive shrug. I am in such a quandary about a lot of things these days that I could use up the supply of shrugs of a whole platoon of "greasers." The worst feature of the situation seems to be the fact that I don't know just what it is that I am in a quandary about. My friends, and their name is surely legion, are as good to me as ever, and, when my day's stint is done, I can look forward with reasonable confidence to a pleasant evening with some of the most interesting people I have ever met. As to the work itself, it goes swimmingly, as you shall see with your own eyes one of these days—and not far in the future, I hope. My health is perfect, as it has always been, thank Heaven, and I eat like a plowboy and sleep like a tree.

"Then what in the name of all the Nine Worthies are you grouching about?" I hear you query impatiently: That's just what I should like to know myself, and therein resides the head and front of my dissatisfaction. If I were home, and showed such symptoms, Mother would give some kind of nauseous dose warranted to cure anything short of a bad disposition, but, fortunately or unfortunately, I am not at home, so there you are!

Your friend Miss Thomasine is my one consolation. Anything I may say or may have said derogatory to women, I withdraw as far as that dear girl is concerned. She is as constant as the pole star, the same yesterday, today, and forever, though, as you well know, there is no monotony in her consistency, but just a fine, splendid dependableness which one knows he can count on to the last breath. I should no more expect an unworthy action from Tommie Dawson that I should from my dear mother. I have never met a young woman who more completely commanded my absolute respect. Not long ago I heard a group of college students singing *"Integer Vitae,"* and I thought of the lovely Thomasine. Sometimes, reflecting on her physical and moral beauty, I wonder why I have not fallen in love with her, for we have been close friends from the first minute we met, but strange to say, our friendship seems to be troubled by no undercurrents of more stormy emotions. Since you have become so violently interested in her, I am glad this is so, for it would not be a happy situation if we should be rivals.

While Tommie, in these last days since Dr. King has been carrying on such a whirlwind campaign of wooing, has not been so much at the house, still I am always seeing her at some function or other, and I never fail to have a chat. She is a most comforting sort of person, though, if one wants information in which any friend of hers is involved, he will waste a lot of time trying to pump Tommie Dawson. I know, for I have tried it. She is patient, and considerate, and courteous, and she lets one down, oh so gently—but *down,* nevertheless! "True blue" is an accurate characterization of that young lady. Different as they are from each other, she and Caroline would, I verily believe, fight for each other, or, if need be, die for each other. Tommie, though little, if any, older than her friend, is more serious and more mature, and she seems to protect Caroline from the consequences of some of her mad pranks, and to dissuade her from others. Caroline, even in the short time I have been here, has changed perceptibly in one or two ways. Sometimes I feel that, in the case of most girls, this so-called flapperism is only a passing phase, sometimes even merely a *pose.* Most of them, I am fully persuaded, affect certain petty vices, just as a small boy at a certain age tilts his cap over one ear, swears, swaggers and smokes, and imitates, in his juvenile way, in externals at least, the toughs and rowdies in the neighborhood. How many of us have seen that, and how many of us have *done* it, and lived to laugh heartily over it? Human nature is a curious conglomerate!

Well, as I have said, Caroline has changed in certain outward manifestations, if not in anything deeper. Certain of the more notable flapper characteristics and mannerisms have, temporarily at any rate, disappeared. Whether just naturally, as parts of a passing phase, or whether because of some definite cause or reason outside of her own whimsies, who can tell? One might, quite reasonably, attribute some of these changes to a serious interest in the wooing of Dr. King. Constant as he is, and ready as she seems to accept his attentions, I somehow am not convinced that she loves him. Tommie might help me at this point to form a conclusion, but, as I said above, that is just what Tommie will *not* do where a friend is concerned, though I feel that she likes me very well and trusts me implicitly. But she is true to Caroline *first.* I have always been taught by worldly-wise people that women are not so true to each other. If so, this is an exception that proves the rule.

Failing to elicit any information from Tommie, I have studied Caroline and the Doctor for myself. One thing is certain—he is crazy about her! Aside from that, nothing seems to be perfectly clear. Contrasted with his very evident infatuation is her serene calmness. That she likes him very much is patent, but I have never noted anything in her manner which corresponds with his evident adoration. She takes him for granted, so it seems to me. However, I have seen women act that way even with men they loved. So I suppose that proves nothing.

Caroline has one active and I might even say aggressive rival for the Doctor's affections, and that is none other than Miss Billie Riddick, whom you met at the Benedict's ball. As you will probably agree, she is not a bad-looking girl, with a superb figure, and she has style and "pep" to waste. I recall distinctly that, when I was first introduced to her by the late Mr. Jeffreys, I found her a most entertaining young person, and she is the type that makes men turn in the street to look after her, and makes the women take an extra clutch on their male escorts. If she were a movie star, she would be featured in the descriptive literature as a "V-A-M-P" in large capitals. Give her a mantilla and a large black fan, and she would run Nita Naldi a close second for the love of the young matador, or whoever happened at the moment to be the fair Nita's intended prey. Of course, I don't mean to say that she's as handsome as the seductive Italian woman, but she *is* good looking, and she has that swing to her hips and that "come-hither" look in her green-gray eyes that has changed the course of many an empire since Adam's descendants ceased to be cave-men and went to dwell in cities. Oh, that side glance from under the long lashes, from those curious light eyes in the dark face! The average man seems no more able to resist it than a bird can resist the charming of the snake. I guess I have not told you, I have heard more than once that Miss Billie has fascinated a well-known benedict of my acquaintance. I won't call his name, for one hears so much idle gossip about here that has absolutely no foundation in fact.

Well, Miss Riddick is terribly in love—so everyone says—with the handsome Dr. King, and they say further she has tried to take him away from Caroline. Billie's weakness in that contest is that, if she *is* in love, it does not show on the surface. Knowing your own sex, Bob, you will realize that Billie has not a look-in, as they say. I don't know any more pitiful sight than that of a woman who is so much in love with a man who does not reciprocate that she does not care who sees it. Somehow one feels that there is something sacred about a woman's dignity, and that in such a case it is being dragged in the dust, so to speak. I really feel sorry for Miss Billie, though, with her record as a "vamp," I suppose she might not naturally call forth much sympathy.

At the fraternity dance I attended Monday night, many of the gay younger set were present. Numbers of the fellows asked for you, and said they were sorry you had not stayed over. I took Tommie, and Caroline and the inevitable Doctor were on hand, of course. Billie Riddick came in with the Baltimore man Lacy, whom I mentioned in connection with the passing of Jeffreys. Miss Billie had on a ball dress, which for elegance, beauty, and stylishness, I have never seen surpassed anywhere. Every woman in the room watched her, many, of course, with covert sneers, but they all watched her just the same. She has a stunning figure, and carries herself like a queen. Indeed, Verney, who was present, dubbed her the "Queen of Jazz," and the title suited her exactly. It was Billie's big evening, and she had wit enough to realize it and make the most of it. It was as interesting as a play. She was very much sought by the men, danced every dance, and it was fascinating to see how cleverly she tried to turn everything to account in her attempted conquest of the Doctor. She exerts some fascination over him, that is plain, and she has evidently left nothing undone to increase her hold.

Naturally, I watched Caroline, too, thinking I might see something to give me a line on her real feeling toward Dr. King, but, when the evening was over, I had had my trouble for my pains, for I saw nothing to help me decide either way. Indeed, she seemed not to notice Miss Riddick's efforts. In the course of the evening, a little thing happened which puzzled me somewhat. I had danced with Miss Billie, complimented her on her looks, and as I escorted her to a seat when the music stopped, she said:

"We have not seen much of each other, Mr. Carr, have we? But we ought to do so. We might help each other. What do you say?"

I am afraid I looked blank.

Then she said, as Verney came up to claim the next dance:

"Oh, Mr. Carr, and you have a reputation for wit!"

As the music started rather suddenly, I had to move quickly out of the way of the dancers. But, as I passed her and Don on the floor a few minutes later, she looked at me mischievously, said something to Verney, and they both laughed. I have not gotten it yet for, somehow, I had not the nerve to ask her what she meant!

I danced mostly with Tommie and Lillian Barton. For the first time since I have been here, I failed to get a dance with Caroline. As there were no dance cards, it was hard to keep the dances straight. I asked for one, but in some way got mixed up about it, and lost it so I did not try again. When we were in the crowd coming out of the hall, the Doctor and Caroline happened to be side by side with Tommie and me. Caroline was so close to me that our elbows touched. I started to say something to her, but she seemed not to notice me, so we walked all the way to the entrance without a word. I never had such an experience with Caroline before. Could she be offended because I did not dance with her? Hardly. As I said above, I tried to get a dance, and it was by no means all my fault that I did not succeed. But, as I have said before, women's reactions are peculiar, and not to be forecasted accurately. Such is life.

Tommie was very silent as we rode home in the taxi. When we alighted in front of her door, I tried to break the spell.

"Whatever in the world are you thinking, my dear friend," I said.

She fitted her key in the lock without a word, and then, when she had unlocked the door and pushed it open, she turned and looked down at me from the vantage point of the top step.

"I was thinking, Davy, that for all their supposed natural endowments and for all their training, men are such simpletons!" And Tommie beamed at me in the most friendly fashion.

"And apropos of what, dear lady, do you so scandalously slander the sex to which I have the honor to belong?"

She looked at me again and smiled, and tapped me roguishly under the chin with her white-gloved fingertips.

"Apropos, dear Davy, of nothing at all!"

And she turned and went into the house without another word. Bob, she's a sweet, beautiful, wholesome girl, if there ever was one! I don't blame you for being so fond of her.

The work is going well again, after the interruption of the holidays. I expected to have a harder time getting back into the swing of it, but I have been most pleasantly disappointed. In my description of the "big house" on the shell road, I have used almost to a dot my recollections of one of those striking old places near Mobile that we both admired so much. But I must study Charleston and its environs at firsthand, for the books do not give me all the help I want, and I lack a certain confidence, which is an absolutely indispensable prerequisite to precision of touch. I can do Charleston and Columbia in one trip, and then run down home to see Mother.

Thomasine is looking fine. Indeed, she is so blooming these days that I am beginning to suspect that you are continuing by letter the campaign which you waged so vigorously during the few days you were here. When I tease her, I get nothing but a laugh and a blush. In fact, the most suspicious circumstance is that she seems rather to enjoy being teased. What about it?

Davy

The coast of Bohemia. Even as you and I.

January 8, 1923

Dear Bob:

We surely missed you at Lillian's last night. Everyone spoke of you, and most pleasantly, too, young man; I should think that your right ear must have burned quite perceptibly. You let no grass grow under your feet for the few hectic days you spent in the Capital City, to judge from the impression you left behind you. Almost everyone present sent you a special personal message, beginning with our charming hostess. Somehow, I feel that the one you will value most is the one from the stately lady with the interesting gray eyes—yes, you have guessed it—Mary Hale.

She was looking especially stunning. Of course, I cannot describe her costume except to say that she wore a very handsome black gown, with the most beautiful embroïdered silk stockings I ever saw, and slippers to match. However, as you well know, though she has exquisite taste in dress, and the style and dash of a Parisienne, there never was a time when Mrs. Hale's fascinating self was not far more attractive and interesting than her clothes. But last night her attire seemed especially suited to set off her physical beauty, and I confess that as I looked at her it was not difficult to understand why our friend Don is subjugated so completely. As for that gentleman himself, on the occasion in question, he sat like one enthralled, and was unable to take his eyes from her.

With those he regards as his friends, Don acts with absolute naturalness, and so when Mrs. Hale, during an interval when we three were rather apart from the others, took note of his admiring glance, and asked him how he liked her new dress, he made one of his characteristically frank answers.

"I think, Mary Hale, that you are the most beautiful thing I have ever seen!"

And Don's look and tone gave one no opportunity to doubt his sincerity.

So Mary blushed most vividly, whether more from embarrassment or pleasure I shall leave you to guess, and thereby heightened her beauty by several points.

"You bold man," she said, "don't you know you must not say such things? In the first place, they are flattery of the most brazen sort, and then, suppose someone else should hear you!"

Don shrugged his shoulders lazily.

"Suppose they should hear? Would it be anything new? Would it not be a good thing for seasoned Washingtonians once in a blue moon to hear the simple truth spoken without varnish or evasion?"

Under ordinary circumstances this should have been the signal for me to withdraw, but I realized that in this instance my presence saved the situation for them, so I showed my friendly spirit by acting the part of heavy chaperone. That Don worships Mary Hale is apparent even to a dull observer, and she blooms under his evident admiration like a flower in the morning sun. It is lucky for them both that she is a woman of character, for I verily believe that if she expressed a desire for the moon, Don would try to get it for her.

When we were having tea, somewhat later on, Mrs. Morrow and Lillian Barton had a mild argument over the use of the words "love" and "adore," Lillian insisting that they were not in any sense synonyms. One of them appealed to Don.

"No," he said, "they are not synonyms. Adoration is infinite love plus infinite respect," and as he spoke he looked at Mary Hale as if in exemplification of his definition.

The statement was so matter-of-fact, and the look so candid, that Sophie Burt strangled over her tea, and almost had hysterics as the result. I confess that if Don and Mary were not, both of them, high-minded people, and both possessed of more than average good sense, I should fear the possible outcome of the so-evident affection. But both are so calm that most folks seem to accept the situation as perfectly natural.

Yes, the soulless Sophie was there, with her eternal Russian cigarettes, and that affected air of blasé sophistication which would make one dislike her if she were not so good natured with it all. And Wallace was there, and—you would never guess it in a hundred years—that very lively little matron who flirted with you so boldly at the Merry Coterie's party. Of course, you have not forgotten her. I shan't call her name in this letter, for reasons which will appear later. She just "happened in," as they say, and Miss Barton insisted on her remaining for tea.

In the course of a rather stimulating conversation, Wallace brought up the subject of the recent revival of interest in the Negro as a subject for writers of fiction. I say "revival," for he was a legitimate subject for such treatment in the generation preceding the Civil War, not only in works like *Uncle Tom's Cabin,* but in many other works long since forgotten. There were conflicting views as to the sentiments expressed or implied in Stribling's *Birthright,* Shands's *White and Black,* and Clement Woods's *Nigger;* and of course, most of those present read Octavus Roy Cohen and Hugh Wiley out of the human race altogether.

Don, dismissing the last two as professional humorists not worthy of serious discussion, held that it is better to be written about in almost any fashion than not to be written about at all, and that in modern writing of the realistic type we must not expect the writer to hold a brief for this or that race or group, but merely to paint the picture as he sees it. But, he went on, the most significant and interesting thing is that we are once more regarded by the literary world as material suited to the uses of the imaginative writer. He recalled the time—not so many years ago—when nothing about colored people was acceptable to practically any American magazine unless it had the unmistakable stamp of Tuskegee upon it. One or two writers of both promise and performance beyond the average were caught in this trough between two waves—and he cited Charles W. Chesnutt as an instance.

But today, with Clement Wood, for example, setting forth in bold terms the ofttimes dramatic relationships existing between the races in the South, it is quite conceivable that in the near future Americans may learn to treat any subject imaginatively which exists actually within the borders of their own country. In their provincial attitudes and in their persistent tabooing of certain subjects, the Anglo-Saxon writers, and especially the American Anglo-Saxons, have shown themselves to be far behind the writers of continental Europe.

I, for one, feel very sure that Stribling, Shands, and Clement Wood are merely the vanguard of a small army of writers who will soon lay hands on the unusually dramatic material which has been lying so long unused within the borders of our Southern civilization. Somehow, I feel, too, that Southern white men may handle it better than the writers of our own group. We are too near to it, and feel it too keenly, to achieve the detachment necessary for work of the highest artistry. That is the reason why, in my own work, I have chosen a period so remote from the present that I can get the necessary detachment and the proper perspective.

But perhaps the thing in this letter which will interest you most is not this literary discussion, for the ideas set forth are surely not new to you, but the conduct of your flirtatious friend, whom perhaps it were wise to designate as "Madame X," in the event that this letter shall fall into strange hands. Recalling what you said about the lady and her actions at two of the holiday dances, I was probably somewhat more interested in her than I should have been under ordinary circumstances.

She was most becomingly attired. I wish I might describe her, but once more this yawning hiatus in my descriptive powers shows itself. Really, if I have any faint hope of devoting myself to writing, and especially to imaginative writing, I must train myself in this particular branch of the descriptive art. It is curious how I stutter and stammer and hesitate when I attempt to describe personal attire or adornment, though I am ready enough in other phases of writing. Sometimes I think it is due, in part at least, to my ignorance of materials and colors and shades, and of the terminology of dress. Whatever the real reason, I must make a studied effort to supply this lack.

To return to your little friend—she was becomingly attired as usual and, if I am any judge, she leans a little toward the striking and bizarre. I think her complexion, unassisted, is not very good, but she was a perfect specimen of the modern art of beauty culture, flawless in every detail. She must spend a small fortune keeping herself white. Aside from this artificiality, which to me is exceedingly repellent, she is too thin to suit my special taste. But let that pass, for it has nothing to do with the incidents of the evening. At the beginning of the talk about the Negro and literature, in which Don and Wallace figured as the principals, she paid some attention, but it was quite apparent that her interest soon flagged, and she was plainly bored and yawned repeatedly, though surreptitiously, behind her pretty hand. Once, catching my eye, she winked and smiled, and, as you will in all likelihood recall, her smile and her dimples are not entirely without attractiveness.

Then the little game of the evening began. As she sat beside Mary Hale, with one arm resting easily on the back of the divan, one of those pretty plump hands—so unlike the rest of her—was right under my eyes, for I sat immediately in back of Mrs. Hale. Somehow, reflecting on some of the things you had said, the notion seized me suddenly to try an experiment, so I rested my hand near hers, and allowed my fingers to stray. When our hands touched, she first started as if surprised, but the surprise was evidently of short duration, for she promptly squeezed my fingers! So you were right in your estimate of her.

Such a game, as you can readily imagine, was too easy to be even mildly interesting. However, it often happens that a personality once evoked is not so easily revoked. (Who said that? I seem to be quoting, but for the life of me I cannot recall from whom.) So for the rest of the tea hour at Barton's I was conscious of her interest. When tea was served she sat beside me, and gave me a most cordial invitation to come to her house any Sunday evening after ten.

"We have some good times," she said, and she named two or three of her very gay friends who, it seems, would be sure to be present. To judge from the little I have seen of them, and the much I have heard, it would indeed be lively.

"Bob Fletcher says," she added, "that you are a better dancer than he is. If this is so, you would enjoy our little Wednesday night parties. Just a select few," she added, flashing that dimpling smile at me.

By the way, what did you *not* say to her during those few dances you had together?

Well, to make a long story short, she suggested that I might take her to the Rhodeses' from the Bartons', for she had a committee meeting of the Merry Coterie to attend, and from there I might go to her house for a late supper. As I had heard of these late suppers, I decided to fall in with her suggestion. So we went to Caroline's accompanied by Sophie Burt, who also had to attend the meeting.

When we arrived we found Tommie and Dr. King present and these two entertained me in the parlor while Caroline, Sophie, and "Madame X" held their committee meeting in the library. Dr. King and I sang to Tommie's accompaniment, and "Madame X" twice or thrice left the committee meeting and joined us, much to the irritation of Sophie and Caroline, and especially Caroline. When the committee had finally finished its work, and we were all assembled around the piano, while I, at Tommie's request, sang "O Sole Mio" to my own accompaniment, the lady with the dimples stood close behind me and rested both arms on my shoulders. I could not help wondering what the others thought of this, but as my back was turned to the rest of the company, I had no means of guessing. But when I had finished, Caroline insisted that Dr. King sing a new "blues" song which is now the rage, and, as soon as he had seated himself at the piano, she beckoned me into the library. I went, wondering.

"Dr. King is going to take Tommie and me driving after a while, and then we are going to Marston's for supper. Don't you want to go, to complete the quartet?"

"I surely should like to go," I said, "but I have an engagement for supper."

"Can't you break it?" teased the lady, in her most purring, kittenish manner, playing with the lapel of my coat, and looking up at me with those sparkling black eyes.

"No, I'm afraid I can't," I said, though I heartily wished I could.

"It's the first time I ever asked you to do anything," she went on. "I think you might be nice for once."

"The loss is mine, I assure you. I wish, indeed, that I could."

"You are like all the rest of the men," she retorted, rather tartly, it seemed to me. "You do everything that you want to do, and when you don't want to do anything, you never lack an excuse!"

Finally "Madame X" said she must get home, and I helped her on with her coat, and slipped into my own. We were all standing about the door, and Caroline had her arms around "Madame X," and the ladies were, as is usual, all talking at once. Suddenly, "Madame X" gave a start and a little suppressed scream. We all turned to look at her.

"What's the matter?" asked Caroline.

"You pinched me," said "Madame X."

"Oh, did I?" said Caroline innocently. "I am so sorry. I certainly did not mean to."

What do you think of that, Buddie? Women are queer creatures. Don't you think so?

So I went to "Madame X's," and it was lively, take my word for it!

Perhaps I should not, once more, call names. There was "Madame X's" particular crony, the little lady who wore such a sketchy costume at one of the parties you attended, and the handsome Baltimore matron who seems to have fascinated one of our Washington friends, and last, but by no means least, that slender vamp who raised such a fog last summer trying to take a well-known politician away from his own wife at a certain party in Newark. Do you remember her? Who, once seeing her, could forget her?

In addition to the ladies, and to "Monsieur X," our host, there were present the husband of the lady from Baltimore, and my good Washington friend, who shall be nameless. The vamp lady very purposely kept the Baltimore man busy, while my friend entertained the Baltimore lady. The liquor was good, and was plentiful. The Baltimore lady drank more than any of the men, though "Madame X" ran her a close second! The vamp lady is a bad one, there is little doubt of that, but she is not outwardly coarse, but the other two are unspeakable, when one thinks that they pose before the outside world as social leaders.

As none of the persons present was anything to me, I enjoyed the opportunity which the occasion afforded for an intimate study of another side of this complex social organism. It was hard for me to realize that just a few minutes before, so to speak, our hostess had been a guest at Lillian Barton's table.

There was no light in the parlor, and the Baltimore lady and my Washington friend spent most of the evening sitting very close together in the darkest corner, engaged in a whispered conversation punctuated by long silences, though perhaps it would be more accurate to characterize it as long silences punctuated at intervals by whispered conversation. The Baltimore gentleman and the clever coquette from Washington had a very lively time in the dining room. To judge from the sounds, they spent most of their time shooting craps on the dining room table and mixing highballs at the sideboard. He was feeling very "rosy" long before the evening was over, though he was to drive his own car back to Baltimore that night. How he managed it, I can't for the life of me imagine. I know I should not have trusted myself behind him. However, he must have made it all right, for I have heard nothing to the contrary.

While "Monsieur X" entertained "Madame X's" pal with some very lively gossip, in the course of which I heard one or two well-known New Yorkers' names called quite frequently, "Madame X" amused me with her very spicy conversation. She told me more about the dancing club which she had mentioned at Barton's, and again insisted that I come to the next meeting. Meanwhile, she asked me if I did not want to help her and the vamp prepare the supper, or rather, look on while they prepared it. So we three retired to the kitchen, and made salad and sandwiches amid a running fire of very racy gossip. Since the vamp is witty to a degree, it was not entirely without interest. But I shall not weary you with a detailed account of the evening. One incident, which I think I shall relate, is typical. For a person of your imagination and training, it will not be difficult to reconstruct the rest.

During the process of preparing the supper, the vamp had to go into the dining room for some salad dishes. When she returned I happened to be standing at the entrance to the kitchen. Having nothing better to do at the moment, I indulged in a bit of foolery, and teasingly barred the way.

"You can't pass," said I, laughing, "without paying a toll."

She smiled that curious fascinating smile. She leaned toward me. I never before noticed what remarkable eyes she has, big and unfathomable; nor what a curious pallor; nor what a red and sensual mouth, in strange contrast to the colorless cheeks. Then I felt her lips against mine, a long, lingering kiss, which was so much more than a mere kiss that—well, if I could describe it, I should do so, and I am willing to wager that the description would be a distinct contribution to emotional psychology. How long this performance would have lasted, I have no means of knowing, but I was brought to my senses by the voice of our hostess.

"You quit that fooling, Pauline, and give me those dishes. First thing you know, you'll break them."

So I awoke, but all evening Pauline's unfathomable eyes and full red lips seemed to hold me bewitched, and I could not shake off their influence. I have never before cared for her and, indeed, I have always felt that her type of woman had absolutely no attraction for me, but I am not so sure. Of course, I am not going to put myself in a position to be made ridiculous, so, under the circumstances, I shall avoid that lady now for a reason, whereas before I avoided her for no reason. However, I can, at least, sympathize with those who fall under the spell of such an enchantress. But enough of this!

This evening I met Caroline in the hall, and she was very saucy. I asked her if she and Tommie would not like to go to a show during the early part of the evening, and have Dr. King come after his office hours.

"You're too frivolous," said the pert young miss. "I have to go to my classes, and then I have to study. You had better hunt up some of your gay friends."

So I have spent the evening writing to you. However, Caroline herself, for all her pretended industry, came home early from class, and a little later went out arrayed like the lilies of the field, with her swain. So that's that!

Tommie sends her "cordial good wishes"—I quote her very words! I leave you to interpret them. Don says, "Hello!"

Davy

TEN

The story of Genevieve. The rivals.
All's fair in love and war. The return of the wanderer.
And they lived happily ever after.

Sunday, January 14

Dear Bob:

During the past few days our household had been the scene of a very romantic little episode. It is so very conventional that if you were to put it into a story or play the critics would hammer you for using a too-hackneyed theme. There is a hero, misunderstood, a very conventional villain, and a heroine, deserted, suffering in silence and waiting in vain for the hero's return. It is the age-old story of the rivals and reminds me of a play I saw when a very small boy from the gallery of the one-horse, one-night theater of my old hometown. Did you ever see *Jim, the Penman*? Well, the story I have to tell you is the story of Jim, the Penman, minus the forged letters.

All of which reminds me that, by one of those curious coincidences which are not at all uncommon, we were talking at Lillian Barton's only Sunday night about the element of romance in everyday life, and Reese, who is a rather modern product of American business life, contended that there was no such thing, outside of books, or movies—or words to that effect; and Mrs.

Morrow said, "What romantic elements could one find in life in a town like this?"

Three of us took the other side of the question, and we had a very lively debate. I am looking forward to the pleasure I am going to have tonight at the expense of Mrs. Morrow and Reese. But let me get on with my story.

You may recall how, on more than one occasion during your stay here at Christmas, you voiced the thought that Genevieve Rhodes looked like a woman who had had a most unhappy love affair. I myself talked with Tommie the evening after you went back to New York, and she confirmed your diagnosis. She gave few details, but her version was about as follows:

When Genevieve was at Wellesley, she met a chap who had graduated from one of the smaller colleges in the pie belt, and was at that time at Massachusetts Tech taking an engineering course. He was a very clever fellow, and his name was Paul Thomas. I myself recall hearing years ago some of the New England boys talking about him as a youngster who was going to make a big name someday. One of his old college mates said that if he would only consent to give up his family and boyhood friends and cross over the line, that there would be nothing to which he might not aspire. He seems to have been a "bear" among the ladies, but for all they were so crazy about him, he never lost his head, but remained a steady, hardworking, serious fellow.

Now, Paul Thomas had a chum, an alter ego, a sort of shadow, in the person of one Oliver Drew. Thomas and he had met in their freshman year in college, and in the natural isolation of two colored lads in a big Northern school, their intimacy had grown and deepened until they had become such inseparable friends that they were known in Boston and Cambridge as Damon and Pythias. They shared their books, their clothes, their money, and even their joys and sorrows. When Thomas entered Massachusetts Tech, Drew matriculated in law at Boston University and thus they were separated only by the Charles River for the length of each day.

It seems that it was Drew who first met Genevieve, and it was through him that Paul Thomas first saw her. To make a long story short, it appears to have been a case of love at first sight, or something very like it, for both Genevieve and Paul, and with the arrival of Pythias on the scene, Damon seems to have been relegated to the rear.

Thomas was assiduous in his attentions. They spent their winter vacations in the same city, they corresponded when apart, and, with the exception of an occasional flare-up, for both were quick-tempered to a degree, the course of their love ran as smoothly as one could reasonably wish. Then Genevieve graduated, and commenced teaching in the high school here. She had been teaching a year when he finished Tech, and got a pretty nice position with an engineering corporation in New York. Meanwhile, the war had broken out, and the plight of the French had excited his interest and sympathy, as it had that of so many millions of Americans. He seemed, however, from all the accounts, to have been a bit more deeply stirred than most folks and more than once had talked, rather carelessly, of course, of going over and helping. This was before we went into the war, you will understand. At Easter 1917, he came to Washington on a visit, and renewed his wooing of Genevieve with the utmost vigor.

Now during the months prior to this visit, Oliver Drew had come to Washington and set up his law office. Naturally, as Paul Thomas's closest friend, he resumed friendly relations with Genevieve, who was only too glad to see him, if for no other reason than that he could, and did, talk much of Paul. So he was a frequent and welcome caller at the Rhodeses' house, and such was the estimate of him that Paul had succeeded in passing on to Genevieve that, next to Paul himself, he was her closest and most trusted friend.

During the time of Paul's visit, he lodged with Oliver, and all the time not spent with Genevieve was devoted to his old friend. Never, apparently, had their relations been more cordial. Indeed, Paul had told his inamorata that she might trust Drew just as she would himself.

Just before the close of Thomas's visit, he and Genevieve had a quarrel, a misunderstanding about something or other—Tommie did not know what, though she assumed it was merely another case of temper—and two days later, Thomas left town, and from that day to the Monday of this week just past—a stretch of almost six years—Genevieve had received no word or message from him or about him. When, swallowing her pride, she questioned Drew, he merely shrugged his shoulders in silence, with an expression which seemed to Genevieve compounded of regret and surprise. Finally, when approached rather insistently by Mrs. Rhodes, who was alarmed at the reaction of Genevieve to the incident, though he professed absolute ignorance of his friend's whereabouts, he showed the greatest concern, and begged Mrs. Rhodes to suspend judgment, as he was sure all would soon come out right. For weeks Genevieve faded visibly, until her family feared she was going into a decline. Then, by some curious revulsion, she seemed to get hold of herself—pride, I guess—but, though soon restored to her normal health and vigor physically, she seemed to have become a confirmed man hater, if, indeed, the word "hate" can be applied to the cold indifference which usually masked her gaze. So, she, who a few years before had been an acknowledged belle, devoted herself to her work, withdrew almost entirely from society, and spent her summers at Northern universities studying. In the interval America went into the war, sending her two millions across the seas.

In September 1919, nearly two years and a half after Genevieve had last seen or heard from her lover, the first division of the great American overseas force, quartered temporarily at Camp Meade, was ordered to Washington with its complete war equipment, to take part in a monster parade in honor of General Pershing. The first division was composed of regulars, infantry, cavalry, artillery, engineer corps, with their forges, shops, and field kitchens, and last but by no means least in impressiveness, the tanks. There were about 25,000 men in all, and they were hours marching from the Peace Monument at the head of Pennsylvania Avenue, through cheering throngs, past the reviewing stand in front of the White House. Genevieve, Caroline, Tommie, Helen Clay, and a group of their friends, including among the men, Don Verney, were occupying a point of vantage not far from the head of the parade, when suddenly Helen Clay, with something very sharp, like a suppressed shriek, clutched Tommie's shoulder, and in a low tone said, "Tommie, look where I am pointing! Isn't that Paul Thomas?"

Tommie was considerably startled, but managed to look as directed, and sure enough, in front of an engineering battalion, in the position of command, sat a big man, with a captain's bars on his shoulders, who, allowing for dust and tan, was the very image of Paul Thomas. While she was looking, the battalion moved, and the officer's face was lost to view.

While the two girls were afraid to mention this startling phenomenon to Genevieve, it was whispered about in the crowd, and, after a few hasty questions put to Helen Clay and Tommie, Don Verney slipped quietly out of the crowd and cut through a side street, moving with the speed of a man who has a definite objective and is in haste to reach it. The parade moved on to its close, and the crowd dispersed. At seven o'clock that evening, Verney turned up at the Rhodeses', and was ushered into the dining room, where Tommie, Caroline, and Genevieve were dawdling over their dessert, Mrs. Rhodes being absent for the week at her sister's, in Baltimore. Tommie and Caroline had ventured to tell Genevieve of the exciting event of the afternoon, and, as the girls had a suspicion of the meaning of Don's errand, they watched him anxiously as he ate the salad which had been set before him. From time to time each of the three stole furtive glances at Genevieve, who had become very pale, showing plainly the strain she was undergoing. Somehow she seemed to sense what was in their minds, for after a while she turned to Verney, and said:

"The girls have been telling me that one of the officers in the parade today was the image of Paul Thomas, and I doubt not, from their manner of looking at you, that they feel that you left the crowd today to make sure. If I am right in that conjecture, I thank you most heartily for your friendly interest and any trouble you may have taken on my account. I know you well enough to be sure of the generous spirit in which any such quest was undertaken. But I think it only fair to myself to say that I was living in this very house when Mr. Thomas last saw me, and I have been here ever since. Had he desired to see me, or to communicate with me, he might easily have done so, provided he is still living. If he *is* living, and has *not* done so, it is because he did not elect so to do. I could not, therefore, welcome any act which might be construed as an attempt by me or any of my friends to get into touch with him. You must see that it would be subjecting me to an undesirable and undeserved humiliation."

As Genevieve spoke, she seemed to grow paler, if possible,

and her face more drawn, and—to quote Tommie's words—her eyes took on an unearthly bigness. The violence of her emotion seemed to be wracking her to pieces and her suffering was so evident that all three of her auditors were stirred to their depths.

Caroline went to her and put her arms around her.

"You are very right, sister dear," she said, "and we are terribly sorry we mentioned the matter at all. It was probably a case of mistaken identity, anyway. Let us forget all about it!"

After one look, Don never raised his eyes from his plate, but kept on eating, as if he had not heard, and as if he had no part in the scene. But to the onlookers, who knew very well his sensible nature, it was apparent that he was himself very much shaken, and was endeavoring to hide his emotion. It was a very trying few minutes, according to Tommie, and everyone felt the strain.

It was some minutes later that Verney suddenly spoke, as if he had just come to a decision.

"As Caroline says, it's probably a case of mistaken identity, anyway, but we are all dreadfully sorry it had to occur, and so renew a forgotten unpleasantness."

Genevieve soon excused herself, and, when her steps had died away in the upper hall, the two girls gazed fixedly at Verney.

"Don," asked Tommie, "was it really Paul Thomas? Was it really?"

And both young women looked at him as if they would read his innermost thoughts.

"Don Verney, I knew when you entered that door that you came to bring us news!" said Caroline.

"How prone you women are to see a sensation where none exists! I came, dear ladies," said Don, taking out his wallet, and fumbling about in it, "to ask you to honor me with your company at the theater tonight."

And, as he spoke, he spread four tickets out on the table.

"But," said Tommie to me as she concluded her story, "both Caroline and I feel that Don really did see Paul Thomas, and that he identified him, and strange as it may seem to you, we both believe that Genevieve thinks so, too, and that she spoke as she did to keep him from telling her. I never realized until that evening how much she must have cared for Paul, and how terribly she was hurt by his disappearance and his silence. I have asked Don more than once since that night to tell me the real results of his quest, but he always laughs and evades. He has never yet asserted explicitly that he found out nothing."

Such was the story as told to me by Tommie, and between September 1919, and last Monday evening there was nothing to add. Of course, as the result of Tommie's narrative, I observed Genevieve more closely, and felt a stronger liking for her, through sympathy for her trouble. Only a woman capable of the deepest, truest feeling could have been so affected. And somehow to my way of thinking, she was not at all *bitter*. She was simply a woman capable of *one* abiding love. When that was killed, or thwarted, there was nothing left. There was in her gaze cold serenity and supreme indifference. As I compared and contrasted her with her sister, Caroline, I sometimes felt that, if she had had the sparkle, the dash, that wonderful *joie de vivre* which is Caroline's distinguishing characteristic, she would be a remarkably handsome woman. Mary Hale told me once that she did have that sparkle in a very high degree when she was a very young woman. I recall also that in Tommie's memorabilia book there was a newspaper clipping telling about a big charity bazaar, at which Genevieve was designated by popular vote as the most beautiful woman present.

"And," said Tommie, "almost everyone was there, and some

of the girls really *campaigned* for votes. Genevieve sat in a box with her mother, and, without lifting a finger, was chosen by a very large plurality over her nearest rival."

The night after Tommie had narrated this story to me, she smuggled into my room a photograph of Paul Thomas, which Caroline kept hidden in her personal keepsakes. He surely was a fine-looking chap, with clear, honest eyes. As I gazed at his photograph, I could not help thinking that it would not be hard to recognize him again if one had once seen him.

I realize that I have been a long time working up to the climax, but the exposition is a very necessary part of a dramatic story.

On Monday there was a club party at Mary Hale's, at which an out-of-town visitor of Mrs. Morrow was the guest of honor. As at many of the affairs I have mentioned, the ladies played cards early in the evening and the men came in later to dine and dance. Genevieve has been a member of this club for many years, and it is the one social function in the month which she regularly attends.

What happened at Mary Hale's forms a very clear picture in my mind, and I shall never forget it. I had just come down from the upper room where we men left our wraps, and had gone into the back parlor. As luck would have it, there were only a few people there, for most of the men had either not arrived , or were stopping for a cigarette and a chat in the room upstairs, and practically all of the ladies were gathered around a table in the parlor where two or three tellers were casting up the points to determine who had won the prizes. Three or four men were grouped about the door opening from the parlor into the hallway. Genevieve was in front of the fireplace in the back parlor talking to Mr. Hale and Tommie Dawson, and Miss Billie Riddick and a

New York chap whose name I cannot now recall were standing in the middle of the room. I had just greeted Mrs. Hale and turned to speak to Genevieve when I heard an exclamation from Dr. Dill, who was one of the group standing in the hallway by the parlor door.

The doctor has a clear, high voice which carries over any ordinary hubbub, and I heard what he said very distinctly.

"Well, by all that is holy, if it isn't Paul Thomas!"

This was followed by sounds of noisy greeting from the other men, and exclamations from some of the ladies in the front parlor. I turned quickly, and saw towering above the heads of the men about him a stalwart form attired in the uniform of the USA. One glance at his face showed me that it was indeed the original of the photograph Tommie had shown me. Then I thought of Genevieve. She had been standing facing the door, and must have seen him almost before anyone else. Never have I seen such a transformation. Her face, which but a moment before had looked at me with a serene smile, was now pale and drawn, and she was shaking all over. In a flash it came to me what it would mean to her to have to meet this man under the battery of a hundred curious eyes. I looked at Tommie inquiringly. She—oh, rare girl that she is—caught my meaning instantly and nodded. In the fraction of a second that it had taken all this to happen, Mary Hale had stepped close to Genevieve and had taken her arm, and with the same motion seemed to screen her from the gaze of those in the front parlor. These ladies, however, were so startled by the apparition of Paul Thomas that for the moment at least they forgot everything else. Unresistingly, and as if in a dream, Genevieve let Mrs. Hale and me pilot her out into the back hall. There our hostess quickly opened a closet door, motioning me to move on into the dining room. In a second she had overtaken us, bringing her fur coat, which she placed affectionately about Genevieve's shoulders, at the same time giving her a kiss.

"Captain Carr will be glad to see you home, dear!" she said. "You can go out the back door. I will wait here while you get your coat and hat," she added, turning to me.

Now I knew that every second spent under that roof would be an eternity of torture to Genevieve Rhodes, and I felt that it would be far easier for me to stand the little discomfort of the out-of-doors.

"It isn't cold," I said, "and we haven't far to go."

Mrs. Hale protested, but I would not listen. As for Genevieve, I don't believe she heard a word we were saying. Except for her trembling, she seemed perfectly numb.

So I led her out of the back door onto a porch, and thence through the alley gate to a side street. After the warm house, it was cold, and I shivered in spite of myself, but I was so glad that we had succeeded in escaping without observation that I minded the chill but little. It was only when we were actually in the hallway of her house that the poor girl noticed that I was bareheaded and without a topcoat.

"You poor Davy," she said, "you should not have done it! Come in by the fire at once."

As it somehow seemed to do her good to take some thought for me, I made no protest but followed unresistingly into the back parlor, where the cheerful open fire, a permanent fixture in the Rhodes household in the winter season, gave me a most cheerful welcome.

There Genevieve fell into the corner of the big davenport as if exhausted, her sudden interest in my welfare having flickered out as quickly as it had flared up, and left her as numb as she had been when we left Mrs. Hale's house. However, she let me remove her fur coat, and then, as if she were quite oblivious of my presence, she fell into a reverie, looking fixedly into the fire. As for me, I knew not what to do or say. As you well know, I am the very last person in the world to wish to intrude upon a private grief of any other mortal, but somehow in this instance it did not seem right to leave. I don't know exactly why I felt so, but I did. Perhaps I felt that if she had wanted to be alone absolutely she would have sought her own room. The fact that she had not seemed to indicate that perhaps I might better remain.

So I sat quietly beside her, taking her hand, which I held in mine. She made no effort to withdraw it. After a while she began to cry softly, and big tears coursed down her cheeks unrestrained. This was too much for me. So I released her hand, put my arm about her, and drew her head down on my shoulder, where she wept to her heart's content. Now as I write these words of cold description, I marvel, first at my temerity in doing such a thing, and secondly, at her calm acceptance of it, and you, who know Genevieve Rhodes so well, will marvel with me, I know. But it is all true as I relate it, and, strange to say, at the time it happened it seemed absolutely natural.

After a few minutes of quiet tears, and a few minutes of calm, she straightened up, and said, with her old calm smile:

"You're a real comfort, Davy! I cannot tell you how I appreciate what you and Mary Hale did tonight, I really can't. I shall never forget that you were sympathetic enough to realize what I must feel, and generous enough to do what you thought I should want done, when I myself was too paralyzed to think or act. Sometimes we are inclined to believe that the present generation is going to the dogs, but whenever I get too pessimistic, I love to recall the fact that I have seen you under fire more than once, and I have never known you to fail to act as becomes a gentleman."

And Genevieve took my hand in both of hers, and held it fast. I have never had a compliment which pleased me more than that little speech. I say this without reference to the question as to whether I deserved it or not!

At this juncture there was a noise at the door, the rattling of the knob, and the sound of voices. Genevieve arose as if in a panic, and as I stood by her, looking inquiringly, she put her arm through mine, and clung close to me as if for protection. It is a queer thing how in moments of real emotional stress we slough off the purely conventional forms. So interested was I in Genevieve's troubles that I quite overlooked anything else, and was brought to my usual senses by the startled glances of both Caroline and Don, who now entered the parlor. Caroline's eyes when they fell upon us standing there had a look of real fright—I can think now of no other word which so aptly characterizes it, and Don's expression was not far behind. After exchanging a puzzled look with one another, Don said:

"I have had a talk with Paul and what he says convinces me that you have done him an injustice and owe him at the least a hearing. I say that with a full recollection of what you said in my presence the last time I heard you mention his name."

There was a moment's silence. Genevieve's look was unfathomable. Finally she said, and as she spoke she seemed to draw closer to me:

"Tell us quickly what he said. If Davy thinks I ought to see him, I will."

Again Don and Caroline exchanged glances of some bewilderment. But Don is a cool one, and in a moment he was his usual calm self.

"Surely!" he said. "To be brief, after Paul went away, angry, he sent you messages through his friend Oliver Drew. From you directly he never received any answer, but he did hear indirectly through Drew, and the message was most unfavorable. He sent another message through the same source, and the answer was still more unfavorable. Then he heard nothing more for some time, and then came a letter from Drew intimating that he (Drew) was very hopeful of bringing his own suit to a successful conclusion. Paul himself has been absent from the country since the summer of 1917, with the exception of a few weeks in 1919, and has never heard your name called until today. He convinced me of the truth of all these things, and I feel he can convince you. Since this version of the story did not seem to tally with the one which evidently sticks in your mind, I ventured to ask you to hear him. I hope Davy agrees with me."

"I certainly do—and most heartily," I said.

Genevieve looked from one to the other of us. Finally she said:

"All right, if Davy thinks it is the proper thing to do, I agree."

"I am glad," said Don simply. "We shall go back to the Hales', and send Paul over."

So I asked them to wait while I ran up to my room to get a cap, and we all three set out together, with Don carrying Mary Hale's fur coat. Caroline clung to Don's arm and said not a word during our short trip. When we reached the Hales' we slipped in the back way, and Caroline and I mingled with the dancers, leaving to Don the delicate task of telling Paul Thomas that his mission had been successful, and getting him out of the house unobtrusively. This, with Mary Hale's efficient aid, he managed to do, for Paul had been gone some time before anyone noticed his absence.

I was conscious during the rest of the evening that Caroline was irritable, and that she seemed to be trying to "start something." During the moment's interval between a dance and its encore she said, as if she wished to provoke an argument:

"I fear, Davy Carr, that you are in the way of being badly spoiled."

I smiled serenely.

"Certainly *not* by Miss Caroline Rhodes," I countered.

"No, I was like all the rest of them for a while, but I stopped in time."

"What has suggested these remarks?" I asked, still smiling.

"Genevieve! She's the last person in the world of whom one would expect it, but she is just like all the rest, evidently. I am disappointed in her! Indeed, I am! I thought she had saner judgment."

"And now you're sure she has not?"

"Quite sure! There is only one person in the world who is more spoiled than you, and that's your friend Bob Fletcher. It's a positive crime the way the girls spoil him!"

There's one for your account, my friend!

"Well, you had no hand in spoiling him, and surely no one can accuse you of any share in the impairment of my disposition, or character, or whatever it is that suffers from spoiling. From your superior heights, then, you can well afford to look down in a spirit of charity and forbearance upon those weaker and more susceptible than you."

This in my best manner—imperturbably.

But Caroline only turned up her pretty little nose in the most ladylike manner possible, and moved away abruptly. What has gotten into the girl lately, I really can't fathom. She is a regular little vixen on occasion, and seems to take special delight in baiting me. Nor am I able to please her in any wise.

Just before "Home-Sweet-Home," Mary Hale sought me out to say that Genevieve had telephoned that she wanted me to ask Tommie Dawson and Don to come over for a few minutes after the dance was over. They did not have to be asked twice, I assure you, for both were wild to know what had happened.

No *words* of Genevieve's were needed to make us aware that she and her long-lost lover had been reconciled. Never before have I witnessed such a transformation. Happiness to the point of exaltation is surely a stimulant, and it would be difficult to realize that the radiant woman before us was the sober, serious, unbending Genevieve whom I had known for the past few months. Nothing can show more clearly how great a change had taken place in her than the fact that she had sent for us that she might tell us the result of the interview. I suppose she felt she had to tell someone. The story was simple enough. The message she had confided to Oliver Drew—as Paul's best friend—Paul never received, and the messages Paul sent to her through the same channel she never received. It may seem incredible to some, and a curious coincidence to others, that *both* confided in Drew, instead of writing directly, but I suppose that can be explained by the tendency of two proud, high-spirited people who have quarreled to avoid direct communication with each other, and to send messages indirectly through an intermediary. At any rate, they *did* so act, with the sad result we have noted. When Genevieve had finished her story, she cried for sheer happiness and relief, and Caroline and Tommie cried, too. Then, in that perfect manner peculiar to Genevieve, and in the happy phrase characteristic of the Rhodeses, she thanked us all for our interest and sympathy, and for what we had done, or tried to do, in her behalf. She kissed the girls, and gave her hand to Don and to me.

"As for Davy," she said, "I have a dreadful desire to embrace him for what he did tonight. I am sure Paul would not mind, if he knew all the circumstances."

At this moment as I write I cannot recall my answer, but it

was, naturally, something more or less jocular. I was embarrassed beyond all reason, for I was most conscious of a smile of sarcasm on Caroline's face.

"Well," said that saucy young person, "before this meeting degenerates into a kind of sentimental debauch, I think I shall withdraw. Excuse the expression, Genevieve dear, but really, Davy is quite insufferable now, and I don't believe I could stand seeing him much worse. I didn't mean to rebuke you, but I don't believe you realize just how bad he is."

Don looked from Caroline to me, from me to Caroline with a puzzled air, and then burst into a perfect gale of laughter. Genevieve, who was too happy to be oversensitive, laughed, too.

"Do you know," said the latter suddenly, "I have just discovered I am dying of hunger. I have had nothing to eat or drink since my early dinner, and it must be one o'clock. Who wants a cup of cocoa?"

Her newfound happiness was so evident and so unaffected that, though none of us was in need of cocoa, or anything else to eat or drink after having partaken of the very generous cheer offered by Mary Hale, we all fell in with her suggestion eagerly, and trooped down to the dining room. While we were sipping our cocoa, Don was taken, rather suddenly, with a fit of laughing. Genevieve, Tommie and I were mystified completely, but, for some strange reason, Caroline seemed to understand him.

"I don't know whether it is the water we drink, or something in the air, which seems to be turning everyone silly," she said, rather tartly, I thought.

But Don only laughed the more, and our party broke up when he arose to go, with his merriment in no wise abated. It was a very jolly ending to a most exciting evening.

4 P.M.

As I write these closing lines, from the parlor two floors below I hear a rich, beautiful voice singing love songs. It is Genevieve entertaining her lover. I, for one, had no notion she had a singing voice at all.

I have met Paul Thomas, and he is an unusually attractive man. It is not difficult to see how a woman might lose her head over him. He spent part of an evening in my room, and we fought the war all over again. He was in long before we were, and was one of the last to leave France, since he was with the regulars. Realizing, of course, that no record, however fine, can make an American of *known* colored ancestry welcome in the Engineer Corps of the U.S.A., he has forestalled the inevitable unpleasantness by resigning his commission. This he did two days after the meeting, which resulted in a reconciliation between the lovers.

As for Genevieve, she is radiant. That is indeed the only word which describes her. I can think of nothing more beautiful than the sight of the supreme happiness of a fellow mortal. I have seen nothing more charming or more moving in my life. Since the Baltimore incident of ill-starred memory, Genevieve has always treated me with consideration, but since last Monday her manner has an added element of friendliness—indeed, I might even say affection. I feel sure that I have *one* loyal friend in this house. Thus richly, sometimes, are our very mediocre deeds rewarded!

But if I don't stop writing, I shall have to send this letter to you in two sections.

I wish you could be at Lillian Barton's tonight, to hear me annihilate, with my best irony and sarcasm, my good friends Mrs. Morrow and Reese! No romance in modern life indeed!

Davy

ELEVEN

Davy reflects. What price happiness? Rouge and lipstick. Cultivating Billie.

Sunday, January 21

I think it is old Juvenal who says, "He who begets children gives pledges to fortune," or words to that effect. From all I have observed, that is indeed a true saying, but, when you think it over, the establishment of every kind of human relationship is fraught with responsibilities which cannot be eluded. Very often we can decide as to whether or not we shall make this or that tie, but once it is made, the matter is largely out of our hands. Once we have set up our gods, though with our own brain and hands we may have fashioned them out of the clay of the roadside, and by taking, though, have invested them with life, the creature becomes master, and we can no more control what it shall do. It is the age-old experience of Frankenstein all over again!

Life is indeed a curious and an interesting thing. Our so-called freedom of the will seems confined, at least so it appears to me, to initiating things. Once they are initiated, they slip from our hands, and withdraw from the circle of our domination. We are continually setting up these little spheres of influence, only to have them pass from under our control. It is no wonder that certain men have tried, by resolutely avoiding the making of ties and the persistent refusal to take on responsibilities, to find a sort of negative happiness, only to discover, in their turn, that there is no such thing. Do you remember the story of Dechelette in Daudet's *Sapho*? That illustrates in part at least the point I am trying to make.

Another angle of the same question is expressed by a character in Mason's *The Witness for the Defence*, who says—I cite from memory—that we can have anything in this world we want, if only we want it hard enough, but we cannot control the price we shall have to pay for it. And he might have added that we cannot, indeed, know beforehand what the price is to be, nor the time when payment will be exacted.

"Step up, gentlemen," says life, "help yourselves with both hands. Don't be stingy with yourselves. The price? Oh, let's not talk about that now. It's a small matter between friends. Only satisfy yourselves. We can talk about the rest later." And, being human, we poor fools, in our greediness, often dip in to our very elbows, and carry off what we will, without a thought of the day of reckoning. All the tenets of the gospel of thrift deprecate buying on time, but did you ever think that in the great scheme of life, we are compelled to take everything by that process, and must enjoy first and pay afterward? Not only that, we must, as it were, give a signed note of hand, undated, and with the amount blank. No wonder so many human lives go bankrupt.

These thoughts went through my mind the other night as I sat in the Rhodeses' back parlor and waited for Thomasine to come down. We four, Caroline, Dr. King, Tommie, and I were going to the Zeta Lambda dance, and Caroline had a new rig in connection with which she had called for Tommie's assistance. A professional call had delayed the doctor, so I sat in the back parlor, and amused myself with the books of the late Mr. Rhodes. I don't suppose, in your hectic hours here, you had a chance to notice them.

I noted, among other things, standard editions of Balzac, Daudet, and Dumas, a large paper French edition of Victor Hugo, Daudet's work in French with the Leloir illustrations, the original French edition of De Maupassant, the Prothereo set of Byron, one of the most satisfying editions I have ever handled, practically all of Edith Wharton's works, and the definitive English editions of Thackeray, Defoe, and Dryden. I figured casually that there were at least seven or eight hundred dollars' worth of books in sets like those I have named, not to mention the hundreds of single volumes. The fact which struck me was that every set present represented the very best scholarship and was what one would call the standard or definite edition, and in the separate volumes I noted practically every one of the best English and American works of imaginative literature, both prose and verse, for the period between about 1890 and 1910. All of the books showed signs of use, the dates in those I happened to open showed that they were bought at the time of their first appearance, and the selection was an eloquent tribute to the owner's taste. No wonder Caroline, for all her occasional "jazzy" manners, has such an unusual speaking vocabulary. It must have been a liberal education to live with her father.

The whole room, in my opinion, is very satisfying to the eye. The pictures, though too many suit the modern taste, which insists on light woodwork, expensive wall coverings and a paucity of detached ornament, were very good, the bookcases simple and unobtrusive, and the rest of the furniture of the most comfortable description—the last touch in "hominess" being produced by the open fireplace, the big davenport conveniently near, and the long Italian table with its two reading lamps just behind it. I have always liked this room.

It was the pitiful story of Dechelette and poor little Alice Doré, which I leafed over idly as I sat there, that started me on the train of thought set forth at the beginning of this letter. Here I am in a house whose inmates were utterly unknown to me a few weeks ago, and now my life seems in some curious fashion inextricably bound with theirs. It's that same old story over again. We initiate actions or relations, and in so doing may exercise to the full our free will, of which we are so inordinately proud, but, once the action is started or the relation entered upon, Fate steps in and takes it out of our hands. Maybe you don't agree with me in this thought, but at any rate you will have to acknowledge that there is something in it.

Here am I, having of my own free will made new relationships in this house, now suffering more or less discomfort because of them—disturbed—yes, I shall have to acknowledge it—disturbed because of the actions of an irresponsible girl whose very existence was, only a few weeks ago, a matter of the utmost indifference and unconcern to me. And such an atmosphere of unconcern I might have maintained throughout my life if I had not allowed any new relationship to be set up between us, but I did, and now I am troubled, forsooth, because she no longer continues to do the things which at first were a source of annoyance to me. Why I should care what she does or does not do is a mystery to me, but I do.

While I sat reflecting on the uncertainties and whimsicalities of life, Caroline came in looking like a dream of almost unearthly loveliness. I really believe she grows more beautiful day by day, and surely she must be bankrupting herself buying new clothes, for she seems to have a new gown for every party. This last one was dainty beyond words, and she emerged from it—her shoulders are the superbest I ever saw—like some wonderful tropical flower. Sometimes I am almost overpowered by her beauty, and this time I was speechless.

"How do you like my new dress, Godfather? I made it myself—every little bit of it. Don't you think it's pretty?"

I murmured some banality or other. Then I noticed what I had not seen before, that the rouge which in her case has been rather conspicuous by its absence, was quite noticeable. I do not know whether or not I should have said anything, but I did not have to decide, for her uncanny power of perception made it unnecessary for me to break the ice. She caught my glance almost before I was conscious myself that I had directed it at her.

"It's impossible to please you, Godfather. You're a perfectly merciless critic, and your eyebrows have the worst manners imaginable. Of course, I've got rouge on tonight. I should look a fright if I did not. I've been out six or seven nights running, and I don't sleep any too well when I do get to bed, so what is a poor girl to do? You must realize that most folks are not as hypercritical as you are. Some of your very-much-esteemed friends use enough, Heaven knows! I should think you would be used to it by now."

The acerbity in the last words was apparent. As she talked, she stood in front of the big mirror over the mantel and looked at herself, and then looked at me from the mirror with a smile unmistakably defiant.

"I said nothing about any of my much-esteemed friends, and I do not recall saying anything about you," I rejoined very coolly, though her manner was most irritating.

"Of course you didn't—in *words.* You never do. In fact, I think I should like it better if you did *say* right out what you think. You certainly get it over. And I repeat, why should I be criticized for doing occasionally what your wonderful friends do all the time? That's a question I should like you to answer if you can."

She had turned, and stood looking down at me with a manner almost belligerent. There was a bright spot on either cheek which showed red even beneath the rouge, and the black eyes snapped dangerously.

My first impulse was to meet her halfway, and in the same spirit. But I stopped long enough for a second thought, and so said nothing. Just at that moment the doorbell rang, and I took advantage of this diversion, and answered it, letting in Dr. King, for whom we were waiting. Tommie, who had been delayed through helping Caroline with her dress, was not quite ready, so I insisted that Caroline and the doctor go on ahead. He hesitated, and looked at Caroline.

"Yes," said that saucy young lady in a tone which made her escort look at me inquiringly, "we might as well go on. I think it will be pleasanter."

And, gathering her fur coat about her, she swept royally out of the room, while Dr. King followed, looking puzzled.

The Zeta Lambda dance was very pretty, and, as most of the girls present were college students, with all the bloom and zest of youth, we had a lively time. Caroline was quite cool at first, so pointedly so as to make Tommie stare at me inquiringly. But I ignored her manner, and started in with a will to have a good time. As at the party of which I wrote you in a previous letter, Miss Billie Riddick and Caroline were the acknowledged belles, but this time Lillian Barton pressed them hard for the honors. I have to take off my hat to Miss Billie, for she's a game loser. If persistence and a "never-say-die" spirit will win for her, the doctor is going to be a sure victim. It's a curious fact that since the doctor's arrival in town, Billie has suddenly sprung into prominence as a favorite at all social affairs, a fact due entirely, as I see it, to the efforts she has made to please. The girl has something besides mere physical attractiveness—she has brains and resourcefulness. For some reason or other she seemed to have worked me into her plan of campaign, for this particular occasion at any rate. In some way, difficult for me to see, I was drawn into her circle, and in my first dance with her I was conscious that she was making an unusual effort to be pleasing. She is better at repartee than any girl around here except Lillian Barton or Caroline, and, even when she is making no special effort, she is interesting and entertaining. But on this occasion she outdid herself. She complimented me, and flattered me, quite shamelessly, and laughed when I tried to call her hand. As she is clever, her compliments, if broad, were so cunningly conceived as to hit hard. They were just the kinds of things, which of all others, I might wish were true. She's a clever one, there is no doubt of that, and she has me sized up perfectly.

The whole thing struck me all in a heap, and just before the end of our dance, I commenced to laugh. Then Billie, for whom you need not diagram your feelings to have them understood, commenced to laugh, too, and soon we had attracted the attention of several of the dancers, including Caroline, Tommie, and Lillian Barton, who looked at us with all the evidences of curiosity. During the intermission for refreshments, Miss Riddick and her escort, who was none other than my friend Scott Green, of Baltimore, got Tommie and me in a corner, where we had a very lively time, indeed. Green, as I have told you before, is very much taken with Miss Dawson. But you need not get jealous, for I don't believe she has anything but the most ordinarily friendly feeling for him. We had hardly gotten seated when here comes Lillian Barton, towing my friend Reese, and they had hardly seated themselves when Caroline arrived with the doctor, and, when the smoke had cleared away, Caroline was sitting between me and Miss Barton, with Tommie on the other side of me and Dr. King in front. Caroline took the door and held it against all comers, and she treated me as if I were a long-lost favorite brother. She gave me part of her salad, sweetened my coffee herself, adjusted my napkin, and overwhelmed me with little attentions. The whole thing puzzled me not a little, it was in such marked contrast to her conduct of the past two or three weeks. But, as I have learned to take women much as they come, I attacked the good things on my plate without letting my state of puzzlement interfere with my appetite.

But in the midst of it all, something struck Miss Riddick as funny, and she commenced to laugh, at first quietly, then staccato fashion, in convulsive sobs. The men all stopped eating to look at her, but I noted, even in my perplexity, that the women, except Billie herself, ate on steadily, as if they would ignore this diversion, though both Caroline and Lillian Barton were flushed and they looked distinctly irritated and annoyed. Finally Billie, unable to control herself, had to be excused, and departed, still laughing helplessly, for the ladies' dressing room, whence she emerged only just as the music started up again.

There seem to be a lot of crosscurrents moving under the surface of our social sea. Just as the music started, and I was looking about for Tommie, up comes Don Verney, who had arrived very late, and, after two or three words of greeting, he made these mysterious remarks.

"Are you a good soldier?" he asked suddenly.

"What do you mean?" I asked.

"Can you follow directions without asking questions?"

"Surely," said I.

"Then cultivate Billie Riddick," he said, looking inscrutable, as only he can look. Then he turned away to greet a lady, and left me gaping. At this moment, Tommie appeared, and, noticing my blank look, asked me what was the matter.

"There seem to be a lot of things going on here which I don't understand," I said.

"Yes?" said Tommie with a rising inflection in her voice, and a very merry twinkle in her eye. "My dear Davy, it's an old, old saying that 'There are none so blind as those who will not see,' and there's another one goes with it: 'Ears have they, and hear not.' The trouble with you is, Davy, that more, perhaps, than most people, you absolutely require perspective to see at all. But, come on, that music is too pretty to waste."

One thing is sure, and of that I have no doubt whatever, namely, that Tommie Dawson is a perfectly heavenly dancer. I believe you agree with me in that opinion. So I soon forgot for the moment all those things which were overworking my curiosity, and enjoyed the moment to the full. Don't you envy me, Bob? Well, just to make you feel a little better, I'll tell you something she said. When the music stopped, I said to your dear friend:

"Tommie, that was an absolutely perfect dance, don't you think so?" And what do you think she said? I won't make you wait longer. She said:

"It was almost perfect, Davy. There's only one person in the world with whom it would have been as enjoyable, and that is our soldier boy. I wish he were here. I miss him a whole lot."

Now I know you'll be glad you waded patiently through all of my puzzles and perplexities to reach this point. It was worth it, don't you think so?

Well, I took Don's advice, or perhaps, I should say better, I followed his order, and cultivated Billie Riddick, and I was perfectly amazed to see how she responded. If you had seen us, you would have thought we were sweethearts of long standing. For a few minutes I was tempted to think that it was I she liked, so cordial was she and so eagerly did she meet me halfway, but soon something set my mind at rest as to that. But everything in its own time.

I had a very lively evening, and the air was electric with flashing crosscurrents. Indeed, I was quite overwhelmed to find how interesting this merely momentary cultivation of Miss Billie seemed to be to a number of people. You can guess who they were, so I need not mention them. There was not a moment when we seemed free from some kind of surveillance. Stimulated by this interest, I threw myself into the game with zest, and the evening, which had begun rather unpleasantly, was not half bad after all. Miss Riddick and I furnished the climax of the evening by actually sitting out one dance in the balcony, while she opened her heart to me about Dr. King. It is curious how love seems to transform some people. While she is talking of him, she seems an entirely different person from the hard, sophisticated young woman to whom I was first introduced by Morris Jeffreys so many weeks ago.

I got one interesting point at least from this interview. She does not believe that Caroline cares very deeply for the doctor. While we were sitting up on the balcony with our heads together, I was conscious of many inquiring glances directed our way. Don Verney, especially, seemed to get a lot of fun out of the situation, and smiled widely at us each time he passed within eyeshot, dancing with Lillian Barton. I discovered in talking with Billie that she was going next Friday night to the Merry Coterie's card party, to which I had been invited also. It's another one of those affairs where the men come in about ten-thirty, when the games are over. So, still following Don's lead, I asked Billie if I might not take care of her for that evening. Her eyes flashed visibly as I voiced my invitation. She said Scott Green had asked her, but she had not given him an answer, so that she could fix it all right. I might consider the matter settled. I was to call for her just before eight to take her to the card party, which began early, and then I was to come back at ten-thirty.

When we were putting on our wraps at the entrance to the coatroom, Billie and Scott Green came up to where Caroline, Tommie, the doctor, and I were standing, and bade us good night most cordially and effusively, leaving me for the last.

"Au revoir, Mr. Carr," she said, "don't forget it's a quarter to eight." And with one of her dazzling smiles, she slipped her arm through Scott Green's and left us with a flourish. As I struggled into my overcoat, I stole a look at the others. As Dr. King's back was turned to me, I was deprived of the possibility of seeing his reaction to Billie's remarks, but Tommie's brow was drawn into deep thought wrinkles, and Caroline stood openmouthed. As they, by one impulse, turned to look at me, I made a point, in my effort to get into my coat, to turn my back on them.

It was a silent party in Dr. King's car, though the thoughts were almost vocal. Just before we drew up at the Rhodeses' house, however, Caroline broke the silence.

Smothering a yawn with her hand, she turned to Tommie, and in the coolest, most matter-of-fact tone in the world she said:

"Did you notice how old Billie Riddick is looking? She really ought to stop going so much."

What Tommie would have answered, I really cannot guess, for at that moment the car stopped in front of the house, and Dr. King swung the door open.

When I was at Tommie's last night for a few minutes, I saw the new photo. It is a good one, there is no doubt of that. I told Tommie that I thought she had enough pictures of you, but she answered that she wanted one in civilian attire, for all she had were taken in uniform. I suppose if she expressed a desire for the moon you would rush and try to get it. Buddie, I fear your days of freedom are over, for this time you have swallowed hook, line, and sinker, and there is little or no use in trying to wiggle, even. Tell Sallie Cole that I say she is wasting her valuable time being nice to you. You are what my old nurse used to call "a gone goose." But no doubt you endure your hopeless state with remarkable serenity.

Davy

TWELVE

Saturday, January 27

Dear Bob:

In my last I told you that I had made an engagement with Billie Riddick to go to the Merry Coterie's meeting at the house of Mrs. Dill, a very gay matron, and the wife of Dr. Dill. Well, if I had realized what was to be the outcome of that engagement, I guess I would have called it off on some pretext or other. But it's too late now to think of that. So like Pangloss in Voltaire's *Candide,* I can only keep saying, "Everything is for the best in this best of all possible worlds." Maybe if I say that often enough I shall really come to believe it. As things stand now, however, I can't say it with anything like a ring of conviction in my voice, for things are in a pretty mess. Don no doubt meant well when he gave me his advice to cultivate Billie, but at this moment as I write I am wishing most fervently that he had kept his advice to himself. But you don't know what I am raving about, do you? Well, I'll set it down for you in chronological order.

For some reason, known only to herself, Billie Riddick decided to meet me more than halfway in my little campaign entered upon the other night at Don Verney's instance, and she has kept the 'phone going in the interim. In practically every case it happened that Caroline answered the 'phone, and, from what I can gather, in each case Billie told her name. So I conducted protracted and lively conversations with the voluble Billie, and, as a result of one of these talks, I called for her, and took her to the movies where, as luck would have it, I saw pretty nearly everyone I know, including Caroline and Dr. King. That was, indeed, a lively evening. The following evening Tommie, who had been in Caroline's room during the hour just after dinner, came up for a few minutes to talk about you, but during our conversation I once or twice noted her eying me very seriously, with somewhat of a puzzled air.

But I must get to last night's party, for—to distort Hamlet somewhat—"the party's the thing!" First of all I called for Billie at about seven forty-five and took her to the Dills' house. When we drove up, as luck would have it, we ran into five people going in, including Mary Hale, Caroline, and Mrs. Morrow. It was a moment full of possibilities, and I shall have to give it to Billie—she certainly made the most of it, without in the least overdoing it. Whatever may be her faults, and one or two of them seem fairly obvious, stupidity and lack of savoir faire are not among them. The more I have seen of her, the more I am compelled to admire her resourcefulness. Well—to hasten on a bit—our entrance into the scene and my exit were dramatic in the extreme, and we got the maximum effect. As I had not yet dressed for the evening, I rode home and dismissed the taxi. After an hour of reading I dressed leisurely, and strolled back to Dr. Dill's, picking up Don on the way. When we arrived everything was in full blast, for the Merry Coterie is the most boisterous crowd in town, and they were making enough noise to wake the dead.

By the way, I almost forgot to tell you that Paul Thomas, after ten days of strenuous devotion to Genevieve, has left Washington for the West. He has very definite plans in connection with which he expects to put to use his unusual engineering education and experience. He has some capital of his own, he told me, and he thinks in a short while he will be on his feet. As soon as he sees light ahead, he and Genevieve are to be married. They are almost the happiest people I have ever seen.

The lady with the gray eyes wishes to be remembered.

Billie—and this was something I had not counted on—was standing where she could see each one as soon as he entered, and so my entrance lost nothing of its dramatic possibilities. She enveloped me with that green-gray glance of hers as if I were the only man in the world. Helen Clay was looking right at us, and I know the scene lost nothing in the telling, nor was the telling delayed overlong. I decided, somehow, to follow my present plan for a while longer, so I still "cultivated" Billie, and we danced, and we flirted, and laughed together interminably, for she is humorous beyond words. I think everybody noticed us, for the few who might otherwise have overlooked our little play had their attentions awakened by persons like Helen Clay. And thus we basked for this one evening in the spotlight. It was not such bad fun, either. Miss Riddick was once more a strong contender for first place in the eyes of the male contingent, and Caroline and Lillian Barton certainly had to divide honors with her. Sometimes I think that in a very gay party the "vamp" type of woman makes more of a hit than she might elsewhere. At any rate, in this case, Miss Billie was surrounded at the close of each dance, and her curious gray eyes worked havoc. As on other occasions the women looked on scornfully, but, they looked nevertheless! As Tommie said to me, in a moment of quiet, every woman in the room was studying the cut and effect of that fetching gown that hung so gracefully from Miss Billie's beautiful shoulders, and wondering what in the world there was in her walk which so fascinated the men. It is interesting to record that among those who buzzed around her, Dr. King and Will Hale were conspicuous.

I asked Caroline twice for a dance and each time she said she was engaged. As neither time did she suggest an alternative, I let it go at that, so, for the second time since I have been here, a whole evening passed without a dance with her.

When the refreshments were served, Billie and I happened to get places in a specially attractive little "cozy corner" in the Dills' back parlor, where we carried on a very private conversation, as if we were dead to the world about us. If the rest would have been able to hear what we were saying, our little tête-à-tête would have lost much of its interest for them, for Billie was telling me, in the most serious way imaginable, the story of her life.

It's queer how much more we like people when we really know something about them. Silence, ignorance, and aloofness seem to be almost absolutely necessary for the growth of a real dislike. To know a person, to talk with him intimately, seems a very sure way to create an understanding, and then in its time, a liking. I sometimes feel that one could find something good in even the worst person one knew, and that even the most repellent man must have some good points, if only we have wit and insight enough to discover them.

I have tried to sum up Miss Billie from these few days of more or less frequent companionship, and I find her an interesting conglomeration of contradictory qualities. First as to her virtues: She is fearless, honest with those she respects and from whom she expects honest dealing, and generous to a fault; as to her defects, if such they should be called, she is headstrong, quick and vicious of temper, too prone to follow her impulses, bad as well as good, extravagant, and oversophisticated. With all her hardness, and all her reputation as fast, I think she would be unswervingly true and loyal to one of whom she was very fond. But the quality which strikes one most of all is the sense of fairness, which shows itself even in her attitude toward Caroline. How often would one find a woman free from a trace of personal hostility toward an acknowledged rival who stood between her and the man she loved. Jealousy, with most of them, would be almost sure to show itself in malicious words or acts. But thus far I have detected nothing of the sort. Sometimes she watches Caroline with a wistful earnestness, which is quite touching, as if she would learn from observing her what may be the secret of the fascination she exerts over the doctor.

While we were talking I was tempted to draw her out. We sat where we could observe Caroline and her escort, who were having a hilarious time with Tommie, Lillian Barton, Reese, and Scott Green. Miss Barton and Caroline were giving an imitation of an argument between two well-known local characters, somewhat noted for their acrimonious attitude toward one another. Needless to say, the performance was a histrionic success, and provoked spasms of merriment in the onlookers, both by the excellence of the matter as well as the manner of the doing.

"What," said I, almost casually, "do you really think of Caroline Rhodes?" The question, the moment it was out, seemed such an idle one that I would have recalled it if I could, expecting, as I reasonably might, only a perfunctorily polite answer. But I was a little surprised when I got it—after a short pause, and a nervous laugh from the lady, who looked at me curiously with her penetrating eyes.

"Well, I can't affirm that I love Caroline overmuch these days, but if I must tell the truth, I shall have to admit that she is the squarest little girl I know. You can trust her with your money, your reputation, and even your life if she cares for you. What more could one say?"

"What more would one need to say," said I. "You're a good sport, Billie. One must surely give you that!"

She showed red a bit, I thought, even under her "war paint." "Thank you," she said simply. "Everybody, even I, must have some good points. I have never seen any fun in a fight which was not fair."

"Nor I," I answered. "It's a lot more fun hitting the other fellow when he is looking you in the eye." At this juncture our tête-à-tête was interrupted by Will Hale, who, as if to show his intent to make a third, brought over a chair and sat down by us. It was apparent that he had been drinking, though he was not the least bit defensive, but only somewhat too animated.

"What have you two been talking about all evening?" he queried, good-naturedly enough, but as if he really expected an answer. I recalled what I had heard and seen of Hale's interest in Billie.

"Men, and women, and things in general," I responded, without hesitation. Then I looked quickly at Billie, but her expression was one of the greatest serenity.

"We have been discussing the question of fairness in fighting. Do you believe one is ever justified in fighting unfairly?" I added.

Hale laughed noisily, as is his way when he has had a drop too much.

"You know the old saw about 'love and war,' don't you? The recent European unpleasantness is a precedent surely for the latter, and, as for the former, well—did you ever see women fight fairly when they fight at all?"

"How about *ladies*?" asked Miss Billie tartly.

"Ladies?" Hale laughed still louder. "It takes 'ladies' to give the crowning touch. Nowadays they use a hypodermic when you are not looking, instead of a dagger, as in the Middle Ages. You never know you are hurt until you drop. Oh, yes, for nice, fair, clean fighting, give me 'ladies' by all means!"

"You're a most objectionable person, Will Hale!" exclaimed Billie.

Hale laughed again.

"To change the subject somewhat, I came over to tell you that you are looking stunning tonight. That's the prettiest gown I've seen in many a moon. Don't you think so, Carr?"

"Miss Riddick," said I, "has already heard my views on her appearance in general, and her gown in particular. I quite agree with you."

Hale's methods being a trifle too direct for my taste, I was glad when the orchestra struck up once more.

The rest of the evening was very enjoyable. For sheer grace, feathery lightness, and "spirit of the dance," few women in any crowd could equal Tommie and Miss Riddick, and two or three of the dances I had with them were inexpressibly delightful. On one occasion Billie and I stopped just in a crowd of my own particular friends. Said Mrs. Morrow with a rather mischievous smile:

"There is one person in this room who is having the time of his life, and that is—Mr. Davy Carr. How is it, my friend?"

"Right you are," I responded with enthusiasm. "How could I help it?"

As I turned, almost involuntarily it seemed, toward Caroline, she turned her head away, and thrusting her arm quickly through Don Verney's, she said, with a laugh:

"Come on, Don, old dear, let's take a stroll!"

When I had taken Billie home, I dismissed the taxi, for I wanted the few blocks' walk in the frosty air, and I wanted to smoke. It was nearly two when I got in, and I was surprised to find Caroline standing in front of the grate fire which is always burning in the back parlor. Something told me to go right up to my room without seeing her, but a strange spirit of perversity seemed to take hold of me. So, instead of going up promptly, I strolled, with a carelessness which I now realized was feigned, into the parlor, with overcoat open and hat in hand.

Caroline glanced at me for a second, and then her gaze returned again to the dying fire, while she tapped idly with the toe of her little gold slipper on the fender, and held with either hand the folds of the coat which hung loosely from her shoulders. Once again—as before in the past few days—her beauty seemed to strike me full in the face, as it were, and I felt a curious mixture of embarrassment and irritation. Since something had to be said, I opened the conversation.

"Did you have a good time tonight?" Thus conventionally I began.

She looked up at me quickly, and I should almost say saucily—impudently. Then her eyes again sought the fire.

"Yes, I had a very good time, but no thanks to you, Mr. Carr."

It is impossible for me to convey to you in written words any adequate idea of the coldness and the cutting sarcasm of her tone. For a moment I hesitated, then I answered very calmly, so it seemed to me then.

"If you refer to my failure to get a dance with you, I think your remark is most unjust, and its tone quite uncalled for."

"Oh, you think so, do you?" was the very crisp rejoinder from the otherwise motionless figure in front of the grate.

"Yes, I think so."

A long silence—interminably long, so it appeared to me as I stood there beside her. Finally—

"Others—and some who are not quite nonentities—asked me more than once, and more than twice. Don Verney asked me three or four times before he got a dance."

"That was his privilege of course," I answered, coolly enough, though something within me warned me to say good night and take my leave before a possible explosion. But the imp of perversity which was hovering about urged me to stay, and I did.

"Neither time that I asked you did you give me the slightest encouragement to ask again. So uninterested were you that I hesitated even to ask you the second time."

"Indeed! I suppose you consider it kind in you to put it that way—to let me down easy, as it were. To give your due, I should expect you to do that, Mr. Carr, and I assure you I appreciate it. It's really much nicer than saying or intimating one is too busy with new friends to bother with the old. Don't you think so, Mr. Carr?"

Her tone was irritating, almost maddening. I had an almost irresistible desire to shake her until her teeth rattled. How is it that a woman can persist in reiterating what she does not believe, and could not believe, as if it were the chief article of her creed? I had heard it done before, many times, but that makes it no easier to endure in this case. Suddenly I seemed to lose myself, provoked beyond control by her cool, sarcastic manner. While I am not quite certain what happened, I shall put it down as I recall it now, to the very best of my ability. It does not sound quite rational, but, alas, I fear it is true.

I seized Caroline by both arms and shook her.

"Why do you persist in saying that?" I said. "You know it is not true."

"Let me go, Davy Carr, you hurt me!" She tried to free herself, but the heavy cloak impeded her.

Then some blind impulse seemed to seize me with violence and rushed me headlong to my own destruction. I let go her wrists, which I had grasped in the folds of the cloak, and holding her in a close embrace, I kissed her again and again. For one brief second in my delirium, it seemed that she yielded to my embrace, but suddenly every muscle seemed to stiffen and she became rigid in my arms.

"Let me go, Davy Carr, let me go!" she panted. "How dare you! How dare you! Oh, I hate you! I hate you!"

Brought to my senses, my arms relaxed their hold, and she wrenched herself free. Her face was ablaze. Without warning, she struck me with all her might with her left hand. The blow, centering its force in my right eye, blinded me completely, and then she struck me again, this time with her right hand, the set from her ring making a long, deep scratch on my left cheek running from my eye to mouth. When I was able to see again, I was alone in the room, and Caroline's fur coat lay in a heap on the floor just where it had fallen from her shoulders, and a few feet off her handbag and a handkerchief, signs of a hasty, headlong flight. My first impulse was, of course, to follow her, but a second's reflection showed me the futility of that, and then, suddenly, I felt almost ill. The scratch on my face burned fiercely, my eye pained me not a little. I slumped rather limply on the davenport, and my incurable propensity to make a jest, even at my own expense, asserted itself almost automatically, as it were.

"The little vixen—a regular fierce little two-fisted fighter!" I tried to smile.

Then I put my hand to my eye, and winced, and touched my handkerchief to the long, stinging scratch, and brought it away with streaks of red upon it. I piled up the beautiful coat, and held it at first idly, between my hands. The delicate fragrance of Fleurs d'Amour enveloped me until it seemed that I held Caroline herself in my arms. And then it struck me all in a heap what has been the matter with me all these days and weeks. What a purblind fool I have been, groping about with my eyes shut, when all I had to do was to open them and then look. But, true as I live and as I write these words, I never realized until that minute, sitting there before the dying fire in that still room, nursing my hurts, that I have been wildly in love with Caroline all this time. In trying to think it over calmly, and discover just when this distemper seized me, I find it difficult to disentangle things. But my present state is perfectly clear, and I see, too, that others have known it for some time—Don, for example, and you. Why did you not say something about it? Or did you think I knew, but was trying to keep it from you?

But what a mess my dullness has gotten me into! If I had realized before what was ailing me, I could have acted differently. But after my brutality of last night, I don't know how I am ever going to straighten things out. I really don't. If ever a woman was offended, Caroline is that woman. And God knows, I can't blame her. Even supposing she could forgive my brutality, could she care for me as I care for her? I wonder. Does she love Dr. King? Poor Billie Riddick—ah, that brings another pang! When I recall how I have been carrying on with her, it makes me sick! If Caroline ever cared for me, would not that have killed off any budding affection? Billie insists that Caroline does not love the doctor, but could not give satisfactory reasons for her faith. Tommie preserves a very discreet and noncommittal silence when approached on the subject. A shrug of her pretty brown shoulders is the most I have been able to get from her. So there you are!

I have been going over my diary since the painful event of last night, and I find that Caroline, when she seemed to like me most, treated me more like a brother than a possible lover. She has always thought me a slow coach, safe company, a personable escort, and all that, but not much fun. Since Thanksgiving she has changed. She has come to my room only on definite, and brief, errands, and she has seemed to take no more pleasure in the teasing pranks which used to delight her so much. As I look over the record, this change of attitude is almost exactly coincident with the return of Dr. King. The prospect is not a cheerful one. I have always prided myself on being a game loser, as you know, but this is different somehow. And then to end in such a disgusting mess. I wish I had gone to Columbia last week, as I originally planned to do. I see now why I stayed on, though up to last night I was not aware of my own motive for the delay.

What I am going to do, exactly, I don't quite know. I have been in the house all day, having 'phoned to the restaurant to send me in my lunch. My eye does not trouble me, for plenty of hot water and a nice witch hazel bandage fixed it all right. The scratch is not so easily camouflaged. I have kept it touched up all day, and it is fast losing its conspicuousness. But I should confess to you what I would not want to confess to anyone else, that I would rather face a nest of German machine guns than meet Mrs. Rhodes or Genevieve. Not that I think Caroline would say anything to them, but I should just feel horribly self-conscious, especially with this shrieking scratch down my cheek.

But I must see Caroline alone, if possible. She seems not to have been home all day, for I have not seen her or heard her since early morning. At about noon, when Mrs. Rhodes came up on some errand in the front room, she knocked at my closed door, and asked if I were ill. When I responded as cheerfully as I could that I was quite well, she went away satisfied.

I shall have to go out this evening, for I have an engagement to play cards at Lillian Barton's. As there are to be just eight of us, I dare not send regrets at this late hour without the very best of excuses. So it is up to me to make the best of it. Nothing by any chance escapes the sharp eyes of Lillian Barton, Don Verney, nor Mary Hale, for that matter. So I expect to be an object of interest this evening. What can be deduced by keen observation will be elicited by that crowd, you may be sure. Whether I am a match for them all, or not, time will tell.

In one way I am glad to have to go, for I think I should explode if I were shut up here all evening. I am sure I should.

7:30 P.M.

As this letter is so long already I think I shall mail it as I go out. If anything of supreme and vital concern occurs in the next few hours, I shall write you tomorrow. Who can tell what may happen? The air is electric! Up to this moment as I write, there has been neither sight nor sound denoting Caroline's presence in the house, nor have I seen or heard Tommie all day. That reminds me to warn you not to breathe one word of what I have told you to Tommie, at any rate not until I give you explicit permission. Things are bad enough as they are, and I cannot afford to risk complications.

Your disfigured but still smiling friend,

Davy

THIRTEEN

Love troubles. "Madame X" once more. What Billie Riddick thinks of the flappers. Don and his Mary.

Sunday, February 4

Dear Bob:

As I pen these lines I am still on Uneasy Street—to quote the slangy Miss Riddick. Several things have happened since I mailed you my last letter a week ago yesterday on my way to Lillian Barton's, but they are not such things as serve to make life more endurable. In a hackneyed phrase, "The plot thickens!"

To be sure I omit nothing, perhaps I might better begin at the beginning, and take things in order. My story starts, then, just after I had dropped your letter in the mailbox at the corner, and set out for Lillian's. As you may recall, Dr. King's office is two doors down from that very corner, and his car was standing at the curb as I passed, a sign that he was keeping his office hours. I was looking idly at the car when I almost collided with two people who were coming from the opposite direction, and who should it be but Caroline and Tommie.

Tommie stopped, of course, and greeted me warmly, but Caroline, with a look in my direction, walked over to the doctor's car and opened the door. Tommie explained that they were going out with Dr. King, and had decided, to save time, to sit in the car until his office hours were over, which would be in a few minutes. As she talked, she looked inquiringly at Caroline, and I gathered from her perplexity that the latter had said nothing to her about our little disagreement.

"Come and keep us company until Dr. King comes out," she added, "if you have nothing better to do."

But somehow I did not want to force myself on Caroline, and when I did see her, I wanted the interview to be without witnesses. Until I could see her alone, I preferred to see her not at all. So I thanked Tommie for her invitation, pleaded an engagement, and with my best bow took my leave, quite aware that the look of perplexity on Tommie's face had deepened, as Caroline showed, neither by word or sign, that she noticed me.

I did a lot of thinking as I moved on up the street, but it was motion in a circle and got me nowhere at all. I had planned to stop at Don's, and pick him up, but changed my mind and went instead straight to Lillian's, and so I arrived a little early. As during my walk I had been so deep in my reflection that I had forgotten to button my topcoat, the chill of the night had begun to strike in, so I enjoyed to the full the grateful warmth of the blazing wood fire in the big parlor, where the alternating light and shade played hide-and-seek in the dark corners. My hostess looked particularly handsome in the yellow light, her welcome was unusually cordial, and I began to be glad that I had come.

"Shall I snap on a light, or will the firelight suffice?" she asked as we came in from the hallway.

"I like nothing better than this," I answered. "It suits my mood perfectly."

"Oh, do you men admit moods? I thought that they were reserved exclusively for the weaker sex."

"Sometimes I wonder just which is the weaker sex," I responded. Then, after a pause, I continued, "I was afraid I might be too early, but I took the chance, hoping that I might not be too troublesome."

"You are never too early, my friend," said Miss Barton, with every appearance of sincerity. "It is nice to think you wanted to be early."

"But you may be busy with something or other. If you are, don't let me keep you. I can enjoy the firelight and—my own musings," I smiled.

"The 'something or other' can wait. But what have you on your mind?" She looked at me keenly.

I think I have discussed with you Miss Barton's perfectly uncanny faculty of "sensing" things. Now and then it is somewhat disconcerting, but on this occasion I was expecting a manifestation of it, and so was prepared.

"Cannot the power of perception, which tells you there is something on my mind, also tell you what it is?" I parried, smiling serenely.

"No, it does not carry that far," she said. "But I knew the moment I saw you in the hall that something was worrying you."

"You have sharp eyes," I said.

"Where my friends are concerned—yes. In your case it is easy to see that you have been puzzling over something for quite a while."

"Indeed! That is interesting."

"Yes, it *is* interesting." Miss Barton's brown eyes looked at me keenly, as she held the match for my cigarette, and then lighted one for herself. "And a great many people are interested," she added, as she tossed the match into the fireplace and idly watched it burn.

I took advantage of her momentarily averted gaze to look at

her. She is surely a beautiful woman, with her soft brown hair, her lovely color, and the graceful poise of her handsome head on the snowy shoulders. The hand, too, which held the cigarette, and the rounded arm, which gracefully flicked the ash toward the hearth, would not be far from the top in any beauty contest. But, for all that, I like Caroline's type of beauty best. And, as I sat there, I reconstructed her in my mind's eye, with her satiny brown skin, her raven hair, sloe-black eyes, and the dainty but substantial prettiness of her, from the slim fingertips to the *"petits pieds si adorés."* Lillian has a sparkle like champagne, but Caroline radiates a sweet, warm vitality which intoxicates no less than champagne. I had lost myself entirely in my dream, and must have been looking through or beyond my hostess when she brought me out of my trance in a jiffy.

"Gracious, Mr. Carr, whatever is it? I am not used to having gentlemen sit in my parlor, and forget my presence completely. You will have to give me the very best of excuses this time."

She laughed teasingly, but there was more of pique than of mirth in her tone.

"Did it look like a trance?" I asked, sparring for time to collect my wandering wits.

Just then the doorbell rang.

"I know you are glad," she said with a short laugh, as she rose and tossed her cigarette into the fire. For neither Reese nor Betty Morrow, it seems, approves of cigarette smoking in women, and Lillian is somehow afraid of Betty Morrow. As for Reese—well, she seems anxious not to displease him too much, so she respects his prejudices.

The newcomer turned out to be Reese, but the greetings had hardly been exchanged before the Hales arrived, and, in a few minutes, the Morrows and Don. When the card tables were brought out and the lights turned up, I had to stand the battery of sharp eyes turned on that long scratch on my cheek. Don broke the tension—and somehow I think he did it deliberately—by asking me how the fight came out. This caused a laugh all around, and gave me a chance for a humorous rejoinder, and so I did not have to lie to get out of it gracefully. In a moment or two we were busy playing bridge, and one might think the matter quite forgotten.

But I could not forget it, my mind was certainly not on the cards, and I played an execrable game, much to the annoyance of my partner, Mary Hale, who looked at me quizzically from time to time. Finally, in playing one hand, I failed to apply the most elementary rules of whist.

"I should like," said Mary Hale, with a smile, "to know just where Mr. Carr's mind really is. It certainly is not on this game."

This remark turned all eyes on me once more. Miss Barton chimed in with one of her characteristic sallies, which was so clever that in the laugh which it provoked I was momentarily forgotten, but after the merriment had subsided I caught her looking at me with more than casual interest in her keen glance. However, I survived the evening, and really did feel somewhat cheered by the lively company.

When I got home at a few minutes after eleven, there were several folks in the parlor, and, judging from the sounds, preparations for a supper were being made below stairs. Tommie was coming up from the dining room just as I turned to ascend the stairs after greeting Dr. King and one of the Clements girls, who were standing near the parlor door. Tommie greeted me as cordially as usual, and asked me if I would not join them. Before I could answer, Caroline appeared behind her, but when she saw me she turned quickly and went into the back parlor. So, naturally, I declined Tommie's invitation, with the excuse that I had just eaten, which was true, and that I was tired and sleepy, which was just about as true as one half of the conventional remarks one makes in gay society.

Between Saturday and Wednesday nothing of special note happened. It was plain that Caroline was avoiding me, and that she intended to give me no opportunity to see her alone. She goes early every evening to her classes at the University, and when she returns remains in her room, unless Dr. King comes. It may seem strange that I have been unable to see her, but it is nevertheless true. By Wednesday I had made up my mind that I should not let her put me off any longer, so on that evening, I sat resolutely in my room until she returned from the University. This was about ten minutes of nine. I knew that Mrs. Rhodes was down in the dining room, and that Genevieve was out. The moment seemed favorable. So I plucked up courage enough to descend the stairs, and knock at Caroline's door.

"What is it?" The voice was hard and incisive.

"It's Davy," I said. "I want very much to talk to you for a few minutes. Won't you come down to the back parlor? I shan't keep you long. Please come!"

There was a short silence, while I stared at the unwinking panels of the cold, unresponsive door. Then came her answer, in the same hard, incisive tone, and, to judge from the sound of her voice, she had not moved from her first position.

"I can't come down now, for I am dressing to go out, but I have no desire to talk to you anyway, Mr. Carr."

It was like a slap in the face, I assure you, and it's the most I have been able to get from her since Friday a week ago.

On this same Wednesday, after Caroline's rude rebuff, I returned to my room quite disconsolate, and was smoking and, between puffs, as it were, chewing the rather bitter end of reflection, when I heard the telephone ring in the lower hall, and then my name was called by Mrs. Rhodes. I hurried downstairs, and was surprised to hear the voice of "Madame X."

"Hello, Mr. Davy, don't you want to join us tonight? Our little Wednesday crowd is expected in a few minutes. Some lively folks will be here, and I know you will enjoy it."

Under ordinary circumstances, I presume I should have some excuse for declining, but, longing as I did for some distraction, I accepted with eagerness. As I felt at that moment, the livelier the crowd, the better I should like it. So a little after ten I made my appearance, and I assure you the affair was quite as advertised. Except our special friend and the two Baltimore people, all of those mentioned in connection with the famous Sunday supper of three or four weeks ago were present, with several additions. One notable person was the chap Johns, whom I think you met at the Benedicts' ball during the holidays. He had been drinking too much on that occasion, and he was in the same condition on this. There were two or three flappers present, with whom he danced constantly.

When I first entered, I was a little scandalized to see a mature man, supposedly of some class, deporting himself in such a manner with such young girls, and I was a little shocked to realize that "Madame X" would tolerate their presence. But after I watched them dance awhile, and saw them drink, and caught a few fragments of their conversation, I decided it was we maturer folks who needed protection. For of all the damned little hussies you ever saw, they were quite the most tiresome. If they are a sample of the present crop, Heaven help us!

As types—as such they were—they interested me, and I studied them all evening, but it remained for Billie Riddick to sum them up in a few trenchant words. Just before eleven o'clock three or four college boys came in and of course that settled the party for me. I was just meditating what excuse I should give my hostess for such an early departure when in came Billie Riddick. So I decided to stay a few minutes longer. We had a couple of dances together, and during an intermission I asked her what she thought of the flappers.

The saucy Billie regarded the two who were performing across the room from where we sat. After a few moments of silence, she spoke.

"If they had any manners, one could excuse their morals, and if they had any morals, one could forgive their manners, or, if they had any sense, one might overlook both the other things. As it is, they're a total loss, in my opinion!"

While we were talking, Will Hale came in feeling pretty "rosy" to begin with, and, judging from the way he began on the punch bowl, it would not be long before he would be more than "rosy." As he attached himself to Billie Riddick, I took advantage of his coming to hunt up my hat and coat, and took a rather cavalier leave. It was nice to get out in the fresh air, and to walk alone under the brilliant winter stars.

Mary Hale is ill, and our good friend Don has been like one possessed of a hundred imps of unrest. If I had had any doubts as to the depth of his regard for her, I should have them no longer. The white bears at the zoo have nothing on him when it comes to restlessness. Mrs. Hale had been ill for two or three days when first I heard of it, and on Thursday noon I dropped in to see Don to inquire about her. He was on the point of going out as I arrived, and asked me if I should mind accompanying him on one or two errands.

So we walked about the downtown district while he made purchases. He spent a half hour at a bookstore, making a selection from the recent novels. He usually knows very definitely what he wants, but on this occasion he seemed unusually hard to please.

"I want something for a friend who is ill," he said, "something cheerful, of course. A romantic love story, maybe, or, if you have something with a touch of humor, that would be nice. But it must be good—nothing cheap or trashy."

The clerk, who was a most obliging young person, suggested a dozen best-sellers, but Don had a very definite objection to most of them, and somewhat vaguer doubts as to the rest.

"No," he said, in answer to a suggestion of the clerk involving one or two of the most approved works of the most advanced type of realism, "they won't do. I want something clean and normal. They are for Mary," he added, turning to me. "I could not give her any of that rotten stuff, could I? Help me find something, won't you?"

So after much hunting we finally located two books which would pass muster, and when I insisted on adding a third to the package on my own account, Don was as pleased as if I had made *him* a present.

Then we stopped at the corner newsstand, where my companion bought all the latest magazines, a real armful. I wondered if these, too, were for Mary Hale, but of course, I did not ask. Our next stop was at the best florist on F Street, where Don ordered the most beautiful roses he could find, and I a bunch of sweet peas. Then we wandered along the street, talking and looking in shop windows. I supposed our errands were over, but I was mistaken, for on our walk we noted a most attractive window display of nuts, fruits, and candies. After a few moments of silent looking, Don went in, and I followed, like the faithful Achates. He seemed bent on buying everything in the shop, and, as it was not my province to make comments, I merely looked on with keen interest. Some of the things he ordered sent to Mary Hale's, and some to his own address. Then we divided up our remaining parcels, and walked uptown together.

That evening I called at his lodgings, and was told to come right up. Don was writing, and resting against a stack of books before him was a beautiful portrait of Mary Hale. It was a stunning picture, and I had never seen it before. Indeed, I had never before seen any photograph of her in his room.

To my comment on the picture he answered:

"I got lonesome tonight, and brought it out for company. It is beautiful, is it not? *I* think it is the most beautiful picture in the world, but I suppose my judgment might be called biased, eh?"

Then we got to smoking and talking, and, as I showed a disposition to discuss the original of the portrait, he seemed in no wise loath. It was touchingly intimate, too much for me to repeat even to you. This much I can say, it was an eloquent tribute to the lovely lady with the interesting gray eyes.

As I said above, Don was writing when I came in, and the table was littered with papers and books, and his famous diary was open in front of him. As I looked interested, Don pushed the papers toward me. They were some of those random thoughts which he delights to jot down for his own amusement. One attracted me, not so much by its contents, as by its title, or rather, I should say by the combination of title and contents. I asked Don if I might copy two or three bits, and he said I might, so I append it for your edification. Here it is:

THE SUMMIT OF LIFE

The boardwalk stretched away into the darkness, flanked on either side by the soft sand. She leaned heavily on his too-

willing arm, and so narrow was the walk that they had to keep very close together, and he could feel the warm contact of her body against him. She held both arms clasped over his forearm. He looked under the big hat, and down at the beautiful face, which showed so pale, so pale in the gathering darkness, and, in the smile of love which greeted him he savored for the first time the joy of this world and the world to come. The winking lights in the cottages they passed seemed to understand, and to flash a friendly greeting. They two were, so it seemed, in the midst of countless friends, and yet alone—as alone as Alexander Selkirk on his uncharted island. Alone! She and he, alone! What a thought! As the realization of it welled up in his consciousness, as her beloved hands clasped his arm still closer, and as she returned his look of love with one of absolute trust and absolute surrender, he knew, indeed, that for this one moment of all time and all eternity, he stood, godlike, upon the topmost pinnacle of life!

I wonder if this bit will pique your interest as it did mine, and I wonder—but what's the use? Besides, there are times when it is neither discreet nor friendly to wonder too much, *n'est-ce pas, mon ami?*

My affair is as yet in status quo. If you are one of the righteous, pray for me, for Heaven knows I need it just about now. I caught a glimpse of Thomasine this evening, and she stopped long enough to send you her very best regards.

Yours, in deep trouble,

Davy

FOURTEEN

The pangs of unrequited love. Davy packs his trunk.
The vainest of all vain things—vain regrets.

Monday, February 12

Dear Bob:

It is very late. I have just finished the task of getting my things in some kind of order preliminary to packing for the long trip South. I note that I say "finished," but that is not quite correct—I have just *stopped* because I am tired and "out of sorts." There is still much to do. Never before have I been in such a mood, my friend. I trust you may be spared such an experience. It may perhaps give you an idea of my state of mind when I tell you that for the first few minutes after Thomasine showed me her ring, my only feeling was one of almost unalloyed *envy*. When you reflect how fond I am of you and how deep is my affection for Tommie, you can plumb, approximately at least, the depths of my dejection. Then, too, I had so long looked forward to the time of your engagement, for I foresaw weeks ago that it was coming, coming none the less surely, if slowly, and yet I got out of it for the first moments no shred of joy, but only just the bitterness of envy. I am ashamed of myself as I write it down, and maybe it is just because I am ashamed that I do confess it and write it. Of course I rebounded quickly from this extreme of baseness, and, my ordinary normal nature asserting itself, I was properly and sincerely glad, though I fear that Tommie was a bit surprised and hurt at the somewhat conventional tone of my first words of congratulations. She looked at me very queerly. Utterly cast down as I was, I caught that look, and it brought me to my usual senses. So I acted as a normal being should when one of the loveliest girls in the world shows him the ring which symbolizes her betrothal to his dearest friend. As might be expected, I tried to make up for the most unnatural coldness of my first words, and succeeded so well that she immediately brightened up, and the look of surprise faded quickly from her eyes—*almost* the most beautiful, the most honest eyes in the world. I know you will understand and pardon that "*almost.*" I congratulate you, Bob, from the bottom of my heart, and I think you are the luckiest man I know. Nothing could make me happier than this, except the quite impossible happening that the girl that I am mad about, and who evidently despises me, should open her heart and consent to look with favor on me.

As I said in my opening lines, I have been putting things in order preliminary to packing up. This preparation process was necessary, for some things go in my trunk, some in my bag, and some are to be boxed and marked for shipment by freight. I have asked Mrs. Rhodes to let me pay for my room for two months after I leave, in the event that I should find it necessary to return here for a short time. I have no idea how long I shall be in Columbia and Charleston, for so much depends on what luck I have. If the records are rich in grist for my mill, I may find it profitable to remain longer. As to the islands along the South Carolina coast, that special quest should not take many days. When that is done, and sufficient material collected, I shall want to go somewhere to work it into shape. It is possible that I may return here for that, but unless the atmosphere changes a great deal, I imagine it might be a most unprofitable venture. So disturbed have I been for days on end that my work has suffered a great deal. If such a condition should persist, it would be far better, I think, to go elsewhere. Don't you agree with me? I am wondering if one of the small towns near New York—in Jersey, up the Hudson, or on Long Island—would not give me the quiet I need, with the chance of running into the city whenever I wished. Think it over, won't you?

Sometimes it appears as if I have been here but a few short days, and then again, when I reflect on the multitude of friends I have made, the functions I have attended, and the work I have accomplished, it seems a long, long time since last September. I am sure now, if I can judge from the exquisite torture I am undergoing these days, that I have never been in love before. I have only *thought* I was. I can no more get Caroline out of my mind than I can stop breathing by merely taking thought. I know you wonder why I have not come to a settlement of some kind with her, but there are two good reasons why I have not. In the first place, I am deadly afraid of the outcome of such an interview. I can readily understand the feelings of a man who is convinced that he has a mortal malady, but is afraid to undergo an examination to settle the matter pro or con. I am reasonably sure Caroline does not love me, certainly not in any such wise as I love her, but I just have not the nerve to hear her say so. As long as I don't ask, I can at least hope, and while there is hope, life is still worth living. Then again, even if I had the nerve to face the music boldly, there is, short of using actual force, no way in which I could have obtained an interview with Caroline. As I have said before, I don't feel equal to talking to her confidentially in the midst of a crowd of people, and she just won't let me see her under any other conditions. The last three times I have begged for a hearing she has said, with a coldness which is so unlike her that it cuts me like a knife, "I have told you more than once that I don't want to talk with you, Mr. Carr!" And she has shown me so plainly that my presence is obnoxious to her that there is nothing a self-respecting man can do but clear out and let her alone. This I have done so far. I have thought of writing, too, and have made several attempts at starting, but it was so unsatisfactory that I gave up trying, and decided to reserve it for a last resort.

Last night I took a notion to read over my diary before turning in, and what a host of delightful memories it brought, or memories which should be delightful if it were not for the feeling of sadness and regret which seems to tinge everything in these latter days. I realized, in reading over this record of my Washington life, that Caroline has always had a warm place in my heart, even when I was utterly unconscious of it. The events of each day, after I had been a week or two in this house, are sown thickly with references to her, and few dates lack completely any mention of her. I remarked, too, a little thing of which I was quite unconscious at the time of writing. It will interest you, I think, though maybe it is purely accidental. In the earliest references to her, I always entered her as "C. R.," later further abbreviated to "C." About the first of December, I note that all the references are to "Caroline," written out in full, and that from that time to this, her name is no longer abbreviated. Are you psychologist enough to interpret that?

I was almost appalled when this evening I began to collect and assort, for further preservation, or for consignment to the wastebasket, as the case might be, all the programs, cards, invitations, and mementos of various kinds which I have accumulated in my five months' stay in this town, to see how many had to do with Caroline. Though not conscious—I can swear to that—of collecting them as such, I don't believe I threw away a single thing, not even a scrap of paper, which referred to her. Among these keepsakes, I note the following: several handkerchiefs, all of them embroidered daintily with "C.R.," and having the faintest trace of the Fleurs d'Amour sachet; a ring; five dance cards; a paper napkin with the autographs of Caroline, Tommie, Lillian Barton, Mary Hale, Don, and several other folks; another napkin with a note from Caroline scribbled in one corner; the faded remains of a red rose which she wore in her hair at the fancy-dress ball the Saturday night after Thanksgiving; a bunch of violets she put in a little vase on my table about the same time; a gold automatic pencil which she gave me; and about ten personal notes.

I experienced a curious sort of painful pleasure in reading the latter over, and noting their almost *affectionate* familiarity—I think I do not exaggerate when I use this phrase to characterize them.

One is as follows:

Very dear old Godfather:

Just a little scribble to say that the Merry Coterie is going to have a "shout" at Sophie Burt's Thursday evening, and you are expected by

Votre affectueuse filleule,

Caroline

Another reads:

Dear Old Grouchy:

What is the matter with you anyway? Tommie says you don't seem to understand that we are looking for you at the dinner party tonight. Such a formal gentleman you are! What did you expect—an engraved invitation handed in on a silver tray? Did you think that Tommie and I discussed all the details of an affair of that kind before you, unless we expected to invite you? How do you get that way? Of course *it would not be a party without* you, *Old Bear!*

Having used up all my question marks and exclamation points, I must stop. I hope, however, that I have made myself clear.

Your devoted godchild,

Caroline

P. S. I agree with Tommie. In some things most men are blind, and those that are not blind are feebleminded.

A third, which accompanied a gift of a copy of Dorland's *Age of Mental Virility*, reads:

Godfather Dear:

I had to go to Lowdermilk's today to get a French text, and happened to see this little book on a bargain table. It seemed so exactly the kind of thing you would like that I ventured to get it for you. It has one advantage over your beloved Westermarck—it is shorter. At any rate, I trust that it will contribute something to the cultivation of your massive intellect, which I properly admire as a dutiful godchild should. A very pretty friend of yours says, however, that she thinks you would be lots more fun if you would cultivate your heart. *A word to the wise!*

Your affectionate ward,

Caroline

It has just occurred to me that you are not as interested as I am in the tenor of these notes, and I shall spare you any further renderings. Most of the others are much in the same vein. When I contrast their natural and unstudied warmth and friendliness with the lady's present attitude toward me, I could tear my hair. Then, apparently, I was indifferent. Now, when I would give a little bit of my immortal soul for a smile or a kind word, I get nothing but cold words and averted looks. Isn't life just like that?

You suggest in your last letter that it is inexplicable that a woman could change so completely in a such a short time. Inexplicable or not, she *has so changed,* and it would be a little consolation if I could persuade myself that the change had taken place following my very outrageous conduct of the other evening. But it began sometime before that, as you yourself must admit, for you will recall at least two instances during the Christmas holidays in which the lady showed temper toward me. I must say that I don't understand it at all. What I have done that could have offended her, or changed her opinion of me, prior to the one overt act of the other night, is a complete mystery.

But I won't burden you any further with my troubles, at any rate not in this letter. Let me charge you once more, in all seriousness, not to communicate anything I have told you to Tommie. I realize you will be under a special temptation to do so, but I ask your forbearance and patience for a little longer. Something must happen soon, but the whole affair is at such a critical stage that I have a really maudlin fear of a possible bad result from the intervention of some well-meaning friend. That's why I have not let out a syllable to anyone but you, much as I trust Tommie and Mary Hale and Don Verney, and friendly as they are to me.

Let me close with something pleasant. It is a beautiful ring, Bob, and it is well in place on Thomasine Dawson's hand. If ever a girl was genuine, honest, high-minded, "true blue," it is Tommie, and she has mental and physical charms far beyond most women. Next to my mother and Caroline, she stands before all women in my heart, and before all men but you, and I had accorded that place before I knew that you cared so much for her. Can I say more? I repeat—you are the luckiest of the lucky dogs! I wish for you both all the best things that life can give to mortals here below, and my wish is not mere words, as you well know. I feel that I am guilty of no indelicacy when I say that Thomasine loves you very dearly, and is always glad to talk about you, indeed that is about the only subject which seems to interest her very deeply these days. Oh, fortunate mortal!

I forgot to tell you what happened when I asked Mrs. Rhodes to keep my room for me for two months after my departure. Well, the dear lady did not want to hear of letting me pay.

"But," said I, "it is just as if I were occupying it. I am preempting it just as surely. You could let it to no one else."

"I am not planning to rent it to anyone else," said she. "It is yours whenever you want it."

Exactly what that last sentence might imply, I cannot see, but the upshot of the whole matter was that Mrs. Rhodes finally compromised the matter with me by letting me pay for half the usual rental for the two months in question. When I stood up to leave the room—we were in the back parlor—she came over and joined her hands about my arm.

"Davy," she said, and it was the first time she had ever called me anything but Mr. Carr. "Davy, we have enjoyed having you, and you are welcome in this household whenever or however you choose to come."

I thanked her in some embarrassment, and went up to my room, reflecting somewhat sadly on the fact that in this mortal life it is so often the case that we can have warm good wishes and kind words from all but the one from whom we most desire them.

I guess I might stop here and turn in. I am not getting any too much sleep these days, and I am beginning to feel it. I hope I may have more cheerful news next time. At any rate I hope to have something more interesting to record than this dead level of monotonous misery. Almost any change would be desirable. If you suffer in reading this letter, console yourself with the kind thought that it has relieved me somewhat to write it.

Davy

Our old friend Jeffreys in the spotlight once more. Caroline to the rescue. Last hours.

Wednesday, February 14

Dear Bob:

For a few minutes last night, I really thought I was going to have some pleasing news to tell you, but Fate was only playing a practical joke on me to see how I should take it. My news then, while interesting, is not especially pleasing.

There was a little dance given at Carroll's by the Merry Coterie, and the usual crowd was present. It was lively, as their affairs always are, and one of the noisiest and most frivolous of that noisy and frivolous bunch proposed going to a newly discovered cabaret which was touted as being especially obnoxious. Most of us did not want to go, but one or two of the women raised so much "sand" about it that the rest finally caved in, and so we went. There were more than a dozen of us including the

Dills, the Burts, Caroline and Tommie, Billie Riddick, Reese, Dr. King, Verney, Scott Green, your humble servant, and three or four others. Our party took up four tables. I need not describe the place, for it was like most of the others, except perhaps to say that it was decidedly second-rate. It was pretty well filled, and there was a plenty of bootleg liquor in evidence. However, it was orderly enough, on the surface at least, when we entered.

We had not long been seated when Verney stepped on my foot to attract my attention, and, following the direction of his eyes, whom should I see seated over in the corner, with his old familiar pair of Baltimore cronies, but Jeffreys, he of the faultless tailoring and the golden smile! By a curious coincidence, his two friends saw me just as I looked, and so did two other persons seated at an adjoining table. These last seemed familiar, but I could not place them, and I have since come to the conclusion that they were at the party in Baltimore the night Jeffreys and I fell out so hard. I did not like to stare, so, after one look, I dropped my eyes, but Verney, who had not the same reason for being cautious, kept his eyes on the party, and, in a low tone told me from moment to moment what was going on.

According to him, they were all drinking heavily, and two or three of them were already pretty far gone. Soon the rest of our party noticed the group which so interested us, and one or two, to my regret, were at some pains to turn about in their seats to get a good look.

Personally, I am not easily intimidated by a crowd of sober men, even if they are hostile, but any man who is filled with this modern moonshine is a source of danger wherever he may be, for he is a trifle less responsible than a maniac for what he does. He is filled with a wild spirit of recklessness unrestrained by any feeling of responsibility whatever. As Jeff and his friends drank, it was apparent from their glances that they were discussing our party. Several of us became aware of it. Tommie, usually so calm, was noticeably nervous. Caroline was at another table, and as her back was turned to me, I could not tell how the situation affected her. After a bit Jeff's party grew noisy, and certain remarks made in a loud tone were plainly intended for our group. At Don's instigation, the word was passed around that on a given signal, we should withdraw, leaving Don and Dr. Dill to pay the check. I wanted to stay with them, but the others would not hear of it.

"You are the one against whom Jeff's malevolence is directed, and it would be inviting trouble for you to stay," said Don in his quiet, insistent tone. "They won't make any trouble for the doctor and me."

So, as was sensible, I agreed, and we all arose at about the same moment. I think we should have gotten out without any trouble, if Fate had not decreed that Sophie Burt should lose her handbag, one of those gold mesh arrangements which are tolerably costly, and which their owners are likely to cherish accordingly. Besides the bag itself, there were the contents thereof, a matter of fifty-odd dollars and several valuable trinkets. So Sophie, who is excitable anyhow, made quite a fuss, and in a few seconds our quiet, undemonstrative exit, as planned by the wily Don, was converted into an excited jamboree of persons looking hastily under chairs and tables, and each one in the way of all the others. While we were in the midst of this, with Don and Dr. Dill looking on with evident impatience, our wild search was interrupted by a harsh voice, and the calling of my name followed by a string of abuse, all of which I did not hear, I am glad to say, and which I would have no occasion to repeat if I had heard it. After a second everybody stopped and turned toward the speaker. We were all more or less startled, because there were outcries from patrons seated near at hand, many of whom jumped up and ran for the door, knocking over tables and chairs in their hasty exit. In a moment I had taken in the cause of the general consternation.

Jeffreys was standing a few feet from me, with eyes inflamed and wild, face flushed, and features contorted into a wicked grimace. This sight did not worry me especially, but my pulse dropped a beat or two when I saw in his right hand the dull blue steel of a long army automatic. To you, who have looked down the barrel of one of those devilish things in time of war, I have no need to say that it was not a happy moment, for well I knew that if once he locked his finger on that trigger, somebody in the crowded room was going to be badly hurt, unless, indeed, a miracle should happen.

The women screamed, and scattered right and left. After the first shock, my wits commenced to work fast, and I figured that my best move would be to throw one of the small chairs at him, and follow it up fast. Of course I have taken much longer in the telling of this than it took in the happening. I had just placed my hand on the back of a chair when there was a cry and a scuffle behind me, something flashed between me and the chair knocking it out of my hand, a sturdy little figure planted itself squarely in front of me, and I was aware of a glossy black head against my chin and the faint odor of Fleurs d'Amour in my nostrils.

"Drop that gun, you coward! Are you afraid to fight like a man?" Caroline panted, her breath coming quickly and with evident effort.

The menacing blue steel barrel now pointing straight at Caroline galvanized me into life, and grasping her by the shoulders, I swung her about, aware as I did so that if Jeffreys would only fire at that moment, he would have a point-blank target. What he would have done in another second I have no means of knowing, for as I braced myself to feel the tearing of a bullet through my vitals, something hit Jeffreys from the side like a catapult, and he went down with a crash, while the pistol fell far from him. My good friend Scott Green had executed a flank movement with the happiest results. The proprietor of the cabaret took possession of the automatic and threatened to telephone the police if Jeffreys and his friends did not leave. Jeffreys himself was a bit groggy from Green's vicious tackle, and suffered himself to be led away unprotestingly.

Order being restored somewhat, we resumed the search for Sophie Burt's bag, and had about concluded either that she had lost it outside or that someone had taken advantage of the confusion to pocket it, when suddenly she exclaimed, "Here it is in my pocket!" and fished it out from some mysterious recess in her fur coat. There was some low murmuring from the men, and a laugh from the women, and then suddenly Caroline dropped into a chair, pale as a ghost, with everyone looking on more or less startled.

"It's nothing—just a normal reaction," said Dr. Dill, coolly, and he whipped out a little pocket flask and held a spoonful of something to her lips. In a few moments the color flooded her face as she realized that we were all standing watching her. She laughed unsteadily, rubbed her eyes, and finally rose to her feet.

"Too much excitement for one of my tender upbringing," she said, with a saucy laugh. "Come on, folks, let's go home! And, Sophie, the next time you bring that bag, please let Will carry it."

This sounded natural, and we all started for the door, laughing. The trip home was uneventful. I escorted Tommie, and she was very silent. At the door she merely gave me her usual friendly handshake, and went in with no more than a "Good night, Davy." In fact, she acted all the time as if her mind were busy elsewhere. When I reached home, the house was dark, and a light showed through the transom over Caroline's door. I was determined that she should not prevent me from thanking her for what she had done, or tried to do, to protect me in the dangerous emergency of the evening, so I sat down at my table and expressed my feelings as well as I could, and added a line to voice the hope that she would let me thank her face-to-face, and also let me say what was on my mind with regard to our misunderstanding. I wanted to add more, and it required all my resolution to keep from putting down all that was in my heart. But I refrained, and I feel now that the event shows my wisdom in so doing. I wrote and destroyed three letters before I finally succeeded in satisfying myself reasonably well. Then I went to bed with a happier heart than I had had for many, many days.

But, alas, my comparative happiness was destined to be of short duration. I left the note on the hall table this morning when I went out. Tonight when I returned, I found this brutally curt little note in its place:

Dear Mr. Carr:

There is nothing for which to thank me. We are quits now, that's all, and I am so glad, for I dislike intensely being under obligation to—anyone. As to the "misunderstanding" to which you refer, you must be laboring under a delusion. The misunderstanding is all yours, for I am sure that on my part there is none. I understand you perfectly.

Sincerely yours,

Caroline Rhodes

P.S. I almost forgot to say that Miss Riddick telephoned this afternoon, and I asked that you call her as soon as possible after you came in. I promised to give you the message.

To say that I was stunned by this note is to put it mildly, very mildly indeed. It was like a slap in the face. I had been hoping all along that Caroline's attitude, so unnatural and so unlike her, would change, so to speak, overnight. This note bordered on discourtesy, to use no stronger word. What am I to infer from the dash inserted between the words "obligation to" and "anyone"? What, except that she meant to write "you," and it sounded so insulting that she decided to substitute "anyone," but wanted me without fail to realize that it was only a substitution for politeness's sake. Under the existing circumstances there can be nothing between us but the fondest formalities of speech. It is embarrassing to be in her company, for, knowing we have been such good and familiar friends, everyone notices the change. Already several people have asked me what is the matter between us, and I have lied most glibly about it. Strange to say, neither Tommie, nor Mary Hale, nor Don Verney have said a word to show that they have noticed anything, but each one of the three has *looked* volumes. Tommie looks really puzzled. I would give my head almost to know what Caroline has said to her. However, as I have remarked before on the same subject, there is absolutely no forecasting with any accuracy just what Miss Caroline Rhodes will or will not do. She is no conventional doll baby, who cries or shuts her eyes on someone else's motion. She has a mind of her own, originality, and courage. I don't know anyone who could better carry out a fixed purpose, and keep her own counsel while doing it. This is not the first time in our acquaintance that I have felt this about her. Indeed, she is a type of whom Jane Austen never dreamed, for all her dainty feminine beauty. All of which only makes me feel just that much more certain that she is the one woman in the world for me. What I shall do without her, it frightens me to think.

Thursday

My boxes are filled, nailed up, and duly marked, and my trunk practically packed. I have decided to stay over for the party given by Les Oiseaux tomorrow night. As it bids fair to be the smartest affair of the year, everyone says I should not miss it, so I shall wind up my Washington sojourn in a blaze of glory, and pull out Saturday morning, early. As I want to examine certain records in the State Library at Richmond, I have bought my ticket for that place and will go through from there to Columbia, taking only hand baggage, and having my trunk expressed from here after I have decided what I shall do. I am restless as a lost soul. The big white bears in the zoo have nothing on me, Bob. I seem to be spending most of my hours marking time. At this moment I should pick up my bag and go, if it were not that I have to be Thomasine's escort to the party. I have regretted a hundred times today that I decided to stay over. I suppose that, away in the back of my consciousness, there is a glimmering hope that some miracle may happen. As things look now nothing short of a miracle would be of any service to me, for I have about come to the conclusion, reluctantly, that whether or not Caroline despises me, at any rate, she does not love me.

Don Verney is a queer chap. He knows there is something wrong, but, for all we are together quite often and are such good friends, he has never said a word. I have taken one or two walks with him lately, and he has spent most of the time smoking, with an occasional quick side glance at me, and now and then a queer throaty noise like a grunt. Yesterday I was in his room, waiting while he dressed to go to a Valentine dinner at the Dills'. He was all ready to go, with hat and topcoat on, when he stopped me at the door while he looked up a passage in the Bible, which it seemed would not wait. As Don does queer little things like that, I only smoked my cigarette and waited patiently. He found the place he wanted and read it attentively, puffing his cigarette violently and giving his characteristic little grunting sound. He was making a mark in the margin of the book when the telephone rang, and while he answered it, I strolled over to the table to see what it was in the Bible which could so interest him. It was open at the thirty-second chapter of Genesis, and there was a pencil mark opposite the last line of the twenty-sixth verse, which reads: "I will not let thee go except thou bless me!" Then I strolled back to the door and waited.

In a moment Don hung up the receiver, and we went out together. He said not a word as we walked along. As we turned into the walk leading up to Dr. Dill's door, he spoke suddenly.

"Jacob was a most interesting character. He was the first 'go-getter.' He must have been an American. He was 'strong even against God.' No one beat him without a real fight. I like him."

Friday evening

Well, there is nothing more for me to do in this town, except escort Thomasine to Les Oiseaux. Under normal circumstances I should look forward to it with such pleasure, but I assure you that under existing conditions it is sheer misery—at any rate, in anticipation. I don't know whether or not I have done the wise thing, but I have not told a soul that I am actually going tomorrow morning. Most of my friends think that I shall go in a few days. On Wednesday, the Morrows invited me to dinner for Sunday, but I begged off on some pretext or other, and said nothing about leaving before that date. So they said they would see me at Lillian Barton's Sunday evening, and I let it go at that. I dislike good-byes intensely anyway, and in the present state of my feelings, they would be nothing but torture to me. How I am going to leave without saying good-bye to Caroline, I have not yet figured out. But the bare thought of a cold look such as she has given me more than once in these latter days is more than I can endure. So I *think* I shall go without saying anything, and then write her what I have to say. I am counting on seeing Mrs. Rhodes and Genevieve in the morning. They will be early astir, since it is Saturday, and Caroline will be sleeping late, after the party. As for Tommie, I have made up my mind to tell her, and put her on oath not to divulge my secret. If she says she won't tell, she won't.

As I write, Tommie has just come in. I can hear her voice from below stairs. She promised to come and give Caroline the "once-over" in her new party gown. I know there are going to be some beautifully dressed women there tonight. I wish you might be here, for more than one reason.

Tommie interrupted me just as I finished the preceding sentence, to say that she would be ready to go in a half hour, and that Caroline is going to be the belle of the ball, unless, to use Tommie's own words, "the men are stone blind." Then, when I said I was writing to you, she added, "Give all my love to Bob, and tell him I am going to miss him a whole lot tonight." She started to leave the room, then stopped suddenly, and came over to me, and sat on the arm of my big chair, just as Caroline used to do. She put her right arm over my shoulder and with her left hand tilted up my chin and looked me hard in the eyes. It took all my willpower to return her gaze without flinching.

"What's the matter, Davy dear? Something has been worrying you for days, and it is beginning to worry me, too. Can't you tell me?"

I had a dreadful temptation to tell her everything. But that innate quality of stubbornness, which seems a permanent attribute of the Carr family, whispered to me to hold on a while longer. So I forced a smile, and shook my head.

"Not even *me,* Davy?"

When Tommie said that, I almost succumbed, for she so seldom uses the power of her personal charm that when she does, the effect is well nigh irresistible.

"No, Tommie, not even *you,* and when I say that, I am saying about all there is to be said. But it is sweet in you to be interested, and to ask."

"It is nothing more than natural. I am very fond of you, Davy—for three reasons."

"Thanks! *Three* is a lot, Tommie! Name the first one."

"You!" she responded, smiling. I sketched a bow as gracefully as I could from a sitting posture.

"Thank you kindly, dear lady! Name the second."

"Bob Fletcher."

"The third."

Tommie smiled and shook her head. "I can't tell you that," she said. Nor could I budge her from her determination. She sat for a moment looking at me, with her pretty forehead in a pucker. Then she ran her fingers caressingly through my hair.

"Davy, Bob says you beat the original army mule for stubbornness, and sometimes I think he is right. What a hard, unyielding jaw you have, my friend." And as she spoke, she rapped playfully with her velvety little fist on what Dr. Morrow would call my inferior maxillary, and leaving her perch on the arm of my chair, hastened downstairs to Caroline.

So Caroline is to be the belle of the ball. God knows I know that without being told, and I might be happier tonight if I were stone blind. For it's going to be torture to see her swinging on another man's arm, and dancing with other men, and receiving their admiring glances, and laughing at their flattering speeches, while I have to sit like an owl—it was an owl, was it not, to which she compared me?—and eat my heart out without even one of the easy smiles she lavishes upon all comers! Feel sorry for me, Bob! I feel sorry for myself!

I am going to smoke now until Tommie calls me. I would give half of my kingdom for a drink, but I have a particular dislike for a man who drinks before going to a dance with nice women, so I shall have to buck up without using any stimulant. Thank goodness, in a few hours it will be over! After that—*quien sabe, amigo*? I feel, somehow, like a man with his foot on the lower step of the gallows, or like the gladiators entering the arena and saluting the emperor: *"Nos morituri vos salutamus!"* It is nine forty-five, and Tommie will be calling me in a few minutes, I know. So I shall stop here.

I had planned to hold this letter open until I return from the party, but on second thought I guess I shall close it now, and mail it to you as I go out, so that it will reach you tomorrow. If there is anything of particular interest to add, I shall send you a few lines by special delivery in the morning.

Wish me good luck, Old Pal! The zero hour held nothing compared to my feelings as I write these lines. I can easily imagine the sensations of a poor devil when the sheriff, accompanied by the gallows party, comes to read the death warrant. Well, you see I can joke, anyway. So here goes with a smile!

Your unfortunate friend,

Davy

FIFTEEN

All's well that ends well.
An extract from Davy's private diary.

Feb. 16–17 (Friday and Saturday)

I am too excited and elated to sleep, and nothing seems more reasonable than for me to put down a detailed statement of the events leading up to the happiest hour of my life. I sincerely doubt if I shall ever experience a happier one. Indeed, if I thought I might, I should be almost afraid to face it, for I honestly believe that I have been through moments since leaving the party shortly after one o'clock this morning when the slightest acceleration of my pulse beat would have resulted fatally. No one can make me believe, henceforth, that a human being cannot die of joy. The shock caused by my sudden rebound from the misery and unhappiness of these latter days was terrific, and I still feel the strain.

It is now nearly five o'clock Saturday morning, and all the world, except the milkman, is asleep. After I left Caroline at her door an hour and a half ago, I lay down and tried to sleep, but I just could not make it, for my brain was whirling like a merry-go-round.

Yesterday, Friday, I believe I touched the lowest depths of misery possible for a human creature. Most of the day was spent putting the final touches on my boxes and trunk, returning books to the Library of Congress, buying my ticket for Richmond, and doing errands preparatory to my departure this morning. How I got through the afternoon I really don't know, for it all seems now like a horrible dream, or like something which happened to me in another world, or a thousand years ago. After a dinner at which I went through the mechanical processes of eating, I came home, and kept myself from going mad by finishing a letter to Bob, though I have not the slightest idea now what I said in that letter. While I was writing I could hear Caroline whistling and singing in her room. This is a practice in which she has indulged a great deal in the last two or three days, and for some reason, the exact nature of which is not clear to me even yet, this seemed to add a touch to my madness. Once I got up and shut my door. Then I got up again and opened it. As to a man with a toothache, one situation was about as uncomfortable as another.

While I was writing Tommie came up to say that she would be ready to go at ten o'clock. Tommie knew that I was unhappy about something, and she tried to pump me, even going so far as to sit on the arm of my chair and run her fingers through my hair, something the like of which she has never done before. "I surely must look badly," I thought. When she had gone I took a peep in my shaving glass, and sure enough, I looked like an extra edition of the morning after the night before. I finished, sealed and stamped Bob's letter, which I decided to mail last night instead of this morning as I had first planned. Then I smoked cigarettes until I felt dopey, and idly tried to recall the author of the *The Last Day of a Condemned Man*, a book I have not read. Finally, it came to me that it was Hugo, and I resolved at the earliest moment possible to get a copy, and see how accurately he had done the job. Then Tommie called me. I had wanted to take a taxi, but Dr. King had invited us to go in his car, and Tommie insisted that we accept his invitation. So I picked up my wraps and went down to the back parlor where I found Dr. King. Even absorbed as I was with my own troubles, I was struck by his evident preoccupation, for he is usually very cordial to me. But on this occasion he spoke rather absentmindedly, and sat looking into the fire, puffing slowly at a cigarette. As the girls came down in a moment, I had no time to notice him further. Thomasine was beautiful, as she always is, for with her handsome face, perfect figure, and her exquisite taste in dress, the result is a foregone conclusion. But Caroline—I have no words to describe her! I have seen her many times when her beauty was almost overpowering, but on this night of all nights in the world—whether or not it was due partly to my own overwrought nerves, I cannot say—the shock of her beauty was like a blow in the face. Her color was unusually high, even making allowance for the rouge, her eyes were big and brilliant, and from her becoming coiffure to the soles of her little slippers she was perfect, in face, figure, coloring, and dress. I have never in my life seen anything so lovely—never! And my lover's estimate is approved by the verdict of the other men at the party, as appeared later. As far as I was concerned, indeed, the impression she made on me was so overwhelming that after that first glance, I would not look at her again. Dr. King jumped up when the ladies entered, and said something or other complimentary, but, as far as any outward expression was concerned, I might have been the proverbial "bump on a log." As I am usually ready enough with the small change of social conversation, the girls seemed to notice it, but I was in such a state of dejection that I did not care about anything. This last evidence of the exquisite beauty and consequent desirability of the one woman seemed to finish me.

With all her social experience, Tommie is not a bit good at

pretending, especially when she is with her close friends. Dr. King seemed to be in a semi-comatose state, and Caroline's mood, though quite evidently not a normal one, was beyond my power of diagnosis. It was a silent party that climbed into Dr. King's car. One might have thought we were going to the funeral of a dear friend. Certainly no one would have guessed we were on our way to what promised to be the most elaborate party of the season. Dr. King had some trouble with his ignition, which delayed us a moment. Then we got under way, but stopped for a second at the corner while I mailed my letter to Bob. Caroline has a peculiar wit, which would assert itself, I verily believe, in the very face of death. We were proceeding more slowly than usual, because of a momentary obstruction to traffic, and in the midst of an unbroken silence, when Caroline piped up.

"Just when do they spring the trap?" she asked, in the driest voice imaginable.

Dr. King started and almost lost control of the car, and Tommie laughed. But for once my sense of humor had deserted me entirely. On the whole the sally fell rather flat, and we entered the hall as silently as we had left the house. While we were waiting at the door of our dressing room for the ladies, Dr. King again relapsed into his state of semi-coma, and as I was not in a loquacious mood, we stood side by side, each thinking his own thoughts. Mine, I can testify, were not the best of company.

Our entrance into the dance hall, between two dances, was made with all the éclat which anyone could desire. The men flocked about the two girls, and Caroline was swallowed up, so to speak, in the crowd of her admirers. One young chap who is a newcomer, I believe, exclaimed to a couple of his friends, "That little Rhodes girl is the prettiest thing I've ever seen on two feet!" Don pushed his way out of the throng and came toward me.

"Hello, Davy," he said. "You asked me once if I thought Caroline Rhodes could be called beautiful. I believe I hesitated somewhat over my answer. I was wrong to hesitate."

"I knew it at the time," I said, laughing. Then I realized my duty toward my twelve hostesses, and hastened to pay my respects as best I could between dances, for the formal receiving line had been broken. I danced with Tommie, Lillian Barton, Mary Hale, Billie Riddick, Sophie Burt, and I should have had a delightful time if I had not been so miserable. The hall itself was beautiful. The floral decorations were lavish and in good taste, and from the center of the ceiling was a huge birdcage containing birds of various colors. The favors of the ladies were unique—winged silver crowns, and altogether the affair was an unusually brilliant one. I regret now that my state of mind was such that much of the charm of this most auspicious occasion was lost on me. I heard Don say that it was one of the prettiest parties he had ever attended, and I am willing to take his judgment on it.

As Tommie predicted, even in that crowd of handsome women, Caroline was the acknowledged belle. Her every movement between dances was followed by a host of young men. As I was taking no more chances on being rebuffed, her popularity was the source of no inconvenience to me, but Dr. King seemed to be having his troubles. As on other occasions in recent weeks, there were strong undercurrents moving below the surface of things. Lillian Barton, queenly in a gown of black velvet, was quiet, for her, and as I was winning no medals for airy persiflage, our first dance was rather tame—for us. Tommie, too, was very serious in her manner. Not content to let well enough alone, as I should by all means have done, I had to stir up things by a question.

"What is the matter, Tommie? Who's dead?" I queried, between a dance and its encore.

"You ought to know, Davy," she countered quickly, "you're acting like a chief mourner."

And she looked at me searchingly with her brilliant black eyes.

Then an impish impulse possessed me to "start something."

"Tommie," I said, "this is almost our last dance together. I am going away tomorrow morning."

If my object was to "start something," I had surely achieved it. Tommie caught me by the lapel of my coat, and swung me about until I was facing her.

"Do you mean you are going for good?"

"Going for good, Tommie!"

"But no one knows it," said she.

"No—no one but you, and I am asking you to regard as confidential what I have told you."

"You mean you are not going to tell anyone?"

"No, no one but you," I repeated.

"But is that fair to your good friends?"

"I think so. I don't like farewells, and never did. I would rather slip away quietly. I shall write them all, of course."

While we were talking we were standing in front of a group of people among whom was Billie Riddick. I noticed Billie turn her head when Thomasine Dawson raised her voice in one of her queries, and I was afraid Billie had overheard. Just then the music started, and Scott Green came up to claim his dance with Tommie. My dance was with Billie Riddick, and I was wondering whether or not to ask her if she had overheard Tommie and me, when Billie brought me out of my state of wonderment by a question.

"So you're going away tomorrow?"

"Yes," said I, knowing there was no use in fencing with Billie. "You overheard?" She nodded.

"Are you going away without telling your friends?"

"Yes, I like it better that way."

"When are you corning back?"

"Probably never," said I.

"Never?"

"Never."

"Have you told Caroline?"

"No," I answered.

"Going to?"

I shook my head.

"Why not?"

"She would not be interested," I said, somewhat coldly.

"What makes you think that?"

"Everything. She hardly speaks to me."

"So I have noticed," said Billie. "What is the trouble?"

"I really can't make it out."

Billie said no more until the dance was over. Then she stood looking at me shrewdly, and I never realized before how penetrating are her green-gray eyes. Then, with that racy diction which makes her so popular among the men, she said:

"You look like last month's drunk, Davy Carr! What is the matter with you anyway? Can't you tell me? I'm your friend."

"I know it, Billie," said I, squeezing her arm, "but I see no good in telling you, nor anyone else."

Again Billie pierced me with her green-gray glance. She gripped me by both shoulders, and, as she did so, I was conscious that several people were taking interested note of us.

"Do you trust me, Davy?"

"To the limit, Billie," said I warmly.

"Have you the next dance engaged?"

"No," I said, on recollection.

"Then do something to please me!" As she spoke, she put her

arm under mine and steered me, half yielding, half resisting, toward a secluded corner of the slightly raised balcony which surrounded the hall on all sides. On the way she caught Scott Green by the arm. He turned.

"Scott, cut the dance with me, and ask that pretty little college girl you're so crazy about. I have something to say to Davy, and it's important."

Scott demurred slightly, as a man might, but he is a good fellow and a good friend, so he grinned good-naturedly, and said, "All right!"

We continued our road to the corner of the balcony. When we had finally seated ourselves, and Billie had pushed a table into a position which would make it impossible for anyone to sit too close to us, she turned on me with another searching glance. Then she smiled. And if striking eyes, and a beautiful mouth, and a dimple which comes and goes make an attractive smile, Billie Riddick has one.

"Davy Carr, I am really fond of you. When you can stand off and look, you can see as much as anybody in the world, but you are farsighted. You can't see anything close to your own nose. I've been expecting to see you wake up and notice things any time within the last two or three weeks, but I think that hope is vain. So I am going to tell you something—and ask you something. First I guess I'll ask. What's the trouble between you and Caroline? I'm not fooling. I'm in earnest. I have the best of reasons for asking. You can trust me—you know that, don't you?"

"Yes, I know that, Billie."

"Then, don't hesitate! Let me say this much first. You are crazy about Caroline Rhodes, and you are going to be crazier before you are any better, or I'm a poor judge of your kind. Now come across!"

So I, who was dying to tell somebody, told Billie everything, from the very beginning down to the kisses which had been my undoing, and the sad rebuffs which had followed. Billie interrupted with questions which sometimes seemed irrelevant, but I answered them patiently. Then she said:

"Now I'll tell you everything. Caroline Rhodes does not care a fig for Will King, except as a friend. He knows it, and I know it. And I did not say 'think.' I said 'know.' As to whether Caroline cares very much for anyone else or not, that is not for me to say. She's been a spoiled darling all her days, and the boys have always made a big fuss over her. She's used to it, and she appreciates herself thoroughly. But what you say about her treatment of you since the night you stole the kisses gives me an idea. I may be wrong, so I shan't tell what it is. So you run along and dance with the girls, and have as good a time as you can, and keep this in mind: As long as a girl is not in love with someone else, you have a chance. So promise me you won't turn on the gas until tomorrow morning!"

She laughed and I laughed, and she shook my hand, and wished me good luck. And the next minute I saw her lithe figure moving gracefully through the crowd in the direction of Don Verney. Of course I was interested, and when she corralled Don, and she dragged him off into the corner we had just vacated, my interest grew. Their interview lasted a long time, and I saw one gentleman looking vainly about the room, after the music had started, for his missing partner, and I strongly suspected that the missing one was the lady with the green-gray eyes who was sitting in back of the post in the gallery talking to my friend Don.

What other things happened during the evening I did not see, except that I saw Billie talking with Caroline a short time after supper was served. Caroline looked at Billie, it seemed to me, a little belligerently, but Billie said what she had to say in a low voice. Caroline answered, still with her rather belligerent look. Then Billie said something else somewhat at length, and turned and left her, and I plainly saw Caroline's expression change to one I could not fathom, and she started looking absentmindedly at Billie's retreating form. Then Caroline turned to Tommie, and asked her a question, and Tommie turned away without answering, leaving Caroline with this same curious look on her face.

That was all I saw. The rest of the evening I danced mechanically, and it is all a kind of haze to me. A last dance with Mary Hale and the "Home Sweet Home" with Tommie I shall always remember. I wanted so much to tell Mary Hale good-bye. Tommie danced like something possessed, and when it was over, and the rush for wraps had begun, I said, "Well, Tommie, if it is the last, I'm glad it was with you. That, at least, is something to remember!"

She smiled at me wistfully, and pressed my arm. Then she turned away to speak to someone while I hastened to get our belongings.

I had told Dr. King not to wait for me, that I should get a taxi for Tommie and me. He looked at me rather questioningly for a second, and then shrugged his shoulders and said, "All right!"

When Tommie stood in the doorway of her home to bid me good-bye, I felt as if I was leaving my last friend in the world. There was so much in my heart to say that it almost choked me. For one thing, I regretted suddenly not having taken Tommie into my confidence about Caroline, but it was too late now to remedy that. So with all the beautiful things welling up in me to say, the best I could bring forth was the most conventional little sentence. "It's been a greater pleasure than I can express to have known you, Tommie. Good-bye!"

"Thank you, Davy. I can reciprocate that sentiment, as you well know. But you talk as if we are parting for good." She looked at me sharply.

"Well, maybe we are," I said, with a poor attempt at easy jocularity.

"Don't you care for us enough to come back to see us?"

"It's not a matter of caring. But I don't believe I shall come back, unless to dance at your wedding, Tommie."

"Davy, don't you mean to tell Caroline good-bye?"

"No, Tommie. That is, I shan't try to make an opportunity. She will understand why. Will you do something for me?"

"Surely. What is it?"

"Thank Dr. King for me. He has been very kind."

"Indeed I shall, but," she persisted, returning to the previous subject, "if Caroline gives you a chance, will you take it?"

"I guess so."

She sighed, and looked at me closely. "Good-bye, Davy. I think you are acting foolishly, somehow, but I am puzzled about so many things I am not sure just what to say. If you see Bob before I do, give him my love. I am going to miss you horribly."

And without a word, evading my outstretched hand, she closed the door and left me standing rather awkwardly on the steps. I had a curious feeling that she was going to cry, and had left thus abruptly to prevent me from seeing it. I walked to the curb mechanically, paid the taximan, and sent him off, looking at me queerly. It was only minutes after that it came to me that I had given him a fiver for a few blocks' ride, and had waved away the change.

I wanted to walk in the air and think. Well, I got the walk, but Heaven knows what I thought about in that interval, for I cannot remember, except that I looked fondly on the now-familiar streets, which I had trodden so often in these past months in such jolly company, and on such pleasing errands. And here I was taking my last look at them!

Before I came abreast of the house, I looked up eagerly to see if there was a light. There was a faint one in the lower hall, and the outer door of the vestibule was open. That meant that Dr. King had come and gone, and that Caroline had left the outer door open for me, and had left the light for me to turn out. But I saw no light in her room, which is the front one on the second floor.

I let myself in quietly. There was no light or sound in the back of the house downstairs nor any light upstairs. I stood for a moment hesitating. Then I thought I would take one last look into the grate fire in the back parlor, before which I had spent so many happy hours. There were usually a few embers still burning, even at this time of night. So I slipped out of my coat, and went quietly into the parlor. Then my heart gave a great leap, for Caroline was sitting huddled in her coat, in her favorite corner of the big davenport.

I stopped halfway, undecided about what to do. Was not this the opportunity for which I had been praying, and yet—the rebuffs of the past few days still rankled in my breast, and my hurt pride strove to assert itself. So, as I said, I hesitated.

"Pardon me," I began as calmly as my throbbing pulses would allow, "I thought you had retired. I don't want to intrude."

I half turned, in that second having made up my mind to go if she did not stop me. My sick pride was fighting now!

Caroline never moved, but she spoke.

"Will you answer one question for me, Davy Carr?"

"Yes. What is it?"

"Are you going away tomorrow morning?"

"Yes, at ten o'clock."

"What time were you planning to leave the house?"

"A little after nine."

"Then you did not expect to see me?"

"No, I did not."

"You were going, just like that, without a word?"

"Yes—why?"

"Well, Billie Riddick said so, but I did not believe it. And I asked Tommie, and she would not answer me, but she didn't deny it. But it's so, isn't it? It's so?"

I was silent for a moment. Then she went on.

"Life teaches us some hard lessons, doesn't it?"

All this conversation without turning her head to look at me.

"For example?" I queried.

I still stood, with my coat on my arm, by the end of the davenport farthest from Caroline. Then I decided to take a hand in the conversation.

"If you will please tell me *one single thing* you have said or done in the past two or three weeks which would lead me to suppose you would be interested in the least either in my going or staying, I will cite you a dozen to show the reverse."

There was momentary silence.

"Have you forgotten what happened in this room? . . . Have you forgotten that?" she said.

"No, I couldn't forget it!"

"If you could not, do you think I could?"

"No, if I thought you could, I should not care whether you did or not, and I should not be here talking to you."

For the first time since I had entered the room Caroline looked at me for a brief second. Then she looked away again.

"Will you answer one question?" I asked.

"I guess so."

"Then tell me, please, why you were so dreadfully shocked because I kissed you. Did no one ever try to kiss you before?"

"*You* never did, Davy Carr, nor had you ever made love to me in any fashion whatsoever, nor had you ever, in any way, told me that you cared for me—nor did you on that occasion, nor have you since that time! Further, you have been for some time at functions of every kind with another woman. Why should you think that you could, without a preliminary word or act, forcibly kiss me—without even so much as a 'by your leave'? The fact that you have not a reputation for doing that sort of thing, and the fact that your reputation, indeed, is quite the reverse, only makes it all the worse in my opinion. How low must I stand in your eyes? I cannot quite visualize you as even thinking of such a thing—much less doing it—with most of our mutual friends. I suppose I must be in part to blame, but after all, that does not make it any easier, does it? I know I have been a little fool in many ways, and I have tried to shock you deliberately sometimes. Well, if I was trying to make an impression along that line, I certainly succeeded, did I not? I had made up my mind that, if you thought that of me, I should never demean myself by any words of explanation. But now that you are going away, I feel differently about it, somehow. I want to treat myself fairly. So I am going to humiliate myself, mortify my vanity, by asking you to believe that I am not that kind of a girl, Mr. Carr. Of course you will have to take my simple word for it."

Her tone, which at first had been incisive and more than a little sharp, had gradually shaded off into a note of sadness and regret. I was stirred to my depths. I started to answer. Then I stopped abruptly.

"Will you wait for me two minutes?" I said.

She looked up at me in surprise and perplexity.

"Yes, but why should I wait? For what?"

"Just wait," said I, "and you will see."

Then I tiptoed rapidly up the stairs to my room, opened my trunk, and took from it the little box containing the handkerchiefs, programs, notes, and other memorabilia relating to Caroline. Then I rummaged in my half-packed bag, and fished out my diary. When I entered the back parlor a minute later, Caroline looked at me with eyes full of wonder. When I drew near I could see, too, that she had been crying. I sat two or three feet from her on the davenport, and placed the little box in her lap. Then I snapped on the light behind her.

"Will you look at those things carefully, please? When you are through with them, I have something else to show you."

"But what have they—" she began, but I interrupted her.

"Just look, please, before you say anything more."

So she took them up, one by one—her handkerchiefs, the programs, the paper napkins with names and inscriptions, and the notes, on monogrammed paper, bits of cardboard, the back of a torn blank check. One by one she examined them, one by one she read them, and little by little her look softened, and a rosy glow suffused her neck and brow and cheeks.

Then she looked up at me in some embarrassment—the shyest, sweetest, loveliest face I ever hope to look upon—and sat with red lips parted as if she would speak, but could not find the words.

Before she could say anything, I held out my diary to her, holding it open with my finger.

"This is my private diary, Caroline, written for my eyes alone. No one in the world has seen it but you. Read from there on. I think there is nothing in those pages you should not see, but if there should be, I ask you to hold it sacredly confidential."

I moved close beside her, and looked over her shoulder as she read, beginning with the night of the stolen kisses, when I first realized that I loved her. Day after day, with nothing but her name, and my hopes, and fears—mostly fears, alas!—and each trivial incident magnified into importance by association with her personality. At first she read steadily enough, then she slackened, stopped short—and, letting the book fall, buried her head in her hands and commenced to cry softly. My impulse to take her in my arms was all but uncontrollable, but by some miracle and self-restraint I waited. In a few minutes she straightened up.

"My cards are on the table, dear lady, faces up. I do not know how I can make myself clearer. If you will tell me how, I'll try to do it."

Her voice shook as she spoke.

"Answer me one question, Davy Carr, on your honor! Do you mean all that—all—literally?"

"All that—and infinitely more, Caroline. There are no words adequate to express *all* I feel."

She sat silent, still looking into the fire. I had to settle things one way or the other.

"Could you learn to care for me—do you think—after a while, maybe?"

"No!" My heart almost stopped as she paused on the monosyllable. "No! I couldn't learn it now, Davy, for I learned it weeks ago."

Then she turned her black eyes full on me, their natural boldness softened by a warm blush which mantled her from throat to brow. Somehow in my rebound from the misery of the days just past, I felt afraid to move, as if I feared by so doing to destroy this beautiful illusion. Then she continued.

"I think I loved you from the first day, but I am not sure. When I was sure, I was in a panic at the thought of the things I had done to shock you. You always treated me beautifully, but it seemed more as a good-natured brother might treat a mischievous little sister, of whom he is fond, but whom he does not take seriously. I don't see how you could have failed to notice things. I stopped smoking cigarettes because of you, Davy; and I stopped drinking with the men because of you; and I stopped coming to your room because I did not want to seem to be seeking you—I had never thought of that before. When I told Dr. Corey I could never love him, I told him that I loved someone else, and I am sure he knew it was you. Then I waited for you to seek me. That's a terribly hard thing for a woman to do sometimes, Davy. Then Will King came back, and I let him come here partly because I had to have an escort, and he is a gentleman through and through, and partly because I was mortally afraid lest someday, if I did not keep myself busy, I might let you see how I felt and you, not caring that way for me, might think I was running after you. And, Davy, I remembered every one of those foolish things I had done. They used to rise up and haunt me nights when I lay awake, and I could not rid myself of the memory of the many times when I had seen disapproval in your eyes. To cap the climax, you started running after Billie Riddick. I don't like to seem to reflect on Billie, for she's always been square with me, and I like her. But, to say no more, Billie's not the kind of a girl one would expect you to run after. If it had been Lillian, now—I was always a little afraid of her—I think I should not have minded quite so much. Well, I don't know exactly why I am telling you all this, except perhaps that you have put your cards on the table for me, and I am not afraid to do the same for you." She paused for a moment. Then, "That's all, Davy," she said softly, and looked up at me from under her long lashes.

"I've been pinching myself, for fear that I might be dreaming," I said. "I wonder if to prove that you have understood and forgiven me for the kisses taken by force, you would give me one, Caroline, freely and from your heart."

"Not *from* my heart, *with* my heart, Davy—my Davy!"

And she did. If I could describe that moment, I would, so that when I am an old man I might read that description, and live it over. But I cannot describe it nor do I need to do so, for I shall never, never forget it!

"What did Billie Riddick say to you that made you wait for me?"

Caroline laughed a merry little laugh.

"She said: 'If I cared enough for a man, Caroline Rhodes, to step between him and a crazy man with an automatic, I should not let him go away tomorrow morning without a word of farewell. And he's going, and he's never coming back. There are one or two nice girls in this room who would be glad to give him that good-bye.'"

Then she snuggled her pretty head close down against my shoulder, and I felt the velvet of her cheek against mine, and I breathed into my eager nostrils the magic perfume of Fleurs d'Amour!

